CRIMSON KISS

CRIMSON KISS

The Ancient Spells Trilogy 1

This book contains varying degrees of the following: bodily injury, descriptions of war, consensual sexual content, and death, including that of a minor. Please read safely and responsibly.

CRIMSON KISS

Copyright © 2024 by Jodie Angell

Cover art and design: Artscandare

ISBN: 978-1-0686881-3-3

ABOUT THE AUTHOR

Jodie Angell is from the rainy valleys of South Wales, whose love (after coffee, of course) has always been fantasy, romance, and a touch of darkness. She lives with her fiancé, but regularly visits her parents and their scrumptious Frenchie, Harvey.

She loves to read, crochet, play cosy games, and keep her plants alive. When she's doing none of those things, she'll be deep in writing or planning her next fictional world.

For Hilmi, the man who raised me as his own. This dedication is homage for everything you've done.

THE BARREN
TERRITORIES

DELLHOLLOW

The
Badla

ZHAH

SOUTHERN
PENINSULA

SOUTHKEEP

The Realm
of
Arogath

SANCTUM
CITY

GALAE POOLS

LAKE
DELENDIL

THE FERTILE
TERRITORIES

VESUVIUS
CAVES

THE
EYRIE

THE HIGHLAND
TREES

THE GREAT
SEA

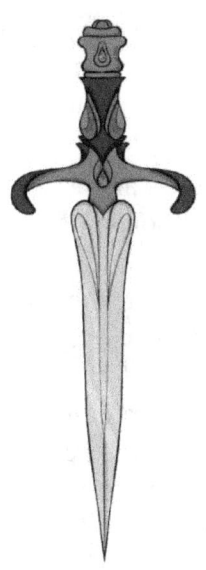

Chapter One

By mid-morning, the preparations for the courtier's ball were underway. Hearty scents of bread and puddings baking in the domed clay ovens wafted through the air. Servant boys lit fires in the small courtyard behind the kitchens and began setting up roasting spits for the feast. I busied myself with hanging garlands of spring flowers around the oak door frames of the Eyrie. The servants hummed as they helped with

1

decorating the castle. The preparations were bringing joy to us all.

Raucous laughter from the council room echoed into the hallway.

As I hung the remainder of the garlands, my hearing perked at the sound of my uncle's voice. "It's not going to happen."

I climbed down from the wooden stool, tiptoed closer, then pressed my ear against the wooden door to get in better earshot of the conversation.

"I can't believe those mindless fools believed you. Send our men to restore the Barren Territories? It would be the *last* thing we do," one of the men said.

I arched my brow and flung open the door, striding across the room.

My uncle was slouched at the council table with his advisors surrounding him. Each gulped their goblets of wine and gestured for the servant boy to refill. A jester danced around them.

His advisors swivelled as one to observe me standing in the doorway. King Atticus followed their gaze, his head wobbling as he turned. Despite his grey hair and dulling skin, his blue eyes twinkled. A smile spread across his face as he opened his arms to me.

"Ah, m-my dear g-girl, good morning!" He sat up straight and beckoned the houseboy. "You, give my niece a goblet of…of wine at once."

"You've refused to fulfil your vow? The Orcs were counting on you." Ignoring the boy who offered me a goblet, I neared my uncle, my footsteps echoing through the room.

"They have food and fish, tools even. The wild beasts don't need anything more." The king gestured to the boy holding a pitcher of wine.

"You enslaved them for years for your own amusement. You divided the lands and destroyed their home because of your greed." I narrowed my gaze on him as he swigged his drink. "You promised them a seat at the table, and you have failed them."

"It was your father who enslaved the Orcs. I, on the other hand, did no such thing. Now dear, why don't you change into something nicer for the festivities?" He wrinkled his nose at me. "Our guests will arrive this afternoon."

"I've already made plans to go to the market. Try to save some of the wine for later." I spun around and left the room.

One the king's guards walked through the hallway, heading to wherever he was stationed for the day.

"Felix, wait!" I hurried after him. "Care to escort me into town? The merchant will be there, and the market will be bustling with locals. It could make for a nice trip." I looked at him through my lashes, hoping he would join me on a stroll through the scenic landscape.

"I'm on strict orders to ensure the event runs smoothly, Your Grace," he said. "I cannot leave, but I can arrange for someone else to attend with you."

"No, I haven't the time to wait around. I shall go alone." I ignored the stab of disappointment and grabbed my shawl and pouch of coins from my chamber before leaving through the tall, arched entrance.

The Eyrie was built from aged granite, surviving countless invasions and sieges over the centuries. Following battles, stones were repaired and replaced, the new ones smooth and stood out against the worn, ragged rocks of its original build. The cold grey edifice in the mountains towered over the surrounding lands, a stronghold for King Atticus. He was unwed, and childless, so I was the only heir to the realm.

The ornate design of the fleur-de-lys, sigil of the Eyrie, had been forged into the tall iron portcullis. Sunlight illuminated the large stained-glass windows of the fortress and ivy grew up its ramparts. This keep was my home.

I smiled at Elijah, the gatekeeper, who hauled the gate open and bid me farewell.

———————⋅☙⋅———————

It took an hour's walk to reach the cobbled street lined with crowded stalls. The sweet, floral scents of hyacinths and lilacs wafted through the town. One of the stands was stacked with trays of dirt covered onions, carrots, and turnips. A loose onion fell from its stacked position, then rolled along the floor until it hit my booted foot.

I scooped up the onion and handed it to the humanoid who manned the stall. "Here you go."

He beamed. "Thank you, Your Grace. Please, let me provide you with some of my freshest picks." He stuffed the vegetables into a paper bag, then gave it to me.

Smiling, I took the gift. "My deepest thanks. Have you seen the silk merchant?"

"His stall is set up farther along the path, Your Grace." He tipped the brim of his hat at me.

I hurried through the crowds in search of the traveller. My cheeks warmed at the prospect of purchasing a new shawl for the ball.

Wicker baskets lined the side of the path. Beside the merchant, a horse stood, tethered to a tree. Five wooden planks supported by two beer barrels formed a makeshift table that supported rolls of silk and a black velvet cushion.

I fumbled in my pockets for my pouch of coins as I gazed at the dazzling ruby pendant on display. It reminded me of my mother's portraits at the Eyrie—each one showed her wearing fine jewellery.

"A necklace for the beautiful lady?" The man gestured theatrically to his remaining selection. He frowned at me, then his eyes widened. "Ah, the princess! How lovely that you should choose to buy from me. Perhaps I can interest you with my finest silks?" He motioned to his fabric. "Whatever colour you choose, I'll take a third of the price. Just be sure to tell your friends that I sell the finest silks in the whole of the realm."

I plucked three coins from my pouch and placed them in his hand. He curled his fingers around the gold. The blue fabric gleamed under the sunlight. "This one, please."

He nodded, cut a length of material from the roll, then handed it to me. "Be careful on your way home, Your Grace. I've seen the Orcs on my travels—

dozens of them. Rumour has it they're after someone from a prophecy, and they're destroying everything in their path. They pillaged a village and burned civilians in their huts. Evil monsters, I witnessed the whole thing."

I clasped my hand over my mouth and gasped. "Were there any survivors?"

"I'm not entirely sure. Some did run from their homes, but I was too far away to see the extent of their injuries." He shrugged.

"How long ago did you see them?" I clutched the silk and bag of roots against my chest, the back of my neck prickling.

"Early this morning. Thankfully, I was on my horse and farther ahead. I heard the ruckus and stopped to spy through the trees."

The mare nuzzled close to me, so I stroked her nose—a welcome distraction from the dread mounting in my stomach. "The Orcs were travelling by foot?"

"Yes, Your Grace." He turned his attention to the nearing customers.

"You're lucky to own a horse; take good care of her. There are very few of them in the Fertile Territories and have become harder to breed since the disease took hold. And take good care of yourself. Good day." I bid farewell. The heat of the afternoon sun beat against my face as I strolled down the cobbles and began the journey home.

At the edge of the forest, I stopped and inhaled the woody scent of pine resin. Blades of grass collapsed under foot as I resumed my journey, and a faint wind rippled the water of a nearby pond, distorting the reflection of the forest.

As I approached the Eyrie, Elijah appeared from beyond the gate. His armour fit him well, and he clutched a sword made from Arogathean steel in his right hand. The gull-grey of the metal glinted under the sunlight.

"Good to see you again, Elijah." I dabbed the thin layer of sweat from my forehead.

"You too, Your Grace." The guard hoisted the chains and raised the portcullis along the vertical grooves built into the stone at either side of the entrance. Once I entered, he freed the chains, and the portcullis thudded against the limestone floor.

I wandered through the courtyard decorated with tended shrubs and topiaries cut into the shape of fleur-de-lys. Guards stood watch upon the Eyrie's thick towers. Quivers were strapped to their backs— arrows poked out from the top.

Elijah unlatched the doors and guided me through a corridor beneath the domed ceiling. Spectacular paintings of my ancestors and battle scenes graced its stone block walls.

The king looked me up and down, wrinkling his nose. "You must have a bath at once and change into your dress. You smell like a town wench, so go and prepare yourself for the ball. Our guests will be arriving very soon."

I beckoned a nearby servant, then handed her the fabric. "Gwendolyn, can you take this, and have it prepared for the ball, please?"

"Of course, Your Grace." She took the folded silk from me, curtsied, then hurried out of the room.

The king reverted his attention to the goblet, gesturing to a servant to refill it. "Fetch my niece a goblet of wine. It's time to celebrate."

When the servant offered it to me, I accepted, for my uncle would only keep demanding I drink it. It was going to be a long night.

A rosewood table with eight chairs stretched across the width of the hall. My gaze fell on a turkey laid bare next to a full pig—its mouth biting an apple. Along with the meats, there were an array of colourful fruits—soft plums and juicy nectarines from the south. Some were dressed and added into pies, others baked into breads. My mouth watered.

King Atticus sat at the head of the table. The hall was spacious, with high ceilings and towering archways. Armoured knights stood beside the open doors. Their hands clasped over the hilts of downward-pointing Arogathean blades. The silver finish of the blades shone in the bright glow of the many candles lighting the hall, and fine engraving along the length of the swords sparkled.

Felix walked to the king's side. "Your guests are arriving."

"Fantastic!" He clapped his hands once. "Have them join us."

Felix nodded. As he strode towards me, his gaze fell on my sapphire encrusted gown. A hint of a smile appeared on his lips but disappeared just as quickly. As he left, my cheeks warmed. I adjusted my silk shawl, shoving thoughts of Felix's perusal aside.

Near the entrance to the banquet hall, hung a commissioned painting of my father, Aneirin, and me. He wore a tailcoat embroidered with the fleur-de-lys and a matching waistcoat, breeches, and lace cuffs. The fineries of life as a royal. Aneirin was the king's older brother, and their relationship had been a beloved one, many years ago. They'd bonded over boar hunts and celebrated in the evenings by drinking the finest wine in the realm. My uncle ascended the throne when my father died, as I'd been too young to inherit the Crown, not that'd I'd wanted it. He grieved his loss for years and had to adjust to his new position as king quickly.

The time I'd spent with my father resurfaced and my heart throbbed. Memories of him lingered in all corners of the Eyrie. We'd sat together at this table, relishing one of his boars. The painting depicted us on the evening we'd danced around the banquet hall to the delicate sounds of vielles. Father and daughter.

"It's a splendid portrait of Aneirin, isn't it?" Uncle said. "Sit. We must eat."

A servant boy pulled out a chair, and once I was seated, he fetched the decanter, then poured red wine into my goblet. I left the goblet on the tablet—just because my uncle wanted to dull his mind with alcohol, didn't mean I had to.

"We imported the finest wine in the kingdom for the celebrations, my girl." Uncle raised his goblet, noticing mine was untouched. "Indulge."

Guests filed in through the Eyrie's entrance, and the violin players began their melodic tunes.

To stop my uncle's pestering, I lifted the goblet to my lips and sipped the wine. "It's delightful."

A moment of silence formed, and my thoughts returned to the merchant. I tapped my fingers against the table's polished wood.

"What is it, dear? You're frowning." Uncle Atticus fixed his gaze on me.

"When I was at the market," I cleared my throat, set my drink aside, and flattened my hands against my breeches, "the travelling merchant mentioned a prophecy. He also said he'd witnessed the Orcs destroy a village. He was lucky to escape."

Uncle Atticus slammed his goblet onto the table, flung his chair back, then rose to his feet. Rubbing the side of his head, he held out his goblet for the servant boy to refill. He swallowed a mouthful of wine before continuing, "Did he say when? How did this happen?"

"He said the attack occurred this morning on his travels into town." I turned in my chair to see the servants handing out beverages to the visitors gathering in the foyer. "Your guests are expecting you to greet them. Now would be the time to do so."

"The damned Orcs!" Uncle Atticus slammed his hands on the table. "Attacking innocent people. I'll have them beheaded for treason. Every single one of them. Evalyn, you must flee. I hadn't planned on telling you this, but given the circumstances, you must know: Shortly after you were born, your father told me about the prophecy. I'm sorry it's come to this."

"What are you talking about?" I frowned. Clearly, the copious amounts of wine he'd consumed had gone to his head.

The merchant burst in through the door. "Your Majesties, the Orcs have arrived within town. I caught a glimpse of them as I was leaving. I rode here as fast as I could. There are dozens of them. They'll outnumber your guards."

The other guests overheard his outcry, and urgent yells rang through the foyer and open doors. Guards swarmed them, uttering orders to remain calm.

"You must leave now. Hurry! You are the one they are after, Evalyn," my uncle urged, gripping me by the arm with some force and hoisting me from my chair. "Pack some food and run. I am sure you already have a blade."

I ignored my uncle and turned to a nearby guard. "Take our guests down to the crypts, right now, otherwise many innocents will die." I spun around to face my uncle. "I think you have had far too much to drink, Uncle. My father would not have kept this a secret. You must be mistaken."

"I'm sorry, but it's true. Your father did not wish for you to know as we had kept you safe within these walls your whole life. And when he died, I decided it was in your best interests to keep it that way. I did my best." With his goblet in his hand, he went to address those who'd arrived for the party.

Felix approached him. "I will accompany the princess and ensure her safety."

"What are your plans, Uncle?" I hurried after him. "You should come with us, find somewhere safe for now."

"I…the guards are well-trained as you know," he stammered, his eyes half closed. "They will fulfil their duty, and I will not abandon our home. Everyone…it's time to leave."

I summoned a nearby guard who crossed the hall in several long strides. "Take the staff into the crypts immediately."

I hurried to my chamber, changed into a shirt, breaches, and fur cloak. My leather satchel lay on the bed. I stashed a map, compass, and a pouch of coins inside, then hauled the bag over my shoulder.

My fingers curled around the handle of my bedside drawer. Opening it, I grabbed the spell book from inside. I traced my fingers over the smooth, leather cover and wondered why my gut had urged me to pick it up. My mother had used it, many years ago, and she'd left to me. A few years had passed since I'd learned and used some of the spells, and although I'd mastered some good spells, some were reckless and dangerous. Without having mastered my magic fully, destruction followed. Regardless, I stuffed it into my bag. Just in case.

Before leaving the room, I cast a glance at the portrait of my mother, which hung above the bed. The pictures, and the spell book, were the only connection I still had to her. Her cheeks were rosy, and her eyes brown and round. She wore a beautiful sapphire necklace and midnight blue gown. My heart panged. I couldn't remember her gracing the corridors of the Eyrie. She was yet another ghost that never wandered too far from me. I'd have to hurry if I didn't want to become one myself.

In the kitchens, I shoved several rolls, fruit, cheese, nuts, and seeds into my bag. The food would last a few days if I was careful.

Guards swarmed the area, gathered their weapons for battle and called orders to the watchmen on the towers. Others ignited fires in pots along the walls, ready for the archers to launch burning arrows towards the approaching enemy.

"Evalyn," Uncle Atticus called to me from behind. "I am sorry. The Orcs have caused so much disruption. Now they bring it to my home."

"You should go to the crypts, Uncle, where it is safe." I squeezed his arm in silent farewell.

He kissed me on the cheek, then faced Felix. "Take care of my niece."

My gaze travelled to Felix, the tall, broad guard to the king. He stepped closer to me—resting his helmet against his hip—and bowed.

The blood in my veins pulsed. If my uncle had dealt with the Orcs, like a king should, they would not be encroaching upon the Eyrie, thirsty for my blood.

I walked away. Felix and I headed north, leaving the Eyrie and the forest behind us.

Hours had passed since our hasty exit, and neither of us spoke more than a few words. The basics were terse: "Watch your step, Your Grace...We'll head for Sanctum City...We must rest soon."

To all of which I nodded. This man had grown and trained within the Eyrie grounds, being my uncle's favourite guard. He could be trusted.

Now and again, he lifted his helm high enough to take a sip of water from his wineskin. He would glance at me as he did so, a frown on his face.

I tugged my cloak tightly around me and turned my face away from the biting wind. We'd travelled into the night; the sky blurring with the horizon, and I strained my eyes to see the outlines of nearby trees. Mountain wolves howled in the distance.

"This is a good place to rest for the night," he muttered, his voice muffled. He pointed to a cave. "I've been here before. There's a hole in the roof so we can light a fire. I'm going to collect some branches. I won't be long."

"Fine." My heartbeat steadied. We would sleep warm and dry.

The cave was hidden by vines growing up its walls, and the stars of the night sky shone on.

Felix returned with an armful of logs, sticks, and twigs, then stashed them under the hole in the roof. He propped the logs up against one another with the sticks and twigs in the centre, forming a nest. I handed him the flint and he lit the fire.

Adding more sticks, he encouraged the flames. Soon, it consumed the entire construction, transforming into a radiant, dancing ensemble of red and orange. He sat opposite me with the fire between us. A few scratches and a dent on his helmet glinted in the warm glow.

He remained still for a few moments before lifting his helmet from his head. Handfuls of dark brown hair fell around his face in a tousled mess. He flattened the mane with the palms of his hands. His hazel eyes glimmered in the firelight, and a thin scar ran down the left side of his face from his high cheekbone into a fine layer of stubble. He prodded the fire with a crooked stick he'd kept to one side and peered at me.

"What?" He rested the stick on the ground, and his expression remained unreadable.

"Nothing." My cheeks burned. There was something beautiful about him. I'd always thought his scar told a story like the dents and scratches on his helmet. There was something mysterious about him, and I wanted to know more, but I didn't think he would appreciate me questioning him given his first priority was keeping me safe, not making conversation.

We ate our bread and seeds in silence, saving as much as possible for the following day. I stared at the jagged stone surface of the cave walls, unable to pluck words from my brain. He made me shrink inside.

Next to the glow of the fire, I brought my knees to my chest, sitting idle in the silence between us. I recalled the one spring afternoon when I'd batted my eyelashes and flirted with him as he patrolled the Eyrie grounds. He brushed me off, and we'd never spoke of it. His rejection had stung, but I didn't know what I'd expected. He was a royal guard after all.

"You should get some rest." He bit a chunk of bread, glancing at me with his piercing eyes. It wasn't a suggestion.

I removed my cloak and bunched it up to form a pillow, the fire warming me. I was no longer able to stifle a yawn.

He removed his armour, shirt, and gambeson, which clanked against the stone walls. The dim, flickering of the fire illuminated the ridged scars across his chest. I pictured him slaying the enemy in previous battles, Arogathean sword in hand. He'd survived them all.

My gaze travelled along his torso. Each scar held a piece of his past, a piece of what made him a royal guard.

"Did you remember to bring a blanket?" His voice jerked me from my reverie.

My cheeks warmed again. "No. I didn't even think of it—my mind was on food. I have my fur cloak to keep me warm."

"You've just created a pillow with your cloak. That wouldn't have kept you warm, would it? Good job I remembered, otherwise we might've frozen to death." A not-quite-a-smile tugged at the corners of his lips before he turned away. He drew a coarse woollen cover from his satchel, walked around the fire, then plonked down beside me.

As I rubbed my hands together, he draped the blanket across us. The material was thick and warm, and combined with the heat of the fire, it would be enough to get us through the night. I closed my eyes, hearing his rhythmic breaths as he fell asleep next to me. My heartrate slowed, and the crackling fire lulled me to sleep.

Birdsong in the nearby trees woke me the following morning. Felix had already dressed. I drew my fur cloak around my aching shoulders, grabbed the blanket, then folded it into his pack.

Sunlight beamed across the cluster of trees; no cloud concealed its splendid glow. A soft breeze carried ashes from last night's fire through the air. I wrinkled my nose at the smell of singed wood.

"Did you sleep well?" Felix swigged the water from his wineskin, then offered it to me.

"As well as anyone can in a cave." I held the wineskin to my lips, letting the chilled water spill into my mouth. "We need to find a spring; our water is low. How many days will it take us to get to Sanctum City?"

"A few. It's as far north as north goes." He rifled through his pack for the remaining pouch of seeds, then shovelled a handful of them into his mouth.

"Are we taking the quickest route?" I rummaged in my satchel for a piece of bread, then bit a chunk. The loaf was stale and dry, but I imagined it with a warm centre and covered with poppy seeds.

He brushed some stray seeds from his mouth and looked at me. "Of course. Your safety is paramount."

My safety was paramount? If the Orcs broke through the Eyrie's defences, they'd assassinate the king. And if I was really who they were after, it wouldn't be long before they pursued me, and we'd both be murdered for a prophecy I knew nothing about.

"It's so hot." I yanked my cloak from my shoulders and tried to loosen my collar.

"Don't panic, Your Grace," he said, the lines around his eyes softening. "I'll get you to Sanctum City. We should get a move on." He walked past the cave, and I hurried to catch up with him. "We don't have time to loiter around."

"I'm worried about my uncle. Isn't there anything we can do to help?"

"I'm afraid not," he said. "The king has bought you more time, to give you a chance to survive. We need to keep moving, Your Grace."

We continued our trek in silence through a field of small, yellow flowers like those in the gardens at the back of the Eyrie. They would conceal our tracks. Birch trees were dotted across the flank, with birds' nests stowed between their branches.

The sun reached its highest point and sweat formed on my hairline, threatening to trickle down the contours of my face.

We neared a bridge. Two wooden beams about three feet apart from each other jutted out of the ground, and frayed ropes hung from holes in the stumps.

"Do you think he's dead?" I blurted. "My uncle?"

He hesitated a moment. "I can't make assumptions, Your Grace. The Orcs were close when we left."

A burning sensation coursed through my body. A bolt of fiery red magic shot from my hands and smashed into the bridge. Chunks of wood erupted into the air, the rope severed, and the remaining planks dangled into the ravine.

"That was our route to Sanctum City, Your Grace," Felix said, raising an eyebrow.

I gasped, staring at my trembling palms. "I'm sorry, I didn't mean for it to happen."

"It's all right." His voice was a trifle softer, reassuring. "There's no safe way across the chasm and no other route to Sanctum City. We need a new plan."

I peered over the edge. Shrubs clung to the white, flat cliff. Chalk crumbled into the powdery blue river below.

"Where else is there to go?" I frowned. "Sanctum City was our only option." I was plagued with images of us starving in the middle of nowhere or being attacked by some wild beast, or worse, the Orcs. "We can't go back either."

He paused as if to consider our possibilities.

"Lake Delendil," he said.

I tried to recall the significance of the location. "You want to go see the High Elves?"

"They serve light and purity, and they'll offer us protection. Nieve is the Chief Councillor, and she will help us. The Orcs wouldn't dream of setting foot on such sacred ground. The lake's magic repels all darkness and causes excruciating pain to those who pose a threat, so we would be safe there. I also have a friend who can assist you with your magic, I'll take you to her," he said. "She'll know about the prophecy, and you can get your answers."

"How do you know about the prophecy?" I narrowed my eyes on him. "If you know anything about it, you must tell me. I need to know what I'm being hunted for."

He looked me straight in the eyes, and his expression returned to its usual unreadable mask. "It's not my place to say, Your Grace."

"You're going to tell me right now." I stepped closer to him and raised my chin.

"Evalyn—"

"Tell me, Felix. I command it." I wasn't one for pulling rank, but when my life was on the line, I didn't have much of a choice.

He sighed, rubbing his chin. "Your uncle decided it would be the best way to ensure your safety. He made me aware of the prophecy to ensure I did everything in my power to protect you if the day came. Initially, I didn't believe it until the Orcs attacked."

"That's when you volunteered to come with me rather than stay with the king." My shoulders relaxed a fraction as the realisation sunk in.

"My friend, the Oracle, will help you to control your magic, and tell you about the prophecy." He looked at me sincerely before settling his helmet back on his head.

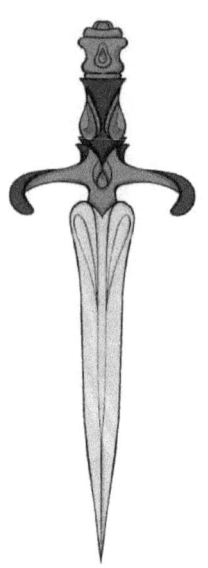

Chapter Two

As Felix led the way through the wildflowers, a citrus hint wafted on the breeze. We were headed towards Westwilde. For centuries, the tranquil village surrounded by tall trees housed one of the Elementals, the Gnomes.

"This route will take us through the main settlements of the Fertile Territories. It'll lead us straight to Lake Delendil." He looked at me with an amused twinkle in his eye as I clutched the map and compass. My breath caught in my throat—there was something intimidating about the way he watched me. It was his job to keep his eye on me, to ensure I didn't fall or injure myself, but I couldn't help but wonder if there was something *more* to it. Especially when his gaze lingered for a few seconds longer than it ought've. "We'll stop off along the way at Bluefair Fort. There, you'll meet my friend, the Oracle."

I nodded. Still aching from the last two nights of travelling and camping, I longed for a room to sleep in for the night. "The Gnomes may be one of our allied clans, but they will turn us away if they are in danger." I bent to rub my stiff calf.

"The settlements of the realm are never within a day's travel of each other," he continued. "It's best you get used to the sore muscles."

Felix and I walked alongside a stream that flowed through woods and fields. Twilight fell across the sky as a cool evening wind stirred the grass and leaves of the trees.

I stopped, placed the map on a tree stump, and strained to read the calligraphy marking each town. Westwilde was in reach, but Lake Delendil was one-hundred-fifty miles away on the western edge.

Sanctum City was inscribed at the top of the parchment. Long before the domination of the Orcs and segregation of the Light and Dark Triads, the city offered shelter to tribes from all walks of life.

The map showed the segregation. Dangerous tribes lived on the eastern side of the continent where the Orcs held a significant amount of power. They'd breached the Fertile Territories when the king failed to fulfil his promise, and destruction had followed. A civil war was inevitable, and the rest of the Dark Triads would obey them.

I shivered at the prospect of another war. Light fighting against Dark. Red staining the ground as the Orcs plundered their way through the territories.

"What is that?" Felix jerked his head and wrinkled his nose. "Smells like burning."

Within a few yards, we entered a copse at the edge of the grassland. On the other side, smouldering ashes, and thick clouds of smoke from Westwilde dominated the skyline.

"What the hell?" He drew his sword from its shaft, then sprinted towards the settlement ruins.

Clutching my own blade in a white-knuckle grip, I followed him. My heart somersaulted in my chest. A shadow moved amongst the ashes. We drew closer as a Gnome poured water over the last dancing flames. Remains of vendors' wooden carts and wagons were strewn across the ground, their vegetables crushed, and trinkets broken.

Gnome children assisted the elders by pouring small pails of water on embers and gathering any ears of corn that could be salvaged. Once they rested the food on a pile of unscorched corn, they filed into an intact house located in the centre of the village.

"What happened?" Felix asked as I handed the Gnome a handkerchief from my pocket. He was no taller than four foot and covered in soot.

"The Orcs." The Gnome wiped the soot from his face. "Who else? The blasted monsters torched the place, destroying everything."

What if they were already ahead of us? Had they found another route? Perhaps they understood Lake Delendil was our last option for safety. We had to press on.

"My most sincere apologies. I fear this is our doing."

Before the Gnome could reply, another appeared, holding a handful of charred crops and a pail of water.

"The king sent one soldier? What good is that going to do?" she raged.

"The king didn't send me to help," Felix explained. "The Orcs want the royal family destroyed. We're looking for refuge."

She stared from Felix to me. "Princess Evalyn. Oh, goodness. We are here to serve you, Your Grace, although we have little to offer you." She dropped her crops and bucket of water to the ground and curtsied in front of me. When she rose, she flattened her crumpled, dirty skirt.

"Water would be appreciated." I offered a warm smile. "We have been travelling for two days now. What are your names?"

"I'm Gnovash," the female Gnome responded. "And this is my husband, Finbrik."

The two Gnomes hurried to show us the well, surrounded by burnt, collapsed houses. Buckets tied with rope were lowered into the depths and brought back overflowing with fresh water. I filled my wineskin, took a mouthful, then placed it in my pack. Beyond the well were rows of corpses wrapped in blankets—those who'd perished in the fire. They'd been no match against the Orcs, and a mixture of rage and grief overwhelmed me. I gripped the edge of the well to steady myself. I wouldn't show weakness in front of them.

All around me, Gnomes poured buckets of water on the smouldering remains of their homes to salvage anything they could.

A gust of wind fuelled the embers flickering on the houses at the outer edges of the village. The fire raged—the strong oaken trusses of the homes were stripped bare.

Flames burst from nearby buildings, shooting smoke above, and lashing out onto the nearby cottages. Screams of children pierced the air as the central house buckled, and a beam collapsed, blocking the entrance.

Felix dashed towards them. Its roof had buckled, and the Gnomes outside struggled to push the door open. The beam blocked the doorway, lodged between the debris from the crumbling walls.

Two elder Gnomes grunted as they attempted to dislodge the beam. One of them lost their grip, then tumbled backwards into the dirt. Felix hurled a beam that blocked the entrance and caved the door in with his foot. He scooped up the children and delivered them to the arms of their waiting mother.

"Thank you! How can I repay you?" The mother held each child in turn, inspecting them for injuries. Sooty tears fell from her eyes as she embraced them and buried her face into their hair.

He watched the mother with a sparkle in his eyes.

"You owe me nothing," he said. "Travel with us to Lake Delendil where you'll be safe until your home can be restored."

"Civilians of Westwilde, please gather around," Finbrik called.

We stood beside Gnovash as she spoke. "As your chosen leader of Westwilde, it is my responsibility to ensure your safety and provide you with homes and food. After the devastation caused by the Orcs, we have no other choice but to seek refuge at Lake Delendil."

The Gnomes in front of us were carrying the few personal belongings they'd managed to save from the fire. Eyes brimming with tears stared back at us.

"How would we protect so many unarmed, untrained civilians?" I asked Felix in a hushed tone.

"We'll find a way," he said, although his eyes had darkened.

"We are blessed to have Princess Evalyn and her loyal companion beside us and the gods in our hearts," Finbrik said.

"You can find peace at Lake Delendil under the protection of the High Elves," Felix added, scanning the crowd, eyeing the devastation before him. "I cannot predict the difficulty of the journey. We may encounter more enemies, more destruction, and we must offer protection to those who need it. The law requires it. Grab anything you can use as a weapon, and ready yourselves to move onwards."

Felix and the Gnomes dug graves while I gathered wildflowers with the Gnome children. Once the dead were buried, we laid the flowers on top of the graves, and the villagers whispered their farewells.

When it was time to leave, the survivors picked up metal poles, knives, and bats. The younger ones formed a phalanx with armed adults guarding them along each side of the queue. A few of them carried bags of salvaged supplies—food, medicine, and tools.

We led the way out of the destroyed settlement, with Gnovash, Finbrik, and their people behind.

Atop a nearby hill, the Gnomes turned to stare at the smoke filling the air. We gazed in silence upon the town they'd resided in for many years.

One by one, the Orcs would raze all the settlements of the Light Triads to the ground. When our souls were hurting, they would attack with all their strength and brutality. If they won, they'd obtain dominion over the territories, and no tribe would question their authority.

I pulled out my map and peered at the neat drawings of each settlement, their names inscribed at the bottom. The route northwards would take us to Bluefair Fort, home of Centaurs. We continued our journey until the blue and purple tinges to the sky meant night would soon be upon us. We needed to rest.

We travelled to the edge of a forest. The canopy of broad leaves would conceal us from the harsh winds of night, and the carpeted forest floor would give us warmth.

I lowered myself onto the grass and stretched out my tired legs. "We still have eyes on the field from here, and we will hear the enemy coming by the crunching of leaves." Felix said, a softness to his voice. "No harm will come to you."

"I trust you," I said matter-of-factly. There was no reason not to.

Gnovash laid out a blanket for each group. The food and supplies the Gnomes carried were set on a flat piece of grass. Everyone collapsed onto the blankets around it.

Felix let out a deep sigh as he sat on the dry floor near an old and frayed bag of supplies. He tossed his helmet to the side, slid onto his back, then propped his head against the bag, looking up at the starless sky through the gaps in the trees. "It's sad, isn't it?" He pointed to the heavens. "No stars. It must be an omen."

"Gee." I rolled my eyes. "Now that's depressing." I nudged closer to him, laying my head beside his and shared his view.

An omen, he'd called it. How long would it be before the stars returned?

A silence fell over the field as the Gnomes slept. Felix's steady breathing beside me eased my stress. A long journey was ahead of us before Lake Delendil would be in sight.

"I pray to the gods we will survive the trip." I rolled onto my side, facing him. Flattening my hands into a prayer, I placed them between my cheek and the bag my head rested on.

He turned to face me, the hazel of his eyes glinting under the soft moonlight.

"How can we live in a world fraught with tragedy and war?" Tears pricked my eyes. The Gnomes snored gently nearby. An icy wind stirred through the forest, so I huddled against Felix for warmth. He was strong and solid. Reliable. His smooth, warm sandalwood scent reeled me in.

He lifted his fingers to his neck, unclasped a leather woven necklace and handed it to me.

I traced my fingers over the ridged beads. "I think it's chipped."

He laughed. "No, the beads are engraved with runes, and the gold clasps are etched with Celtic knots. I've had this necklace since I was a child. Should anything happen to me, I want you to have it. I wouldn't want this to be lost in a field or stolen. Keep it safe. Consider it a lucky charm." He took the necklace from me, fastened it around my neck, then brushed away a stray tear, which trickled down my cheek. "Rest."

"Thank you." I lowered my voice to a whisper.
"What for?"
"For being here."

———————— ❧ ————————

We set out the next morning, arriving at Bluefair Fort after a half a day of travel.

The fort was built on flat ground with sandstone walls and thin, short towers. Two armed Humans guarded the entrance. Archers stood along the top of the wall, drawing their bow strings to their chests as we approached. I raised my empty hands for them to see.

A guard stepped forwards, his hand grasping the handle of his sword. Its dull engraving and tarnishes meant it was not Arogathean steel.

The guard studied my face, a thick frown etched between his eyebrows. After a moment of contemplation, he lifted his hand to the archers, signalling for them to stand down.

"The Princess of Arogath." He doffed his helmet and offered a slight bow. He glanced at the long line of restless Gnomes behind me. "Dear gods, what's happened?"

"The Orcs. They burned Westwilde to the ground, destroying their food and supplies. It is imperative they find immediate safety."

"Where are you headed?" The guard slid his sword into its sheath, gaze fixed on the Gnome population accompanying us.

"Lake Delendil, but I fear the journey is too dangerous for us all to pursue. May I ask that the Gnomes stay here? A great war is coming." I stared back at the guard, keeping my voice strong and confident.

"You'd have to speak to the council. They alone have the power to sanction guardianship of other clans, Your Grace." He pulled the lever to lift the gate. "This fort has been made strong since the Centaurs and Humans joined forces. Two tribes already reside here, so it all comes down to space."

"Wait." Gnovash frowned. "What about Lake Delendil? That's the safest place for our people!"

"It's safer for you to stay here, at least for the time being. The Orcs are tracking us, Gnovash. Your

31

people are not trained in battle and would be at a severe disadvantage when it comes to holding them off," I explained. If the council of Bluefair had space for the Gnomes, Felix and I could continue our journey, and at a faster pace.

"Our original plan was to find refuge with the High Elves. But it has become clear this realm will be torn apart if we don't do something," Felix said to the guard, the muscles in his face twitching. "I'm sure the High Elves will intervene before this turns into a civil war. Do we have your support?"

"Like I said, you'll have to ask the council. I don't speak for them." The guard led us through the centre of the fort towards the main hall. Smoke from a blacksmith's forge hung in the air and Centaurs' hooves lifted clouds of dust as they rode over the cobblestones. Market stalls outside the hall sold pheasants and wild rabbit, legs trussed, hanging from wooden poles. Clotheslines connected each house to the next with garments pegged up to dry under the sun.

The Gnomes congregated outside the main hall, waiting for the council's verdict.

A table, covered by an ancient map of the realm, stretched across the length of the hall. Two Centaurs and two Humans gathered round, conversing.

"Princess Evalyn and her companion," the guard announced. He bowed at me, then left the hall.

The four members of the council lowered their heads in a bow.

A Human with long blond hair tied back moved around the table, approaching me. "We were not expecting you, Your Grace," he said in a baritone voice. The faces of the council were strained, and some held their fingers to their temples. "Why have you come here?"

Felix stepped forwards. "We have come to—"

"I beg your pardon, but he asked the princess," one of the Centaurs said. His hair was black, matching the coat that covered his lean horse half.

A muscle feathered in Felix's jaw, but he didn't say anything else.

I cleared my throat. My gaze travelled from one council member to the next, studying their frowning faces. Had I walked into a heated debate? Wooden figures dotted the map, marking each clan in the Fertile and Barren Territories.

"A civil war is brewing. The Orcs are getting stronger, rallying all the races along the right side of the map." I pointed to the Dark Triads' wooden figures. "I left the king at the Eyrie. We plan to go to Lake Delendil to seek the help of the High Elves. Along our route, we came across Westwilde, which has now been burnt to the ground."

"Bloody Orcs," the blond-headed Human raged. A large steel shield hung across his back, clanking with his sword as his fists hit the table. He stared at the map.

"We ask that the Gnomes live here in the meantime. I am aware your fort is rather full already, but there doesn't seem to be much choice. There's approximately thirty of them."

The other Human with cropped brown hair placed his fingers to his lips. "We already have food shortages—the Orcs have destroyed our food supply lines. We can't house any more, Eric!"

The blond-haired Human, Eric, frowned. It seemed he had the deciding vote. He discussed it with the two Centaurs for a moment.

"Yes, we have food shortages, but we can't leave an entire clan to fend for themselves out in the open." one of the Centaurs said.

"It is decided, then." Eric placed his hand on the hilt of his sword. "They will remain here until the Orcs are defeated and peace is restored."

"I will show them around and make arrangements for their housing," the other Human said before leaving the main hall.

Eric straightened. "I must inform you, Your Grace, we received a letter by bird this morning. The king is dead. Unfortunately, the courtiers, council members, and servants lost their lives too."

I gasped. My airflow was blocked by the lump forming in my throat. A part of me hoped the king and his guards would have fought, attempted to stave off the Orcs, or even reduce their numbers.

How could I make decisions without any guidance from a higher power?

I dug my fingers into my palms as thoughts swarmed my mind, unable to organise them into coherent chains.

"The king's guards were slaughtered so what happens when *we* come head-to-head with the Orcs?" one of the Centaurs asked.

"You must send s-some of your men to the settlements allied to us. Enlist as many people as possible." I stumbled over my words, trying to make a logical decision when an intense wave of grief constricted my chest. I couldn't afford to make any wrong decisions.

"That won't be enough," Felix interjected. "Look at the Dark Triads: Orcs, Trolls, Dark Mages, and whatever else they conjure up. They harness a lot of Dark Magic and because of your uncle's betrayal, they'll want to overthrow the monarchy."

"And now that the Orcs have, there's nothing stopping them. Let's hope we are strong enough to end them."

Eric nodded. His brow wrinkled for a moment before he lifted his hand. "It's time for you to accept your magical inheritance, Your Grace. I see your eyes aren't glowing, and your skin is Human. A mage's power alters the appearance. I'm sure it'll catch up with you soon."

"No. I will not put myself through that or inflict…the gods know what onto the people of this fort." My powers were unreliable, uncontrollable. The risk was too high.

"Forgive me, Your Grace, but you must. For the sake of the realm's peace and stability."

"My abilities have been concealed deep within me for years. I can't." I turned on my heel and left. Out in the yard, I was alone.

I collapsed onto a bench underneath a tree at the back of the fort where there were no buildings. Letting out a shaky breath, I drew my knees to my chest.

Within a few weeks, I'd been strong enough to destroy buildings and injure anybody nearby, if I'd needed to, so I'd disregarded it. I'd banished it to the farthest corners of my mind, allowing me to be as Human as possible. Now Eric wanted me to unleash my power and use it against the Orcs. I shuddered. It would cause more chaos and problems than it would solve.

Felix appeared, walking towards me. He offered a warm smile and sat next to me, holding his helmet on his lap. "Don't worry, Your Grace, I'll take you to meet the Oracle in the morning."

A long moment of silence followed.

"I don't want this," I admitted, scratching some dirt off the hem of my shirt. "My mother was a mage, but she died when I was a child, and I haven't had the guidance I needed to fully control my magic. At such a young age, I couldn't grasp the concept of possessing such power. It wasn't until I was older that the magic surged within me. I could wield bright beams, which caused destruction. You've been in the King's Guard for as long as I've known you. You know what I'm capable of."

"From what I can remember, the king and your father spent several years trying to find your mother, but her body was never found. Then your father disappeared, and the newly appointed King Atticus called off the search. While we have soldiers who can fight the Orcs and the other Dark Triads, we'll need your abilities. You're the only one who has enough power to challenge the Dark Mages. The High Elves will receive word of your uncle's death if they haven't already. They'll want to keep you protected," he said, rising from the bench. "Maybe you might consider using it again."

My heart thumped in my chest, waiting for him to yell or lecture me on the reasons I should do as I'm told for the greater good. His smooth, yet deep voice echoed in my head.

"While the king's decisions have created tension between the Orcs and the Light Triads, you can fix this." Felix balanced his helmet against his hip. "At least give it some thought."

He led the way to a house we'd been allocated to sleep in for the night. As we strolled through the silent pathways of Bluefair Fort, my mind buzzed. I reflected on the day's events. If I unleashed my magic, could I restore peace in the kingdom? Would it be enough to end the Orcs for good?

"I will do it for my people." I nodded. "Regardless of what dangers it may cause. I'll meet the Oracle."

Felix tilted his head, and his mouth curved into that not-quite-a-smile I was so familiar with.

If there was a chance I could save lives and prevent a war, then I needed to overcome my festering fear.

We walked along the cobblestone path towards the terrace cottage, and through the window of the first house, I saw Finbrik and Gnovash huddled around a circular table. A book lay open on top.

When we reached our designated cottage, we were greeted by a Human named Joy who showed us to our rooms.

Felix stopped outside his bedroom door. "I'll see you in the morning, Your Grace. I'll be right here if you need me."

"Goodnight." I smiled, then entered my chamber.

The textured ceiling was low, and the four stone block walls were exposed. I collapsed on top of the thin and worn mattress, each muscle in my body ached. I'd travelled far in a couple of days, and every part of me hurt.

Closing my eyes, I succumbed to oblivion.

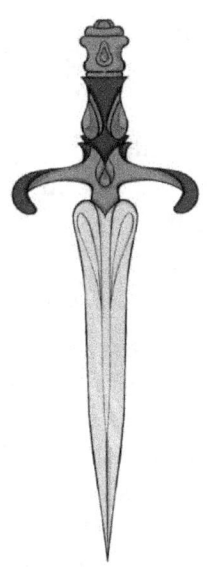

Chapter Three

I stood alone outside the Oracle's workshop. Nausea churned my stomach. Felix had guided me here, muttered he was proud of me, then had left for the blacksmith. My mind buzzed with the fear of war, of death, and of myself and the magic within me. I'd barely had time to process the death of my uncle, and the fate of the kingdom now resting upon my shoulders, and there wasn't enough time for me to master *and* learn to control my powers. Time was my enemy.

I knocked on the wooden door, expecting it to creak open and anticipating the danger lurking behind it. A grey-haired woman dressed in a jewel-embellished and embroidered robe opened the door.

"I've been expecting you," she said.

The magic I'd abandoned long ago stirred in my veins—my arms tingled, and my fingers trembled as blood pumped into my wrists. The scent of molten iron tingled my nostrils. I closed my eyes and relaxed my arms until the charge subsided.

"Felix notified me you'd show. Best come in, dear." She welcomed me into a faint-lit room with deep purple drapes covering the windows.

Peering around the doorway, anticipating a crystal ball and some tarot cards, I arched an eyebrow. Indeed, a crystal ball was placed on top of the tablecloth next to a black velvet pouch. Jars of herbs and roots were positioned on a bookshelf, filling the room with the strong scent of cinnamon. A ginger cat purred and licked its paws as it curled up on the cream rug in the centre of the room.

"Take a seat." The Oracle gestured as she settled into a burgundy chair next to her table.

I held my breath for a moment before reclining into the chair opposite her.

Picking up the pouch, she undid the drawstrings, then emptied a collection of tiny stones in various colours into her palm.

"Gemstones." She lined them in front of me. Her eyes were light amongst the wrinkles around them. "It may seem a bit silly, but I advise you to keep these on your person at all times. They have strong healing and strengthening properties that will aid you in times of dire need."

I picked up the first stone, a purple one with a jagged texture.

"Amethyst," she said. "Develops awareness and intuition. Two things you'll need in dangerous and life-threatening situations."

I placed the stone back on the table and picked up the next one— a deep blue and angular stone.

"That would be the warrior stone—agate—best known for boosting confidence and courage."

She told me the qualities of the rest of the stones, then tucked them into the pouch, leaving a pale rose-coloured one in front of me. The candle on the table pierced the surface and created a prism of pale pink.

The Oracle smiled.

"What?"

"The stone has lit your face in a hue of soft pink," she said. "Just like those beads."

I jolted back as the necklace warmed around my neck.

"Rose quartz," she said. "The stone of love. It will open your heart in your darkest of times, and the purity of love will heal you. But first, you must let it."

"What do you mean?" I touched the beads.

"The stone will encourage you to welcome affection and kindness from those around you, but you must take it upon yourself to do the rest. You must allow love into your heart." The Oracle placed the stone in the pouch, then tied the drawstrings and handed it to me. "If a war happens, which I'm sure it will, you'll need these the most."

"The quality of each stone is a lot to remember." I fiddled with the pouch. My stomach knotted and sweat formed on my neck. The longer I was here for the sooner I'd come face to face with my powers.

"The discussion of auric fields will also be of use." She rose from her chair, the golden bangles on her arm clanking together, then headed to the kitchen. "But we will have some tea first."

A few minutes later, the scent of berry tea wafted through the room.

She returned with a silver tray in her hands and placed the china mugs on the table before taking her seat.

"Now we can continue. One must be at peace when trying to balance one's auric fields. If you're stressed or worried, you might as well leave."

I nodded, the words replaying in my mind. Staring at my shaking fingers resting on my lap, I lifted a hand to grip my mug. I brought it to my lips and sipped the warm, fruity tea.

"There are four chakras that I will talk to you about today. They must be balanced to ensure your magic is being produced to its full potential. The sacral is based in the lower abdomen embodying your emotions and sensuality—your natural desires." She clasped her mug firmly.

My cheeks warmed as the image of Felix crossed my mind.

The Oracle raised her eyebrows. "The heart chakra is our ability to love and find inner peace. The rose quartz I have given you should help you with this." She placed her hand on mine. "I do encourage you to find love, Evalyn, in these dark times."

Every citizen of the Fertile Territories knew the devastation my family faced, and they were dependent on me.

I exhaled. She met my eyes with her own drooping ones. "My priority is my people— protecting them and our homes. Tell me more about these chakras and how they can help me."

"The third eye, the most important of all, is in one's mind." She put her finger between her brows. "It's quite a mystical concept for someone to understand, yet it is said to provide one with perception beyond their ordinary sight. It represents a higher consciousness that allows one to observe other auric fields and use them as they will."

The Arogathean realm was full of magical creatures, possessing Light and Dark Magic and extraordinary abilities. I hadn't witnessed anyone detaching their mind from soul or using their higher consciousness to manipulate another being.

"Exploiting another's auric field seems quite barbaric," I muttered. "Controlling all of their auric fields would mean you'd have total control over their energy flow and have them do whatever you wanted."

"It's awful, yes." The Oracle finished her tea and plucked a leather-bound book from the shelf nearby. She opened it and turned over the thick parchment pages until she reached one near the centre. "It's called the Crimson Kiss, and it has been used before, but many centuries ago. The book tells us the story of when the Dark Mages first used it."

"I've heard parts of the story. The Noble Ones stopped them."

"The Noble Ones were Light Mages, just like you. They conquered evil," she said.

I leaned back against the chair. How in the realm would I save so many lives when faced with such a powerful threat? A chill ran down my spine, and the hairs on my arms stood on end.

"We have one final chakra. The crown, located at the top of your head, represents your connection to spirituality and life. Rather than it being intellectual, it is the convergence of your mind and soul with the universe and nature."

My head throbbed. There were many things to remember and such little time.

"Now to address how these will help you: The importance of the auric fields is keeping them balanced to allow energy to flow. You'll be able to cast stronger spells and harness your abilities." Her lips curved into a smile as she nudged my mug of tea towards me. "Drink your tea, and you can finish for the day. Process what you have learned, and we will resume tomorrow."

"Before I go, I wanted to ask you about the prophecy. Felix said you knew about it." I sipped my tea and kept my gaze fixed on her.

"I have only heard legendary tales on the matter—much like many others. The true prophecy is written in ancient texts at the Citadel. What I believe, is that the daughter of a Mage, a being of purity is destined to rule the realm, and rectify the mistakes made by your uncle and father." She smiled.

"I'll look for the book when I arrive. What mistakes did my father make? How will I rectify them when I don't know what they are?" I frowned. "I've learned some spells from my own spell book, but it won't be enough for us to win this war."

"Don't fret." She placed her hand on mine. "Come back tomorrow, and we will continue. You will be ready."

I found Felix in the local tavern, dressed in casual attire—a sight to which my eyes were not accustomed. A thin cotton vest hung from his shoulders, with the drawstrings around the neck hem untied. The edge of his collarbones poked out from behind the hem, and I had the instinctive urge to trace them with my fingers. My mouth dried—I needed to get a grip. He'd already rejection my flirtations in the past, and I doubted he would welcome my attentions now.

The chatter and bustle of the local Humans eased the twisting sensation in the pit of my stomach. I slumped into a plush armchair and looked out towards an outdoor courtyard.

Flowerbeds bloomed with red tulips, and Humans sat on dark walnut benches. They held steins while deep in conversation with the Centaurs.

"How'd it go?" Felix snapped my attention back to him. He held a half-empty pint of beer in his hands and leaned back into his armchair.

No longer concealed by a helm, his hair stuck up in odd places. Candles were positioned on each table, and their warm glow illuminated his hazel eyes. I swallowed, which did nothing to rid the dryness from my mouth.

A fireplace against the stone wall crackled, warming my skin, and would hopefully conceal the heat rising in my cheeks.

"She said something that puzzled me. She said my father had made mistakes. I learned about the chakras, but I haven't actually practised my magic yet. I fear it will be hard work, and we are running out of time." I propped my elbow onto the armrest of the chair and placed my fingers on my forehead. Tendrils of dark hair hung around my face. "There's so much to learn, and we should be leaving for Lake Delendil within the next couple of days. I haven't used my magic in a few years—who knows what will happen when I unleash it at the Oracle's workshop tomorrow?"

He sipped his beer, and the softness in his hazel eyes dulled the edges of the constricting pain inside me. "I wouldn't let it worry you too much," he responded. "What good will it do you? Besides, I'm sure the Oracle will have you ready in time. I'll bet she said just as much. Have some faith in yourself— I do. I'll get you some food and a drink."

Felix rose from his chair and went to the bar. A few minutes later, he returned with a pint of beer and a bowl of stew for me. I didn't have much tolerance for beer, or alcohol in general for that matter, but I didn't complain.

"What have *you* been doing all this time?" I took a gulp from my dark oak stein, then dug into the hearty meal.

"I spoke to a few of the Centaur soldiers at the barracks— discussed some battle strategies. Nobody has admitted it, but people are scared. They fear the clash of the Light and Dark Triads could lead to perpetual disaster."

"Light and Dark Magic are of equal strength. In the end, it'll come down to tactics. We won't have room for errors if the Dark Mages decide to use their Crimson Kiss spell." I rested my spoon in the bowl.

"Did the Oracle tell you about it?" He grimaced. "I'm hoping this won't be the start of its return—"

"Let's enjoy tonight." I forced a smile. "And for the record, I'm glad I have you as my companion."

After we finished our food and drinks, Felix and I returned to the bench we'd sat on the night before. The smell of stale beer travelled with us, but we left behind the raucous laughter from the tavern. Twilight fell over the realm, yet an orange glow remained close to the horizon. Candlelight in the windows of houses lit the cobblestones, and the scent of roast pig hung in the air as families settled in for the night.

I withdrew the pouch of gemstones from my pocket, clutching the stones between my hands. My neck tingled from the rising heat of the necklace as I drew the pouch closer to my body.

I uttered a silent prayer. *If you can hear me, gods, please make these stones work. Bring me peace during the battles to come.*

"Did you know about this?" I showed him the glowing beads.

"No." He arched a dark brow. "It's never done that before. Perhaps it is your missing link."

"To what?" I tilted my head to the side, studying his face.

"The link that will give your magic added potency." Leaning across, he brushed his fingers against my arm. His gaze briefly lowered to my mouth, and the distance between us grew smaller. I recoiled from the unexpected sign of affection and stared at him, heart pounding.

"We should check in on the Gnomes, and see if they've settled in okay," I suggested. "Perhaps there's something we can do to provide them comfort."

———————— .⌣. ————————

The following day, another cloudless sky loomed with a cool breeze in the shade between buildings. The birds sung from the tall trees framing the fort. I rolled up my sleeves and stretched my arms under the warming sunlight. Centaur children played hide and sought, and their laughter resonated through the fort. Their bottoms stuck out from behind poles which couldn't conceal them.

Felix and I parted ways at the blacksmith's, and I continued down the path until I arrived at the Oracle's workshop.

"I'm sure you've rested, yes?" she asked as she handed me a croissant and a mug of chamomile tea. "Today, you must focus all of your energy. You'll learn how to use and control your magic."

I ate a mouthful of the soft, flaky pastry, then wiped the corners of my mouth. "Eric mentioned something about a Mage's magic altering their appearance. Is it true?"

"Once you've embraced your magic, it can alter the way you look, yes. It's difficult to say how, though," she said.

"We can't be sure how many Mages the Dark Triads have in their ranks." I wrapped my fingers around the mug of tea. "And the likelihood of fighting them during battle is high."

She clasped her hands together. "We will prepare you, Evalyn. For the sake of the realm."

"How?" I voice came out quieter than I had expected. It certainly didn't give me the air of confidence I desperately needed.

"I shall teach you. Come on." She shooed the cat from her seated position in the middle of the floor. "Magic is linked to your emotional state. You need to learn to focus yourself by balancing your chakras. When you're ready, try to create a ball of light between your hands. Clear your mind, picture it, and it will form."

I followed her to the centre of the room, then wiped my sweating hands on my thighs. Taking a deep breath, I cupped my palms and fixed my gaze on the creases along the skin. "It's not working."

"It's not going to straight away. Your self-doubt is blocking your abilities. Felix told me you blew up the bridge—what emotion charged that?"

"Anger." I met her gaze.

"Exactly. Now you need to relax and set aside your worries. Concentrate."

I flexed my fingers and imagined a spinning ball of light. The magic hissed, smoke formed, and a dim light flickered in the centre.

Frowning, I concentrated on it, but the tiny light dwindled.

"See? Progress! Again," she said.

I closed my eyes and composed myself. Magic coursed through my veins towards my wrists. A tingling sensation warmed my palms.

"Great work, Evalyn!"

Opening my eyes, I peered at the brilliant white light emitting through the cracks between my fingers. I relaxed my hands and the light shot upwards, blasting a hole through the ceiling. Chunks of wood fell around me.

I trapped the light in my palm and glanced at the Oracle.

"Breathe, let your heart rate drop, and the magic will go away," she said. "That's it. Slowly in. Hold it. Slowly out."

I sucked in even breaths, focusing on the diminishing light. "There," the Oracle said a few moments later. "It's gone."

"Wow." I glanced at the gaping hole in the ceiling. A cloud of dust hung in the air. "I didn't know what to expect. Maybe my magic would be as strong as it usually is. Or weaker, perhaps. But I didn't expect that. I'm sorry for damaging your workshop."

The Oracle smiled. "This is a place to break and rebuild."

Which was a metaphor, I assumed.

I stroked the cat as she weaved around my legs. "When I destroyed the rope bridge, my magic was red, not white. Why is that?"

She smiled, not even a hint of concern on her face. "White magic is pure. It changes colour when it is charged with an emotion. Now try practicing your magic while keeping your eyes open. If you need to use it in battle, you must be ready instantly."

I nodded, puffing out a sigh.

A clear imagine formed in my mind's eye—each of my chakras took on the form of golden orbs, which aligned side by side. The white light swelled in my palms. My fingers trembled. I tried to steady the enlarging ball by shaping it into a small sphere. It hovered in place, and I grinned.

I practised forming my magic throughout the morning. The Oracle brought us bread and cheese at mid-afternoon, and once we ate our meals, I resumed my training. By the time evening was upon us, my head throbbed, and my eyes ached.

"I think we are done for the day." She rubbed my arm. "Take the evening off and get some rest."

"Thank you for helping me." I traced circles on my temples as I headed towards the door.

She opened it and bid me farewell.

As I trailed along the cobbles towards the blacksmith's, my stomach rumbled. The sun was sinking into the horizon, casting an orange glow into the purple tinge of sky.

Smoke plumed from the forge—the acrid scent of red-hot iron filled my nose. I found Felix deep in conversation with the blacksmith.

"Do you want to grab dinner from the tavern?" I glanced from the newly polished swords on display to Felix.

"Sure. I'll catch you later, Jon." He nodded to the blacksmith, then led the way down the cobbles.

Once we were sat inside the tavern, Felix waved to the owner.

"What can I get you?" the owner asked.

"Beef stew for us, please." Felix handed him two coins.

The man nodded, then dashed into the kitchens. Shortly afterwards, he returned, then placed two bowls on our table.

I stabbed a piece of beef with my fork, dunked it into the soup, then popped it into my mouth. "I don't know about you, but I'm *starving*."

Felix smiled. "You seem chipper. I take it everything went well with the Oracle?"

I laughed around a mouthful of food. "Something like that. I forgot to ask her about my father, though."

Once I finished my food, I pushed the bowl aside and leaned back in my chair. With a full belly from a warm meal, I cupped my hands together and concentrated.

"Are you sure that's a good idea? Indoors?" He propped his elbows onto the table and leaned forward. His eyes gleamed.

"Just watch." I focused on the lines of my palms until the magic sparked and crackled. The light grew brighter. It spun around in a perfectly spherical shape. I grinned as the magic coursed through my being, pouring from me into the sphere and creating a tether.

"I'm impressed—you have more control." He raised his stein and gulped. "You should be proud."

I concentrated on my breathing to keep it steady, and the magic dissipated. "It's definitely a start."

The following morning, I sat on the floor with my back against the bed. I held the gemstones in my hands, hoping they'd give me strength to find the answers to the many questions that plagued my mind. The Orcs were never going to stop. How was I supposed save everyone from destruction and the Dark Triads' tyrannical rule? I'd need help from the Elven council of Lake Delendil to govern the kingdom after the defeat of the Dark Triads.

Once the gemstones were inside the velvet pouch, I tucked it into my pocket.

I steadied my palms and took three deep breaths, as the Oracle had taught me. The ball of light formed. It spun, drenching the room in its brilliant white light.

Someone knocked on the door, then opened it slightly.

Felix peered his head around. "Morning. May I come in?"

"Sure, I was just practising." I dropped my hands, and the magic disappeared.

Lowering onto the floor beside me, he brushed against me, sending a tingling sensation through my arm.

"We can't stay here any longer." I peered at him from the corner of my eyes, trying to focus on our mission as opposed to the scattering of faint freckles across his nose or the long curl of his dark lashes. "We need to get to Lake Delendil and speak with the High Elves. Perhaps they can assist us in negotiating with the Orcs. They'll know I'm not to blame for my uncle's actions. Surely, they will want another opportunity to make things right."

"Not with the prophecy, Your Grace," he said. "They're after you. Did the Oracle tell you why?"

"I'm supposed to unite the people and rule over the kingdoms." I shook my head. "The Orcs gave my uncle one last chance, and he blew it."

"You're not your uncle." The corner of his lips curved into a smile, and he bumped his shoulder against mine in a playful manner. "Although you have a point—we can't stay in one place for too long in case they get wind of us being here. If that happens, they may attack the fort."

I stood, draped my cloak over my shoulder, then grabbed my satchel.

"Before we leave, I have a favour to ask."

"What is it?" he asked.

"When it is just you and me, call me Evalyn. Not Your Grace, or Your Majesty—as I guess that's what I am now. Just Evalyn. I need to feel normal, like myself, and my name without an honorific will keep me grounded." There was something oddly intimidate about asking this of a royal guard, but he was all I had left of my home.

"As you wish… Evalyn." My name sounded like velvet when he spoke.

I turned away from him, quelling the fluttering in my stomach, and headed downstairs.

"Thank you for having us, Joy." I entered the sitting room. "It's time for us to resume our journey to Lake Delendil."

She moved to one side and smiled. "You are welcome here any time. I will pack some fruits, nuts, cured meats, and bread for your journey. May the gods bless you."

"Thank you." I waited while she stuffed the food items into a brown bag, then handed it to me.

I shoved the food into my satchel, then exited the house with Felix leading the way. Outside, sombre clouds threatened to release rain upon the kingdom.

We hurried to the Main Hall where Eric swung open the door, then approached the map on the table.

"We've received news from the Woodland Elves in Rushdale Forest. Their homes have been set ablaze." He pointed to a dense forest region between the fort and Lake Delendil. "Many have died. The survivors have already started their journey to Lake Delendil."

"I know people who lived at Rushdale Forest…" Felix said, voice strained.

Without thinking, I placed my hand on his arm. "We'll help the survivors, just like we did at Westwilde."

Felix nodded, his jaw set in a hard line.

"I cannot accompany you on your travels, although I wish you the very best," Eric said, and bowed his head. "Try to use your magic when you can afford to. Practice is all you need."

I appreciated his words were meant to instil some level of hope in me, but my heart remained heavy. The Orcs were moving too quickly, causing destruction faster than I could master my powers. A couple of days with the Oracle wouldn't be enough, and Eric was right. I'd need to practice whenever—and wherever—I could.

Eric guided us to the main entrance of Bluefair Fort, where the Oracle awaited us.

"I've decided to travel with you, Your Majesty." She clasped her hands in front of her. "I have some business to attend to at Lake Delendil, and I thought it would be comforting to have me with you."

"How did you know that we were leaving now?" I glanced at the small leather bag she held and arched a brow. "What about your roof?"

"I'm an Oracle, remember?" She laughed. "I've already spoken to a builder who's going to take care of it. He'll look after the cat too."

The guards at the gate raised their hands into a salute as we walked through the entrance.

"The Queen of Arogath," a guard bellowed. "May the gods watch over you."

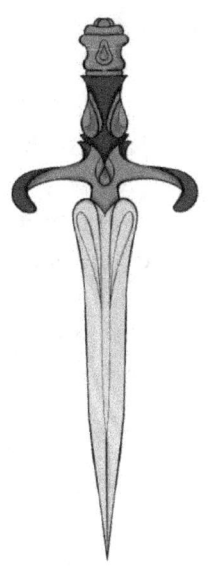

Chapter Four

Turbulent storm clouds crackled overhead as we walked through a wildwood. Rain fell through the canopy, pattering onto the leaves, and dripping icy water onto our heads. Brambles caught and tugged our lower garments as we waded through the pools of water forming between the rampant vines on the forest floor.

Felix wandered along the moss-covered ground. He groaned, changing direction every so often to avoid a cliff-face or a shaft from an underground cavern. He slipped across the sodden ground and fell. My heart lurched.

"Damn it," he huffed, covered in thick mud. Shards of grass and damp leaves clung to his legs.

"Are you okay?" I bent and hooked my forearms under his armpits. I glanced at the Oracle over my shoulders. "Could you give me a hand?"

Together, we hoisted Felix out of the ditch, his body resisting against the densely packed wet mud.

"Thanks," he said, and his gaze lowered to my neck. "Your necklace is glowing again."

As if in reaction to his voice, my neck warmed, and the beads tingled my skin.

"It *is* an interesting necklace," the Oracle muttered.

I changed the subject to avoid making a fool of myself. "You should have worn darker clothing." I pointed at her crepe-de-chine cream pants, spoiled by mud stains. The fabric had been torn by the thorny brambles, and the hems were damp and clinging to her ankles.

The Oracle waved the matter away. "How about a story to keep us entertained?"

Felix shrugged, but the Oracle's sing-song voice relaxed the tension in my shoulders. I wasn't alone. The constant slosh of footsteps beside me steadied my heartbeat.

"Have you ever heard of the Ezen Riders legend?" she asked.

I frowned. "I've heard the name before, but those types of stories aren't usually shared in the Eyrie."

"During the time of the Noble Ones, the legend says that the Dark Mages conjured the Ezen Riders— four deadly women mounted on bears—to do their bidding. They encompassed all evil—the apocalypse—and were extremely powerful, an almighty force to combat."

"So what happened? Was there an apocalypse?" I tugged my cloak around me and scanned my surroundings, letting my magic hum beneath my skin in case I might need it.

"Not that time. Believe it or not, the Light Mages worked with the Orcs and the Trolls to destroy the portal before any damage was done."

"I guess now is as good a time to know as any: What has my father done? What mistakes of his must I rectify?"

The undergrowth rustled. I spun around. The bushes swayed as though as animal swept past them.

"Did you hear that?" I jolted to the left.

"Wait here while I check ahead." Felix freed his sword from its scabbard and trod towards the crunching leaves. Twigs snapped under his feet. I froze.

A fox darted from between the foliage, crossed our path, then disappeared behind the oak trees.

"Blasted animal," I spat.

Felix hilted his sword. "You're okay. These forests are rife with wildlife, but this is getting ridiculous." He removed his helmet. "Everything looks the same in here. The forest is supposed to be a mile long, but we've been walking around for ages."

The Oracle lifted a finger to her lips for a moment. Her eyes widened.

"What is it?"

"It's a labyrinth," she answered. "Yes, that must be it. Hand me the map."

Felix passed it to her and peered over her shoulder.

"The map shows a small forest, as I suspected. We should have reached the edge by now." She traced her finger over the forest on the map. "A spell has been cast to slow us down."

"A Dark Mage?" Bile rose in my throat.

"Yes." She frowned. "Perhaps a reflection spell, so the trees never seem to end."

"How do you suggest we get out?" He kept his voice level, in control. Not a single line of frustration marred the planes of his face "It'll take another two days to get to Lake Delendil, and that doesn't account for a stop in Rushdale Forest. We can't afford further delays."

The Oracle handed the map to him. "There is a counter spell. Evalyn, you'll need to cast it."

"Am I ready?" I squeaked, adrenaline flooding through my veins.

"Of course," she said. "Think of a great force that would have the power to split something in half. Remember what I said—you need to balance your chakras. Focus on your breathing." Her gaze fell on my trembling hands. "You must believe in it for it to work."

I flexed my fingers and closed my eyes, imagining the brambles dispersing. I sucked in a deep breath, held it for a few seconds, then let it out. In my mind's eye, the labyrinth dissipated, leaving a clear route in front of us.

I opened my eyes and grinned at the revealed bristle-moss floor between the chestnut trees and scooped up the nuts that had fallen onto the path.

"Well done." The Oracle beamed. "It's not as difficult as you think, is it?"

"It wasn't so bad." I returned the smile. "Thank you."

Felix shovelled a handful of the nuts into his pocket, then led the way down the curving path. Along the way, I plucked sprigs of nettles to use for tea and stuffed them inside my bag.

Jays perched on swaying branches between masses of leaves. Their song caused me to pause and listen. Felix and the Oracle followed the mossy floor in search of an exit. As soon as they were out of sight, the jays' melody stopped. The trees turned black, and the trail closed in, moss shrivelled, and blades of grass became sharp, pointed stalagmites. Felix and the Oracle were nowhere to be seen.

The labyrinth was closing in on me. My lungs were tight, my heart pounding. I was looking through tunnel vision as the shape of the trees grew farther away from me.

I followed the trail, but I couldn't see them. "Felix?" No response.

Behind closed eyes, I allowed the force of magic to pulse through my veins, but I couldn't summon the path.

I spun around to rustling amongst the decaying greenery. Something lurked in the darkness of the trees. A loud screech pierced my ears.

With my feet rooted to the ground, my gaze darted from one branch to another in search of the threat. Silence surrounded me. I stepped forwards, squinting towards the darkness.

"What is it?" Felix asked, jerking my heart in a somersault. He emerged from lush greenery that was visible again, and I jumped back.

"Where the hell did you go!"

"We've been here the whole time, Evalyn," he said. "I was focusing on the moss floor, trying to find a way out of the forest. When I turned around, you'd vanished. We went looking for you and found you right where we'd left you."

"You were gone! The path was *gone*." My body trembled, and my magic fought against my skin, demanding to be let free.

"Hallucinations," the Oracle explained. "We need to get out, and fast. And Evalyn, if you don't calm down, your magic will explode from you, and we don't want to be caught in that when it happens."

My heart pounded against my ribcage, and despite my best efforts to calm myself, I couldn't see through the block spots in my eyes or shift my legs.

Felix came to my side, his arm around me. Steady and strong. I lifted my hand, gripped his fingers, and didn't let go until my heartbeat stabilised.

"You're okay, Majesty," he soothed. "Look at me. Focus on my eyes and nothing else."

I did as he asked, peering into the hazel depth of his eyes, studying each golden fleck in turn. My lips parted as heat spread through my body. If it weren't for the Oracle a few feet away, I might've kissed him in that moment. The way he looked at me, as if I were the only person in his world, would be enough to bring any woman to their knees. I swallowed, shoving strands of hair out of my face.

"We should get moving," I whispered.

He nodded, letting go of me. The separation between us allowed a gust of cool air to chill my skin. I hadn't missed the heat burning in his own eyes.

The Oracle continued along the route, map, and compass still in hand, with us flanking her.

"What the—" Felix halted, staring at something not quite in my line of sight. "Cover your eyes." He turned to me, holding his hands up. "You don't want to see this."

I shoved his hands away and marched past him. A corpse, with a rope around its neck, hung from a tree. Flies buzzed around the rotting flesh. I pinched my nose to block the foul stench. The Oracle bent double and retched into the undergrowth, while Felix pressed his forearm to his mouth and nose. A sack covered the face, and its clothes were bloodied and tattered. From each tree framing the path, a body hung. Arms and legs were missing; other corpses had gaping abdominal wounds with their entrails dangling free, and the rest of the bodies were bruised and bloodied. My eyes pricked with tears.

They were refused a proper funeral, left there to rot, and be pecked at by birds.

He draped a sackcloth over his shoulder and climbed the trunk of the first tree to pull the corpse down. Lifting the rope from around its neck, he shifted the heavy weight onto his shoulder, and tested some branches with his foot before making the descent. He placed the body onto the path ahead of us. He removed the sack from its head.

The corpse was a Human male. Blowflies flocked to the bodies in search of dead flesh.

The Oracle clasped her hands in prayer. She closed her eyes and muttered something under her breath.

"My uncle, the Gnomes, Woodland Elves..." I shook my head, magic raging against my skin, demanding a release. "Who's betting the Orcs are behind this?"

"The Centaurs are the only ones who've not been targeted so far—they're well protected by the fort for now," Felix said.

"They won't be able to set foot anywhere near Lake Delendil. It'd be a suicide mission." I tried my regain control of my volatile magic. If I didn't, it would burst free, and I didn't want to cause injury to Felix, the Oracle, or the surrounding wildlife. It wasn't implausible that I'd set the forest on fire. "The pure and sacred magic coursing through the ground and the roots of the trees are enough to stop them."

If the Orcs were responsible for this, would they stop killing innocent people if I gave myself over? I was the one they wanted. The murders and mutilations would be over.

I imagined what Felix might say.

'If you hand yourself in, the Dark Triads will kill you and find a way to destroy the High Elves and Lake Delendil. They will have complete control over

Arogath, and the Light Triads will be slaves to their darkness.'

I shook my head to rid myself of the pestering voices and rubbed the tears away. I couldn't surrender to the Dark Triads. I had to find a way to stop them for good.

Clouds tinged in warm hues of pink drifted further into the sky above and blended with the midnight blues of twilight. Felix located another glade within the ever-stretching forest. The roots of the ancient oaks intertwined, leaving small hollow pockets across the ground.

"We should camp here." He pointed to the copper-brown oaks.

I slid to a dry patch of ground protected by an ancient overhead branch and reclined against one of the solid trunks. His gaze fell on me as he swivelled around. His eyes glimmered under the bright shine of moonlight casting through the glade.

"Evalyn," he murmured. "Get some sleep. I'll take the first watch in case anything else happens."

Despite my aching muscles, my mind would not settle. How could I be a leader? He'd taken on the role better than I, telling us where to sleep, leading the way to Lake Delendil.

"I cannot silence the loudness in my head." I tapped my temple with my forefinger.

"Then unburden yourself. Tell me what troubles you." He shifted against the trunk until his shoulder rested against mine. The Oracle relaxed against the next tree over. Crickets chirped in the undergrowth.

"The same things." I shrugged. It was a simple action, and not at all reflective of the whirlwind inside my mind.

"You haven't been given time to grieve your uncle," he said after a pause. "I know you had your differences, but he was the last of your family. With him gone, the Crown falls to you. To top it off, you have to grapple with your magic, and all of it has happened in the last few days. It's a lot for anyone to deal with, and you have dealt with it well. The best anyone could, given the circumstances. But you should rest, gather your strength."

"You're right." I tilted my head to the sky, watching the last rays of sun disappear beyond the horizon. "And I haven't released any of my magic. I'm suffocating it. Remember the bridge? My anger caused my powers to explode, and seeing all those dead people left to rot made me want to unleash everything, but I feared I'd injure you. Destroy the forest, even. I couldn't allow that."

"I appreciate your concern over my welfare." He smirked. "Now get some sleep. Let your emotions calm."

I sighed and nestled between the roots, Felix's sturdy presence a welcome comfort.

The chill of the night nipped at my cheeks, and the breeze stirred the forest. I tugged my cloak around my body and allowed sleep to welcome me.

66

Sometime later, Felix nudged me. I sat up straight against the trunk and rubbed my eyes.

"Sorry," he whispered as the Oracle snored beside us. "But it's time to swap."

I stretched my limbs. "I enjoyed it while it lasted."

"I'll sleep for only a few hours. Wake me if you need me." He closed his eyes and soon, his breathing evened. It hadn't taken him long to succumb to the depths of unconsciousness.

Surrounded by the silence of the forest, I practised balancing my chakras. The white light formed in my palms. I shielded the glowing light with my other hand.

The light disappeared into the sky, and the forest returned to its dusky hues.

A rustle of movement came from the shrubs to the right. I jumped to my feet and scanned the area. A dark shadow headed towards us, leaves shook, and branches rocked as it floated past. A low hum emanated from the object.

I will defeat this Demon.

Focusing on my breathing, I waited for my heartbeat to steady and balanced my chakras. A fiery red ball of light sprouted from my palms. I gaped, realising my magic had changed colour, then launched it towards the monster. It darted out of the way, and the ball collided with a tree trunk, singing the bark.

The supernatural being drew closer, hovering three feet above the ground. The Oracle let out a piercing scream, and Felix bolted upright.

The Demon's transparent energy gripped the Oracle's neck. She wheezed and gasped for breath.

Felix ripped his sword from its sheath, then plunged it straight through the Demon. A bolt of darkness shot through the sword. Felix was thrown backwards.

I conjured another ball of light and steered it towards the Demon. It scowled as the blast of magic grazed past its head. Its talon fingers remained clutched around the Oracle's throat. Her eyes bulged from their sockets, her body limp.

I cupped my palms together, then tried to stabilise my chakras by imagining the purest things the world could know. The sun raised in the east and set in the west, the moon held its place amongst the stars each night and the sacred magic coursed through the grounds of Lake Delendil.

"Hurry, Evalyn!" Felix shouted. "We're losing her!"

I urged the red light to manifest. Through squinted eyes, I glanced at its brilliant glow. My heart thumped and I trembled. My auric fields were not balanced.

'The importance of the auric fields is keeping them balanced to allow energy to flow. You'll be able to cast stronger spells and harness your abilities.' The Oracle's words from our training in the workshop rang in my mind.

Straining my muscles, I embraced the magic— became one with it. It pulsed through my body and burned within my veins like wildfire. When the magic reached its brightest, I hurled it towards the Demon. A red glow seared the being, and it let out a shrill prolonged shriek. Felix fell to his knees, bent double, with his hands clamped over his ears.

The Demon disintegrated.

Where had the creature come from? There was no place for it in Arogath.

I rushed to the Oracle's side and wrapped my arm around her waist to bear her weight. Felix cradled her head and set his fingers to her neck in search of a pulse.

The Oracle gasped as she opened her eyes. Her drowsy gaze fell on mine. "Well done, Evalyn," she said. "You're getting the hang of your magic."

I let out a strangled laugh as relief flooded my body. In the wake of my magic, a coolness spread through me. And hope, I realised. I'd done exactly as the Oracle had taught me.

———⁓———

Later, the Oracle lay limp against a tree trunk with dark bags under her eyes and a deep crimson mark around her throat from the Demon's grasp. After a time, with Felix's help, she climbed to her feet for our onward journey.

We breached the end of the forest, following the path I revealed through the chestnut trees. But as we stepped forth, the edge of the world loomed in front of us. I peered over the cliff to see a large body of water at the bottom. Its foaming torrents crashed against the jagged surface of the cliff face.

"A cliff? Is this even on the map?" I asked.

Felix unfolded the map, looked for a moment, and shook his head. "I thought not," he said. "How can we be sure that what we're seeing is even real?"

"If the Dark Mages are altering the entire realm in our vision, it's going to take us longer to get to Lake Delendil."

"This is no work of a Dark Mage..." the Oracle croaked. "At least, not the work of *one* Dark Mage. I don't know."

"So you're saying it could be the result of *multiple* Dark Mages?" I flung my hands into the air, the words seething from my mouth. "How am I supposed to be able to stop them all when there's just one of me?"

The Oracle shrugged. She had nothing to say.

"We can't go into battle blind," I insisted. "We need to know what to expect, or we are *all* going to die."

"Let's deal with one thing at a time." Felix raised a hand. "We need to figure out how to get to Lake Delendil first."

He walked around the cliffside, his hand resting against the handle of the sword in its sheath. The Oracle and I trailed behind in silence, but I kept my hands out to support her when she needed it. She stumbled and staggered over the rocks, her eyes glassy from her attack. We were on new grounds that weren't on the map, and the reflection spell could change what we saw at any moment.

Phases of the day passed over us. Golden shards of sunlight faded into soft oranges and pinks as the sky transitioned into twilight. We moved along the trail, and I kept my gaze fixed on the crumbling rocks at the side of my feet. Tiny fragments of rock fell into the raging waves below.

"You need to keep up," Felix said to me.

The Oracle drew in sharp, ragged breaths. Loose shale gave way beneath her feet, and she staggered sideways, teetering on the edge of the canyon. I gripped her wrist and yanked her away. A festering wound now spread from her neck to her fingers.

"She's too weak." I held the Oracle up straight. "*I'm* too weak. While I was desperate for my magic to have an outlet, it's taken my energy too. We need to rest."

"We can't camp here out in the open," he huffed. "It'll be too cold when night falls."

I scanned our surroundings for somewhere we could rest. "We can't return to the forest. There's a wooden shack over there." I gestured to a crooked building in the distance.

He put his thumb and forefinger to his forehead and squinted in the general direction where I was pointing.

"Half a mile…" he muttered. "We can make that."

We dragged the Oracle, her feet trailing as we moved forwards, across the remaining stretch of cliff-side, until we reached the shack. Behind our shelter the terrain sloped downwards, stretching into a field. The grass was charred, abandoned, and exposed to the elements. The trees were mere skeletons of their former selves, limp and dying in the wasteland.

The door creaked as Felix pushed it open, then it slammed shut behind us. Inside were two rooms, one of which contained two beds. The other had a few worn cabinets and a fireplace with a rack and cooking pot. Dark patches of damp festered in the corners of the dust covered windowsill and cracks in the walls let in a draft. Broken, uneven floorboards poked out from beneath a tattered circular rug in the centre.

I eased the Oracle onto a bed in the other room and tucked her under a torn blanket, which was dumped at its foot.

In the main room, I poured water from the wineskin into the cooking pot. We had enough water with us to brew some tea, and I'd gathered plenty of nettles from the forest to use. He crouched beside me and used his flint to light the remaining twigs and branches in the fireplace.

"What is this place?"

"It's not on the map. Your guess is as good as mine." He sighed.

"We're blind."

"There must be something I can do."

"We'll think of something," he said matter-of-factly.

When the tea was brewed, I rootled around in the cupboard, found a chipped mug, and wiped it with a rag. Once the tea was ready, I poured it into the mug, then handed it to the Oracle. She stared back through half-closed eyes.

"Nettle tea should ease the pain. Is there any way I can reverse this spell?"

"Do you have your spell book?" the Oracle murmured.

I rummaged through my bag, then pulled out the small, leather book. Its cover was worn and battered, and the paper inside was crumpled and torn at the corners. "I've read and practised some spells in the past, but I fear the damage it could cause."

"You know how to control it now." She rested her arms against her sides. "See if you can find a spell in there that will counteract the distorted visions."

"What about you? Is there something that can help you?" I clutched the book in my hands.

"I'm fine as I am, dear."

Taking a seat on the dirty wooden floorboards in the other room, I opened the book. Spells, enchantments, and even curses covered the pages. The scripture was the tongue of the Noble Ones, each letter curved in elegant calligraphy.

I flicked through the pages, trying to find a spell that could heal her, or at least restore her strength until we arrived at Lake Delendil.

"There's no use," the Oracle said. "I have my gemstones. They'll offer me the strength I'll need. I do not permit you to use any magic on me."

She closed her eyes, then drifted off to sleep.

"There are symbols, like the ones on my necklace, to show ancient magic." I tilted the book to show Felix the runic diagrams as he came up beside me. "These are powerful and dangerous spells."

He handed me a cup of nettle tea. "Come with me. Some fresh air may do you some good, and it will allow the Oracle to sleep peacefully."

"My family isn't magical," he said when we were outside, "yet us Humans still believe in a deity, you know? The gods, the Noble Ones, their extraordinary powers. The Eyrie has the fleur-de-lys everywhere, carved into the gates and stitched into their clothing. My family have those symbols."

"Why?" I was eager to learn more of him.

"As a reminder." He leaned against the water slick wall.

"A reminder of what?"

"What they stand for. My family was all about duty and honour. They were thrilled when I joined the royal guard."

"Do you miss them?"

"Every day," he said. "I haven't seen them for years."

We cradled our cups as a field mouse scurried past. I brought the cup to my lips and sipped the warm tea. An owl hooted in the distance.

I cleared my throat. "Did—"

"Tell me something—" We started at the same time, then he insisted, "no, you go first."

"Did you begin training as a king's guard as soon as you were of age?"

"No, I travelled for a while. I lived at Rushdale Forest with the Woodland Elves. Remarkable people."

I arched an eyebrow. "You? Living with Elves?" I smirked. "I can't imagine it."

"I was close to a lot of them. One of them convinced me to become a knight of the Eyrie. Before that, I was planning to become a blacksmith."

He paused, and his gaze dropped to the necklace warming my neck. "I wonder why those beads glow every time I'm close to you."

"You said it was the missing piece to my magic." I held my breath and stayed very still as he studied me. "What did you mean?"

"I'm sure the Oracle told you about rose quartz?" he said.

My cheeks warmed. "She did. What does that have to do with it?"

"I know what the stones represent—what it encourages your heart to feel." He closed the space between us and tucked a lock behind my ear. "Finish your tea. It's getting late, and we have a full day ahead of us tomorrow. You get the bed sorted, and I'll check the perimeter to make sure we're secure for the night. I'll be in shortly."

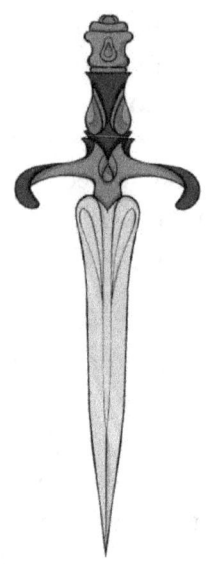

Chapter Five

I stirred awake the following morning, stretched, and turned onto my side. The candle we lit the night before had long since burned out, and only a stump remained. I was alone in the room. Not even the wind creaked the wooden structure.

Had Felix and the Oracle woken to devise a plan in preparation for the day ahead?

Dressed in the same clothes as the day before, I yawned and tucked the stray pieces of hair behind my ears.

Clambering out of bed, I padded across the floorboards to the main room of the shack, but Felix and the Oracle did not greet me. Instead, the silence extended throughout the building. I flattened my hands against my sides.

I wouldn't worry unless necessary.

I opened the door to see Felix with his arm around the Oracle, taking slow steps. He was helping her back towards the shack. Her eyes were sunken and grey, surrounded by wrinkles and dull skin.

"Morning." Her body quivered.

"You don't look well." I pressed myself against the door frame to allow her and Felix past. She sank into the chair against the back wall.

My mouth dried. How could we take her with us? She'd slow us down, cause more problems. Would he think the same?

"Stop frowning, child." The Oracle clasped her trembling hands in front of her. "It ruins your pretty face, and you don't want that."

"Felix?" I glanced at him as the nausea churned my stomach. He shook his head.

My jaw locked, and no other words escaped me. I had to sit by
and let the Oracle wither away. She'd die, and there was nothing I could do to save her.

"Read the words of the Noble Ones," the Oracle whispered. "The saviour is the part you must play in this life."

I flicked through the tattered spell book to the page titled Revelation Spell.

"Reveal the earth and the sun, the mountains, and the waters of the gods. Breathe the air of the Noble Ones and relinquish all evil. Restore the balance of life and banish sin to the underworld." The Oracle closed her eyes and chanted. When she opened them, her gaze fixed on mine. "Now repeat what I just said in the tongue of the Noble Ones with as much power as you can muster."

"*Revela sol terrae, montes et aquas deorum…*" I struggled to pronounce the foreign words. "*Relinquere omnes primores respiret. Culpam releget lubricam inferorum redde vita statera.*"

I repeated it again, allowing the strange words to roll off my tongue until they became easier to say. Once the words were as familiar as my native tongue, I pronounced them loud and clear for the third time.

Nothing happened for a few moments. I held my breath and peered out the window, waiting for the magic to take form. Holes appeared in the vision of the cliff-side, revealing the true terrain of Arogath. I gawked as the hallucination faded away. Once the whole picture of Arogath returned, Felix yanked out my map. He beamed and pointed at it.

"Who would've thought I'd need this damn map?" He laughed, forming lines around his mouth.

"Why didn't you tell me to use this spell before?" I crossed my arms. The Oracle did not respond.

"We're an hour's walk from Lake Delendil," he said.

I relaxed my hands as I adjusted to the scenery. Instead of being on a cliff with deep waters and barren lands, we were on flat ground. However, the burned remains of buildings lingered. They were true to my vision. A dwindling forest fire permeated the air with smoke.

Why had the caster of Dark Magic decided to keep that element of vision in the hallucination? Was this their way of continuing to goad us and show us their strength and power?

We surveyed the land in front of us. A dense forest no longer clustered the settlement of the Woodland Elves. Torched remains of trees littered the ground. Some flickered with the last dance of fire.

"Woodland Elves." Felix peered at a charred body sprawled across the burned grass. Her features were black with soot and burnt in some areas, leaving her unrecognisable. Her wings were left battered and torn. His face twisted. "Of Rushdale Forest. I need to find Alinar."

He jogged into the ruins and surveyed the masses of bodies.

Consumed by the urge to vomit, I turned to the Oracle. "Who is this person?"

"Alinar was the clan leader of the Woodland Elves." She tilted her head towards me, sorrow in her eyes. "Felix mentioned her before. She's the one who encouraged him to become a knight."

I hurried after Felix, who panted as he tossed planks of charred wood onto the beaten trail through the village.

I grabbed his arm. "Let me help."

He nodded, then threw loose stones aside.

"Alinar!" He walked through the debris, scanning the area.

My heart sank, and magic thrummed in my veins, demanding a release. She wouldn't emerge from the wreckage unscathed.

He dashed towards a collapsed hut.

I looked over his shoulder to see a blood-covered Elf crushed between the logs. Her eyes were closed and her body limp.

A piece of burned wood lay across her chest. I bent while Felix gripped the other end, then we hoisted it off Alinar.

He removed her from the wreckage, cradled her in his arms, then swept the remaining strands of hair away from her face. A deep crease knitted between his brows, and his lips were pressed into a thin line. As if holding in a breath, his chest was stiff.

Who had she been to him?

"I will carry her to Lake Delendil where she can rest." Dazed, he stared ahead.

I nodded and stayed close to him, walking past the remaining ruins and the dying trees to our left. The Oracle staggered behind. Before we reached the end of the trail, leaving Rushdale Forest, a faint voice called out.

Jerking to the left, I followed the distant sound to a tree behind the last building on the settlement.

The deep voice croaked once more. "Wait."

At the sight of the male Elf impaled to a tree by a blade, I gasped. He choked on blood spilling from his mouth. His clothes were bloody, and his body sagged from the trunk. His eyes drooped as he fought to stay conscious.

I approached the Elf and curled my fingers around the hilt. Once he was free, I eased him to the floor.

"Save this world," he muttered. He closed his eyes for the last time.

I rubbed my face.

Would this ever get better? Would light once again reign in this
world? I wrestled with my magic, stuffing it somewhere deep within me, in fear that it would explode from every crevice of my being.

After a moment of silence for the fallen Elves, I led the way out of Rushdale Forest. The last stretch of the journey dragged. I stayed close to the Oracle as she struggled to move her legs. Felix followed, carrying Alinar.

I clung to the hope that Lake Delendil would be our saving grace. We would heal there, and the Oracle would regain her strength. We could grieve and rebuild the Fertile Territories.

The sun reached its highest point when we breached the perimeter of Lake Delendil. A clearing welcomed us to a large body of water and a citadel beyond it with tall towers and domes made from opaque glass. Its bright rainbow colours glistened against the rays of the sun.

A mosaic glass bridge arched across the water in front of us, leading to the Citadel of Lake Delendil. With wide eyes, I marvelled in its beauty. The tallest multicoloured towers glinted a bright white where the sunlight kissed its roof. Its glass and marble structure refracted a prism of colours across the water.

Felix crossed the mosaic bridge. I kept my arm around the Oracle, helping her walk. The blistering wound around her neck and face seeped blood and yellow puss and now covered most of her arms.

When we reached the other side of the bridge, two tall male Elves with brown hair tied atop their heads in tight buns greeted us. Silver capes embellished with gold threads were draped over their shoulders and wide golden collars framed their faces. They bowed when their eyes met mine.

"It's good to see you, Your Majesty," the guard said. "We will find aid for you and your companions." He opened the towering glass doors to the Citadel and guided us into the foyer. "Wait here."

The entrance was vast and unlike its glass exterior, tall stone soldiers were carved around the entrance. Their faces resembled the sharp beauty of the High Elves—slender noses and harsh cheekbones. Their ears pointed through the gaps in their helms and each stone soldier clasped a spear.

A male servant approached Felix. "Let me take her from you."

"I will keep hold of her," he said.

I wanted to know his connection to Alinar, understand the bond they shared and what importance she was to him, but it wasn't the time to ask.

I waited as five High Elves descended the curved glass stairs. They stood in front of us, slender-legged and strong postured. They dipped their heads into a bow before the Elf in the middle, holding a ruby-encrusted staff, stepped forwards.

"You've made it. My name is Nieve," she said, voice light and her face framed by ice-white hair. Her gaze rested on Alinar's limp frame in Felix's arms. "Your spirits are low. Let us first say goodbye to your friend, then we will discuss important matters." I glanced at Nieve as she glided across the sapphire glass floor. "Come with me. My handmaidens will escort your friend to the healers."

Two young women dressed in cream robes, their hair tied back into tight buns, escorted the Oracle up the staircase. Felix and I followed the High Elves through the courtyard to the left of the Citadel. Towards the side of the building, gardens of rose bushes were accompanied by a bench. We trailed the path framed by flowers and came to a halt at the sloping lake embankment.

Two Elves in white dresses stood barefoot across from us.

"What is the name of your friend?" Nieve asked.

"Alinar." Felix stared hollow-eyed at her burned face. "Rushdale Forest."

She raised an eyebrow, placed her finger on Alinar's chin, then tilted it towards her. "My apologies. She is difficult to recognise. Now pass her over to my ladies, and they will bathe her before releasing her into the sacred waters."

Felix clutched Alinar and stroked his finger across her cheek.

"Until we meet again, my friend." He kissed her forehead, then held onto her a moment longer before handing her over to Nieve's servants.

They carried her into the lake until the water rippled around their hips. With gentle hands, one of the Elves washed Alinar's hair and face as the other held her. Once she was clean, Alinar's beautiful elven features were revealed: high cheekbones, curved ears, and a slender frame. A few burns damaged her cheeks, neck, and singed her eyebrows. "She is ready," one of the maidens said.

Felix removed his armour, then stood in his undergarments still covered in mud from the last few days of wear. He stepped into the clear saltwater, and the Elves shifted Alinar's body into his arms.

"It is time," Nieve said. "You must give her to the lake now, so she may rest for eternity in the realm of gods."

Felix released Alinar into the gentle waves.

She drifted away, the magic of the water removing her blemishes caused by the burns. She was ready for her afterlife.

"Our great Mother," Nieve began, her hands clasped in prayer. "We thank you for the life and energy you gave to Alinar, and now, we return her to you."

Pure white hands rose from beneath the still water and eased her body below the surface.

"Those hands…" I followed Nieve into the council room. I wanted to ask Felix questions of his history with Alinar, yet I'd no right to pry. "She just…disappeared."

"You have a lot to learn, I see." Nieve flicked her mass of ice white hair off her shoulder. Her fellow councillors stood in silence behind her. "There's a certain point in the lake where life and death meet, and a person makes their journey from this life into the next."

"Did I just witness the afterlife? Did I see the hands of dead souls?" A servant handed me a goblet of water. I gulped it down. Considering I was supposed to be the saviour of the realm and the last royal, I didn't know very much about my world. Living a Human life for so long had left me oblivious to many of the natural and magical wonders of this kingdom.

"We will know the answer for ourselves when we have made the journey to the Beyond," Nieve answered. She muttered something to her councillors that was too quiet for me to hear, then they left through the magenta-coloured glass door.

I studied her for a moment. She stood with her chin held high and the frame of a warrior. Her eyebrows arched on her forehead as she pierced me with her azure-blue gaze.

"The Dark Triads are a lot stronger now." I placed the goblet onto the ornate glass and ruby table. "Their magic is more powerful than we anticipated and it's not the work of a singular Dark Mage."

"Yes, they are stronger." Nieve relaxed in her gold-encrusted chair. "They have their tactics, but so do we." She lifted a finger before I could say anything. "Don't you worry about that, though. I have a plan."

"What did you have in mind?"

"I'm going to infiltrate Zhah," Nieve said. "Guards will escort me through the Badlands, to Zhah. I'm going to meet with the Orcs' leader and bring him back for negotiations. We've paved the way by leaving cattle at the border for them to collect for food. I have an ally on the inside who says the Orcs possess a powerful weapon."

"Do you think they'll agree to negotiations?" I frowned. Considering the way my uncle had treated them, I doubted it. The Orcs had already made the decision to lay waste to the Fertile Territories—cattle would do little to change their minds.

"I must try all options." She waved the matter away. "Please make yourself comfortable. My maidens will show you to your chamber. You will be safe within the citadel grounds."

"I heard the surviving Elves of Rushdale Forest were on their way—have they arrived yet?"

"A few of them made it—they'll reside here until their home is restored." Her gaze softened. She turned to a nearby servant. "Mildred, will you escort Her Royal Highness Evalyn to the healer's room?"

Mildred curtsied, then led me up the grand glass staircase and down a hall with a vaulted ceiling. This level of the Citadel was built of glass in gradients of blue, becoming paler in colour towards the right wing.

Inside the healer's room, the Oracle lay still on a mattress with an Elf leaning over her, dressing her wounds. Beside her, on a diamond table, stood a crystal goblet. The Elf dabbed some of the liquid

86

from the container onto a dressing and placed it on the Oracle's wounds.

I observed the steady rise and fall of her chest. Would she last another night? My heart throbbed with the need to keep her alive, but her life now rested in the healer's hands.

I collapsed at her side. "Please fight this. I need you. I can't do this without you."

The Oracle wheezed and struggled for breath. The corners of her mouth turned upwards into a hint of a smile.

I glanced at the healer as he finished applying the leaf dressing to her wounds. "Will she be okay?" My voice trembled.

The Oracle closed her eyes, dipping back into unconsciousness.

"I have cleaned her wounds with water from the lake, which heals in preparation for the afterlife, but its potency isn't strong enough to recover her." The healer rose to his feet. "I will leave you to have your time with her."

He left the lavender-scented room. She was going to die.

"Evalyn. There is something…your mother… She isn't on the other side." The Oracle writhed on the bed, as if grappling with life itself.

"She's not dead?" I shook her hand. My mind reeled at the impossibility of it. It couldn't be true, and yet, the Oracle had no reason to lie, to spend her final words telling me so.

"No…they told me…"

"Who?"

"The spirits…they wait for me."

"Oracle?" She lifted her eyelids halfway, revealing bloodshot eyes. "Where is she?"

"They…didn't say," the Oracle muttered. "You can't…trust

Nieve…" Her body went still. A last breath escaped her white lips.

The door flung open, and Felix strode in.

"Oracle!" Tears welled in my eyes, and a tight knot formed deep in my throat. "Just as I found someone to guide me, she's been ripped away from me."

"You need to remember what she taught you." He crossed the room. "Carry that with you. I'll be with you every step of the way."

"I don't even know her name…" I stared at her waxy face. The life faded from her, the last touch of pink diminishing from her cheeks.

"Juliette Vrecrai," he muttered. "How didn't you know this?"

"I'm sorry. I can be thoughtless. I should have tried to know her name, and I didn't. I will make sure I respect and honour her memory." I touched his arm to comfort him as guilt burrowed itself deep into my chest.

We stayed with Juliette until the same Elves who'd bathed Alinar in the lake came to collect her. I clenched my teeth to stop the tears from falling and followed the Elves.

Felix stood a few strides away from me and the Elves as they carried Juliette into the waters. When she met the crucial point, departed souls reached out, and her body drifted below into the Beyond.

Juliette's final words echoed in my mind. Nieve couldn't be trusted. I had to tell Felix.

His gaze lingered on the spot in the waters where Alinar and Juliette disappeared, then travelled to mine. Tired circles had formed under his eyes. "What is it?"

"Not here. We need to find somewhere out of earshot." I grabbed his hand, not caring who saw, and led him inside.

In a small room on the third floor, the glass was coloured in gradients of green, resembling beautiful hues of grasslands, mountains, and the treetops. Armchairs dotted around the room with several books abandoned on a coffee table.

"We need to talk." I shut the door so the guards outside couldn't hear. "Nieve is going to Zhah to arrange renegotiations. She has an ally on the other side. Juliette told me not to trust Nieve. She's hiding something, but Juliette died before she could tell me what."

"We'll figure it out. Keep your wits about you and try to keep your distance from her until we know what she is up to." Hew folded his arms across his chest, accentuating the broadness of his shoulders.

"I need to ask her about a book somewhere in the citadel. It contains the prophecy, but it'll have to wait. Finding out what Nieve is up to is more important." I ran a hand through my hair and rested against the wall. my mind whirled.

"Are you okay?" I asked him, noticing the darkness forming in his eyes.

"She was my first true friend, you know," he said. "Alinar."

He crossed the space between us, squeezed my arm gently, then left the room.

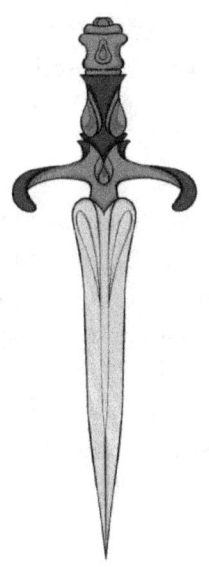

Chapter Six

After we bathed and ate, Felix and I gathered in the foyer as Nieve and the guards prepared for their departure.

The fitted plates of her armour were gold, and a flowing silk cape draped her shoulders.

She addressed her guards. "I will cross through to Zhah alone. We'll be concealed by nightfall."

The guards lifted their hands into a salute. They marched out of the Citadel behind Nieve, then crossed the mosaic bridge, disappearing into the trees beyond.

"I can't shake that something's not right." I tilted my chin to Felix, who towered above me. "Why wouldn't Juliette trust her? I think we should follow them."

"That's not a smart idea," he said. "We can't charge into the night without evidence."

I grabbed his arm, took him up the staircase, then strode into my chamber and clicked the door shut. "Then we'll find evidence. Now is the perfect opportunity to go after her."

Felix frowned as if deep in thought. "Juliette was my friend, and I trust her judgement. If she believed Nieve's motives to be unclear, I won't argue. I'll pack my bag and go alone."

"I will join you." I hurried across the room, then hoisted my armour onto the four-poster bed. "I'm doing it for Juliette, and if Nieve *is* hiding something, then she's a threat to the Fertile Territories, and I want to find out what she's up to."

He shook his head. "You can't go—it'll risk your life. You bear the Crown now."

I ignored his comment and spoke of Nieve instead. "She's gone. I think it is safe for us to look now—surely, we will find something which could indicate what she is doing." I abandoned my armour, exited the room, then paced down the corridor into Nieve's chamber.

Felix lingered in the doorway, a frown knitting his brows.

"Care to give me a hand?" I yanked back the covers on the bed, tossed the pillows aside, then stuffed my hands under the mattress in search of anything that could be a clue.

He rummaged in the drawers and in the jewellery boxes while I checked the wardrobe. I shook each boot and checked every pocket.

Nothing.

"Is this what you're looking for?" he said.

I spun around. He held a small glass vial in his hands. Several drops of a green liquid remained inside. "What is it?"

"It was inside the blue vase on the table." He gestured to the object—the flowers discarded onto the floor. "Have you seen this liquid before? I haven't."

"No. If neither of us have seen it before, it has to have come from the Barren Territories. Whatever this is, it's something. We need to go after her." I strode towards the door. "Are you coming? And don't try to talk me out of it. As you said, the Crown falls to me, and this is my responsibility. I will do what I must to protect my people."

"Fine. I know the way to the Badlands," he said after a moment's pause. "But if I do this, you follow me and listen to what I say. This could be a dangerous mission, and you must give me your word you won't do anything stupid."

"Of course." I nodded. "If we get caught, I'll tell them I want to speak to the Chief Orc, to negotiate with them. They're not going to negotiate with a guard, are they? Leave me to change into my armour, and I'll meet you at the entrance."

Felix was deep in conversation with one of the High Elves as I descended the stairs into the foyer. He turned his attention to me.

"Your Majesty." A council member bowed his head. "An honour."

"What is your name?" I approached him.

"I am Kiirion, Your Majesty," he replied. He wore his black hair in a high knot, which symbolised his rank within the Elven community. "Felix and I were discussing your plans to cross the Badlands. I'm not convinced it's a good idea."

"If Felix has told you what we found, then you understand why I must go. And Felix is an experienced member of the royal guard. I will be well protected." I adjusted my silver armour into a comfortable position.

"I'll have a servant bring you food and water." He gestured to a nearby maid who scurried into the kitchens.

A few minutes later, she returned, then handed Felix a bag.

"You'll find two canteens of water, a blanket, bread, meats, seeds, and cheese." She curtsied to me. "Your Majesty."

Felix and I left and headed across the mosaic bridge, our footsteps beating even against the ground. Crickets sounded in the nearby greenery.

"Are you okay?" He peered at me.

"I'm fine." I needed him to believe those words, because if he believed, then maybe I could too.

We reached the border of a forest where the wind blew icy-cold against my cheeks, raising gooseflesh in any area left bare from armour. I tugged my cape around my arms, shielding me from the harsh wind that whipped through the trees.

Familiar with the vast spaces of open fields, expanses of water and dense gatherings of oaks, I wondered what kind of landscape I would be greeted with when I arrived at Zhah.

The chilly bite of wind against my skin diminished as we entered the trees. Moonlight shone through the gaps between the leaves. An owl hooted in the distance, and a rodent scurried through the undergrowth. The thuds of our boots marked the imminent approach of the Badlands.

The outline of trees around me blurred into a dense, dark mass. I trembled.

"You were right." I curled my hands into fists, nails piercing the skin. "Now I'm here—I'm not fine. I'm angry, and my magic is writhing inside of me, demanding a release. The chief councillor is someone we should be able to rely on, and that's not the case."

Felix patted me on the back. He didn't say a word.

He stepped ahead of me as the oaks narrowed the path ahead. The air was heavy with moisture. My chest tightened. I took in short, sharp breaths.

There were no bodies hanging from the tree branches, no Demons hiding in the shadows; nothing that distorted our vision.

Thrusting my hand into my pocket, I clasped the pouch of gemstones. With my gaze to the skies through the clustering trees, I prayed to the gods to bring me strength.

"I'm still here," he said, drawing me from my desperate plea. "We'll get through this."

I smiled. His gentle gaze rested on mine. His effort to reach out to me was a reminder that we were in this together, woven into the same destiny. "Do you think I'm strong enough? For whatever we may face?"

"You're learning to trust yourself," he said. "It takes time."

"I've been scared to use my magic because I knew what damage it could cause. Maybe I *am* selfish." I frowned.

"Your family was murdered, Evalyn. I'd be scared too," he said. "Juliette told me my mother isn't dead. She could be anywhere. All through my childhood, I thought she was dead. I'd cry myself to sleep. I'd run to the gate and peer beyond the Eyrie. She never showed."

"How do you feel about it?" he asked.

"We've lost so much time together—time we could've built upon that relationship. I'm grateful she's alive, but I don't want to talk too much about it. It's going to take some time to come to terms with it. I'll keep a look out for her from now on. This magic of mine…as much as it's difficult to accept, I'm glad I can use it to help people."

"You're doing amazing. Keep practising."

I cupped my hands together, steadied my breathing, and conjured a brilliant white light. The orb floated through the trees ahead.

"Stop." He shielded the light with his hands. "I didn't mean now. We are headed towards enemy territory. Do you want to get us killed?"

"I'm sorry. I didn't think." The magic diminished, and darkness cloaked us.

"We need to be stealthy." He tucked a piece of stray hair behind my ear and rested his hand on my shoulder. A warmth spread through my body.

Tufts of his brown hair poked out at odd angles from underneath his helmet. His eyes twinkled as he cast me a sideways glance, and a gentle smile spread across his mouth. My breath hitched. I knew of him as a guard, a protector of the royal family, but an unexpected urge inside me wanted to know more about him, his life, and his history.

I walked into the trunk of an oak tree. "Ouch!"

My armour vibrated hollow notes through my inner ears, and my head pounded from the collision.

"Watch your step.." He winked.

We exited the forest and were greeted by the brutal force of the sharp wind rippling from the clouded sky. Nothing grew or lived on the open, ashen plains of the Badlands in front of us. Large rocks jutted out of the ground. The divide stretched to the farthest corners of the barren field, from the northern tip to the Great Sea in the south.

"That's the only thing separating the lands." I glanced at him, heartbeat thudding against my ribcage. Every bone in my body locked, freezing me to the spot. "My uncle created this divide, not that it's done us any good."

Wilted weeds sprouted from the cracked mud. Bits of rubble and wire were dotted across the ground as far as my sight could travel, and once we took our first step onto the dying ground, we'd be isolated from the Fertile Territories.

"Get down!" He yanked me to the ground.

"What is it?" I threw a hand over my mouth to muffle my squeal.

He pointed ahead. In the distance, armour glinted under the moonlight.

"Nieve?" I whispered as stones shifted underneath me.

"Yes, and the guards. Straight ahead," he mouthed.

I squinted and kept my tone hushed. "I can't see anything."

"Damn it, they're gone. Let's move on but keep low." He climbed to his feet, then scurried ahead.

I hurried after him. "Wait!"

Several yards in front, Felix stopped, craning his neck. "I've lost her."

"What do you mean you've lost her? She couldn't have gone far." I grabbed his arm.

"Come on. If we head in this general direction, hopefully we'll see her," he said.

I nodded and pulled my cloak tightly around me. "Do you remember a few years ago when Nieve was appointed chief councillor?"

"How could I forget?" he said. "The last chief died, and I recall the day when your father elected

Nieve. A lot of people disagreed with her title, due to her questionable political decisions."

"I didn't know." A sudden coldness swept over me.

We continued across the width of the Badlands.

My ankle gave way as I stumbled over a stone, and I plummeted into a hole about three foot deep. I wacked my head against a rock jutting out of the ditch wall, and my helmet vibrated from the impact.

"Evalyn." Felix stretched out his hand and hoisted me out. "Are you okay?" He scanned my body for injuries.

I adjusted my helmet, then brushed myself down. "Damn it, I can't see anything. Why are there trenches out here anyway?"

"Left from the previous battle, perhaps. Is your ankle all right?" he asked.

"I think so." I twisted it gently to be sure. "Tell me more about your friend Alinar."

"I met her during my travels, and stayed with the Woodland Elves for a while," he said. "She suggested I do something worthwhile with my life, seeing as I had a predisposition for helping people. I thought it was a good idea, so I went to the Eyrie barracks and trained to become a member of the royal guard."

I bowed my head briefly—their relationship had been platonic. "She's in a better place now." I touched his arm. "If there's anything I can do to help you feel better—"

"No, don't worry about me. I'll be fine." His piercing gaze met mine, and for a moment, the

Badlands around us disappeared. He traced his thumb over my jawline, and I froze.

"Felix," I whispered. My mind whirled with a need to touch him back, but the confusion over his action was even stronger. "What's changed?"

"What do you mean?" His gaze wandered to my lips.

"In the Eyrie, you'd made it clear that nothing would happen between us, that you were not interested. What's changed?" I withdrew from his touch, unwilling to give in to it until I understood his intentions.

He straightened and pulled away. "You're right. I'm sorry."

The space between us allowed a harsh coldness to spear through me.

I shoved the thoughts of him aside, ground my teeth together, and focused on the trail ahead. We came up to a slight hill, covered in rusted, abandoned swords and helmets. I squinted, craning my neck. Amongst the rubble were skulls. Something glimmered—a tarnished silver helmet underneath a red flag. A battle of a previous age.

"We're walking through a graveyard," he exclaimed as I picked up the red flag.

"The flag of the Dark Triads." I scanned the dirty and torn material.

"The last battle was before we were born," he said. "And we've ended up back in the same position."

I tossed the flag aside and stumbled through the skulls, placing each foot on solid mud between them.

"How far do the Badlands stretch?" I eyed wasteland to either side.

"We'll be at the edge of Zhah by morning which means a bitter night's sleep under the open sky."

I'd grown accustomed to sleeping in different locations.

A moment of silence passed between us, and my thoughts turned to my future as a leader. Each decision I made during this war—and any decisions I was yet to make—would affect everyone in the Fertile Territories.

"I'm sorry, Evalyn. I didn't mean to sound harsh," Felix said abruptly as he came to a halt.

I stared at him, my mouth open and unsure what to say.

"Trust me, it was never a question of whether I was interested in you. I've *always* found you interesting, and not because you are royal. In fact, you are interesting for a whole host of other reasons. The way you watch the sunset when you think no one is looking, how you frown when you concentrate. And most of all, your compassion and willingness to be better than those who ruled before you. Those are just a few examples."

My breath lodged itself into my chest, and on a sudden burst of confidence, I asked, "So what's holding you back?"

"You are above my station." He ground out as if the words tasted sour in his mouth. "It would be improper of me."

I laughed. "Really?"

"I'm being serious." His stare hardened.

"I can tell that." I tilted my head to the side. "But I'm queen, and I get a say too. No one can tell me I'm being improper. And if you haven't noticed, there's no one here to see or hear us."

He studied me for a moment, a war raging in his eyes. Then he turned his attention the rubble around us. "Here isn't the place, and now isn't the right time."

I swallowed and tried to ignore the sting of his rejection. Fine. Just as I was about to prepare myself to spend the rest of our journey in silence, he flicked his fingers across mine, allowing his warmth to transfer. Felix did not lock his hand with mine, yet he did not pull away. It would be enough for now.

———⌣———

A dark, starless sky covered the realm. On our journey to Bluefair Fort, Felix had called it an omen. The deep knots in my stomach returned.

"I can't make out Nieve's tracks in the dark, and it's too risky for you to use a ball of light in the open. We should rest here for the night." He slid into a ditch deep enough for us both to fit in, then held out his arms to ease me into the hole. We stood facing each other. His breath tickled my nose. I closed my eyes, and a warm sensation passed through me. He still had his hands underneath my arms, and I hadn't removed them. I opened my eyes, stepped back a little, and he released me.

Even from six feet underground, the wind was brutal above our heads. The rocks and firm mud which formed the structure of the ditch dug into my back at awkward angles.

"I wish Juliette were here." I took off my helmet. She would've had a plan for us, and I needed her words of wisdom.

"Me too." He sank onto the hard earth at the bottom of the ditch and doffed his helmet, placing it next to him.

A few minutes later, Felix shot up, and I jolted against the rough stone. "Wait, where did the Demon even come from?"

"How could we be so stupid to not think about that!" I bolted upright. "If they came from the Beyond, someone had to let them."

He grabbed my face between his hands and kissed my lips. Within seconds, he leaned back and pushed his hand through his hair. Silence formed between us. His eyes darkened. I held my breath and stared at him, astounded by his sudden display of emotion considering our earlier conversation.

"So we know the Dark Mages must be behind the Demons." The involuntary kiss stunned me, and my voice trembled. Our second of delight diminished quicker than I experienced it. "But it doesn't tell us what Nieve is hiding."

"We'll follow her tracks in the morning." His gaze fixed on something to the right of me. "Sleep now, Evalyn."

I fidgeted, wedging my back between slanted rocks. After several attempts to get comfortable, I huffed and gave up. I peered at the faint outline of his figure beside me and listened to the soothing rhythm of his breathing.

———————～◡◞．———————

I squinted at the bright white-gold morning sun. In contrast to the bitter cold from the day before, the air of the new day warmed my cheeks. Felix still slept with his head against the ridge of the ditch. The rising sun cast its light across the right side of his face, creating shadows along his cheekbone and jaw. His eyes fluttered open to meet mine. "Morning." He rubbed his eyes and smiled at the cloudless sky.

A single bird flew overhead. I followed it. No forms of life ever came to the Badlands. It landed next to me—a delicate scroll tied to its leg.

"I've never received a letter by bird." I laughed and untied the parchment from its leg. The bird did not hesitate before flying away.

"It's from Eric, at Bluefair Fort." I flattened the parchment against my legs.

"What does he say?" He leaned forward.

"Orcs invaded the fort. Civilians were killed. It doesn't give any indication of how many. Eric and the Centaurs managed to fight them until they withdrew, but the fort is a wreck."

"The Gnomes are homeless, and barely any Woodland Elves survived the fire at Rushdale Forest," he said.

"We aren't going to survive this." I drew my knees to my chest and rested my chin against them.

"There. I said it. We are outnumbered, and their power is far beyond what we were prepared for."

"Let's deal with one problem at a time. Firstly, we locate Nieve's tracks and find out what she's up to." He donned his helmet, then clambered out of the ditch. He offered me his hand to help me to my feet. Together, we ventured along the scorched ground.

Felix rummaged in his pack for the bread and seeds, then tossed me a crust.

I ate my food, washing it down with a swig of water from the canteen.

"Look over there. Can you see the marks on the mud? Footprints." Felix jogged over to the tracks.

I followed him. "Should be smooth sailing from here." We followed the trail up a slope as we ate.

"See the stone wall? That's Zhah. We need to be careful." He pointed to the structure in the distance.

"I hope you have a plan." The dried mud crumbled underneath my feet.

"From what I know," he said, "the wall is heavily guarded."

We were headed into hostile territory that no one from the Light Triads had explored since the Noble Ones. Other than the Dark Triads living beyond those walls, what else loomed in the Barren Territories?

The large basalt stone wall towered above us as we neared it. I surveyed the length of it, looking for a way in.

He shoved me behind a boulder and covered my mouth. My elbow cracked against a stone. A wooden door with steel bolts was located on the right in Felix's line of sight. Two Orcs patrolled the entrance.

Both stood with hammer-like weapons in their hands. Their chests were bare, and their frames wide.

I peered around the side of the boulder and stared at them. I'd never seen one so close. They were huge beasts with wide jaws and teeth overlapped their lips. Plates of metal covered their broad, bulking shoulders, wrists, and shins. My breath caught.

"What are we going to do?" I ducked behind the boulder and squeezed his arm.

"Keep your head down. I'll have a look." He craned his head and glanced over. "One of them has spotted us." He leaned against the chalky white boulder and sucked in a deep breath.

Within moments, one of the Orcs yanked us both up from behind the rock. I screeched, astonished by his strength. We both hung from each of the Orc's massive hands.

"I want to speak to your chief," I announced, "I've come to negotiate better conditions for the Barren Territories."

"I think you might be too late for that. Our chief is insisting that the Light Triads have had their last chance." The Orc studied my face intently. "Queen Evalyn?" he growled as he lowered us to the ground.

Felix raised an eyebrow at me. The Orc peeled off our helmets.

"Uh…yeah?" I quaked, unsure what in the gods' names to say to an Orc.

"Please don't be alarmed. I'm an ally. I know your face from portraits." He clicked chains around our wrists. I writhed and tugged, but the Orc yanked back. "Don't worry, I'll help you get through. I'll explain everything later."

I jerked the shackles, trying to break free. I couldn't believe an Orc, the kind slaughtering our people. How could I be sure he wasn't sending us to die?

"Stop pulling, Evalyn."

Felix tried to squirm his way out of the chains, but they were made from thick, strong metal.

"Stop wriggling," the Orc ordered in a hushed tone. "Don't say a word."

"What have you got there?" the other guard said as we approached him by the entrance of the wall. He laughed, baring his yellowing tusks. "Humans!"

"They were lurking in the Badlands, looking to be killed," the Orc who carried our chains said. "I'm taking them to the dungeons."

The guard let us through, with his rumbling laugh still echoing behind us. It was a preposterous idea for two Humans to venture across the Badlands, with no clue what to expect and no instructions as to how we'd make it into Zhah without being caught. The idea of an Orc being an ally to the Crown seemed insane.

A great fire pit in the middle of the settlement cooked a large beast hanging above its flames. Orcs passed us, seeming to attend to everyday duties like Humans and other races did. From what they'd done to the people of the Fertile Territory, I'd expected them to be savage and as wild as the creatures they ate.

Our alleged ally dragged us along. The chains that bound us rattled, causing a few Orcs to raise their heads and snicker at us. I lowered my head, avoiding eye contact with anyone.

When we were away from the central gathering, the Orc urged us into a small hut made from irregular sized stones.

"Get out of your armour." He clicked the door shut behind him. "What in heavens were you doing in the Badlands? You could've gotten yourselves killed." His bulky hands clamped the curtains dressing the singular window and yanked them shut. Every footstep he took boomed through the house.

I didn't want to leave Felix alone with the Orc, so without argument, I stripped from my armour, revealing my cream cotton clothing underneath. Shoving my trembling hand into my pocket, I clutched my gemstones, urging them to give me strength.

"Put these on." The Orc rummaged in a nearby trunk, then chucked us clothes. "It is how you'll stay undetected. Dark Mages reside nearby, and these are their robes. The Dark Triads know what you look like, so we best be quick about this."

"Why are you helping us?" Ignoring the clothes in front of me, I balled my hands into fists so the Orc couldn't see them tremble. "Better yet, who the hell are you?"

"I may be an Orc," he said. "But I don't condone their actions. My name is Xurek."

They must be oblivious to his opposition. If they'd known of his betrayal, they would have him killed. Why would he want to form an alliance with the Light Triads? We stood for purity and represented Light Magic, neither of which agreed with the nature of an Orc. By blood and flesh, he was bound to a life of violence and savagery.

I stared at my arms and raised my brows. Scales, in a variety of red and gold, had broken through the skin and transitioned into silver towards the top of my arms. Eric had mentioned that a Mage's magic would change their appearance—was this the start of it?

"First time seeing your scales?" Xurek said.

Felix turned around to face me. His brows knitted into a frown.

"I didn't realise they would appear so quickly." I traced my fingers along them.

I changed into one of the robes provided. When I was ready, I clasped my hands together, and imagined the scales disappearing, replaced with smooth peach-coloured skin. One by one, they faded.

"Smart idea," Xurek said. "That will stop you from drawing attention to yourself. Let's hope the spell lasts long enough for you to get out of Zhah in one piece."

"I wasn't sure I'd be able to camouflage myself…" I muttered. "I keep forgetting how strong my magic is."

"We'll make it quick," Felix said. The black robes hung from his body in odd places.

"That will do." Xurek eyed us. "Beseech the gods to bless your souls. This is a dangerous mission I can't see you surviving."

"If that's true, then you will die with us if the other Orcs catch wind of your betrayal." I narrowed my gaze at him.

"Of course." He flipped the notion away with his hand. "My own people will tear apart my limbs and burn them in all corners of the realm."

I shivered. Felix stood in front of me with a widening stance. While he'd tried to conceal me from the Orc's line of sight, Xurek towered above him.

"How do you suppose I protect myself and the queen's life?" Felix questioned.

Xurek looked at him with a blank expression.

"Out there in front of our enemies?" Felix clarified.

"Here you go." Xurek tossed him a blade. "Shove it into your boot and shut up."

Felix grabbed my hand and held it tight. His muscles tensed, and his jaw locked.

"Right, I'll ask again. Why are you here?" The Orc frowned.

"How can we be sure you can be trusted?" My voice was faint, answering his question with one of my own.

"Because I would have killed you by now!" he growled.

I decided we didn't have much choice but to trust what the Orc said. "We were warned Nieve couldn't be trusted, so we tried to find evidence of whatever she may be up to. After searching her chamber, we found a vial. There were a few drops of a green liquid left inside. We had to follow her."

"There's a Dark Mage you should know about. Her name is Makdou, and she's very powerful." Xurek said. "Nieve *is* Makdou."

"How is that possible?" I gasped.

"She's using something called Milleshar. Makdou is using it to
appear as an Elf, which is why she can walk on the sacred grounds of Lake Delendil. I'm going to hang around for a while to see if I can find out more."

My head spun. "Is this what the vial we found is for? To store it?"

"Quite possibly. Follow me." He opened the door and lumbered out of his hut with us trailing behind him. We kept the hoods of our robes up, hiding our appearances. If Nieve was lurking nearby, I didn't want us to be spotted.

A few Orcs eyed us but made no comments.

A female Orc with a lengthy black braid dangling against her back carved spears as we walked past. She glanced at me with her fierce eyes before returning to her activity.

A group of Trolls with elongated ears and dishevelled hair ripped apart a cluster of roasted chickens and sipped red wine from their goblets. They were too engrossed in their meal to spot us passing.

As we ventured farther and farther south, away from the stone wall, an enormous castle emerged. Large black steel gates surrounded it, and barred windows lined the length of the towers.

"The dungeons," Xurek said. "When you go in, your fate is sealed, so let's hope we never end up there."

My hands sweated, and my gaze darted around. I waited for one of the Dark Triads to throw an axe or spear at me.

Felix squeezed my hand again. I focused on him—his strength—and my hammering heart steadied.

"Breathe," he mouthed.

I sucked in a deep breath, counted to three, and let the air pass through my mouth.

Xurek followed a dirt path away from the main area and into a stretch of tall grass. The route drifted downhill and at the base, there was a wooden signpost. The heat of midmorning created a slick layer of sweat down my back.

"To find what you're looking for," Xurek's thick eyebrows furrowed, and his gaze fell to our entwined fingers, "you need to follow this path to Dellhollow."

Dellhollow was the capital of the Barren Territories, the same way Lake Delendil was our central hub.

"Give us strength," I tilted my head to the sky and whispered to the gods.

"Stay hidden in the trees." Xurek pushed us towards the signpost. "Allow yourself to see what you need to see. I will meet you back here in an hour. The Orcs at the entrance think I've taken you to the dungeons, so I'm going to make sure they're not still there for when you leave. And try not to get yourselves killed."

I didn't know whether to offer my thanks to him, so I opted for silence instead.

"Why don't you just tell us what's there?" Felix squared up to Xurek, although the Orc soared above him.

"You wouldn't believe me if I told you." Xurek shook his head, then left, walking the way we'd came.

Felix and I ducked into the wilted grass before the dying trees. I wanted to call to Xurek, beg him to wait. But what good would he do us now?

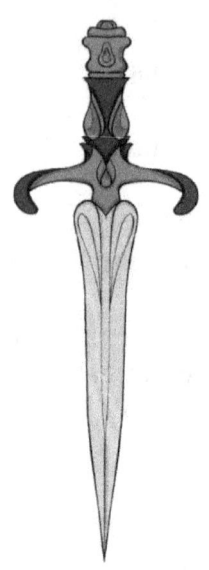

Chapter Seven

The branches of the trees intertwined, forming a shelter from the heat of the sun. The coolness of the shade sent shivers down my spine, chilling the line of sweat covering my back.

I wiped the perspiration from my forehead and pinned up my hair. My tongue stuck to the bone-dry roof of my mouth. Felix tried to roll up the sleeves of his robe, but they slid down his arms again. He huffed and let them hang loose around his wrists.

Deep groans caught my attention. Felix crept forward with his hand up, signalling for me to wait.

He bent and grabbed the knife from inside his boot, then clutched it.

He dropped to the floor and lay flat, then yanked me beside him, jolting my spine into an awkward position. I grumbled in discomfort and pressed myself against his side.

Down the steep hill in front of us, beasts of amber with bright piercing green eyes rumbled and puffed their way across the ground. Their arms were thick and lengthy like an Orc's, but their chests were broader, and their mechanisms were visible through their translucent bodies.

"Machines?" Felix whispered. His facial muscles twitched. "Why would they need machines?"

"I'm not sure but look." I pointed at the congregation of chained, naked people who were being filed into glass chambers.

Orc soldiers played sentry. When they were sealed inside the tubes, a thick green liquid filled the chamber. The same green liquid coursed through the insides of the amber monsters.

One captive struggled as he fought for breath. Then he was still.

Had he drowned in the strange liquid?

Within a few moments, the chamber sparked into life, operated by a steam-generated device behind it.

I'd borne witness to the atrocities of the Orcs. Torched villages and burned bodies. Souls left to roam the land, unable to rest in the Beyond. Hanged Humans in the forests. The skulls in the Badlands. Now this?

"Dark Mages." He craned his neck and squinted at the scene in front of him. "Look at their skin. They have the same scales and markings as you, if not more prominent."

I stretched forward to get a better look, peering between the long grass that concealed us from the hostile eyes below. Sure enough, they had the same markings as mine, yet deeper in colour, accompanied by red eyes. Dark Mages.

"I don't understand." I kept my voice hushed. "Why are they encapsulating Dark Mages?"

"I don't know." He shook his head. He slid backwards until the machines below were out of sight, then rose. "But Xurek does."

Scrambling to my feet, I followed him back the way we'd come. Twigs and branches snapped underfoot, and the nearby bushes caught at my robes. Sweat formed along my forehead as I fought to keep up with him.

What could this mean for the Light Triads of the realm? What were the Orcs intending to do with these machines and the Dark Mages they'd trapped? They'd distorted our visions in the forest, but was this under the Orc's control? Were they enslaving them to do their bidding?

I panted and carved my way through the path of the forest. Felix sprinted ahead towards the signpost where Xurek had left us. Why would he reveal the hidden advantages the Dark Mages had at war?

My head spun. I jigged my legs and flexed my fingers as we waited for him. Upon his return, my mouth opened. I was ready to pounce on him with a flurry of questions.

"Before you say anything, we need to go somewhere out of sight. Your interrogation will have to wait until we are back at my hut. Stay in line with me. Don't give anyone a reason to be suspicious."

My heartbeat pounded in my throat. Sharp pains stabbed the side of my head as the array of questions and demands created a whirlwind inside me.

When we reached the hut, Xurek closed the door behind us. His feet were rooted to the wooden floorboards, gaze fixed on me. I wanted to know every little detail about the giant beasts, the chambers with green liquid, and the Mages.

"Now you can ask me questions." He dropped his hammer onto the table. His fists found a resting point on his hips.

"What the hell was that?" I threw my hands into the air.

"Don't be so loud." He gritted his teeth and glared. "Unless you want to get yourselves killed."

"First of all," I lifted a shaking finger, "why do they have machines?"

"They're soldiers," he said, expressionless and unmoved.

"Why are they binding Dark Mages?" Felix asked.

"They are hosts for the vessels." Xurek's forehead crumpled. "Blood magic."

"So the Dark Mages are hosts for the big containers," I clarified. "What is the green liquid for?"

"That keeps them unconscious, but alive." He paced. "It channels their power. They will become dependent on it."

"It's feeding off them?" Felix asked. "Draining their energy but leaving just enough to keep them alive."

"That's barbaric." I clasped my hand over my mouth. Despite the Dark Mages being one of our enemies, the atrocity wasn't lost on me.

"Yes. Now you have your proof. You've seen it with your own eyes," Xurek said. "The Orcs want total control over the realm—that includes bending the Dark Mages to their will."

"Why would they go to such lengths? Have the Dark Mages even posed a threat to them?" I frowned.

"Dark Mages are extremely powerful, and by nature, Orcs are volatile. Tensions have been boiling between them for a while now, and they are divided by their desires for control," he said.

"Why didn't they stop the Orcs with their magic?" Felix asked. "They must have put up a fight, surely."

"The Dark Mages were weakened as they were unable to stand together to fight. The Trolls and Giants had already sided with the Orcs, leaving the Dark Mages outnumbered. They were incarcerated and bound with chains that mute their magic. I didn't think the chief had it in him to use Milleshar against them."

"Sounds like you feel sorry for them." Felix narrowed his gaze at him.

He shrugged. "Would you like to be in their place?"

118

"I suppose not," he said.

"More importantly, what would happen if they were to break free?" I glanced at Xurek.

"Let's hope that never happens. I can't imagine it'll end well between them and the Orcs," he said.

"What do you propose we do?" Felix asked.

"There's nothing you can do right now." Xurek stood by the door of his hut. "You must go back to Lake Delendil and arrest Nieve. You're lucky she didn't spot you here."

He opened the door with us tailing behind him. Trolls and Orcs alike walked about the main gathering, eating roasted meats. Others were sitting beside a campfire, swaying their heads from side to side, their voices grunting in unison—singing.

I pressed my hands over my ears. I gawked at a pack of wolves tearing apart an animal too covered in blood for me to tell what it was. Some of the wolves eyed us and growled, warning us away from their meal.

We reached the main gate where Xurek found us; the other guard was no longer there. Where had he gone, and what had Xurek done to ensure our safe exit out of Zhah?

"How do the wolves survive here?" I shuddered as one of them howled in the distance.

"Nieve and the guards brought us regular supplies of food— chickens, cattle, and the like," Xurek said. "You're very lucky your stay here was as pleasant as it was." We hurried through the entrance and behind the wall, out of sight. "Now go and be quick about it." Xurek urged us into the Badlands. He guarded the main entrance, scanning his surroundings.

We jogged until we were past the boulder and away from Zhah.

"We'll be fine," Felix said, as if sensing the tension working my muscles into tight knots. "I've got you."

We trekked across the Badlands, the sky descending into darkness. Every inch of my body ached, and my eyes drooped half-closed.

When we reached our ditch, Felix drew me against his chest, his broad arm wrapped around me, enveloping me with his warmth. The harsh winds of the night would soon fall upon us, and we no longer had our armour to protect ourselves from it.

I shifted to peer up at Felix. "They're channelling Dark Mage Magic. Somehow, they let Demons in too. Perhaps…that's what they used to distort our visions and cause my hallucinations?"

"I don't know." He stifled a yawn and rubbed my arm.

I leaned into his touch, thankful for his warmth, and for the comfort it brought.

When we returned to Lake Delendil, I'd have Nieve thrown into the dungeons.

———— ～✦～ ————

We began the last stretch of our journey home when the sun broke free from the horizon and stretched across the surrounding wasteland. We hit the silent forest, which separated us from Lake

Delendil, where we would return to the glistening waters and serenity of the Citadel.

We crossed the glass bridge with the afternoon rays burning the nape of my neck, my hair tied into a messy heap on top of my head. My feet dragged for the last few strides, and my shoulders hunched over. The Elven guards called to greet us, bringing with them a flagon of water. One of the guards held my head back as he tipped the refreshing liquid into my mouth.

"Prepare a meal for Felix and me." I turned to Mildred who carried a basket. Herbs were propped inside.

She curtsied, then dashed into the kitchens.

I rubbed my eyes and headed to the banquet hall. Felix sat beside me. Another maiden hurried to place the napkins and cutlery in front of us, then filled our goblets with wine.

Moments later, Mildred returned with two plates of bread, meats, and cheese. "Is this suitable, Your Majesty?"

"I'd eat anything at this point." I grabbed the bread and bit off a large chunk.

As we devoured our meal, Nieve sauntered into the banquet room.

I stared, mouth open, at the woman. My magic pulsed against my skin, demanding release. I wrestled it into submission and pinned Nieve with a glare.

"Morning, Your Majesty," she said.

"How was Zhah? Where is the Chief Orc?" Felix asked, giving me no chance to respond to her pleasantry, not that I would have.

She stared, lips parted, at him.

I jumped out of my chair. Felix drew his sword, then stood between me and Nieve.

"Guards. Arrest her," I ordered. The guards—my guards— obeyed.

As the guards seized her, Felix faced me. His gaze fell on mine and glinted under the warm golden glow of sunlight streaming in through the window. He offered a smile.

"This is preposterous. How dare you! Release me at once." Nieve tried to wriggle her way free.

"I know who you really are, Makdou." I turned away from her and addressed the remaining guard. "Take her to the dungeon."

"How could you possibly know? Let go of me." She writhed and thrashed against the guard who held her arms behind her back.

"We followed you, and we met a wonderful Orc," I said to her in a sing-song voice, relishing the adrenaline pumping through me. "It seems we do have an ally on the other side, after all."

"That traitor!" she screamed as the guard towed her away. "Tell me who it is!"

Ignoring her, I strode through the hallway, then entered the council room. A map of Arogath hung on the back wall. A red line was painted down the centre of the mainland territories, marking the Badlands and the segregation of the Light and Dark Triads. Daylight streamed in through the glass walls and painted the room with multicoloured hues. A ruby encrusted table was in the centre.

"Your Majesty, you've returned." Kiirion rose from his seat. "May I introduce you to Valneris, Theodas, and Ascal."

"It's good to meet you. Let's sit, shall we?" I clamped my trembling hands behind my back. I was not used to having authority. Perhaps the people were looking for someone new to trust.

I sat in the head chair with Felix next to me. "We have found an unlikely ally in Zhah—an Orc named Xurek."

Kiirion wrinkled his nose. "An Orc?"

"Fear not—he provided me with vital information."

"What do you have to share?" Valneris asked.

"We saw some sort of vessels." With the memories fresh in my mind, I explained, "They were encapsulating Dark Mages and preserving them in Milleshar—a green liquid which drains them of magic. The same liquid is powering their beasts."

Felix cleared his throat. "Xurek informed us that the vessels would drain the Mages until they were almost dead, but not quite."

"Worst of all, Nieve is a Dark Mage. Her real name is Makdou, and she is using the green liquid to portray herself as an Elf."

"How could she fool us all?" Ascal gasped. "I'm sorry, Your Majesty. We had no idea."

I glanced at Felix for guidance, and he offered a reassuring smile in return. Taking a deep breath, I realised the High Elves did not make the decisions. Their job was to advise me the best they could.

"No need to apologise. There's no way you could've known. There's more: Xurek said tensions have been boiling between the Orcs and the Dark Mages for some time. If the Dark Mages manage to escape, they're sure to retaliate."

"What are your orders, my queen?" Kiirion leaned forward.

"You must…search—ahem—contact…yes, contact the remaining knights of the Eyrie, as well as Bluefair Fort. Ask Eric if he can spare any guards and Centaurs. Search for any other surviving Woodland Elves." I cleared my throat. "Enlist as many as you can and bring them here where we will train them."

"We're outnumbered and overpowered," Theodas interjected. "How do you suppose we win this?"

"One step at a time." I rose from my chair. "This meeting is adjourned for now. We have had a long journey. Excuse me." I left the room, with Felix trailing behind me.

"You did well," he said. "You should be proud."

"I'm not doing it for pride, I'm doing it for the people of this realm." I tilted my chin higher.

He rested his hand on mine, pulling me to a gentle stop in the middle of the foyer. Facing him, my breath hitched, for a fire burned in his eyes, catching me off guard.

"Felix," I whispered, glancing over his shoulder at the guards who patrolled the foyer. None of them looked our way in what I could only determine as an attempt to provide us with privacy. "What are you doing?"

"I should never have ignored this," he muttered to himself.

"Ignored what?" I asked, my heart pounding and my skin burning beneath his touch.

"I kept telling myself that I am your guard. Your protector. And I will do whatever it takes to keep you safe. My sword—my life—is yours, should you need it. I will stop at nothing to ensure you sit on that throne and take your place as queen. You *will* rule, and you will make this kingdom far better than those who preceded you. I know my place," he paused, his throat bobbing as he swallowed. "But you haunt me, Evalyn."

My name on his lips was like velvet. Soft, irresistible. Inviting. Everything about him drew me in, and without realising it, my fingers had wound their way around the fabric of his shirt.

"What do you mean?" I whispered. My legs were rooted to the spot, and my magic *thrummed*. It did not rage against me like some wild beast demanding release. It sang beneath my skin, directly under his touch.

"You live in my dreams, and in my thoughts." He closed the space between us and brought his lips to my ears. His next words were a soft purr. "You consume me."

"But I thought," I shook my head, fighting for focus and clarity among the desire spearing through me. "You didn't want this. You feared your station was enough to keep us apart. That it would be improper."

"I have wanted you for as long as I can remember." He traced his thumb along my jawline, then across my lips, where his touch lingered. "Back in the Eyrie. And every day since. I never said anything because I didn't think you'd go for someone like me. You deserve more than I can offer you."

From the corner of my eyes, I peered at the guards who stood frozen like statues. I was pretty sure they could hear every word, and my cheeks burned.

"Come with me." I grabbed Felix's hand and led him upstairs.

When I reached the bathing room, I closed the door behind us. White marble flooring covered the expanse, surrounding a large, oval pool. The sun shining through the turquoise glass walls created shimmering patterns across the floor. Steam permeated the room—the servants must've filled the bath upon my arrival.

Felix walked ahead of me, observing the vast grandness of the room. I kept my back pressed against the door, each breath coming in faster than the one before. There was no going back now. I wanted this. I wanted *him*. And I had done for so long.

When he turned to face me, his eyes darkened. Hunger burned bright there, and my body acted of its own accord. Within seconds, I'd closed the space between us, pushed onto my tiptoes, and pressed my lips against his.

Spearing my hair with his hands, he tilted my head to the side. He trailed lazy kissed down my jaw to my throat, and I gripped on to him, for fear my legs might give out beneath me. I couldn't tell if it was from the building steam from the bath or from *him*, but I was on fire. Every inch of my skin burned. My magic swarmed to the surface of my flesh, chasing each of his touches. The sensation overwhelmed me, and I drew back.

"Evalyn?" He asked, his breathing ragged. "Are you okay?"

"I'm fine." I swallowed. "I just needed a second."

His hand cupped the back of my neck, and he pressed a kiss to my forehead. "We can take as long as you'd like. There is no rush, and there never will be."

The gentleness of his voice, combined with his featherlight touches created an ache inside me, and I needed more.

"Kiss me."

His mouth crashed against mine a second later, and he scooped me off the floor. Carrying me, he pinned me to the wall, his hands on my buttocks as his tongue slid against mine. A low groan rippled in his throat, and my core tightened. Everything else—the deaths, the war—melted away.

I weaved my hands into his hair, gripping onto the tousled strands as he slanted his mouth over mine again. As he held me hostage against the wall with one hand, he trailed his other hand up my chest, exploring.

"Gods, I've wanted you," he groaned against my lips. "And you might be the death of me, Evalyn."

"We wouldn't want that," I teased as I trailed kisses along his jaw, his stubble tickling my lips.

"No." He lowered me to the floor. "I don't think we do." A wicked playfulness danced in his eyes as he stepped back, gripped the hem of his shirt, and drew the garment over his head in a swift motion.

Heart hammering, I remained pressed against the wall and watched as he removed each item of his clothing. When he stood straight, a took in every inch of him. The broadness of his shoulders, the toned planes of his abdomen, and the hardness of him. Heat raised to a boiling point in every inch of my body.

He turned around and padded over to the pool. At the edge, he slipped into the water, letting out a sigh when it rippled around his chest.

"Care to join me?" He quirked a brow, running a wet hand through his hair and slicking it back.

I chewed on my bottom lip. There was no way to ease into this gently. I would be bare to him in a matter of seconds. But the thought did not terrify me. Instead, a thrill shot through me.

Riding the high the confidence gave me, I slipped out of my robe, letting the material drop to a puddle on the floor. then I worked on my cream undergarments, until they, too, landed at my feet. And I did not look away from him as I made my way to the pool's edge.

In swift movements, he pushed through the water until he joined me. Reaching up, he splayed his hands across my thighs, beads of water dripping down him.

"Beautiful," he said, voice guttural.

My heart somersaulted, and I lowered into the water, further into his touch. He pulled me against him, untied the fastening from my hair, and wound his hand through the locks. His mouth found mine again, and I immediately parted my lips for him, welcoming him.

With my body firm against his, he lifted me up and I wrapped my legs around his waist. His hardness pressed against me, and my core tightened.

He bit my lip before breaking the kiss. "Tell me if you want to stop."

"You won't be hearing those words from me," I whispered against his mouth.

Growling, he carried me back to the seating at the edge of the pool. He lowered himself onto it, and my knees gently hit the surface as I straddled him.

His hands travelled up my back, splaying across my skin. My magic sung.

"That feels good." I couldn't hold the words back.

The compliment only seemed to stoke the fire burning in his eyes. "Is that so?" he teased.

"Yes." I arched into his touch, craving more.

"Tell me what you want." He traced his tongue across my collarbones as he rubbed his thumb over my nipple.

"You." I managed. My mind was foggy, and I could barely think through the desire spearing through me. "All of you." Instinctively, I ground against him, relishing the closeness of him.

He groaned and hoisted me up slightly as he guided himself into me. Slowly, I edged down his length, letting out a sigh of my own as I grew accustomed to him. His hands found my hips, and he pumped into me, slowly at first, then mounted in speed.

I gripped onto the edge of the pool for better leverage, meeting each of his thrusts in turn. The ache inside of me intensified, coiling and tightening.

Wrapping my hair around his fist, he pulled my head gently to the side to gain him better access to my throat. He flicked his tongue across the sensitive skin, and I moaned.

"Evalyn," he muttered against me. The husky sound of my name hurtled me towards the edge, and I clamped around him.

"Please," was all I could think to say, and he thrusted up into me harder than before.

I buried my mouth against his shoulder, my teeth marring his skin as I let out a scream. Pleasure rippled through me, and something nearby shattered, but I didn't pull away. Instead, I weaved my hands into his hair and clung onto him as he drove himself into me, deeper. His body tensed beneath me. He was close.

Leaning back, I flexed my hips against him, meeting his gaze with my own.

"Felix," I said, running my fingers up his chest. I could only hope the sound of his name on my lips did the same thing to him.

He wrapped his hand around my wrist and pulled me to him, crashing his mouth against mine as he plummeted into his own release. He groaned into my lips as his whole body trembled.

I ran my fingers through his hair, slicking it back once more.

"I think you broke the mirror," he panted.

"What?" I peered to the side. Indeed, one of the floor-length mirrors lay shattered on the floor.

Clamping my hands over my eyes, I hid my embarrassment. My magic was fuelled by my emotions, and consumed by him, I'd been unable to keep my powers from breeching the surface.

He peeled my hands away, and looked at me with such tenderness, my shoulders relaxed.

"I *did* break the mirror," I finally said. "Whatever will the servants think?"

"I'm sure they probably heard us." He laughed.

"Oh gods." My cheeks burned, and I fought the urge to bury my head in his shoulder again.

"They won't question you about it." He cupped my cheek, tracing the skin with his thumb. "You are queen, remember? You can do what you like here. This place is your home now."

He held me against him for a while, our bodies still connected. Sometime later, he kissed my forehead, then unravelled himself from me. Climbing out of the pool, he offered me his hand. With water dripping down his body, he grabbed a towel and wrapped it around my body. Only then, did he stop to dry himself off.

His gaze lowered to the glowing necklace around my neck, and he smiled. "I must go," he whispered. "But I'll find you later, okay?"

I nodded, clutching the robe against me. The distance between us felt strange, unnatural, but he was right. We couldn't stay in here forever.

He quickly dressed, then slipped outside.

"You will find your bedchamber in the left wing of the Citadel, past the staircase," an Elven servant muttered outside the bathing room.

Felix clicked the door shut. His pattering footsteps dwindled as he moved farther away from the bathing room.

I sighed and dressed in my fresh clothes. The servants had laid out a satin nightdress and robe, presumably when they'd filled the pool. The soft material slid against my skin.

Outside, I found the servant who witnessed Felix leaving a few moments before. "Please escort me to my chamber."

Once I was there, a handmaiden scurried around the room, drawing the thick cream curtains embroidered with gold in an ornate pattern. She peeled back the silk bed linens and fluffed several pillows, placed a water pitcher and chamber pot near my bed, then stood poised at the ready.

Candles sat on top of the oak cabinet next to the window. A fourposter bed with golden vines engraved into its wood was next to the left wall, and a fireplace opposite had been stocked with logs.

"I hope your chamber pleases you, my queen," the servant said.

"Yes." I smiled. "Thank you. You may leave now."

The servant obeyed, closing the door behind her.

One by one, I lit the candles, in memory of Juliette, the king, and my parents.

The candlelight flickered, but it would soon dwindle. Would Felix and I have the same fate? While I hadn't the nerve to tell him, I knew I was falling for him. Deeply. The very feeling consumed me. I traced my fingertips up my arm and along my collarbone—his featherlike kisses imprinted on my skin.

I lowered my hand and crawled into bed. The dancing beauty of the gold and red of the candle flame lulled me into sleep.

Several hours later, I woke when the candles had burned out and the shadows of night swallowed the room.

There was a rap at the door and as it creaked open, a head peered around. I strained my eyes to see Felix's face lit by the moonlight streaming through the window. He lingered in the doorframe before entering. With his back to the door, he pressed it closed. A woollen robe hung from his broad shoulders.

"Can't sleep." He took small steps towards me. "Plus, I am truly under your spell now. Nothing could keep me away."

I grinned, peeling the covers back for him.

He shrugged off his robe, then climbed into bed, tucking me against his chest. After holding my breath for a moment too long, I relaxed against his warm frame. We were exactly where we were meant to be.

We slept through most of the morning. None of the handmaidens, nor the guards, came to wake us.

Felix left before I woke, enveloping me with the serene silence of my bedchamber. I stretched before rising from the bed as a handmaiden rapped on the door and entered.

She braided my hair down the length of my back and dressed me in a pair of dark woollen breeches and a high-necked blouse that was ruched and pinned with a glistening brooch.

I descended the glass staircase to the main foyer below, the smell of warm, fresh food filling my nostrils. I followed the scent into the banquet room. There were delicate pastries and scones with jam and cream, plates of different meats with bread and butter, and a collection of different juices.

"You didn't have to go to this much trouble." I smiled at one of the cooks as she placed the remaining plate of pastries on the table.

"It's an honour, Your Majesty," she said, "to serve you."

"Sit." I gestured to a chair next to me. "Please, join us."

The Elven cook stared back with wide eyes and no words to respond with. She didn't move.

"I've startled you."

"No, my queen," she replied. "I intend not to offend you, but I would like to eat with my family."

"Of course." I watched her leave, then sat at the table.

Moments later, Felix strode into the room, his expression carefully neutral, giving nothing away from the night before. "Good morning, Majesty."

I smiled, then poured some orange juice into my goblet. "What am I supposed to do with Nieve? We'll meet with the High Elves once we finish our morning meal, and deliberate."

"You're beginning to sound like royalty." Felix dumped a load of meat and bread onto his plate. His gaze remained fixed on the plate of food in front of him.

"Is there a problem?" I leaned forward. At first, I'd thought he'd wanted to portray professionalism, which I could've understood, but there was a harsh edge to a tone that made me think something was wrong. What had changed since last night?

"No, my queen." He shovelled a forkful of food into his mouth. "Excuse me."

He shunted his chair back and left with his plate before I could object. Could I order him to stay? I hadn't yet found the courage to order him to do anything. I slouched back into my chair and huffed. How could he behave in such a manner when last night he'd shared my bed?

I pushed my plate of food aside and left the banquet room. Instead of dwelling on Felix, I would attend to an important matter in the council room. The High Elves were seated around the table, deep in conversation over glasses of apple juice. Sooner or later, the juice would turn to wine. They rose to their feet, backs straight, and bent in a bow of greeting.

"Thank you. Please sit." I slipped into my seat at the table, and as my gaze fell upon the empty chair beside me, I wondered why Felix had retreated from the morning meal.

Kiirion cleared his throat, reverting my attention back to him.

"We received word this morning from Bluefair Fort." He held a piece of parchment between his fingers. "The Humans and Centaurs are travelling to Lake Delendil. They mentioned something about Gnomes too."

The memory of Gnovash and Finbrik brought a smile to my face.

"Guards have been sent to Rushdale Forest to look for surviving Woodland Elves, as you commanded," Valneris said.

"We should discuss the other three Elementals," Ascal said. "You've already established a positive relationship with the Gnomes, so they will come to our aid when the time comes. However, the same can't be said for the others. Let's start with the beings of water who reside in the Galae Pools."

I raised an eyebrow, waiting for elaboration. I'd grown up oblivious to many other species that dwelled in the realm, and I'd shunned anything magical to the furthest corners of my minds. Ignorance was bliss.

"Undines and Nereids," Kiirion said. "Undines aren't pure, as they lack souls. Nereids, on the other hand, represent everything beautiful and tranquil about their element, which could come in handy when trying to defeat evil."

"They're frightening creatures." Theodas grimaced, and his mouth twitched. "Half-Human, half-fish, with such haunting eyes."

I leaned forward and placed my hands on the table. "Tell me more."

Laughing, Kiirion eased into his chair and motioned for Theodas to continue.

"I've more than seen one, my queen." Theodas' eyes darkened. "One of them tried to enchant me with her songs so I'd marry her. Marriage to a land being provides them with a soul."

A shiver shot up my spine. "What are the other Elemental clans? If we can gain their allegiance, then we have the natural elements as an advantage. We may stand a chance in this war."

"Sylphs—beings of air," Valneris added. "Delicate, tiny creatures of the Highland Trees."

"And then we have the Salamanders, beings of fire, residing in the Vesuvius Caves." Kiirion held the final piece of parchment. "A humanoid said to be descendant of some sort of lizard. They do not have digestive organs and cannot consume food. They gain their strength from the fire they produce, which also regenerates their scale-riddled skin."

Sweat built on my palms. "How can we be sure such a volatile creature will pledge themselves?"

If the Salamanders could produce fire, they'd be a strong ally to have. Yet, a tightening sensation formed in my gut at the image of the Undines. They were menacing creatures who lured in men for their own gain. How could I trust them?

"If we can guarantee these Undines will support us, then I will accept their allegiance with open arms." I cleared my throat and wiped my hands free from sweat. "But I am led to believe soulless creatures are, perhaps, creations of the devil."

"It seems the Nereids keep them in order." Theodas waved it off with his hand. "Their purity has rubbed off on them, so to speak. After all, they have been cohabiting in the Galae Pools for centuries."

I accepted his counter notion. Felix should be here. He needed to know of our potential allies, of our strengths and increasing odds against the Dark Triads.

"Send them our regards, and a small gift in an act of gratitude. I will visit them when the time comes." I pushed my chair back and rose. "Call upon me if you receive any further news."

"Your Majesty, your skin has made quite the transformation," Valneris said.

"I've noticed." I lifted the delicate sleeves of my blouse. The scales and etchings had deepened and strengthened in pigment. What did this mean for me? "I will reconvene this meeting later. There is something I must do."

I exited the room to find an Elvan handmaiden wearing an ankle length peach-coloured dress loitering in the corridor. "Please escort me to the library."

She curtsied, then led the way up the staircase, and down a long, high-ceiling corridor on the third floor. The library was more beautiful than the rest of the Citadel. Its intrinsic, mosaic flooring twinkled against the colourful glass structure and the high shelves filled with books.

When I was alone, I rifled through the shelves in search of the book Juliette had mentioned. If there was more to the prophecy, then I needed to know.

I lay several open across the floor and table. My gaze flicked between the dusty pages, but I couldn't find anything that mentioned a prophecy. Glancing up at the many bookshelves, I resolved myself to the fact it would take some time to find such a book.

The sound of loud horns caught my attention. I jolted when a repeated thudding at the door boomed through the library.

"You have guests waiting for you, my queen. Allies from Bluefair Fort," the guard called through the door.

Felix was already outside the main entrance with the Humans, Centaurs, and Gnomes. Once I was in the foyer, I hurried to Eric and gave him a quick, tight embrace. I smiled against his chest and inhaled the familiar scent of fresh grass and wood from Bluefair Fort.

"You look well," he said. My gaze locked with his dark, hollow one.

"You must be tired," I said. "We will provide you with food, and I will make sure you have somewhere suitable to rest."

"You sure look like a queen now!" Gnovash appeared, and a wide smile spread across her stout face.

"My friends." I gave a smile of equal measure in return. "The High Elves will show you around.

There is food in the banquet hall. Please help yourself."

Felix relaxed. He smiled and circled me with his arms. The smell of sandalwood clung to his shirt, and my heart fluttered. I couldn't understand his strange mood swings, yet my body melted into his embrace anyway. I'd question him about it later.

"We're going to be okay," he whispered.

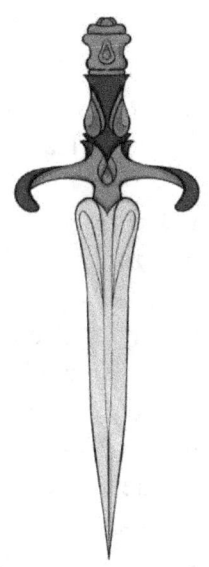

Chapter Eight

Felix held my hand and played the role of guide on our own walk through the grounds of Lake Delendil. We followed the gravel path around the left-hand side of the Citadel and into the gardens behind the castle where we passed rose bushes and a bench positioned in front of them.

Underneath the warm mid-morning sun, tulips bloomed, and the smell of jasmine and roses hung in the air. A framed walkway leading to a grand fountain was heavy with blossom. Cherry trees were dotted around us, the array of colours a significant contrast to the dull and barren Badlands. Lake

Delendil was frozen in a perpetual, blissful state of spring.

"Kiirion told me about this place," he said. "I thought we deserved the pleasure of seeing such beauty."

Why was he making an effort now? Was it because he left at morning meal, then skipped an important council meeting?

The potential answers twisted my stomach into knots. Our relationship—if I could even call it that—was delicate and strained by the war erupting around us. It was unclear if what was forming between us was stemming from a desperate need for escapism, and while I had other important things to think about, I couldn't focus on them unless I had a clear mind.

"Felix." I came to a halt, tilted my chin up, and met his gaze. "We should talk about this morning."

He shifted on his feet and ran a hand through his hair. "I apologise for being so abrupt with you. That hadn't been my intention."

I edged closed to him. "Do you regret last night?"

"What?" Of course not." He cupped my cheek. "Nothing could *ever* make me regret that. If I'd had it my way, I would never have left that bathing room."

"Then tell me what is wrong." I stepped out of his touch. Answers first.

"I had a moment, that's all," he hesitated. "A moment of fear, perhaps. We've crossed that line—we are no longer simply a queen and a royal guard. We've made this muddier with our feelings and physical connection."

"Muddier? That's your choice of words?" I tilted my head to the side, my voice coming out harsher than I'd wanted.

"That's not what I meant, either." He sighed and closed his eyes for a moment before returning his attention to me. "Look, we both know this isn't going to be easy for us. While the staff here at the Citadel might not question our relationship, I guarantee others will. Our allies, the lords and ladies of the kingdom—they will have something to say about you being involved with someone beneath your station."

"Then we face them together," I said. "But if you don't communicate with me—if you shut me out—then we have no chance of ever making this work."

"I know. I'm sorry." He relaxed his shoulders. "From now on, I won't keep things from you."

"Good. I'll hold you to it." Unable to resist his touch any longer, I leaned in and kissed him, savouring the softness of his lips against mine and the taste of cinnamon from this morning's baked goods on his tongue.

When he pulled away, he bent and plucked the head off a rose, then handed it to me. "For you."

I took the flower and inhaled its sweet scent. It tickled my nose.

We continued through the garden until we circled around to the towering back entrance into the Citadel. The mosaic multicoloured glass reflected streams of golden sunlight onto the path.

"Your guests have been taken to the grasslands a few yards west for training, Your Majesty," a guard stationed at the door said.

The beautiful display around me was a distraction, tempting me with fancies I didn't have time for.

"I will meet with the council members," I said to the guard. Nieve's sanctions had to be decided. What was a suitable punishment for somebody who'd deceived us all?

The council room was full when we arrived.

"Felix will join our meetings." I stroked the petals of my rose. "He knows the lands very well and is a member of the royal guard. I trust his judgement, and I hope you'll listen to what he may have to say." Felix sat to the left of the chair at the head, then created a steeple with his fingers.

I paced as I considered her fate. "Nieve is in the dungeons, but a punishment has not been given."

"We can't administer any severe punishment." Theodas stood behind his chair and waited for me to be seated, then reclined into his own seat. "No laws were broken."

"*Yet*." Ascal pointed. "We cannot be sure what she may do if she were free. She's already deceived us, and we cannot give her power to do so again. Is this not crime enough?"

"She has committed treason by having ulterior motives. She has not been the chief for the good of the community," Kiirion said.

"We should hold her in the dungeons until a date can be set for her trial," Felix said, bringing his first opinion to a council meeting. Pride hummed through my body at the sound of his voice, reassuring and confident.

"There are more pressing issues at the moment, Felix. She might be there until the end of the war," I said.

"The war could last years." Valneris frowned, deepening the wrinkles around his eyes. "I don't want her around here much longer. She's a Dark Mage. Keeping her here will taint the holy grounds of the lake."

"Not much else we can do," Kiirion said. His braid of black, shining hair hung from the nape of his neck. "Now, if you will pardon me, my queen, I'd like to return to the training grounds. There's much to be done."

"Ensure they train and rest well. We must be ready." I fixed my gaze on him.

"I will travel to each of the Elementals and ask them to confirm their support. A handful of guards can travel with me," Felix said.

"The Elementals won't answer to you or the guards. If a Dark Mage can fool us all into believing she's a High Elf, only the gods know what else the Dark Triads have up their sleeves. We need to be prepared," Kiirion said.

Valneris sighed. "In normal circumstances, it would have been Nieve who'd deal with the Elementals as she was supposedly negotiating a peace treaty between the Light and Dark Triads. The Elementals must've been fooled by Nieve's Milleshar as they will only deal with the purest of individuals. Someone else must go in her place—someone with access to pure magic."

Their collective gazes landed on me.

"During the last war, your father was sent to confirm the Undines' and Nereids' allegiances. At that stage, nobody knew about the delicate balance of good and evil between the water Elementals, and the impact it would have if a being of less purity were to be sent. Such a fragile magic was thrown askew, turning the Undines feral, and leaving the Nereids without their voice of reason. A powerful mage, known as Mya, was sent to restore the balance, and bring peace to the divided water Elementals," Kiirion said.

"Mya? My mother?" I gasped, pressing my hand to my chest.

"This is why you must go." Theodas tapped his fingers on the table. "We have a stable with a few horses. They're battle trained. Evalyn, please take them."

"How many horses?"

"Six."

"I'll prepare myself for departure and have the stablemen ready the horses and arrange for the guards to join us out front." Felix exited the room. After saying farewell to the council, I followed and turned at the top of the stairs to my chamber.

Once inside, I placed the limp rose on the dresser, dipped a quill into the ink horn, which smelled of burning wood, and used it to circle each of the three locations on the map. The Galae Pools were the closest and a few miles northeast of Lake Delendil before Sanctum City. The Highland Trees were farther away in the south, past the Eyrie, and the Vesuvius Caves were near the Badlands back in the centre of the map. Travelling by horse would take half the time than it would to walk. We'd reach all three locations of the Elementals within a week.

I gazed at the wilted rose beside the map—its sweet aroma faint.

The beads on my necklace warmed my neck.

It was just a rose, I chided myself.

I unpinned my brooch and placed it on the dresser. Kissed by the warmth of the sun streaming in through the window, I walked across the room to change into my armour.

Someone knocked the door.

"Come in," I called.

"I am here to dress you, Your Majesty." Mildred clicked the door shut behind her.

Nodding, I tried to shake the uncomfortable knot in my stomach. I'd spent my whole life dressing myself, and I was still getting used to my position.

"Here, let me undress you." She closed the space between us, then assisted me out of my clothes. "If I may say so, Your Majesty, your scales are magnificent."

I glanced at the indigo ridges along my arms— they transitioned into silver on my forearms and up to my collarbones.

"They grow brighter by the day." I traced my fingers across the scales.

She smiled, then fastened me into my armour and attached the golden cloak of Lake Delendil. The material flowed down the length of my back. Next, she took a brush from on top of the dresser and pulled it gently through my hair. Once it was detangled, she braided it, twirled it into a bun, and pinned it into place.

"You are ready" She smiled again. "I wish you safe travels."

"I'll have Felix and the guards with me."

"They'll keep you safe." Mildred nodded.

"He will waltz into the Galae Pools to be enchanted by the Undines." I laughed without humour. "The trip also gives me time to dwell on other uncertain matters."

Where was my mother at this point? I longed to find her.

"If you will allow me to speak free, Your Majesty," she began, "your necklace is glowing. I've never seen magic of this kind before."

I curled my fingers around the fuchsia beads. "This damn thing doesn't keep my secret very well. It reveals my heart's deepest desires for everyone to see."

"In a time of war, is that so bad?" Mildred placed her hand on my arm.

"I suppose not. Thank you for your company."

"It's my pleasure to serve you. I imagine it's quite isolating being a queen, Your Majesty." She curtsied. "If you should ever need someone to talk to, I vow you can do in confidence. Call upon me if you should ever have need of me."

To serve me...I wanted my handmaidens to respect me and for me to return the respect by treating them the same way I would a friend. This was the beginning of building that. "Thank you. You have my gratitude."

I grabbed my pouch of gemstones, then left the room to meet Felix outside the Citadel. Four guards mounted the remaining horses and waited for instruction.

"Let's move out." Placing my foot into the stirrup, I hoisted myself onto the horse.

The horses trotted along the winding dirt path that took us northeast of the Citadel. My stomach fluttered as I recalled the description I'd been given of Undines and Nereids. I'd never laid eyes on them before, so had no understanding of them. The anticipation to see what they could do gave me hope.

Felix, who rode beside me, held out his hand. He clasped mine and rubbed his thumb against my skin. I stared at our interlocked fingers and the contact calmed the thrumming of my pulse. We continued our route to the Galae Pools with a slight stirring breeze around us.

Our connection broke. I kept one hand on the horse's reins and dug into my pocket with my other, withdrawing my pouch of healing gemstones.

The path wound downhill through small fields and gatherings of trees. We passed a few houses, although they'd long since been abandoned. The rooftops sagged; birds rested in the crevices, rats scurried through broken windows, and doors banged as the breeze turned into a gusting wind.

I wondered who'd lived in those homes. Where had they gone?

I took the map from my bag and gazed at the path we were following. A small tavern where we could stay for the night lay somewhere ahead. I remembered the nights of our journey to Lake Delendil spent in caves or in fields under the cold skies. This time, we'd have a solid roof over our heads and a crackling fire to warm us while we sleep.

Light rain began to fall from the gathering of clouds as we reached the tavern. I climbed from the stallion, tied it to a nearby tree alongside the others, then opened the main door. Once inside, I rubbed the drizzle of rain from my face with the back of my hand. A Human poked the fire opposite, sending embers flying up the stone chimney. A few others sat nursing wooden steins of beer, the Humans talking in low muffled tones.

"We're closed," the man said without turning away from the fire.

Everyone else, however, pushed back their chairs and abandoned their steins before rising to their feet. They bowed, bending halfway over, and a few stumbled while doing so. The strong aromas of hops and yeast hung heavy in the tavern.

The man whipped around. His gaze settled on mine and widened as he scanned the scaled contours of my face.

"Forgive me." He flattened his thinning grey hair with his hands. "If I'd known it was you—"

"It's not an issue, sir." I waved away his apology. "I would like several of your rooms for the night, if it would please you."

"Of course." The tavern keeper rushed towards us. He guided us to a door on the right, which swirled 'round to a steep set of stairs. "Right this way."

He climbed the steps that curved sharp to the left. There were several rooms on this floor and another set of stairs led to the final level of the tavern.

"This room is free." He opened the door. "It's not much for a queen, but it will keep you warm and dry. Your guards can take the vacant rooms on the second floor."

"Thank you." I smiled. "You are very kind."

He lit a fire in an old brick fireplace on the right side of the room, providing a dim orange light and cozy warmth. Afterwards, the tavern keeper bowed, then left to guide the guards to their chambers. The floorboards creaked as they ascended the stairs.

Felix lingered in the doorway. "I can stay here with you. For your protection." Despite the professional tone, which I presume he'd used in case the fellow guards overheard, his eyes blazed.

"Of course." My heart pounded as he stepped into the room and closed the door behind me. I didn't move as he locked the door, drew the curtains, then removed his armour.

Anticipation thrummed through me, and my magic buzzed at his close proximity.

Only seconds passed before I recalled exactly how his hands felt on me, how his mouth against my skin sent my magic into overdrive. Now I thought about it, the smashed mirror was a testament to his abilities, and I wanted more.

"Why are you looking at me like that?" He took a single step towards me, the light between the curtains casting a golden hue across his face and neck.

The breeze coming through the cracked window did nothing to cool the blazing fire erupting through my body.

A line of sweat formed on the nape of my neck, so I swept my hair to the side, twirling it around my hand. "Like what?"

"Like you're thinking about what I did to you in that pool." His voice deepened into a gravelly sound that made me shiver.

There was only longing in his eyes as his gaze travelled up the length of my body, although I was still fully clothed.

"Maybe I am." I raised my chin. "So what?"

He closed the space between us and took my hair in his hands, laying it aside to expose my neck.

"I'll allow it." He smirked against my skin, his warm breath tickling me. "So long as I'm the only man you look at like that. Like I'm the only one you could possibly want."

I pushed back slightly, so I could look him in the eyes. "You *are* the only one I want, and I will tell you that as much as you need me to, if it will get you to believe that I *want* this. My title will not keep us apart."

If he'd had any doubt left, any reservations, my words had chased them away. His eyes burned brighter as he tucked his thumb underneath my chin and brought his lips down on mine.

Relishing the taste of him, I surged up onto my tiptoes, and we stumbled back against one of the bed's posters. He let out a low groan as his back thumped against the wood, but his mouth didn't leave mine.

His fingers worked the buttons of my breeches, popping them open. Kneeling before me, he slowly pulled the material down and lifted my feet out of the trouser legs. Tossing the garment aside, he ran his fingers up my calf muscles and thighs, and he lingered at the edge of my underwear. I shivered against his light touch and ran my fingers through his hair. Having a man at your feet was enough to make anyone weak at the knees.

In a swift motion, he rose, scooping me up into his arms. Spinning around, he tossed me playfully on the bed, and I let out a laugh. Sliding the fabric of my underwear to the side, he settled between my legs, a ravenous hunger in his eyes.

"What are you doing?" I squealed and he yanked me to the edge of the mattress, propping my legs either side of his head.

"Taking what's mine." His gaze flared before he buried his face between my legs.

Pleasure radiated through me with each painfully slow drag of his tongue, and I threw my arm over my mouth to stifle a moan. As his mouth teased me, my body trembled and coiled. Reaching down with my free hand, I gripped onto his hair, feeling the softness of his scalp beneath my nails.

When he eased a finger inside me, I shuddered and raised my hips to meet each of his thrusts. I arched my back off the bed, wanting more of him. It would never be enough—this craving would never cease.

"*Felix*," was all I managed. A desperate plea for more.

He slipped a second finger inside and curled them as his tongue stroked against my softest spot.

Power surged through my bones, my flesh, every inch of my body, demanding a release.

"You're mine," he muttered against my flesh. "Say it."

"I'm yours," I said breathlessly as he picked up the speed of his fingers moving inside me.

I clamp my eyes shut as my magic thrashed against my body like an untamed beast, and I ricocheted towards release. The distinct sound of something cracking didn't go unnoticed.

Felix surged up to cover my mouth with his own as I cried out, tensing and trembling around him.

Grinning, he pulled back to observe me lying in a tousled mess on the mattress. With a gentle touch, he moved the strands of hair out of my face and kissed me again, the taste of me still on him.

Reaching between us, I rubbed my hand against the hardness of him through his breeches, but he took my hand in his and brought it up to his lips.

He placed a kiss on my knuckles. "We should stop before you break anything else." Amusement twinkled in his eyes.

"Oh gods," I grumbled. "What did I do this time?"

"I'm pretty sure you splintered the bedframe." He laughed, peering at the posters.

Indeed, a fissure ran through the entire length of the wood. And I didn't care one bit.

———————⁓———————

In the morning, the tavern keeper prepared some food for us to take on our journey. He handed me bread, cheese, and berries wrapped in brown cloth to put in my bag.

"Keep safe, my queen." The man smiled. "May the gods protect you."

"Thank you for your kindness." I returned the smile.

We straddled our horses, then rode down the path to the Galae Pools. Two guards rode ahead, and the remaining two flanked us.

Far off, mountains stretched into the distance until they disappeared beneath the horizon. Sanctum City would be farther north.

Chin down, I followed his lead. As I rode, I cast a ball of vibrant white magic in my hands. Felix caught a glimpse of the white light I held, and the corners of his mouth tilted into a smile.

"Do you still have the spell book?" he asked. "You should keep it safe."

"Yes. It is in my pocket with the gemstones from Juliette." I closed my eyes for a long blink, remembering her. "I miss her."

My eyes widened at the crisp, bright colours of the tulips and the red berry trees. Enchanted by the beauty of my surroundings, I revelled in the exquisiteness. The tree-lined path guided us towards the mountains. The foliage of the shrubs and flowers were delicate shades of blues and purples.

I stretched from the saddle, reached for the velvety leaves, and plucked one from its thorny branches. The leaf was lined with tiny hairs that kissed my fingertips. The aroma of juicy blackberries wafted through the air as we grew closer to the Galae Pools. The transitional colours marked the area of the water Elementals.

"Do you trust them?" I asked Felix. "The water Elementals?"

"I've never come across them before." He locked his sight on the mountains ahead. "I base my judgement on the council members' words. They said they enchant men for a soul, which doesn't sound promising. The guards and I will lead the way in case there's any signs of an ambush."

The highlands opened in front of us. A breeze blew through the gorge as we entered. Steep mountains towered above us. Clouds gathered and the squawk of nearby birds rang in my ears. Indigo moss and loose rocks shifted as the horses trod along the path.

"Do you know how deep into the valley the Galae Pools are?" I asked.

"I'm not sure." He rested his hand on his sword.

The guards filed into the narrow path ahead of us.

I drew the map from my satchel, then peered at the circular pools, which were about a hundred yards or so ahead. What if the Elementals tried to enchant Felix or the guards with their songs? As we drew nearer to our destination, the muscles in my jaw tensed. I swallowed dryly, unable to wet my parched throat.

I wasn't too late to run right around and go back the way we'd come.

We continued through the pass until a faint blue glow materialised in front of us. At the end of the path were three pools connected. They shimmered a magnificent turquoise. The mesmerising water illuminated the opening, and we inched closer.

"Walk slow." Felix took the lead with the other guards flanking him.

The songs of the Undines rose, their angelic voices echoing through the mountains.

'One of them tried to enchant me with her songs so I'd marry her. Marriage to a land being provides them with a soul.'

Theodas' words haunted my mind. He'd been lucky to escape with his soul. The Undines' melody rose the hairs on my neck. Their voices were the perfect pitch—a tranquilising lullaby.

"You should stay there." I gestured to Felix. "Let me do the talking. The risk to your sanity is greater than mine."

He, and the guards, obeyed. His eyes glazed over, and his face softened as he swayed to the lyrics. I glanced at the surrounding guards, who were all under the same trance.

"I mean it, don't move." I snapped my fingers in front of Felix's face. "Be strong."

I steadied my breathing and took a step towards the pool's edge.

The water was clear yet gave a bottomless illusion. The stones in the walls of the pool glistened, and the turquoise glow lit the spring water plants until they faded into dark depths. The silky voices continued to chant their charms, and I shuddered.

"I'm Queen Evalyn." I cleared my throat and held my chin up.

"I have come to ask you to pledge your allegiance to the Light Triads."

The melodies faded, loosening the hypnotic grasp they held over Felix and the guards. An Undine swam from the back pool into the one in front of me. Her tail was wide and long, adorned with dark green scales, matching her lighter green skin. When she reached the edge of the pool, she emerged from the water and leaned on the side.

Her hair fell away from around her face and revealed her bright golden eyes. There were no irises or pupils, just a solid mass of colour. They were endless and resembled all things I imagined being soulless. Her torso held shadowed curves, all that remained in place of breasts.

"You've brought malessss," the Undine said in a silky voice. "That'ssss a dangeroussss game…" Her voice echoed in smooth intonation.

"They're here to protect their queen," I reminded her, although certain I'd said it to ease my own nerves. "If you agree to an alliance, you will be expected to restrain yourself from your natural desire. The males of the Light Triads are out of bounds to you. Please advise your sisters of this also."

The Undine laughed, creating a wicked, screeching sound that reminded me of Zhah, of its evil—perhaps she belonged there.

More Undines appeared and circled the main pool, and my pulse accelerated.

The Nereids shared the same pools as the Undines, but swam in their own circles, avoiding each other to some extent. The Nereids were the purest of all water beings, and they looked like beautiful mercreatures with hair of all colours.

"We are more evil than good," the Undine said with her hypnotic voice and hollow gaze piercing into mine. "But we are the Elementals, and we are bound to nature."

"So…you will help us?" I shook.

This was a stupid idea, but I couldn't afford for them to say no.

"The battle will allow ussss to ssssing our songssss and enchant the malessss of the Dark Triads. A different song of coursssse." She twirled a piece of emerald hair around her long, curling fingers. "We will have our soulssss. The tales call it marriage." I jerked back.

The Undines laughed again. Flowers around the pool curled up, the ground vibrated, and thousands of tiny ripples spread across the water's surface.

"Marriage issss a Human term," the Undine said. "Our songssss bind ussss to the person they enchant, ssssplitting the ssssoul in half. We'd be bound until the ssssoul has transsssferred from them to ussss, leaving them to die."

"Not the most pleasant of creatures." A Nereid with radiant waves of red hair laughed. Her skin shimmered a pale silver colour, and water droplets glistened as they glided down her body. Their tails were smaller than those belonging to the Undines, and they swam as if one with the water.

The Undine shot her a glare. The Nereid remained silent.

"How long does that take?"

"He speakssss," the Undine said. "Very dangeroussss, indeed."

I shot a look at Felix, and my mouth fell open, shocked he would risk his life by commenting. The guards edged closer.

"A few minutessss..." she purred. I thanked the gods their songs hadn't resumed.

"If we're to call on you for battle, how will you get there?" I focused on their writhing fish tails.

"A ssssacrifice will allow ussss to walk on land for a few dayssss. We mussst return to the Galae Poolssss within four dayss or we face the consssssequences—never to return to the waterssss." She twirled her long finger through the water.

"What sacrifice?" I pressed my hand to my chest, then stepped back.

"It requiressss one male." Her gaze darted from one guard to another.

"No!"

"We will support you providing we can find another," a Nereid said.

My gaze flicked between her and the Undine. "I have your word?"

160

"Of courssse," she said. "Our ssssongs will only enchant our mutual enemiessss. A threat to the Fertile Territoriessss issss a threat to ussss."

"How can you be sure your songs will work on the Dark Triads?" I pursed my lips. "Do you have any proof?"

"Our ssssongs have never failed ussss. I'm ssssure you know your mother hassss ssssstood in that very ssssame posssssition before. We were requesssssted to ussssse our abilitiessss in the last great war."

"While we do not always agree with the Undines' behaviour," the Nereid glanced sharply at the Undine, "we are sisters, and we work together in the face of battle."

My forehead wrinkled. "Do you remember how to get to the Badlands?"

"One never forgetssss." The Undine rested her arms on the edge of the pool and fixed her unwavering gaze on me.

"Thank you. I will send you word when it is time to gather. Meet us at the camp." I took Felix's hand. "It's time for us to leave. Come on."

He moved with me but kept his stare on the Undine. "What is your name?"

"Sssseara," the Undine whispered.

Her eyes glowed.

The choir started singing again. I grabbed Felix by the back of his cape and pulled him. His heels dug into the soft ground beside the rocks. I yanked harder. Seara let out a shrill laugh. He jolted back into reality.

"Let's get out of here now," I commanded. "Guards, leave!"

We forged our way back to the grassland as the songs faded in the distance.

When we were out of the gorge, I leaned against the rockface and panted. Sweat beaded on my hairline. They were terrifying creatures, but to win this war against the Dark Triads, we needed a little evil ourselves.

"Are you okay?" He gripped me hard and shook until my gaze rose to meet his.

I'd been more concerned for *his* safety. They could have enchanted him, leaving him for dead. "I could ask you the same thing. The High Elves left out a few details. They downplayed how evil the Undines are."

"We'll be all right," he said. "They will help us win this war, and we don't have much of a choice."

He was right, but I hated the idea of using evil— the one thing we were trying to overcome and prevent from destroying this realm.

I flattened the map I'd scrunched in my hand. The Highland Trees of the Air Elementals were deep in the south, below the Eyrie.

"Let's get a move on." What would I gain from fretting over something I couldn't control?

He nodded. We mounted our horses, and I cursed the gods.

As we rode, the purple tinge of twilight returned to the sky, and we needed to find somewhere to spend the night.

"Have you ever wondered what else is out there?" Felix gazed through the gaps in the canopy of leaves above us. We passed through a gathering of chestnut trees, and the chilled breeze of evening cooled my cheeks. "You know, what lies past the Fertile and Barren Territories?"

I'd never once before wondered what else there was to the realm.

I wasn't sure if there *was* anything more. The world seemed to end outside of the territories. I shrugged. "Wilderness. Or nothing at all."

He didn't respond. There was something final about the words I said. The idea of there being anything more to the world made the hairs on my neck stand on end. What uncharted lands lay beyond the Great Sea?

"Nothing at all..." he repeated a few minutes later. "I don't believe it."

The sun sank beneath the hills, and we stopped at a small, empty barn. The doors hung from their hinges and the roof sagged from weathering and age.

The guards trapped rabbits for supper, then prepared them beside a glowing fire outside the barn.

"I'll call upon you when food is ready, Your Majesty." One nodded to me.

"Thank you."

Felix guided me inside the structure. A thin layer of hay covered the concrete floor and there were several divided sections where horses or cattle were once kept.

"When this war has ended," he sat on the floor with his back against the barn wall, "and you are crowned queen, you'll never have to sleep like this again."

"It's not a burden," I admitted, and it was true. "I won't take this power for granted. And this journey allows me to see all corners of the realm I will rule over. I will not neglect it like King Atticus."

"You know, when I was a child, I was terrified of the dark." Felix chuckled, his tone uneasy. "I hated it and wouldn't go anywhere without a candle. My mother would put me to bed and blow out the candles. I would scream every time."

"You have fears?" I raised an eyebrow. "A knight of the Eyrie…scared of the dark."

"I *had* fears," he corrected. "My father put a stop to that. He would march me to the barns and lock me inside with the horses. I wasn't allowed out until morning—until I was free from my fear."

"That's cruel." I clasped my hand over my mouth, unable to stifle a laugh, and leaned forward. "Did it work?"

"Well, here I am now, without a candle and about to sleep in rotting hay." He winked.

"The rabbits have been roasted, Your Majesty." A guard poked his head around the barn door.

We rose, then joined the others around the firepit. One of the men grabbed a metal pot from the bag, pulled the cooked meat from the stick above the flame, then handed it to me. "Here you go."

I smiled, then tucked into the lightly charred meat. Together, we remained close around the warmth of the flickering flames until a cold wind whipped through the trees. We retired to the barn— the guards sleeping closer to the entrance.

When the light of the morning sun shone in through the open door of the barn, I awoke. The warmth of looming summer set off a desire to strip free of my armour and allow my skin to breathe.

Felix stirred and surfaced from his slumber. He smiled at me with groggy eyes.

"Morning." I gently pushed the hair back from his eyes.

"Good morning." He kissed me, his lips lingering on mine before he rose from the hay.

After a hasty morning meal of berries and stale bread, we untied the horses from the trees, then set out. A thin layer of dew covered our path. The freshness of a new morning instilled a confidence in me, and I rode with my shoulders back and my chin held high, ready to meet the Sylphs of the Highland Trees.

A series of bangs and groans caught my attention, and I jerked my head in the direction of the sound. I tugged on the horse's reins, then lifted my hand to halt the guards.

Concealed by the trees, I slipped from my saddle. Felix and the guards followed suit and drew their swords.

A horde of Orcs marched down the path, their boots thudding in unison against the stone. They bared the same sharp tusks as Xurek and wore similar leather armour around their shoulders. Each Orc carried a giant hammer with ease.

"I've never seen them within our territory before." Felix frowned.

I yanked him to the ground as one of the Orcs shot a look in our direction. The guards stood behind trunks, waiting for the all-clear. The smell of burning flesh singed my nose. I grimaced and shrank further into the mud.

After they were out of sight, I ran through the trees, following the scent of burning flesh. Felix and the guards flanked me.

I came to a halt, and my gaze fixed on a dozen or so bodies stacked on top of one another. They were burned and no longer recognisable. I couldn't tell if they were Human, Elf, or other.

Tears formed in my eyes, and I didn't try to stop them from falling. Felix took me in his arms and cradled my head away from the charred bodies.

There were no settlements this far south that were designated to just one tribe, so trying to figure out what clan these bodies belonged to was impossible.

"What are we to do with all of them?" I leaned back to look at Felix, to the other guards, then back to him. He stared in silence at the pile of corpses, his face pale. His silence confirmed there was nothing we could do. We had to leave them there to rot.

"My queen, we ought to leave in case the Orcs come back," one of the guards said.

I nodded, took one last glance at the dead I couldn't help, then returned to my horse.

We rode down the path and around the bend until the stench of rotting flesh had long since diminished.

I stroked my horse's mane. My breath caught in my throat. I wanted to strip out of my armour and curl up in a ball somewhere dark and pretend this nightmare wasn't happening. But it was. It was raging on and showed no signs of ever letting up.

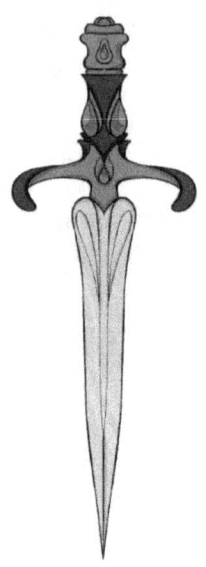

Chapter Nine

It took us two and a half days to reach the route to the Highland Trees. The Sylphs were settled on top of a cliff overlooking the sea. We travelled to the very south of the Fertile Territories with the uncharted Great Sea ahead, stretching into the unknown.

We reached the top, then dismounted the horses. I glanced at the sea—large wooden boats were abandoned on the rocks below. My heart lurched at the lurking shadows of beasts swimming beneath the surface. The waves crashed against the jagged rocks, spraying water up the cliffside.

I couldn't help but wonder what lay past the horizon. If I took a ship across the dark water, what would I find? How far would I travel and for how long?

Fresh green grasslands stretched along the top of the cliff with yellow flowers dotted here and there. A chilled breeze stirred the tall grass and whipped my hair around. I clasped my golden cloak tight against my face and hurried to the shelter of the trees.

Ancient oaks blanketed the cliffs, their roots gripping the rocks like claws. The stony path ended as we breached the perimeter of the Highland Trees.

"I'm preferring this to the pools. The forest is peaceful." Felix traced his fingers down the ridged bark of an umber-brown trunk.

"Let's hope you don't succumb to the songs of the Sylphs. I don't want to have to save you again." I laughed.

He lowered his head and peered at me from beneath his eyebrows. "Their sweet singing is nothing compared to the wrath I would receive from your tongue, should I err in my duty to protect you, milady. Do you have anything in your pouch I could use to cover my ears?" He threw his head back in laughter.

I prodded his ribs through a small gap in his armour. The guards followed, remaining silent.

The cliff-side behind us disappeared, and the waves grew silent as we moved farther into the forest. Like the songs of the water Elementals, the Sylphs' music transfixed me. We were surrounded by blissful tunes—light and airy notes lulled me into comfort.

I took a few steps between the trees until the small flying creatures were visible as they weaved their way through the intertwined branches above. The mossy floor was spongy underfoot, and golden light dappled the leaves. Fungi grew along the path, and beams of sun illuminated the jagged bark on the trunks of nearby trees.

"My name is Evalyn." I raised my gaze towards the Sylphs who were gliding in the breeze around a gnarled tree branch. "I've come to ask for your allegiance."

The song ceased, and the air remained silent until a buzzing sound began. A small Sylph appeared and hovered in front of my nose.

"It's the queen!" she squealed.

Other Sylphs emerged from the canopy and assembled in front of us. They formed straight lines and flew six feet above the ground.

Amongst the wilderness encompassing me, I became one with the soul of the Highland Trees, a single unit with the air I breathed. I closed my eyes and inhaled.

Is this what it was like to be an Elemental being?

"You are more beautiful than I imagined." A Sylph flew through the crowd, buzzing around my head. A sheer material hanging from her shoulders glistened like a spider's web coated in drops of rainfall against the moonlight. "Are you a Mage? I've seen one before, and her skin was gold and red like yours."

"That must have been a long time ago. I am the last Light Mage." I wondered if my mother visited the Sylphs, like she had the Undines and Nereids. Here I stood, in what may have been the same position as her, history repeating itself.

"Then I shall thank the gods that we have you." She picked up the corners of her dress, attempting to curtsy, but her wings fluttered faster. She somersaulted and stifled a laugh. "Aren't you a pretty sight…the scales on your face…glorious!"

"Fascinating," Felix said. "Since we arrived here, your scales have changed colour—they're perhaps deeper—and your hair is red."

"Perhaps this visit has strengthened my magic." I smiled. "What
should I call you?"

"Falaya," she responded. "It is an honour to meet you, my queen." Her bee-sized wings fluttered as she spoke.

"If I may, I'd like to discuss your role in the war, as we need to prepare our strategy." I clasped my hands.

"What are your abilities?" Felix added.

"We are bound by blood and flesh to the winds of the sky," Falaya said. "We have the ability to manipulate it. The Dark Triads won't be expecting it, my queen. Will you be speaking to the other Elementals?"

"Of course." I nodded. "The Gnomes have become dear friends of mine, so I believe their word is true, and we have visited the Galae Pools."

A few of the Sylphs shook their heads and tutted.

171

"The Undines are vile creatures." Falaya hissed. "Whether they like it or not, they are bound to Lightness. The Nereids are free to choose their loyalty. They are a yin yang entity at its finest meaning."

"Nonetheless, they have agreed to assist us in battle. Will your abilities to control the wind be strong enough against the Dark Triads?"

"Certainly. During the last war, we manipulated a tornado that wiped out a quarter of the Dark Triads' army. You can place your trust in us, my queen." She bowed her head graciously.

"There's the Salamanders of the Vesuvius Caves left," Felix said. "What should we expect from them?"

"They are very powerful—more so than the rest of us," Falaya explained. "They are one with the fire of the world."

"It's been an honour meeting you." How could the Sylphs coexist in a world with such evil? "I will send word to you when you're needed at the Badlands. Meet us at the camp."

"See you soon, my queen," Falaya said as the crowd of Sylphs dispersed amongst the trees. "May the gods protect you."

Throughout my journey, I'd received this prayer from the Gnomes and the Sylphs. I'd prayed to the gods myself along the way. When we confronted our enemies on the battlefield of the Badlands, I prayed, too, that the gods would hear me.

On the fifth night of our journey, the guards set up camp nearby while Felix and I sat against tree trunks. The fire drenched the forest in a deep, orange glow, and the scent of roasted squirrel wafted on the slight breeze.

"You should eat," Felix said, "here, have some." He gave me the cooked meat, hauled out his pouch of seeds, then poured some into a metal bowl.

I bit into the squirrel leg and fidgeted against the oak trunk. "No stars *or* moon tonight…is this an omen?"

"No, just a cloudy sky. I'll stay awake a little longer." He circled me with his arms and tucked me against him. "Lean your head on me and rest."

Birds rustled the canopy of leaves above as they flew into their nests for the night. Branches snapped, and something shuffled in the foliage around us.

I jolted upwards; my gaze dashed from one tree to the next. "Something's out there." My arms tensed. Gooseflesh raised along my skin.

"It's a badger." He soothed and stroked my hair.

"It wasn't a badger last time." I shrugged him off and scraped the hair out of my face. "I fought a Demon!"

"No, I'm serious—look!" He pointed to the black and white creature sniffing amongst the fallen leaves before it scurried under a bush.

I laughed, tugged his arm tighter around me, and buried my head against his chest, his sandalwood scent filling my nose. His heart pumped beneath his

173

armour, and its steadiness soothed the knots in my stomach. I closed my eyes and drifted to sleep.

I stirred awake when the heat from the morning sun caught my cheeks. We took the horses to graze on a nearby pasture, then we ate the remaining trapped squirrels and prepared to journey onwards.

Near the grassland, we found a narrow spring of water and took advantage of the rare opportunity to bathe and refill our wineskins for the trek. The guards lingered nearby, bathing themselves.

I wrenched off my armour and boots before wading into the stream. The cool water lapped around my feet. Birds sang their morning songs as they flew overhead.

Cold water bit into my face, and I trembled. Felix stood in front of me, soaking wet and grinning.

"Did you just splash the queen?" I gasped with mock horror.

"Of course, not—I'm...er...bathing the queen," he managed between laughs. He thrust his hands through the ripples and splashed me again.

I stomped, thrashed, and kicked the water until his hair hung sodden around his eyes.

"Okay, okay!" he shouted. "I beg your forgiveness, Your Majesty." He smirked.

"That's it!" I leapt onto his back and rustled his hair.

He locked his arms around my legs and shifted my weight onto
his back. "Hold on tight."

I clutched him as he trudged through the water and stumbled on the pebbles underfoot.

"Put me down!" I laughed and pounded his chest with my fists. "I need to wash my hair."

He set me down and cupped the back of my neck. He studied my face, interrogating me with his eyes before his lips met mine, slow and lingering.

Once we bathed and dressed, we pursued our route northeast towards the Vesuvius Caves. I moved the heavy armour into a comfortable position as sores developed on my shoulder blades and hips. I longed to return to Lake Delendil, to the safety of my new home and under the protection of the High Elves.

"Are we close?" I glanced at the path that turned black farther ahead.

"Yes. We'll need to leave the horses here as the ground will be too hot for their hooves." He swung his leg over, then jumped from his horse and tethered it to a tree. His boots scraped across the uneven path.

The guards filtered ahead of us with their swords poised. I dismounted, then followed Felix.

The path turned to solidified lava—solid black and cracked. The encroaching heat seared through my armour, and beads of sweat ran down my spine. He jumped sideways, avoiding a blast of steam that jetted out from the rocks. A foul rotten stench filled my nostrils and I dry-heaved. He tugged a couple pieces of cloth from his pack and handed one to me. I clamped it over my nose and gasped.

Coughing, he wiped his reddened face. He made his way along the narrowing route towards the entrance of the cave. We crossed the thin trail between the pits of boiling lava bubbling around us.

"Be careful, the path is crumbling away, and we can't have you falling into lava," he said, his voice muffled by the cloth. I nodded and grasped his hand.

I squeaked and clung onto Felix as the ground trembled beneath my feet. The path ascended as we pressed on through the blistering heat, and I wheezed, trying to suck in breath through the smog.

Through a break in the smoke and bubbles of lava, I saw a pack of Salamanders gathered outside of the caves.

'A humanoid said to be descendant of some sort of lizard.'

They had the bodies of Humans, covered in thick scales the colour of sand. Their eyes were beady and alert, and a sack hung from their chins like a bearded dragon's. Would they flare when we approached them?

A Salamander came forward. He scraped his long, thin claws against a boulder. Felix stood in front of me as the rock sliced beneath the Salamander's talons. A few of the creatures behind him hissed; smoke tendrils escaped through their nostrils.

"A Human *and* a Mage..." The Salamander whistled. His tall frame and curved spine loomed over us. "The queen and her companion."

My heart lurched. Our allies were terrifying to witness. The other Salamanders around him retreated from their territorial threat display and the smoke from their noses diminished.

"I've come to ask you to form an alliance with the Light Triads." I ignored the image of them roasting me alive and pushed my shoulders back.

"A pleasure." The words rolled off his tongue in a lull like the bewitching voices of the Undines. "My name is Ignatius," he hissed.

"What do you intend to do with the Dark Triads when the battle begins?" Felix stepped backwards, moving away from the Salamander's shadow.

Ignatius scowled at him. "We do not answer to you." He spat.

The Salamanders who flanked Ignatius glared at Felix.

"I understand." Felix nodded, but kept a protective hand on my arm, his sword poised forwards.

"Please tell us how you plan to use your gifts against the Dark Triads." I gestured to Ignatius.

He tilted his head towards the sky, took a deep breath, and exhaled a fierce burst of fire, flaring his beard. I shielded my eyes from its bright red light and thanked the gods for presenting us with a strength against the Dark Triads.

"We can release large blasts of fire at our enemies and create deep cracks in the ground, which can be useful if we become surrounded by enemies," he said. "We were called upon during the last war, and such powers did not fail us then." Ignatius curled his tongue and whipped it out the side of his mouth. "Now why don't you show us what *you* can do? You are a Mage, after all."

The guards remained close, keeping their gazes locked on the Salamander.

I manipulated a ball of white light within my palms and threw it at a boulder, and it shattered upon impact. I followed this by the red light I used to ward off the Demon in the forest.

"Almost as magnificent as our fire." Ignatius eyed the ball of red light spinning and twirling in my palms.

"I've used this on a Demon." I dropped my hands to my side, and the magic disappeared.

"Demon?" He arched an eyebrow. The other Salamanders, whose ears pointed with interest, drew nearer.

"One killed a friend of ours," I said, recalling the memory of the night she died. "This red light didn't slay the Demon, but it suffered excruciating pain before it disappeared."

"Interesting…" Ignatius muttered. "Our fire may have a similar effect. When will you call upon us?"

"I will send a letter when it is time for us to ride out to battle. We will be setting up a camp nearby. Find us there."

"So be it. Come sit and rest. You must be overheating out here."

I glanced at Felix who edged closer.

"We won't hurt you." Ignatius's tongue lapped at the corners of his mouth.

Felix clasped my hand and guided me into the dry caves, following Ignatius and the pack of Salamanders. Inside, we were sheltered from the jets of sweltering steam, and the rocks were cooler beneath my feet.

We sat on boulders away from the group. Felix opened his bag and withdrew two pieces of stale bread. "It's not much, but it won't be long before we're home."

I took the bread from him and bit into its rough surface.

Home. He'd called Lake Delendil home.

"When the war is over, do you plan on staying?" I peered at him.

"While it is my sworn duty to protect you, I fear you are now in possession of my heart and mind." He grinned. "Nothing will keep me away. I am yours as much as you are mine."

His declaration made my heart somersault.

After finishing our meagre meal, we left the Vesuvius Caves and headed along the path that would lead us westward to Lake Delendil. The trail returned to its normal dirt colour as the purple tinges of evening fell across the realm.

That night, we set up camp in an open field underneath the clear sky. Guards hunted rabbit for dinner. Felix and I lay on our backs and gazed at the vast heavens above us. The horses grazed in the grassy pasture.

"These are the first stars we've seen since the war started." I pointed to the glowing balls of fire above.

"You hear that?" He turned on his side and smiled. The silver glow of the moon lit his face.

"What?" I returned the smile.

"Nothing." He closed his eyes and breathed. "Nothing at all. Peace."

He circled his arm around my shoulders. His breathing evened, and with my head against him, the steady sound of his heartbeat fluttered in my ears. He stroked my hair away from my face until my eyelids fell heavy and sleep welcomed me.

The sun found its highest point in the sky when we passed the pine trees that stretched along the south side of the glistening waters of Lake Delendil.

"It's good to see you home safe, Your Majesty," an Elven guard said as we stopped outside the Citadel.

"It was a successful mission—the Elementals have accepted my request to meet us on the battlefield."

The guard opened the entrance doors, and we crossed the foyer to meet the Elves in the council room. Theodas, Valneris, and Ascal were seated around the council table while Kiirion signed a scroll.

"You have returned, my queen." Kiirion glanced up. "Although it frustrates me you put yourself in so much danger."

Eric entered the room in a brisk walk and drew me into his arms. A servant stood nearby with a decanter of wine in her hands.

"You're safe." He let out a sigh as we embraced, his voice low and gentle.

"Indeed, I am." I let go, then sat at the head of the table, Felix taking his position at my side.

"The Elementals are quite the bunch of allies to have." the council members laughed.

"You had the pleasure of meeting the Undines," Theodas added. "I told you they were grotesque."

Eric sat next to Theodas. Although Theodas' features were pointed and sharper, little differed from Eric's. Their hair hung from their shoulders in golden waves, and their eyes shone a bright sapphire.

"The main thing is the Elementals have guaranteed their support, regardless of their disturbing qualities," Felix said. "They each have abilities that will prove useful on the battlefield."

"The Centaurs and Humans have made progress at Bluefair Fort. Kiirion has made a ledger of all those who have completed training." Eric pointed to the signed parchment. "I will send them word when it is time for them to meet us."

"The cooks are busy in the kitchens preparing a meal, Your Majesty. We understand you must be famished and exhausted," Ascal said.

I rubbed my forehead. "It's been a long journey, and a tiring one at that."

"Perhaps we should share a goblet of wine in your honour, my queen," Theodas said.

"I appreciate the offer, but I'd like to rest." I turned to the servant. "Have Mildred draw me a bath, please."

He bowed, placed the decanter of wine on the table, then exited the room.

Felix cleared his throat. "I would like to change out my armour, also." When we were both outside the council room, he said, "Perhaps we can enjoy some of this wine over dinner together."

"Of course. I'm looking forward to seeing you dressed in finer garb." I gave him a quick kiss before meeting Mildred at the top of the staircase.

She flung open the bathing room door and began filling the marble bath.

Free of my armour, I submerged into the warm, soapy bath and let out a deep sigh. I swirled my hand through the water, watching it ripple outwards. I needed a hearty meal, then to curl up in bed with the covers pulled to my chin while a fire crackled in the hearth. It would only be made better by Felix's presence.

Sometime later, Mildred returned, then hung fresh clothing on the divider and waited for me to finish bathing.

"I'm ready." I stepped out of the bath.

She gave me a cotton sheet. I wrapped it around me and patted myself dry.

She dressed me in a silk blouse and woollen breeches. I picked up the pouch of gemstones and spell book, then tucked them into my pockets.

"Please escort me." I gestured to the door, and she led the way at once.

She guided me into the banquet hall, the largest room within the Citadel, where Felix and the Elves gathered for dinner. Its high glass walls and domed ceiling offered a picturesque place for celebratory events, and I imagined a splendid coronation after the war was over.

The table was garnished with plates of sliced boar meat. Fresh loaves of bread were dusted with flour and complimented with butter and cheeses. Blackberries were baked into tarts and served with cream and fresh fruits were drizzled with honey. Magnificent candles hung from the chandelier.

The council members stood in conversation with Felix and Eric, all clutching a goblet of wine. A houseboy handed one to me as I approached him. A musician played a violin, filling the hall with its soft tunes.

Felix's gaze met mine, and his eyes shone.

"Let's eat." I gestured to the table.

Everyone slid into their chairs as I took my seat at the head of the table. Food was stacked onto my plate by a servant. I grasped my cutlery, ready to sink into a hearty meal.

As I lifted a forkful of meat to my mouth, a guard flung open the heavy glass doors of the hall and paced towards me. The music halted. He gave me a scroll sealed with the wax crest of Zhah.

I peeled back the wax seal and unfolded the thick parchment.

Felix placed his hand on my thigh, leaning closer to get a look at the letter. "What does it say?"

As I read the paper, a lump formed in my throat— I couldn't produce the words to answer his question. I stared at him with my mouth open.

He took the paper from my hands and scanned the writing.

"The Dark Triads want Evalyn to submit herself to them," he ground out, voice laced with rage. The room fell silent.

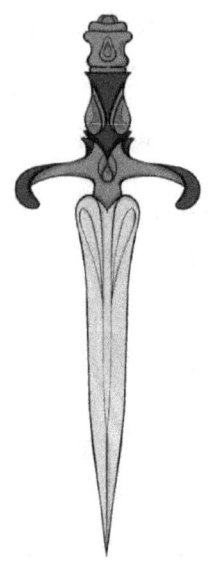

Chapter Ten

The colour drained from Felix's face. I grew lightheaded, my vision blurred, and my limbs weakened.

"If Evalyn doesn't submit herself to them, they'll burn everything to the ground," he said.

"There's not much left for them to burn," Kiirion said. "We'll protect you."

"Innocent civilians are already living under our protection," Theodas argued. He was right. The Citadel had no room for more. "If more towns are torched, there could be an onslaught of refugees seeking shelter."

"I will think of a solution." I shunted my plate away, no longer hungry, then placed my spell book on the table. "There must be something in here that will offer us additional protection."

The council members looked at each other, speechless.

An incantation could buy us more time, yet I couldn't see one.

I pleaded silently with the gods to give me a spell that would help us.

After a few moments of flicking through the book, I located a charm that would protect the whole of Lake Delendil from the impending invasion, though it wouldn't protect the people living in the Fertile Territories outside of the lake.

"There is a protection charm here." I tapped my finger on the page. "Although I'm not sure if I'm strong enough to cast such a powerful incantation."

"It's all right, my love. You can do this. Take a moment to steady your breathing, then decide what you think is best," Felix said.

"I'm worried for my people." I rubbed my temples, then closed my eyes for a moment. "I can't afford to make any mistakes."

"I have faith in you—we all do." He gestured to Eric and the Elves. "Tell us about the spell."

I sucked in a deep breath, then flattened the curling pages. "The spell will enchant the stone soldiers."

He arched an eyebrow. "That's impressive."

"But more people will die." Ascal dropped his gaze to the table.

"Don't forget the large populations of Humans residing in the other settlements near the Eyrie," Eric said.

"I want the guards and some volunteers to take night shifts around the Citadel grounds." I glanced at the men around me.

"I will take the first watch." Eric raised his hand.

"Me too," Felix added.

The council members took it upon themselves to partake in the watch at the main entrance to the Citadel. They'd be accompanied by other guards for further protection.

"I will bring the stone soldiers to life, but I must warn you—it will have a temporary adverse effect on me." I showed them the relevant page. "See here? My eyes will glass over, and my body will turn to stone. I'll be trading some of my life, so to speak."

Felix frowned. "You're sure it's temporary?" He took the book, then scanned it. "Of course, I can't understand a word of it."

"Trust me." I departed from the main hall and made my way into the entrance of the Citadel. The stone soldiers towered above me, their suited armour thick and carved with the intricate detail of chainmail.

Please, gods. If you are to give me strength, give it to me now so I can give my people further protection.

I could bring them alive. We could slow the Dark Triads advancing around us.

Clutching the book with my trembling fingers, I scanned the words of the Noble Ones. My handwriting was scribbled down the side of some of the pages, although this one I'd left blank. How could I have known I'd need a spell of this scale?

I cleared my throat and pushed my shoulders back. A ball of white light formed, hovering above my cupped hands. It glided across the room and fused with the stone soldier's chest. The magic set my veins afire as each ball came to life.

The foyer glowed with Light Magic. A low hum rumbled the marble floor underfoot and a solid gripping sensation shot up through the soles of my feet. Rooted to the spot, my knees locked—the magic shot up my spine and into my arms. They were icy cold and solid, unmoving.

I attempted to move my arm but was frozen in time. As the chill moved into my neck, my vision blurred.

A sensation of warmth spread from my head into my arms. I flexed my legs and my arms until the muscles loosened. The light dwindled and at first, nothing happened. I tried again until I could lift each foot out of the magic's solidifying grasp. I peered over my shoulder at the council members.

Theodas beamed—the corners of his mouth turning up into a huge grin. It was a small act of kindness that reminded me to have faith and to keep trying—the kind of support we needed to survive this war. "Did it work?" he asked.

"It has to." Kiirion glanced at the stone soldiers who remained fixed to their podiums. The white light disappeared, and so did the magic.

"We must give it time to work," Felix said.

I bit my lip and stared at the helmed heads of the stone soldiers. "The blasted spell failed." I huffed and spun around to see the council members staring, mouths open, at me.

"It's all right, take a moment," Felix said, steady and reassuring.

The low hum resumed and shook the ground throughout the hallway.

"Evalyn...turn around." He grabbed my shoulder and pointed me in the direction of the stone soldiers.

One by one, they stepped down from their pedestals. Their movements boomed through the area and the soldiers aligned in front of me. The stone soldiers dispersed, exited the Citadel in pairs and took up posts across the main bridge.

"Splendid!" Eric said as I returned to the crowd.

A servant carried a tray of food towards the door that led underground to the dungeons. As she opened the large door, clanking shackles rang through the Citadel.

"What in heavens is she doing?" I hurried towards the servant.

A guard ascended the stone steps, blocking my access. "She demands to speak to you, Your Majesty."

"I'll go with you. We can't be sure what she'll try when you're down there." Felix appeared at my side, then scooted past the other guard and servant. I followed him.

Underneath the Citadel were the cold and damp stone cells holding Nieve and several other prisoners.

Water dripped off the walls into puddles and a fusty smell hung in the air.

When she caught my gaze, she smirked. She didn't fear me. But I pitied her.

"What can I do for you, *Your Majesty*?" She crawled towards the gate, rose, then wrapped her fingers around the steel bar. A snarl formed on her mouth.

"Get back," Felix warned.

She laughed but stood back and inspected her nails. "Now, now. Is that any way to speak to someone who has information you need?"

"What information?" I narrowed my gaze at her.

Felix gestured to the servant holding the plate of food. "If you don't share it with us now, you won't be fed for the next week."

"There's more to the prophecy than you know," she said, ignoring Felix.

"Tell me." I edged closer.

She glared through wide eyes. "The daughter of a Mage, being of purity, will conceive a child who is destined to rule the realm."

"What does that mean?" I gripped the bars until my knuckles turned white. My voice rang against the stone walls.

"Well." Nieve grinned. "You are with child."

"You're lying." The words caught in my throat. It hadn't been that long since Felix and I had lain together. It was impossible.

"The prophecy is woven in the constellations of stars, within the dirt and sand and dark saltwater," she said. "Did no one tell you those who wield magic result in pregnancies that progress *much* faster than normal?" She laughed, her words echoing like a riddle. "It is written in the songs of the Noble Ones. The father is in this very room!"

"It can't be true." My voice quivered. I refused to believe it.

"I've an aptitude for finding ancient texts." She flicked her hair over her shoulder. "The Citadel library is brimming with scripture written in the foreign tongue of the Noble Ones. Folk tale labelled you as the person in the prophecy, as you are the daughter of a Light Mage. It didn't matter so much when you were a child. You understand where I'm going with this, don't you? Of course, you do. When I was appointed chief councillor, I looked for spells that would change it and make me the chosen one, knowing you'd be a threat once you came of age. I didn't know a fragment of the prophecy was missing. Turns out, it wasn't you at all. The literature mentioned a child, and as no one else in your family is alive…" Her head tilted towards the ground, and a wide grin spread across her lips.

My hand throbbed from a tight grip on the bar. "No, that's not right. It can't be."

Nieve cackled.

Felix tugged me away from the cell, then guided me to the stone stairs. "We'll be okay. Let's talk to the council."

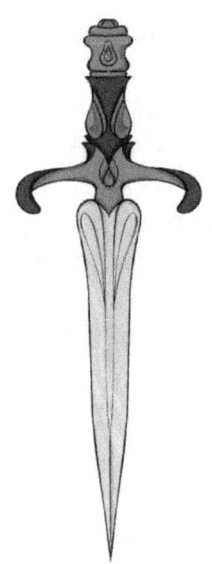

Chapter Eleven

Silence fell over the council room once I'd shared Nieve's revelation. Everyone turned their heads to me.

"Is this true?" Kiirion raised from his chair.

In the periphery of my vision, Felix's face remained frozen.

"She's got to be lying." I spoke with as much conviction as I could muster, willing them to believe me. I'd know if a child developed within me. Felix, pale faced and silent, stood rooted to the spot before taking a seat. "Conception wouldn't happen that fast."

Nieve must be taunting me. I wasn't pregnant. Not at a time like this.

The council members traded glances.

"Who did you lay with?" Theodas asked, his words confirming his belief in the prophecy. His voice, however, held a soft ring, accompanied with gentle eyes, pleading for private information to be shared.

Tears threatened to spill from my eyes as warmth crept up my cheeks.

I looked at Felix, then fled the room to seek the comfort of my chamber. Crashing on my bed, I shook my head in disbelief. A war raged around us, and people were dying in all corners. I could not bring a child into this world.

With trembling fingers, I removed my healing crystals from the pocket of my dress and laid them across the bed. If Juliette were here, I wondered what she'd say. Other than Felix, she'd been a source of support, and I needed someone to tell me what to do.

Someone rapped at the door. Mildred entered and closed it behind her. She curtsied before rushing to my side.

"Perhaps I could help you undress—the corsets are tight, and it may ease your discomfort to wear something less restrictive," she said.

I wheezed and clawed at my corseted dress. "Yes, this thing makes it impossible to breathe!" I rose.

As I stood, hands planted on a pillar of the bed, she unlaced the back of my dress. No words were shared. The mirror opposite me revealed a small swell in my belly that had gone unnoticed before. I'd been preoccupied with the Elementals and the Orcs, I hadn't realised my own body changing. Was my magic speeding up my pregnancy?

She draped my silk dressing gown over me.

"Thank you." I tightened it around me as she left the room to bring some chamomile tea.

When she returned, I sat on the bed with the crystals in my hand. I fiddled with them, wondering when they would bring me strength. Perhaps the crystals were based on superstition, and nothing more.

She left a tray of tea on the cabinet next to the window. On her way out, she crossed paths with Felix.

"May I come in?" he asked.

"Of course." I plucked a handkerchief from atop the dresser and dabbed it to my eyes.

"I came to see if you were okay," he said, his hand still on the door. "But I can visit you in the morning if you would prefer time alone."

"No, I'm okay. Just overwhelmed." I offered him a seat adjacent to the little mosaic coffee table next to the full-length mirror. I brought over the tray of tea and poured him a mug. "Have tea with me."

It sounded like an order, but more than anything, I wanted to sit in his company and know what he thought of the pregnancy. I was hopeless with no plan and needed his words of guidance.

"What's going through your mind?" Felix perched in his seat, and his brows furrowed.

"All sorts." I crossed, then uncrossed my legs. "I don't know what to do. What are people going to think? Their next queen is with child outside of wedlock; it's scandalous."

He closed the gap between us, then drew me into his arms, resting my head against his chest. "I'll be with you every step of the way. We're in this together, no matter what. You are not alone in this."

The vivid memory of my passionate night in the bathing room with Felix replayed in my mind. The night that caused my pregnancy. I hadn't acted like a queen then. I'd indulged in pleasure, but if I could've done it all over again, would I have walked away from him?

No. Definitely not.

"We have spent so much time together." Tears rolled down my cheeks. "And now I have a child with you."

"I love you, Evalyn. Nothing will change that. After the war, we can raise the child, together, in court." He stroked my hair.

"I love you too." My nerve endings tingled with the admission.

A bolt of warmth shot through me as he pressed his lips against mine and swiped away my tears with his fingers.

Despite his affection, my mind reeled. "The child is a bastard and therefore cannot have my throne." I clutched on to him, needing his security to keep me on my feet.

"You needn't worry, my love. As I've said before, there's nothing in this world that could keep me away from you. I am yours, and you are mine. We will bring this child into the world together, and we will lay out a better future for them. I will stand by your side—as your husband—if you will have me," he said.

I peered up at him. "Marriage? You would do that for me?"

"For *us*." He leaned over and relaxed his palm against my abdomen. "I was going to ask you when we were at peace—after the war. It has just happened a little earlier than expected."

A knock at the door startled me. I placed my tea aside.

"Come in."

A guard stepped in. His eyes were hollow.

Felix shifted his attention to the guard. "What is it?"

"It's Nieve," he said. "Your Majesty, I swear to you the cells were locked."

"Tell me what's happened." A wave of nausea rushed over me.

"She's gone. We've checked every cell, and we've searched the grounds. The High Elves are still looking, but there's no sign of her," the guard said.

"How could you let this happen? Who was on duty in the dungeons today?" My voice cracked, and I fought to keep my emotions under control.

"I am, Your Majesty." He shook his head. "Forgive me. She was there, I made sure of it. Then moments later, she was gone."

"How is this possible?" Felix asked.

"Wait." I lifted my hand as I frowned. "Nieve hasn't had any recent doses of Milleshar. Does this mean..." I placed a hand on the guard's armoured forearm. "It's nothing you could've foreseen. Notify the council members to meet me in the council room in five minutes."

"I will, Your Majesty." He bowed, then rushed away.

Felix waited while I changed into breeches and a shirt. Once I was ready, he took my arm, then guided me downstairs. "What do you think caused it?"

"The Milleshar allowed her to appear as a High Elf. Once the liquid wore off, the lake's natural magic must have sensed her true evil form." I hurried the last few steps towards the council room.

He stepped ahead and opened the door for me. "So the lake made her vanish?"

"Your Majesty, a guard informed us of Nieve's disappearance," Valneris said, his face pale. "I'll order them to continue the search until she's located."

"You won't find her." My voice didn't waver. "There's no need."

A few moments of silence fell in the room.
Theodas frowned. "So she just disappeared into thin air?"

"No, she's right." Ascal leaned forward. "It's a defense mechanism. It keeps evil away."

"Have the guards join the stone soldiers around the perimeter. I guarantee Nieve will be telling the rest of the Dark Triads about my pregnancy."

"At once, Your Majesty." Kiirion nodded.

I left the room, my heartbeat ringing in my ears. Each breath came shallow as I clutched onto the staircase. My vision blurred.

"Evalyn?" Felix draped an arm around me, then helped me up the stairs. "Come on, let's take you to your room. You'll be fine, okay? Just take deep breaths."

"Felix." I grabbed his arm, halting him in the doorway of my chamber. "The Orcs—they're going to come here. Our baby."

"Hey, calm down. Nothing will happen to the child. Here, sit down and drink the rest of your tea, okay? I'm going to join the other guards, and your handmaidens are outside your room, so call on them if you need them."

I gripped the mug between my trembling fingers. Felix placed a kiss on my forehead, then dashed from the room, leaving me alone.

I'd been searching for two days for the book that contained the prophecy, only stopping to eat and sleep. The library was vast, with shelves that ran endlessly, as far as the eye could see. Nieve had taken it upon herself to disclose the missing element—my child. The book with the information about my child was nowhere to be found. I was also right about her—she still hadn't been located.

Felix cleared his throat. I spun around to see him standing in the doorway.

"Apologies if I startled you, my love," he said, "But you have been up here for so long. Perhaps Nieve might've hidden the book or destroyed it."

"I can't give up. Not now." I focused on the books in front of me—their spines were worn and faded with age.

"I've told the Elves of our plans to wed." He crossed the space between us and slipped an arm around my waist. "Preparations will be made at a more appropriate time. Let our marriage act as a beacon of hope in a dark time."

I pressed my forehead against his, breathing in his warm scent.

"Why don't you come outside and get some fresh air? You'll see what the others have done in preparation. Eric is helping the guards and archers. They are on high alert," he said.

The sound of horns boomed through the Citadel, tearing my gaze from Felix. "What was that?"

"Stay here. I'll find out." He dashed from the room.

I hurried to the window to see the stone soldiers standing side by side and slashing Orcs in half. Swords clashed against hammers as the Orcs tried to breach the protection spell and cross the bridge. Elven guards drew their swords of Arogathean steel and marched forth to battle the invaders.

Rangers were at the top of the towers drawing arrows, freeing them into the chaos below.

The council members, Eric, Felix, the Humans, and Centaur soldiers joined in to hold back the encroaching Orcs. A group of Orcs fought another Orc, but I couldn't see his face. I opened the window and leaned out for a better view. Xurek tried to push his attackers off.

Several of them succumbed to the natural magic coursing through the ground and staggered, yet they did not retreat. One stumbled, hunched over, his face contorted by the pain caused by the lake's natural magic. *'The lake's magic repels all darkness and causes excruciating pain to those who pose a threat.'* Felix was right.

The Orc let out an earth-shaking, terrifying roar.

The remaining Orcs withdrew and hurried away from the lake. I fled from the window to meet injured soldiers and council members.

"Take the wounded to the healers for treatment at once." I urged the guards towards the hunched men with wounds.

"Why have they come here?" Kiirion shoved his sword back into its scabbard.

Felix's footsteps boomed through the foyer. "Xurek is out there on the bridge. You need to order the guards to free him. They've got his arms bound and have confiscated his hammer."

"I saw him from the window." I hurried out of the room, through the arched doorways, then pushed past the guards.

One held out a hand and blocked me. "It is not safe, Your Majesty."

"Let me pass." I shoved his arm away. "I know Xurek well, and I trust him."

I jogged across the mosaic bridge, then found him with his hands bound in front of him with rope. If he'd wanted to, he could have fought off the guards. But he wasn't here to cause damage.

"Step back, Your Majesty," the watchman warned.

"Stand down. He is an ally."

The guard slid out of the way.

"Xurek!" I untied his rope. He rubbed his freed wrists and shot a glare at the guards.

"What are you doing here?" I turned to face the guard. "Go to the kitchen and ask the cook to prepare food and refreshments for him at once. Also, arrange for a healer to check him over. We don't know what damage they have done to him." He nodded, then returned to the Citadel.

"I've come with important information, Evalyn," Xurek responded, his voice the low hum I remembered. His face was strained, creating a thick frown between his brows. "It's better I tell you face to face."

I tugged on his large arm, trying to hurry him towards the castle. "Tell me. I'll have your wounds tended to."

"I'm hardly scratched—the healers can wait until I've spoken to you. Makdou is channelling Dark Mage magic to summon Demons," Xurek explained as we hurried across the bridge. "Through blood magic."

The words chilled me. "Blood magic is the most dangerous of all. What implications would this have?"

"The lake's defences won't hold, and it's unlikely to ward off this level of evil. We need to speak with the council immediately."

"It would have been her who brought the Demon to us in the labyrinth—the one that killed Juliette. She must have thought it would kill us both. Come with me."

Xurek's footsteps thundered as he followed me through the main door. He turned sideways and stooped to fit through the doorway of the council room. Kiirion and Eric hurried inside after us.

"How did he get past the protection spell?" Ascal's posture stiffened. "And, more so, the natural magic coursing through the ground of Lake Delendil to ward *off* beasts such as yourself."

"Protection charms work against those who pose a threat," Xurek explained. "The lake protects purity. I entered with one desire: to be of aid to the queen."

"We have no time for this, Ascal, please remain silent." I tapped my foot on the floorboards.

"I don't trust you, *Orc*." A vein throbbed in Valneris' neck. He was the oldest and wisest of the High Elven council members and wrinkles lined his forehead.

"Calm now, Valneris." My tone was sharp.

Despite my best efforts to reassure Valneris, his scowl lingered. He remained silent. A healer arrived to tend to Xurek, although his attention was fixed on retrieving his hammer from a guard who struggled to wield it.

"There's more you need to know." He clutched his weapon, his eyes feral and full of rage and more Orc-like than I'd seen before. He dumped the weapon on the ground where it made a loud thud. His face softened, his eyes lightened, then he faced the healer. "Not now."

Valneris rubbed his temples. Kiirion, however, sat up straight with interest.

"What is it?" I dragged the chair back, then eased into it.

"Everyone had the prophecy wrong except Nieve. Why do you think that is? Your library is filled with ancient texts from the Noble Ones, is it not? Her disguise has given her ample time to research. Although her Milleshar wore off, she used it to her advantage and went straight to the Chief Orc to tell him." Xurek offered me an unnerving look, his eyes dark and hollow.

Felix rose immediately, stood by my chair, then rested a hand on my shoulder. "Nothing will happen to Evalyn or our baby. I give you all my word."

"Make sure your guards don't remove my hammer again—I will need it to fight off the Orcs as they'll keep coming here. And next time, they will bring the Dark Triads." Xurek's lips pinched together. "They will descend on the Citadel and annihilate every single one of you."

A servant arrived with a tray for Xurek, set it on the table, then left the room.

He eyed the plate of food and grabbed a piece of crispy bread. He wedged a piece of meat between two slices, then ate a large bite.

"Your Majesty, I've found something." A guard paced the room towards me. "One of the Orcs must've dropped it."

He uncurled his fingers and revealed a silver talisman necklace. Three emeralds were fixed between claws, but the surface was scratched and dull.

I took the object and traced my fingers over it. "Why would the
Orcs have this?"

Valneris' eyes darkened. "I've seen that before."

"Where?" My voice hitched.

"Your mother," he said.

"What do you mean, my mother?" My heart pounded.

"That's her necklace," Kiirion said. "She wore it all the time, and no others were made like it. It's hers."

"There's portraits of her hung up in the Eyrie, and I've never seen it before." I trembled.

"She wouldn't have needed it within the safe confinements of her home," he said. "When the last war broke, she had it made to harness her magic. I'm telling you, that's hers."

"If that's true, we must go to her. Why else would the Orcs have it unless they have her captured?" My head spun. The possibility of my mother being alive after all this time seemed greater than before. I couldn't ignore this sign.

"We will head out at first light and find her for you," Ascal said. "You must stay here."

"It's my mother we're talking about. If you think I'm going to stay here, you're wrong. I'm the queen now, so what I say goes, and I'm going. End of discussion."

The High Elves exchanged glances.

"We'll find your mother together," Felix said. "You'll have skilled warriors protecting you. We'll have a better chance of keeping you safe."

"We'll put a stop to this. Send a bird to each settlement, summon our allies to the Badlands— we're going to need as much support as we can get."

When the first lights of dawn cascaded across the lake and in through the glass of the Citadel, I glanced out of the window. Soldiers gathered across the bridge along the treeline.

An Elf came into my chamber to dress me for my journey to Zhah. She brushed the knots out of my hair and plaited it tight at the nape of my neck.

Once I was ready, Felix accompanied me from my chamber.

"Stay close to me at all times," he said. "I will do everything I can to keep you and our baby safe."

I squeezed his hand. "I know."

Outside, we met the council members. Bows and quivers rested over their shoulders. Although it was legend an Elf was at his strongest with a bow, they wielded Arogathean steel swords for close combat.

"We've brought all six horses from the stables. These are all the ones we have, and we must reach the Badlands as soon as possible," Kiirion said. "The guards will carry canvas to set up a military camp. Bags of food have been strapped to the saddles. We've filled enough canteens to last the journey."

"What of our allies?" I asked.

"We've sent word. No doubt the Humans, Centaurs, and Gnomes will meet us. If the Elementals mean to keep their pledge, they will be on their way."

I shivered, wondering whose poor soul was traded in exchange for the Undines' and Nereids' ability to walk on land.

The council members mounted stallions. Hooves thudded against the ground. Kiirion grabbed the leather bridle and tugged it. His horse threw its head back, and foggy breath snorted from its nose.

I climbed onto one of the two remaining horses. Eric, left without one, hoisted himself onto the back of mine.

Xurek mounted the last horse, then glanced at Felix. "Looks like we're sharing."

Although he still wore his traditional Orc attire of thick armour covering his shoulders, elbows, and knees, he'd tied golden ribbons around his leather to mark his alliance with the Light Triads.

Felix hesitated a moment before he put his foot into the stirrup, then flung his leg over the horse.

We rode along the wide path through the silent trees.

Felix offered a reassuring smile. "We'll bring your mother home safe."

———— ～⁚～ ————

The following morning, a harsh wind whipped across the Badlands, fluttering the canvas tents.

Guards roasted game on spits above open flames. The horses grazed on the sparse, dry grass sprouting from the cracks in the mud.

Felix drew me closer to him, then rubbed my arms. "You should eat something. Today will be a challenge for anyone, let alone someone with child." He handed me a stick with an impaled piece of charred meat.

"I'm worried about my mother. If she's alive after all this time, they would've kept her imprisoned. I can't imagine what she's going through." I drummed my fingers against my leg.

"I know, my love. We won't leave without her, but you ought to
eat." He nudged me.

I sank my teeth into the meat, finished the meal, then wiped the corners of my mouth with my fingers.

The Gnomes arrived by late morning clutching batons, knives, and pitchforks, standing as strong and as tall as they could, ready for war. Gnovash and Finbrik were at the front on the back of a Centaur. They held their chins high in honour.

Centaurs towered over the foot soldiers. Metal plates curved over their backs and stretched down to the top of their strong legs, leaving their defined muscles exposed. Each Centaur wore chest and back plates with gold engravings to mark their allegiance. Many wielded Arogathean steel swords, however, there were several Centaurs who'd taken Elven bows. Some squatted to allow Gnomes to climb onto their backs.

The Salamanders joined us like a pack. Fire flickered from their skin, the same territorial display they'd given us upon our first meeting.

The Sylphs gathered like a swarm of wasps ready to control the wind.

"Where are the water Elementals?" I turned to Felix.

He kept his gaze fixed on the distance as we waited for them to join us. Did the sacrifice work? Did they have enough time?

As we prepared the horses to move out, a shimmering glow appeared in the distance. A dozen or so figures emerged. They were tall and slender, and silky fabric flowed down the length of their bodies. Their dresses shimmered iridescent against the morning glow of the sun. One female led them all as they neared us, barefoot.

"Your Gracsssse." She curtsied, and the rest of the females copied.

"Seara?" I frowned.

She lifted her rippling skirts to her knees, then stretched her leg, pointing her toes.

"It worked," I breathed.

She narrowed her gaze on me. "A traveller, looking for new trade. Our ssssongs enticsssssed him."

Her fingers brushed a ruby pendant clasped around her neck. The same one I'd seen in the market.

I gasped, stumbling back. Felix caught my arm and steadied me.

Seara smiled coyly. "The pricsssse we musssst pay for freedom."

Felix tugged on my arm, pulling me away from the Undines and Nereids.

Reeling from the sacrifice, I stared ahead as breath caught in my throat. My hands shook as I clasped my horse's reins, put my foot in the stirrup, then hoisted myself onto the saddle. He patted my leg gently before mounting his horse.

We rode across the remaining stretch of the Badlands with our allies flanking us.

Far in the distance, near the wall of Zhah, Orcs, Trolls, and Giants gathered, clutching hammers, batons, and large clubs. They formed rows that stretched the length of the wall.

"What's going on?" My gaze darted from the battle ahead to Xurek. "We need to find my mother."

His face paled as he lifted his hand and halted all movement. "I don't think they have her, my queen. I think they used your mother's pendant to lure us here."

"What do you mean, they don't have her?" I trembled. "We have her necklace—she *is* here. With them."

Without warning, the Orcs charged towards us—their mighty roars rippling through the air.

The mechanical beasts, who were controlled by the Orcs, thundered across the Badlands. All the possible outcomes of the battle spiraled in my mind as I imagined a deathly duel against a machine which towered high above me.

"Here they come!" Valneris bellowed. "Prepare yourselves."

We galloped across the barren land to meet our enemies. As we neared each other, an army of Dark Mages sprinted towards the Orcs from the southern entrance to Zhah. Their Demons followed them.

Why were the Dark Mages charging at the Orcs? Who'd freed them from their Milleshar fuelled pods? They must've regained their strength once they were reunited.

I turned to face my army. "They're fighting each other. Let's hope it will divert the Dark Triads' attention from us to them. Let's pray the Dark Mages don't use the Crimson Kiss."

"Leave the rest to usssss," Seara said. "Our sssspecial ssssongs will affect our enemiessss, not your men."

I nodded. The Salamanders formed the front line of our army, their flaming skin creating clouds of smoke above them. The Undines and Nereids took elegant steps across the cracked ground. Their dresses flowed behind them like waves. They hummed in unison.

We rode to battle, drawing closer to the Dark Triads. Dead Orcs, Trolls, and Dark Mages littered the terrain. Some were injured—blood spewing from chest wounds.

The Salamanders stomped their feet, fire flaring from their bodies. Their eyes flashed a bright red as they pounded their fists into the ground, causing the earth beneath our feet to crack. The fissure rippled towards the Dark Triads, dividing the Badlands, and leaving the Dark Mages on the same side as the Orcs.

The split in the earth deepened and widened, and Ignatius began a chant the rest of the Salamanders enhanced with their bellowing roars. They sang the words of their haunting hymn and the deep ravine soon filled with bubbling lava.

The Undines and Nereids joined in—their hums turning into melodic high notes. Trolls and Orcs stopped fighting, gazed at the Undines with hollow eyes and wandered in their direction. Other Orcs roared, dropped their weapons, and clamped their hands over their ears long enough for the water Elementals to wrap their arms around them in an embrace, whispering their hypnotic tunes into their ears.

Then Finbrik and Gnovash emerged with the other Gnomes. Gnovash cleared her throat and turned to me. "It is an honour to serve you," she said, then muttered something in a foreign tongue.

A huge beast made of mud and grass emerged from the ground, growing and forming a shape as it rose. It would be a match for the Giants of the Dark Triads.

"How did you do that?" I gasped.

"We spent our time at Bluefair Fort studying the ancient magic of the earth." Gnovash beamed.

The Salamanders shot bolts of fire at the enemies who hadn't fallen in the lava. Seara and the other Undines manipulated water to wipe out a row of injured Trolls who crawled and dragged themselves across the Badlands.

The Centaurs fired arrows from the back line of the army, piercing the hearts of several Orcs who were out of earshot of the Undines' songs. Xurek led us around the lava-filled crack and attacked many of the Orcs head-on, crushing their heads into the ground with his own hammer.

The earthen creature of the Gnomes' creation marched forth, taking on the Trolls, fighting like wolves and tackling each other into the ground. Golem continued onwards to the next enemy.

I left my sword in its sheath and headed straight for the Dark Mages. Felix and the council members followed me on their stallions, slaying any enemy who approached me from the sides. An Orc grabbed Ascal by the shoulders, ripped him from his stallion, stabbed the horse, then launched his blade through Ascal's stomach.

I screamed. My horse reared.

"Move, Evalyn!" Kiirion urged.

The Salamanders incinerated the enemy with their blazing skin. I coughed, desperate for air as thick smoke hung in front of me.

Although I tried to steer the horse towards Ascal, Felix leaned over, grasped my reins, and tugged me away from the scene. "We need to keep moving."

Falaya, the leader of the Sylphs, directed the swarm of air Elementals. Her tiny hands swirled around, whisking the wind into a tornado that rose above the army. The tornado whipped across the Badlands, taking out a line of Trolls.

Towering, menacing amber creations churned and crunched with every step. They had florescent green eyes, fuelled by Milleshar, and were something possessed, inhuman, and lethal.

Earth creaked and strained underneath their feet. Golem approached one of the mechanical beasts after taking down several of the Giants. The machine clamped its large hands around Golem's head and crushed it inwards, obliterating it.

Mud and stone shifted in the distance, forming giants. Gnomes chanted nearby as their own Golems towered above them.

I pressed forth, surrounded by the council members and Felix, to a Dark Mage who stood on top of a small mound to the right of the wall to Zhah. He turned to face me while the other Dark Mages fought the Dark Triads.

"Your skin is as red as mine." He seethed. "Therefore, you are as evil as I."

I sent a red bolt flying towards him, but he ducked out of the way. The bolt demolished a mound and shards of dried, cracked mud burst free.

Kiirion challenged the Dark Mage with his blade. The Dark Mage gave a wild grin and formed a ball of swirling black mass. Before he could end Kiirion's life, the Golem crushed the Mage with his foot.

"Where is Felix?" I swivelled around in search of him, noticing he was no longer in our formation.

"He's helping the guards from Bluefair Fort—you need to keep moving!" Kiirion resumed his place at the front and urged me forwards. The smoke parted in intervals, whenever the Sylphs created tornadoes. The spinning clouds threw the enemy aside, destroying the Trolls and Orcs in its path.

I shot balls of magic towards Trolls who surrounded several Gnomes. Gnovash lay on the floor, covered in mud. I offered her my hand, then hoisted her off the ground.

The Undines continued to sing their songs of enchantment, enticing enemies into their arms.

Amongst the clash of weapons, screams and bursts of fire, came the loud thud of footsteps. Behind the marching machines, annihilating many in their way, were smaller machines made of dark jagged amber with wicked carved faces, fuelled by the same substance as the larger ones.

Sweat trickled down my spine.

Machines crept forth, then buried themselves deep within the ground. They launched several feet into the air before coming back down. They plummeted into the mud between the Humans and Centaurs, attacking them with blades built into their arms.

The last remaining Giant stomped his way towards us, pushing members of both armies out of the way. He ripped Humans and Centaurs up from the ground, crushing them within his fists.

A deafening rumble shook the ground across the Badlands, halting enemy and ally alike. The rumble grew louder, and a dark mass came from the eastern horizon, high into the sky. It grew ever nearer to the sun.

The mass swirled and twisted, forming tentacle-shaped features that crept towards the sun. Within a few moments, the sun fell behind the darkness, and the Badlands were blanketed with shadows.

I strained to see.

My council members clustered around me, clutching their swords.

Four beings emerged from the trees in the east. Their forms were ethereal, and I shivered. Four females straddled giant silver bears. The bears roared, exposing their sharp teeth. Were these the Ezen Riders from Juliette's story? The Dark Mages stood beside them as one army. Were they responsible for conjuring them?

"By the gods!" Eric emerged from the crowd, marked with blood and dirt.

"We must leave *now*, my queen," Theodas said.

No one moved. The sky was pitch-black, covered by a swirling, never-ending mass.

The Dark Triads fell back to the safety of Dellhollow. The Trolls and machines were also quick to withdraw from the scene, hastening back to Zhah. A Dark Mage stood next to his demonic creations and raised his arms.

"We must hurry," Kiirion said. He stared straight at the Riders, unable to peel his gaze away.

I noticed the water Elementals had already abandoned the battlefield. Likewise, the Sylphs and Salamanders had disappeared at the appearance of the Riders.

The Gnomes remained, although they cowered behind the slender legs of the Centaurs. Within a few moments, the Orc army dispersed, retreating to the Barren Territories. Had they realised the threat the Ezen Riders posed?

———— ～～ ————

"Sound the retreat!" I gripped Valneris and shook him.

"Retreat to Lake Delendil for safety!" he ordered the others.

"We will need to rest at the camp—we can't ride through the night without food, and the injured must be tended to." I jerked my horse's reins. He neighed, bucked, then galloped away. My army followed, sprinting in the direct of the military camp.

When we reached the camp, the guards tended to the horses, providing them with water in large bowls. Torches were lit in bamboo stands. A hazy glow of orange fire surrounded us.

Kiirion ushered me into one of the tents, then draped a blanket over my shoulders. He brought a canteen of water, and once he unscrewed the cap, he handed it to me. "Drink this. I'll get you some food."

The canvas flapped shut behind him as he disappeared from the tent.

Moments later, he returned, and rummaged in his bag. He drew a crust of bread and handed it to me. "The guards have gone to hunt. Have this bread for now."

He paced the length of the tent with his hand pressed to his forehead. "I can't believe Ascal's dead. If I'd stayed closer to him, perhaps I could've saved him."

"I'm sorry, there wasn't anything we could do." What else could I say to bring him comfort?

He shook his head. "The war is bigger than we thought. The Ezen Riders' apocalypse will destroy the world."

"Did you see the Dark Mages standing beside the Ezen Riders?" I kept my gaze fixed on the billowing canvas tent entrance. My body trembled.

"I did. The Dark Mages were fighting the Orcs. Is this their retaliation against them? The Ezen Riders could be their ultimate power play." He pinched the bridge of his nose.

"Xurek warned us it wouldn't end well between the Orcs and Dark Mages if they were ever freed from their Milleshar pods. I will find Felix and speak with him." I then exited the tent, scanning the camp for my knight as I searched for Valneris.

When I spotted him, I grabbed him by the arm. "Has Felix returned?"

"I haven't seen him, my queen," he said.

"Guards, search high and low, and do not stop until he is found. Search the surrounding area. Check everywhere," I ordered the nearby guards.

"I haven't seen him, my queen," Theodas said as he slid his sword into its scabbard.

"What about Eric?" I trembled, adrenaline flooding my veins.

"I'm here," he said as he came up beside me, then drew me into his arms.

"Ensure the injured are tended to, and we will move out at first light. If anyone sees Felix, alert me immediately." I withdrew, shoving my way through the crowd of gathering soldiers. Felix was nowhere to be seen.

What if he was being tortured, or worse, dead?

The following day, I dismounted on the mosaic bridge, then turned to face the stone soldiers aligned in front of me. "Defend the perimeter in case the enemies attack the lake."

My gaze darted from one end of the bridge to the other. Servants bustled past me to aid the soldiers and Gnomes inside. Healers guided Centaurs to the stables.

The image of the Ezen Riders emerging from the darkness etched itself into my brain. This whole time we'd been focusing on the Orcs and their control over the Dark Triads, and we'd never once taken a moment to consider the sheer strength of the Dark Mages.

When the Ezen Riders started the apocalypse, they cast a curse upon the land, the likes of which had not been seen since the dawn of the Noble Ones.

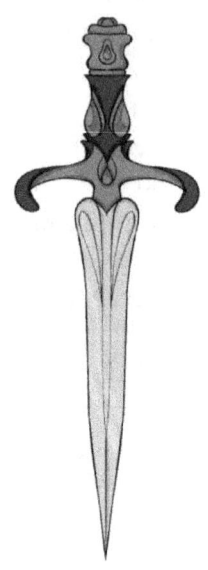

Chapter Twelve

Darkness swelled around the main entrance to the Citadel. Burning torches were dotted across the grounds of Lake Delendil. Faint twinkles of light moved with the water ripples on the lake. I conjured a spell that imitated the sunlight and cast a shadow over the sundial, indicating the first hours of morning.

Eric stood beside me with his arms crossed, face pale and lips pressed into a thin line. Brooding, he stared at the dull tree line.

"Has Felix returned?" I tugged my necklace, which was cold and unresponsive against my skin.

"Not yet, my queen." He sighed. "We have soldiers still out looking for him."

"I've been pondering overnight...Juliette was killed by a Demon in the forest of hanging men." The memory pulled at my heart. "Do you think the Demon could be connected to the Ezen Riders and the retaliating Dark Mages? Nieve could be helping them—after all, she *is* one of them."

"I would imagine so." Eric hung his head.

"In the lake, there is a certain point where the dead drift into the other side, the place for them to rest." I paced as I tried to connect the pieces. "Is it possible there is a portal somewhere in the realm that lets Demons and the Ezen Riders cross over? I mean, where else would they come from?"

"A portal..." Eric's brows wrinkled. "Perhaps. The Ezen Riders are in the Badlands and very real. And so are the Demons. Anything could be possible, and the Dark Mages are responsible for it. Why didn't we see this coming? Is Makdou behind the release of the Mages?"

I scratched my head.

"If the portal exists, it must have been conjured by a dangerous type of Dark Magic." I trembled. "The Dark Mages created the portal and let the Demons and Ezen Riders through?"

"Seems that way," he said. "I'm guessing they wanted something strong enough to overthrow the Orcs—the ultimate revenge for enslaving them and draining their magic."

"Even if the Ezen Riders obey the Dark Mages, Juliette said they will bring an apocalypse." I cradled the child who grew inside my womb.

"I have some basic knowledge of the apocalypse—it's easy to learn these things when I lived for so long with an Oracle in my fort. The first stage is seemingly upon us—asphyxiation of life. It suffocates us from any light from the sky and casts the gods aside," Eric said, his words sending a shiver down my spine.

"We can't sit around and wait for the next stage. We cannot be sure what else we will face during the apocalypse."

"It is time to cross the Great Sea, my queen," he said. "Put some distance between us and our enemies."

"We can't leave without Felix."

He placed his arm on mine. "I'm sorry, my queen. We have no other choice."

"I understand." Although my words were honest, my gaze flicked to the trees across the bridge, longing for Felix to emerge.

What lived in the sea or lay beyond it? A voyage hadn't taken place for decades. People speculated, of course, that great, fearsome monsters dwelled deep within the uncharted waters. Maybe there was an undiscovered city along the seabed of merpeople.

Were they any other prospects at all?

"I fear they will follow us wherever we go." My shoulders tensed. "I suspect that the Dark Mages are after control, and the Ezen Riders will do their bidding."

"Perhaps. You should meet with the council members," Eric suggested. "I know you fear for Felix, so I shall wait here to see if he returns."

I hesitated before marching to the council room where the High Elves and Xurek circled the wooden table in the centre.

"I need your input. Eric was saying we should voyage across the Great Sea." I gazed from Kiirion to Valneris and Theodas. "What are your thoughts?"

"It's absurd," Theodas said. "We cannot risk the journey. We are unprepared."

"We have no other choice," Valneris said with a calm voice.

The map sprawled across the table didn't show anything past the sea. We would be sailing, blind, for weeks potentially, until we found anything. If there *was* anything.

"My friends." I held my hand up to signal a break in conversation. "Wherever we go, the effects of the apocalypse will follow us."

"Crossing the sea will not do us any favours, my queen." Theodas shook his head. "It is undiscovered territory; we have no idea what we'd be facing out there."

"And we will die if we stay. The Ezen Riders are far too powerful for us to fight right now. Putting some distance between us will buy us time to plan."

"You're suggesting we flee, my queen?" Kiirion asked through gritted teeth—his hands bunched into fists.

"There's no alternative. Makdou has returned to Zhah, and the sheer volume of evil magic from the Dark Mages could reduce the lake's capacity. It might've been strong enough to eject Makdou from the dungeons, but it won't be strong enough to hold back the Ezen Riders and the Demons." I pressed my hands onto the edge of the table. "I think the Dark Mages raised the Ezen Riders to retaliate against the Orcs who drained many of them for their magic. We could use their feud to our advantage. How many boats do we have?"

"I'm not sure…a few. They have been used to sail the shoreline for fishing, but I can't recall the last time they were used for a long voyage," Theodas said. "If ever."

"As a child, I went out to sea with my father. He taught me how to sail the boat," Valneris said. "From memory, the ones down south are large vessels, so should be fine to carry the local civilians, cattle, and our supplies."

"I may be of use," Xurek said. "The Barren Territories largely rely on fishing for food. I can share pointers on the way." I pondered in silence.

"We'll lead the soldiers south to the Great Sea." I touched the route on the map. "I pray to the gods we survive the journey. Gather the people. We must prepare." Without another word, I left the room.

I found myself in Felix's chamber, tracing my fingers across the sheets where he'd slept. He'd been a soldier and a lover throughout my journey and would remain so. He said this necklace would strengthen me, but it remained cold against my skin. All I could do was hope we'd find our way back to each other.

I tore the jewellery from my neck as tears pricked my eyes. Back in my own chamber, I tossed it into a drawer and slammed it shut.

The council members gathered everybody into groups for departure. Gnomes hurried about, grabbing pitchforks and batons whilst the Humans carried sacks full of medicinal herbs, flowers, ointments, and bandages. Children clutched their mother's hands and stayed within the formation for protection. Each Human wielded a sword or axe. Centaurs drew carts, which were stocked with barrels of water, secured by rope and heavier bags containing more weapons and food for the long journey south. Guards went to the stables behind the Citadel and gathered the horses and cattle. Gnomes mounted donkeys and cows.

The council members led the various clans.

I addressed the civilians. "Ladies and gentlemen, please stay within your groups and with your designated leader."

"I will lead my group first." Kiirion mounted his horse.

Valneris' cluster of Centaurs followed, then Theodas' group of Elves. Eric's hollow gaze fell on me before we'd even left Lake Delendil.

"I have unfortunate news, my queen. Felix still has not returned," he said.

"I thought not." A lump formed in my throat, but my heart burst with courage when Xurek appeared at my side.

"If I know you at all by now," he said, "you'll find your way back to him."

"And what about the Dark Triads?" I lowered my voice to a whisper. "What if they decide to cross the Great Sea?"

"The apocalypse is a force greater than the feud between foes," Kiirion responded.

I gave one last longing look at the other end of the bridge. I yearned for Felix to emerge from the forest and join us on our journey to a new land. It would be a long ride south, at least a week's travel, venturing past anything I'd explored. There were numerous fields along the way where we could camp, and I'd keep a look out for him at every given opportunity.

Xurek, Eric, and I followed the other groups eastwards around the lake where we would head south. We left the burnt remains of Rushdale Forest and its dead behind.

No light led the way, other than the fiery torches each leader held. The grass and plants withered away, and petals disintegrated on the ground alongside dead leaves from nearby maple trees. We rode through a barren field, weaving around corpses of birds that had fallen from the sky. Flies swarmed the corpses, attracted to the rotten flesh.

The grass had turned to straw, thick and harsh when I brought my fingers to touch it.

"It's happening." I peered at my companions. "And quick."

"I can only wonder what the world will be like when disease strikes, whatever form it may take," Xurek said. "Let's hope we aren't here to witness it."

We carried on through the fields rotting into wastelands. The carts rocked each time they were drawn over loose stones. Valneris' group of Centaurs were ahead of us. Their heads hung low.

I feared we would be greeted by the Ezen Riders before we could reach the Great Sea. Why hadn't they come looking for us? I was glad they hadn't but still wondered why not.

After a day or two of travelling, and disoriented from perpetual darkness, we reached the ruins of Westwilde, the former home of the Gnomes. We'd caught up with the other groups as the Gnomes stopped to mourn their loss. We lingered for a while, then continued the route farther south.

"What do you think is out there?" I turned to Eric.

"I have no idea," he replied. "Do any of us? Hopefully, the distance will give us time to find a way to stop the apocalypse."

There were several legends written and speculations of the Noble Ones who were too scared to venture out past known territory. Most of their writings were of terror and danger lying beyond the Great Sea, past the monsters that lived within the water. To my regret, I'd spent next to no time in the Citadel library, which may have prepared me a little for what awaited us.

"I wonder if there is anything in my spell book…" I grabbed the book out of the satchel bag hanging over my armour and flicked through the pages.

Adrenaline coursed through my veins in anticipation. "Nothing…typical."

"The sun has also been blocked for several days," Kiirion said, "and I'm assuming the temperature will begin to drop."

"Even more reason for us to set sail as soon as possible." I shoved the book into my bag, then dragged my hands over my face.

I paused for a moment when the Eyrie came into sight upon the mountain. The crowd stopped and gazed up at the high walls of the keep.

The council decided we should push forth into the Human village not far from the marketplace, where we might rest for a while.

The Orcs had ransacked the village huts, and the people were crucified on the streets. I screeched, unable to hold back my horror.

I begged the gods and hoped the Demons could not follow us across the Great Sea. The stretching waters could offer us the refuge we needed and a life away from the Dark Triads, to recuperate and look for an option to end the darkness and the Ezen Riders. Perhaps the glowing torches were symbolic of each life we'd lost as we marched towards the village. Each dancing flame was an eternal soul resting in the Beyond.

After regaining our strength at the desolate village, we proceeded farther south, advancing on the barn where Felix and I spent the night on our journey to the Highland Trees of the Sylphs. From their home, we could overlook the Great Sea. It wouldn't be long before we arrived at the shoreline.

People coughed and sneezed. Dead birds dotted the ground. Deer decayed in a ditch beside the bridleway.

"The next step of the apocalypse is disease." Kiirion shuddered. "I read about it in one of the ancient texts. Wild creatures are already succumbing."

I rubbed my brow. "We ought to stay calm. Keep an eye on everyone and have them tended to if needed. I'll ensure each group is able to hunt what wildlife remains and refill their canteens at the nearby streams."

We reached the pile of burned innocents Felix and I found on our journey to see the Elementals. Shreds of clothing hung from their bones and shoes had fallen to the ground. Parent Gnomes pulled their children close to them and shielded them from the sight.

The stench of dead bodies still lingered in the air as we passed. Gasps of horror broke the silence. I doffed my helm in respect. My heavy heart hung in my chest. Soon, the corpses disappeared behind us.

My stomach had turned at the foul scent of death, beginning the sickness that came with pregnancy. I feared the days I would not be able to hold down the bile.

I needed Felix. I needed his comfort. His support. His arm on mine to assure me that everything would be okay. But he wasn't here, and I didn't know if he would return to us.

Eric squeezed my arm, his sombre gaze connecting with mine. We traded no words. Nothing could be said.

When we reached the Highland Trees, the Sylphs were quiet. I could not hear them talking or singing amongst the oak. I wondered if they'd hidden within crevices in the trunks for the canopy of leaves would shield them from the darkness, and the spread of disease.

There was a bank parallel to the cliff tops of the Highland Trees where we all descended. The boats were docked below, waiting to be filled with civilians and soldiers.

"We do not have a map to show us what lies past this point." I addressed the council members. "So we keep sailing until we see land."

"We could really do with those pointers, Xurek." Theodas eyed Xurek.

"The first thing you need to do is check the lines that raise and control the sails. Make sure they are separated and knotted at the ends. The sails will need adjusting for the wind direction. You'll need people working the ropes to ensure the sails are pointing the right way," he said.

The Elves ushered their group onto the ships. There were five cargo vessels in total, none of which were designed to carry masses of people. The civilians filed on board, and the horses were guided below deck. Once the sails were raised, the ship was ready.

Eric stood by my side as I surveyed the tree line one last time.

"We cannot wait any longer," he said. "Perhaps he will find his own way across the sea."

"We only have these five ships." I rested my hands on the rail. "What's the likelihood of him discovering another way?"

I averted my gaze from the trees before boarding my ship in the centre. Xurek lumbered onto the deck. My ship was the first to set sail, leading the way for the others to follow. I peered overboard at the ominous ocean, and nothing could be seen within it. The dark swell covering the sky would make it hard to navigate the seas.

"You will be okay." Xurek patted my hand.

The gentle, lapping waters of the Great Sea steadied my heartbeat.

Would the Ezen Riders appear, levitating in front of us to block our voyage? Would they end our journey here?

Xurek steered the ship as I stood beside him, eyeing the gloomy surrounding sea. What if the water went on for miles and miles and miles and disappeared into nothing afterwards?

Although it was daunting to sail into nothingness, it outweighed living in constant fear of the Ezen Riders and the apocalypse. Time was a friend on this mission. We could find a way.

No rain had fallen upon us on our trip, and no sunlight broke the darkness. The life of the realm was draining.

"How long will our journey be?" Gnovash fidgeted, and her voice trembled. "Two days have passed since we left the lake. We now have little to drink, and even if we had purifiers, they wouldn't remove the salt from the seawater. Oh my, we could die of thirst, especially with the horses needing so much."

"We have to keep sailing until we see land. As soon as an island comes into sight, we will dock and find a source of water. Until then, ensure what we have lasts for as long as possible. Tell the crew to drink only when really necessary." My words rang clear as I walked across the deck. "I will keep count of how many barrels have been used throughout the journey."

Gnovash and Finbrik retired to the cabin where they slept, cramped with the many other Gnomes who boarded my ship.

"You ought to get some rest," Xurek said.

I obeyed, left the helm, then made my way across the deck to my room. My eyelids hung heavy, and my feet were swollen from the travel. My stomach somersaulted with the bobbing of the ship. I heaved into a nearby bucket and collapsed onto my bunk.

When I awoke a while later, groggy and restless, I returned to Xurek who slouched over the ship's wheel. I'd never seen a tired Orc before, but his exhaustion softened his stern, harsh features.

"How long was I asleep?" I rubbed my eyes as they adjusted to the torchlight.

"A few hours maybe, I can't tell." He sighed.

In the silence that formed, I remembered Ascal, who'd been killed within a matter of seconds. Due to the panic and chaos of the battle and the intrusion of the Ezen Riders, I'd little time to reflect on his death. I grimaced at the image of his body left in the Badlands to rot. He deserved a traditional funeral. Anger raged through my veins. All the people who'd died at the hands of the Orcs were decomposing out in the open and had not been laid to a peaceful rest at Lake Delendil.

Tears swelled in my eyes. They deserved so much better, so much more than what the end of their lives had given.

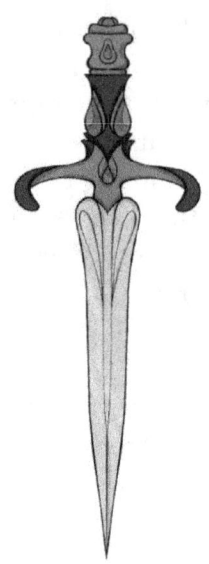

Chapter Thirteen

On our travel across the Great Sea, time dragged by with no indication of day or night, with the darkness of the apocalypse hanging over the realm. My sundial spell was unreliable but suggested late afternoon. As the ships grew ever-nearer to our mystery destination, the undiscovered territory emerged as a shadowy strip across the horizon.

"We will be dropping anchor soon," Xurek called to the civilians onboard.

Murmurs of panic and uncertainty spread across the deck. People shared words of anxiety at the prospect of disembarking in a new land. Xurek and the others prepared to dock.

"We must stick together." I surveyed the many wide-eyed faces above deck. "We may come across species and populations we have not seen or met before."

We neared the shoreline, surrounded by shallowing waters.

Xurek whizzed around the ship. "Prepare to unload! Gather your belongings."

The ship grew closer to the island's beach with a scrape and groan of wood against the seabed.

Each council member filed their groups of civilians off the boat. The wood creaked under our feet. My heart lurched. I hurried along the boards until safe on the firm ground of this new, strange island. Would we find inhabitants nearby?

The horses were guided off the boats. When my horse approached me, I smoothed his hide, then used the stirrup to hoist myself onto his back.

A path inclined upwards, leading away from the sea, farther south. The council members now held torches to guide their groups through the darkness. This confirmed my suspicions—this new evil, indeed, *did* blanket the *entire* world. At least, as far as we could see. For additional light, I manifested a harmless white ball of magic and let it hover above our heads as we walked. Quartz dotted the ground and sparkled under the white light.

"How beautiful." I gasped, tugging on Eric's arm for him to look at the quartz.

"I've never seen anything like this before." He raised his brows skyward.

When the ground flattened, my heart sank at the sight of empty space ahead of us. Perhaps I'd been naïve to think there would be a settlement, home to a kind, generous population. Why had I allowed myself to believe such dreams?

A few feet ahead, the dead remains of elm trees were dotted here and there. The soil was hard and dry, seemingly devoid of life under the darkness.

Xurek wandered off, grumbling under his breath in disbelief, his gaze scanning the environment. The rest of us followed cautiously.

He stopped in front of a small wooden structure submerged in a cluster of dead, broken birch trees that sank into the boggy ground. The hinges were rusted from age and rain, and the building bowed at the roof.

I dismounted, walked up to the door, then extended my hand to turn the handle. Loud sirens pierced the silent surroundings. I jerked back. A beam of light sprouted from the ground and aimed at us.

A whooshing sound filled the air and a voice spoke. "Who are you? Why have you come here?"

Where was that coming from? How were they communicating? What magic were they using?

I looked at Xurek before mustering the nerve to respond. He clutched his hammer high, ready to smash an enemy to pieces if need be.

"I am Queen Evalyn." I showed my palms—my people would not cause any harm. "We've come seeking refuge from the darkness that has plagued our land."

234

No other words were uttered via the strange magic. A click came from the door. Was this their acceptance of our request?

"Our council would like to speak to you, Queen Evalyn," the voice said, "alone."

"Not happening!" Kiirion slipped from his stallion, then yanked my arm. "We cannot let you go in without protection; we don't know these people."

"Take a look around." I waved at the barren surroundings. My

feet ached from the swelling, my pregnant belly crooking my spine in an awkward angle. "There's no other choice."

I clasped the door handle between my fingers. Its cold surface crackled. Inside, a set of wooden stairs descended into the ground. Before I took the first step downwards, I glanced at the council members and bit my lip. They exchanged helpless frowns in response.

The steps groaned as I moved down them. Dimly lit torches hung from walls in iron brackets, leading farther into darkness. The stairs declined ten flights before I reached the base. A guard in black armour with a helmet disguising his face checked me for weapons and removed my sword. He placed it into a hutch, out of sight.

The guard led the way, without conversation, down a narrow passageway. The hallway extended into a complex network with several different routes stemming from it, creating a great underground lair. Who'd built this place and how? Intrigued, I followed with knots of anticipation forming inside my stomach.

"In here." He hauled a door open.

Four individuals waited inside the room. My gaze fell upon the Mages, and my heart thumped. Were my eyes telling lies? Was she another Light Mage?

She wore the most beautiful ruby red robe with gold and crystals embellished across the fabric in intricate patterns. Her scales were different than mine, lighter in colour, and ice-white hair hung around her face. A Light Mage with High Priestess healing abilities. An asset when living underground.

The room, like most of the structure, was made from the rough surface of stones, mud, and steel beams. A round table took centre of the room where the four individuals gathered.

"Evalyn, I presume." The Mage with ice-white hair waved a hand, dismissing the guard, who shut the door behind him after he left. "Take a seat."

I studied them before obeying. I found it difficult to take my gaze from the Mage, mesmerised by her iridescent skin. It glowed and shimmered whenever she tilted her head.

"As you may be aware…ahem…the apocalypse has begun." I faltered. My nerves caught in my throat. "I have come seeking refuge for my people."

"*Your* people?" The Mage flicked a strand of silver hair over her shoulder.

I winced at her words. The magnitude of her healing magic made me more cautious of her Mage abilities and her power. I flattened my hands against my thighs and took a deep breath.

"If you seek refuge, then you have no throne to rule from. Everybody is equal here."

"Calm now, Sofia," said the Human in the middle of the table. "She is our guest."

There was something familiar about the Human male who sat in front of me. He had a pleasant face with soft features, but several scars lined his right cheek. His blue eyes were etched in my memories.

"My name is Aneirin—your father." He offered a warm smile. "It's good to see you, Evalyn." He walked around the table, then opened his arms to me.

With wide eyes, I stared at the man. I stood and backed away. I did not trust the people before me.

"You're lying." My cheeks burned with anger. "My father died."

"I did not die, Evalyn," Aneirin explained in a soft tone. "I left the Fertile Territories almost two decades ago."

"You think I'll blindly believe you? I don't even know you." I crossed my arms to hide my trembling fingers.

"I know what you must think, and I'm not surprised, but you have nowhere else to go." He was a middle-aged man with dark hair, the same colour mine had been before my appearance changed. "And you have a lot of other people to take care of."

I remembered the crowd of the various races above ground waiting for my return, and a decision had to be made. "If you are who you say you are, then you owe me and my people your protection. Consider it an apology for leaving me when I was a child."

Aneirin pressed his fingers to his chin. "Who have you brought with you?"

"Gnomes, Elves, Centaurs, and Humans." I kept my gaze fixed on him. "We also have horses."

"The Gnomes can stay, as they take up the least space, but the others will need to remain on the boats." He returned to his seat. "We can arrange a patrol to ensure the animals have enough hay and water also."

Flattening my hands against my thighs, I took a deep breath as anger bubbled in my veins. "It will be all of us or none of us."

My father, if I were to believe him, remained silent for a moment, then waved his hand. "If they are to stay here, they will be allocated jobs to contribute around the hideout, but the horses cannot come underground. We do not offer shelter for free."

I nodded, then left the room, squeezing past the guard who took up a huge amount of space in the doorway. At the top of the stairs, I cranked the steel door handle and reunited with my people.

"Who are they?" Kiirion scanned me, presumably looking for any injuries.

"I'm not too sure. Other than a Human named Aneirin, who claims to be my father."

The council members looked at each other and gaped.

"I don't believe it…" Theodas gasped, and a light appeared in his eyes I hadn't seen before. "It's been so long."

"We were acquainted with your father before our roles were appointed," Valneris added. "We fought alongside him in the last great battle between the Light and Dark Triads, and that'd been the last time we saw Aneirin."

"They are to be trusted," Kiirion said at once. "Aneirin is a good man."

The council members filed past me and entered the underground hideaway. I stood to the side, frowning. How could they trust a man they'd not seen or heard from in twenty years?

A surge of something resembling jealousy flooded through me. These men were my closest friends, my advisors, yet they were old friends of my father. There didn't seem to be even a hint of resentment in them.

"Xurek, can you take the horses back to the boats, please?" I turned to face him. "Aneirin will arrange a patrol to check their hay and water."

He nodded, gathered the horses' reins, clicked his tongue, then guided them back the way we'd come.

I hurried in after the men while the groups of Humans, Centaurs, Elves, and Gnomes swarmed the entrance behind us. There were five ships full of people now crammed in the narrow hallway at the front of the hideaway. I sucked in each heavy, musky breath with difficulty as I squeezed through the crowd. I glanced across at Kiirion. One hand was on Aneirin's shoulder, and the other was pulling him in for a hug.

"Let's take you all into the canteen," he said. "We will introduce you to the people who live here and explain everything to you."

He led the way down the straight corridor, past the winding paths that broke away from it, into the open area.

This new room was much like a cave, and several brackets held torches to the jagged wall. No natural sunlight flooded in. How long had these people been subjected to surviving underground, in such confined conditions?

Elves and Humans, dressed in loose woollen trousers and shirts, gathered around wooden tables. People removed their shawls and scarved made from scrap pieces of wool.

I stood at the front of the cave with my council members, Aneirin, and his advisors. The groups we'd brought with us made the food hall cramped, and people removed their capes and unbuckled their armour as their faces turned red. The Centaurs took up a large proportion of the hall, and they grunted in discomfort, squished between other people, children, and the cold, wet surface of the cave walls. The original residents of the breakaway muttered with annoyance as the Centaurs blocked their view.

"This is going to be a hard adjustment," Aneirin said loud and clear for all to hear. "It will be cramped and claustrophobic, but we have welcomed these new residents into our home to shelter them."

The hall remained quiet. I scanned the crowd before me and took a deep breath. Although I had no voice here, I wouldn't let these strangers see any weakness.

"We have four sections of residency depending on your role: the Developers, the Harvesters, the Seamstresses, and the Healers. Our new residents

240

will all join these groups to help strengthen and rebuild our world." Aneirin's voice echoed in the cave and resonated with pride and certainty.

Where was Felix at this moment? Did he wander and roam the lands above in search of his pregnant queen and friends? Hidden away from the world, it became a very real possibility— Felix may never meet his child.

"We have important things to discuss." I turned to Aneirin.

He nodded and led the way back to the room away from the crowd. I brought my council members who sat alongside me opposite Aneirin and his supporters.

"Welcome." He beamed at my council members. "It has been a long time, my friends. I know I have some explaining to do, but we'll leave it for a later date. Let me introduce you to Sofia, Katrin, and Laurent."

The two females were Katrin and Sofia, while the Human, Laurent, sat, brooding, in the corner. His hair covered the length of his back in a few shades darker than his olive skin and was twisted into thick dreadlocks.

"Sofia has refined High Priestess abilities alongside her Mage magic. She offers protection and provides the best training for our healers. She is most vital to our survival. Laurent makes sure the developments of the hideaway are carried out, as well as ensuring we have enough food to eat," Aneirin explained in an upbeat tone. "I manage defense and security. Our residents have been trained in combat in case a situation arises where they may need it."

"What of my advisors and me?" My voice was small and fragile. What power did I have in this new place?

"I said you were not a queen here, Evalyn." He sat straight in his chair. "You are not a queen of vast lands and territories, but instead a future leader and a symbol of hope for the people I have offered protection to for the last two decades."

"I'm grateful for the shelter you've offered me and the civilians we've brought with us. I'm with child, so I may require some further assistance." I smiled slightly.

"Ah, the confirmation we need. How splendid! I can tell you're showing, but now it's out in the open, we can make arrangements for you." A wide grin spread across his face, somewhat softening his scars. He lifted his arms into the air in celebration.

"I'll tend to you myself," Sofia chirped, seemingly pleased with this revelation in an equal measure. "How long have you been with child?"

"A few weeks maybe. I'm not sure. The pregnancy is faster than I expected."

"Let me take you to your chamber; it's not spacious, however, it will provide you with the comfort you need." Sofia gestured to the door. "It's perhaps time for you to rest. You have travelled many miles."

I wanted answers from Aneirin. How could he leave alone to figure out the ways of the world without a father? However, my body ached from exhaustion, and I couldn't find the words. A heated conversation with him would only distress the others.

I followed Sofia out of the room, hearing Aneirin explaining himself to my council members as I walked farther away.

She guided me through a long, winding walkway, the torches providing a warm orange glow that danced on the cave walls. Along the corridor were several wooden doors leading to other rooms. At the end of the passageway, she opened the last door.

"Your chamber," she said. "There are some clean clothes for you. I'll come back in a while to show you to the washroom."

She shut the door behind her. I turned to scrutinise the room designated to me. The ceiling was dome-shaped, a mini cave sprouting from the main one. A fireplace was built into the right wall. The fire crackled and glowed, and its warmth soothed me.

Where did the smoke of the fire travel? Up through the ground perhaps?

I removed the armour I'd been wearing for too long.

What would happen to the other Elementals, and how long would they survive? How much time would pass before the Galae Pools dried and the Vesuvius Caves burned out?

A floor length, plain robe was draped across the bed. I tied it around my waist, sitting snug above my bump, just as something rapped on the door. It opened and revealed Sofia dressed in an elegant, embroidered robe. Her eyes travelled to my swollen belly.

"My magic is speeding up the pregnancy," I said.

"You're right about that," she replied. "Yours will be much shorter than a Human pregnancy."

A towel was draped over her arm, and she held a few sprigs of lavender between her fingers. "For your bath. It will relax you."

She picked up the clean clothes laying neat across my bed. "I'll show you the way to the washroom now."

She directed me back down the corridor, past the crowded canteen, and through another winding route. A single doorway graced the walls.

The washroom was far from the rest of the hideaway. A natural pool glistened in the dim light, filling with water that glided through small holes on the left-hand side of the cave room. When the pool overflowed, the water drained through a deep hole, leading further underground.

"The Developers built this whole network, securing many passageways for natural, fresh water to channel to wherever it is needed." Sofia beamed as she placed my clothes on a crooked chair in the corner before exiting.

The washroom resembled much of the rest of the hideaway— cave-like features with burning torches hanging on the walls, yet it was peaceful. With my naked feet against the cool stone ground, I eyed the water, imagining its ice-cold contents sending shivers across my body. Gooseflesh now covered me.

I dropped the lavender into the pool, then untied my robe and let it fall to the floor. With one hand on my bump, I edged over to the pool, letting each toe rest on the ground before taking another step towards the rim.

In small movements, still cradling my belly, I dropped to the floor and dipped my toes in. My eyebrows shot skywards. Instead of the shocking numbness of iciness, my toes were caressed by the lukewarm water.

The lack of light in the washroom made it difficult to see the true depth of the pool. I clutched the side, inching myself in and allowed the warm contents to ripple around me. My feet flattened against the stone-covered bottom. Once comfortable amongst the ripples, I let out a deep breath in relaxation. My toes uncurled since I no longer feared a slip against the smooth edges of the stones below.

In the sweet haze of warm water and loosening muscles, I reflected on how my life had progressed over the last few months. I'd experienced every possible emotion. Pain, anger, fear, grief, passion, love, familiarity. How could so much light and dark coexist within my mind at one given time?

Every single event hurtled past without a moment to reflect or allow myself to rest. Now, comforted by gentle lapping waves, I could sift through each event and understand its significance. I drifted through life and war in a haze with no real understanding of what the future might hold for any of us. I don't think anyone did—not even Aneirin.

That evening, the canteen was bustling with chatter from the day's events, and Eric and my council members surrounded me. On the table between us, were plates of corn, cabbage, and carrots, with small, ration-sized portions of wild boar. The Elves had changed from their golden, bejewelled armour into cotton clothing, yet it allowed their sharp, striking features to further stand out. The contours across their faces were deepened by dark shadows from the torchlight.

"Our people have been categorised already," Kiirion said. "Most of the Gnomes have found themselves in the Developers group, as they are notorious for their craftsmanship with the earth. The Centaurs have also been assigned to the Developers group, and the Humans have joined the Harvesters and Seamstresses. All will undergo combat training."

"It is time we say our words for Ascal. He was taken from us, and we have not had the chance to toast in his memory." I'd not known Ascal well. He'd not voiced his opinion as much as my other advisors. But as a queen, I understood the importance of my advisor and his relationship with the other High Elves. "It maddens me that we cannot give him a proper funeral in the lake."

"We have not had a chance to mourn our losses." Kiirion stared at his hands on the table. "Ascal was a true friend."

The air between us fell silent and heavy. My gaze wandered to the Gnomes who chatted amongst themselves.

"We are so grateful to have found refuge from the raging war above ground," one said to a Human companion.

The Centaurs gathered at the back of the room, nestled amongst bales of hay, and eating a mixture of carrots, potatoes, and meat.

I held up my cup and began a toast. "To Ascal. May you find peace in Elysium."

Finbrik and Gnovash dug into their food as they continued to talk away with their new friends. My heart sank. Felix was not there to enjoy this feast. It consumed me with an urge to break free from the hideaway and search for him, no matter the cost but doing so would jeopardise my health, my baby's, and our hope of finding a way to end this apocalypse.

After food, I retired to my room, hollow and empty from Felix's absence and the struggles my people still faced.

Sofia arrived once I lit the fire in my bedchamber.

I stood in front of the hearth, staring at the flickering embers as the room glowed with burning reds and oranges.

"You must lie down," she said.

I obeyed and padded to my bed, stretching across the sheets. She poked and prodded at my swollen belly. She plucked an ointment from her pocket, along with another small vial, then placed them both on the cabinet next to my bed.

"This ointment is made of many healing herbs," she said as she rubbed it into my belly with a light touch. "Our supply is running low and isn't to be restocked any time soon, so this will have to do for now. The salve will help the baby develop and grow."

"And the vial?" I yawned.

"It contains a liquid that needs to be consumed every night before you go to sleep," she said. "It will ease any discomfort you may experience and allow you to sleep well."

"Thank you." I squeezed her hand. "Felix, the father of my child, is missing. I don't know if he will find his way back to me."

Sofia remained silent. Her glinting eyes met mine. Pity, perhaps.

My eyes burned with the need to cry, but my fatigue could not bring forth any tears. My body longed for Felix's touch, for his fingers to trace my pregnant belly, our child.

Felix, I beg you, I implored, *survive this. For me. For our child.*

Sofia left me. I stared at the fire as I sank further into the sheets beneath me. I had to work to build something new from this broken, burned world. It was either that or stumble through life in a blur with no real idea of how to survive without Felix. Maybe I was beginning to understand Aneirin's optimism. If he gave up, everyone else would too.

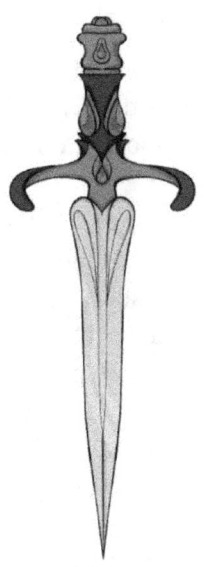

Chapter Fourteen

Over the next few days, the underground compound bustled with people fulfilling their orders and errands. The Developers were extending the hideaway, adding in extra bedrooms, and beginning the construction of a new washroom. The Harvesters seeded the ground for new vegetables that received their energy from large clusters of quartz in the cave's roof. The Seamstresses continued to make new clothes for everybody to wear and mended those damaged.

One day after being underground for a week, I weaved my way through the crowds, careful not to knock over the stacked stones of the Developers or the wicker baskets of fabric and thread. Aneirin was in the meeting room with his advisors, discussing strategy. My own council members accompanied him.

Once free from the active canteen and construction corridors, I entered the meeting room, then clicked the door closed behind me.

"We should consider forming a new group: the Defenders. They can take post above ground to protect us from the Dark Triads," Aneirin suggested. "We'll choose our strongest combat-trained citizens. Orc scouts have been spotted patrolling the area. There are more than I'm comfortable with."

"Good idea," Laurent said. "I can recommend several combat-trained Humans who have passed each section of their training at the highest rank."

"We can't let the scouts locate the hideaway. It is our safe place, and they are not welcome." Aneirin eyed Laurent. "Does it appear the Orcs found the boats? If they have, it is only a matter of time before they find us."

"They are not looking to co-reside with us." I lowered into one of the chairs and rested my hands on the table. "The Dark Mages and the Ezen Riders will be too powerful for the Dark Triads to fight, especially with their influx of Demons."

"What do you suggest we do?" Kiirion crossed his arms. "If the Orcs do come, who's to say more of the Dark Triads won't find their way here too? If they see the trail of footprints leading to the hideaway, they could report back to the Chief Orc, and our position would no longer be a secret."

"We can't know for sure what will happen." I pressed my lips together and rubbed the side of my head.

"Even so, we can't risk them finding us or the hideaway," Aneirin said. "We have to think of another solution."

It was all well and good discussing the issues of the hideaway and those we would face every day due to the Riders, but we weren't producing a workable, strategic plan to overcome those issues. The Dark Triads would seek a place to live away from the grasp of the Dark Mages and the evil they'd manifested.

Xurek, who'd been busy helping the Developers with the expansion since he returned from the boats, joined the council meeting. His eyes bulged from his skull. He hated the Dark Triads as much as us, but he had a price on his head. He'd betrayed his own kind, and they'd be out for his blood.

"The Orcs are too close. They will find us soon enough. We need to destroy the doorway above ground," he suggested. "It's an obvious giveaway."

"And seal us all in?" Laurent recoiled in his chair. "Are you mad?"

"It won't be permanent," Xurek explained. "Some of the men from the Developers were suggesting it amongst themselves, and I said it was a brilliant idea."

"What's the plan?" Aneirin placed his fingers on his chin, perplexed. "How are we going to seal ourselves in?"

"See, this is the part I was most impressed with." Xurek arched a thick brow. I'd never seen him speak in such an animated way before. "The Developers and I will knock the structure down. That's the easy part. Then we have the help of the Harvesters. They are making a flat doorway that seals us in and looks like barren grassland above."

"You're hoping a disguised door is going to keep the Dark Triads from discovering us?" Laurent laughed. Something about the man terrified me. Perhaps the chill tone to his voice. Why would Aneirin trust him? "That's pathetic."

"Do *you* have an idea to put forth?" Enraged by his dismissal, I clutched my hands into fists at my side.

"There *is* an alternative option…" Aneirin muttered, his eyes hollow and dark. "Magic can reveal an escape room. It was built by the Developers upon arrival, and Sofia can open and seal it with magic."

"Why wasn't this mentioned earlier?" Xurek probed, distaste in his voice.

"It is only now that we were presented with a threat from the Orc scouts," Aneirin said.

"I will reveal the passageway, and once everyone has been guided through, I will seal it shut from the other side," Sofia said.

"Let me know if there's any way that I can help you." I glanced at her. "I can use my magic to assist you."

"You are carrying a child, and I won't put yours or the baby's life at risk." She smiled. "All will be fine."

My friends trailed me out of the meeting, and we wandered the dim lit passageway back to the canteen.

"Change into your armour, then have Aneirin and his advisors meet us in the food hall when they are ready," I said to them.

"I have a theory as to why the Orc scouts have come here," Valneris said. "You said their machines were powered by Milleshar, right? The substance that drains Mage magic?"

"Yes…" I cocked my head towards him, my curiosity piqued. "What of it?"

"Well, you know by any large number, Mage magic can be very powerful," Valneris said. His eyes dilated with excitement. "Perhaps the Dark Triads are coming here with their machines to give themselves more time. They could be preparing to fight the Dark Mages and the darkness themselves. I'm not sure it will be enough to close their portal, wherever that might be. Demons will still be able to cross over until it's destroyed."

"Let's hope the feud between the Orcs and the Dark Mages destroys them without causing the Light Triads anymore suffering. It's wishful thinking, I know. The likelihood is we will still be involved. I'll meet with you all once I've changed." I headed down the winding corridor towards my chamber.

After dressing in our armour, the High Elves and I entered the food hall and formed a line in front of the rows of tables. Sofia stood beside us with Aneirin, Katrin, and Laurent.

Sofia cleared her throat. "Everybody, gather around. We have an announcement to make."

The citizens formed a crowd in front of us, abandoning their

tasks and tossing their hammers or sewing needles aside.

"We have seen many Orcs coming nearer. We have decided that we need to travel farther underground to find safety. There is a concealed passageway."

"Is it safe?" a Human asked.

Sofia nodded. "Yes. We have no other choice. The threat is too close."

The food hall rang with questions and murmurs which overlapped each other, and I couldn't distinguish one question from another.

"Order, please," she called to the crowd. "Please pack your clothes and essential items only. The Harvesters will collect our food supply—as much of it as we can fit in our baskets and able to carry. Katrin and I will get the medicinal supplies. The Developers—please gather candles, water canteens, blankets—anything you can carry. Meet back here in one hour."

Our set time to collect our belongings went quickly. I'd left my chamber with a bag over my shoulder. Inside, I'd placed my gemstones, spell book, spare clothes, and my blanket.

The canteen bustled with civilians, carrying baskets of food and supplies, who waited for Sofia.

When she arrived, she led the way through a stretching corridor. We came to a halt at the dead end of the passageway. Masses of people waited, their unsettled murmurs stirring around us.

"What lays beyond the wall?" one questioned, yet no answers were given.

I scanned the faces in the crowd. Sweat lined their foreheads.

"Once I've revealed the room, take the people down to the stairs, all the way to the end," Sofia instructed. We couldn't risk staying in the hideout with the possibility of the Dark Triads hunting us down. "Aneirin, do you have the gold?"

"Right here." He jingled a pouch.

"Where did you get these?" I glanced at him.

"There is a tribe called Krears who live in a temple underground. The fee is for safety," he said.

Sofia started her chant and cupped her palms together until a glistening light appeared. She then separated her hands, allowing the light to expand as she continued to cast her spell. The light floated towards the wall until it was absorbed by the stones.

A few moments passed, and nothing happened. I rubbed my sweaty palms against my chest as the wall crunched and churning noises sounded through the corridor. It shifted and dissolved into nothing.

An opening appeared before me, revealing a narrow tunnel leading to a stone stairway as Sofia had described.

"Magnificent, as always, Sofia," Aneirin said, then turned to his advisors. "Laurent, Katrin, lead the civilians to the temple."

They obeyed, and queues of citizens filed through the secret opening and into the damp, slick tunnel.

I pressed myself against the wall with its wet surface dampening my hair as the crowd filed past.

Sofia moved towards me, then turned to face the opening of the passageway. She chanted her spell, and the wall flickered into reality.

We descended the stairs, travelling farther away from the surface. I wheezed, my chest tight and each breath heavy in my lungs. Pipes ran the length of the walls, allowing fresh air to reach us far beneath the ground, yet I longed for a large opening to bring more air to travel through.

"Stay close," I said to my advisors.

The High Elves obeyed, taking positions behind me with Xurek and Eric next to them. Aneirin led the civilians after us, leaving the room empty.

"The deeper we go," Kiirion started down the steps and frowned at the air pipes in disbelief, "the harder we'll find it to breathe."

"Then let's hope Sofia or I can conjure a spell that'll give us all oxygen. The air pipes should suffice for the time being." I turned my attention to Aneirin. "Should I be worried about the Krears?

"No. I've lived underground a long time—almost twenty years. Not long after I settled in the hideaway,

I heard them. I went down to speak with them. Over the years, we made an agreement—we would provide them with a share of food in exchange for peace and the safety of the people who lived with me."

"I hope they keep their word." I continued onwards, hemmed in by dark, cave walls.

After five flights, a stretching, narrow corridor lay ahead of us.

The Gnomes moaned and gasped for breath, their airflow above blocked by those taller than them.

"I know a spell that'll make it easier for them to breathe." Sofia gestured to the wheezing Gnomes.

"Thank you, but I'll do it." I pulled out my spell book, flipped through the pages and found a spell for manifestation. Shrugging a shoulder, I sucked in a breath in preparation.

Once I was sure of myself, I repeated the spell loud and clear, picturing fresh air in my head. I imagined it having a visible form—a rippling layer floating around us.

After the spell was complete, an ethereal shimmer materialised like a shield, and the panting stopped.

"We ought to pay our fee," Aneirin said. "Katrin, stay here with the civilians."

We pressed on with my advisors but who would meet us? My skin tingled with anticipation and my heart thumped.

"I must warn you—the creatures you will meet have been imprisoned underground for centuries. They may not be so pleasant with strangers." He wrinkled his nose.

"Perhaps we should lead the way," Xurek suggested, although he left no option for argument as he held out his arm like a barrier in front of me. "You need to be protected."

As we walked through the corridor, the pitch of the ceiling changed, subtle at first but as we journeyed on, the tunnel tightened.

"Loosen up, guys." I became claustrophobic from our tight formation. I wheezed, faint and light-headed as I clutched my pregnant belly.

The corridor opened, and the space loosened, revealing an ancient underground temple made of sandstone that was layered in shades of brown, tan, and burnt orange. Thick vines wove around the stone pillars, hiding a slight crack that ran from base to ceiling. How had the structure endured so many years?

No noise disturbed the temple. Blazing torches were affixed to the walls, offering our new location its source of light. I took several cautious steps forward, waiting for a few seconds between each one. Knots formed in my stomach.

Kiirion's gaze rested on the enormous piles of gold stacked around the cave and in front of the temple entrance.

Great beasts emerged from within the centre of the building, some on ground level and some above, weaving their way around the pillars. Their skin appeared tough, rubbery, and was the colour of dark tar.

Xurek's face twisted as his lips peeled back in a growl. He lifted his hammer in front of him. The

High Elves drew their swords and braced themselves as the creatures formed a semi-circle around us. Eric, although of smaller build, held his rigid stance with his sword pointed forward.

The beasts reared their round heads with accentuated, carved cheekbones and beady, gold eyes. I jolted backwards at the sight of them, unable to stop myself from cowering behind my companions as my heart pounded in my ears. Chains of gold hung from their necks, draping across their golden breastplates, and multiple bangles adorned their wrists.

The creature who wore the most jewellery, a dozen or so bangles on each arm, stalked to the front of the pack. He approached us on all fours, shuffling along like a gorilla. The others assembled behind him, grunting.

"Don't make any sudden movements." Aneirin slowly bent, then dropped the pouch in front of the brute.

I sucked in a breath.

"Ah, Aneirin." The beast picked it up and sniffed, then poured the coins into his hand and fumbled with them one by one. "Why are you here?"

"The world above ground is no longer safe," he said.

"What makes you think you're welcome here?" The assumed alpha snarled, displaying his sharp, jet-black teeth. "We have a deal, but that does not include permission to live in our temple."

"The world is plagued with darkness. A portal has been opened, connecting the world of the dead to this realm." I squeezed through the formation.

The beast raised a crooked eyebrow.

"Darkness…" Another animal approached their leader. "Could it be?"

The alpha shoved him and roared, making the ground shake beneath my feet. The smaller one cowered behind a chipped pillar to the right side.

"This gold is not enough," the leader said. "Not if you are hiding from the darkness. If you want to stay here, I need *more*."

The alpha raised onto his hind legs and approached us, growling. He sniffed us and snatched at whatever he deemed worthy of payment, including the gold encrusted armour we wore. The Elves cautiously began removing their armour. Kiirion gestured for me to do the same.

I unclipped each piece, then placed it on the floor in front of me.

The alpha pushed his way through my guards and bared his teeth as he searched me for gold. He peered at my ballooning belly and fell back onto his haunches.

Resting my hands on my bump, I stepped back.

"What is your name?" He stared at me with beady eyes.

"Evalyn." I cleared my throat. "Queen Evalyn."

"If you may allow it," Kiirion gave a cautious half-smile, "she needs to rest."

The alpha nodded before returning to his pile of gold where he sprawled and fiddled with each coin and treasure. His eyes were wide, and he grinned.

As my guards led me to a quiet spot in the temple where no beasts were lurking, Valneris and Eric retreated to the corridor to inform Katrin and the civilians it was safe to enter the temple.

"What are they?" I flicked my gaze to the alpha.

"Goblins," Aneirin explained. "You'd be surprised to know they were once a peaceful humanoid race."

"What happened to them? From what I've seen of them so far, nothing in them resembles anything human."

"During the time of the Noble Ones, there was a period of perpetual darkness brought about by a clan of Dark Mages who delved a little too deep into blood magic. They attempted to open a portal that links this realm to the Beyond," he said. "They were stopped by the Krears, a humanoid race of kind nature, and the Dark Mages got their revenge by placing a curse upon them."

"Turning them into Goblins." I shook my head in awe, not quite believing the story. "So they're living underground out of fear? The time of the Noble Ones was a millennium ago."

"Yes, but they're still cursed." Xurek crossed his arms. He'd become our encyclopaedia of Dark Triads' knowledge, now an invaluable ally. "The Krears are aware of their millennia-long feud with the Dark Mages."

"You're going to need to break the curse." Kiirion shook his head.

Would there ever be a time when a silver lining would emerge from the darkness?

"What for?" I stifled a yawn.

"We don't want to live underground forever, and I can't imagine they do either," he explained. "The gold will only satisfy the Krears for now. They'll consider your help payment for our stay. You'll need to find a way to close the portal and destroy the last of the Dark Mages."

"Are you serious?" I laughed at the sheer ridiculousness of his proposition. "You underestimate the power the Dark Mages have acquired. Their very feud with the Orcs is the reason *why* their magic powers the machines."

"Perhaps we need to find out what kind of portal we are dealing with," Kiirion suggested. "We need to know its powers and how to destroy it before more Demons and other evil entities find their way through. Let's hope we can stop the Dark Mages again like the Krears did a millennium ago."

As the civilians filed into the temple, gawking at the Krears in awe, I re-joined the leader of the pack who still lay on his bed of gold. I cleared my throat. "We ought to talk."

I mustn't seem afraid of him or any of the Goblins who lurked in the darkness behind him.

"You do not get to tell me when I ought to do *anything*." He glared as he wrapped a golden chain around his hand, holding a brilliant red ruby in his palm.

"It might free your people." I ignored his jibe. The possibility we could find a solution to the apocalypse and destroy the Dark Mages at the same time was unfathomable, but I wasn't about to waste the opportunity to at least try. "From the darkness *and* the Dark Mages."

"After so many centuries, a chance of freedom presents itself. Who would I be to pass up on such an offer?" The Goblin's ears pricked. He sat up straight and offered a wicked smile, revealing a set of sharp teeth that could rip flesh apart.

I shivered. I couldn't imagine what they would have once looked like as humanoids.

"Follow me." He pivoted towards a dark corridor full of Goblins.

I shot a quick glance at Kiirion and Xurek who hurried to my side. The others remained silent as they navigated their way around the temple for a suitable place to sleep. The elders clasped hands with children and guided them away.

Finbrik and Gnovash surveyed the scene with wary eyes, perhaps unsure whether to stay or leave with the leaders for sleeping arrangements.

"You'll be fine," I mouthed to them before they disappeared out of sight.

"Stay close." I looked at Kiirion and Xurek. "We're going to discuss a plan."

Three burning torches lit the dark room at the back of the temple. I chewed my lip and took each step slow.

"We suspect the Dark Mages have opened a portal. They've let Demons and the Ezen Riders cross through. Do you know anything that can help us?"

Something in them still resembled humanity. Flashes of hope brightened their eyes, and they alternated from walking on all fours to their two hind legs.

The leader shuffled his way through the crowd, disappeared into a dark room, then returned with a large, dusty book in his hand. He threw it in front of me.

"We cannot read," the leader grunted the words. "This book is centuries old and may be a bit worn, but I believe you'll find what you're looking for."

I struggled to pick up the book and kept a hand on my back as I
bent to grab it. When I had a firm grip on the ancient, dusty book, I stared at its cover. *The Chronicles of the Noble Ones and Arogathean Beasts* was scrawled on the front cover in a faded calligraphy.

"There should be a short passage somewhere inside which describes the portal the Dark Mages tried to open. Once you've found it, return and we will begin devising a plan." The leader turned to walk deeper into the shadows. "We're unable to leave the Temple in our cursed form, but you can."

"What should I call you?" I asked.

"My name is Zander," he answered with weary, half-closed eyes. It was those expressions that made him look more Human than Goblin. Perhaps Xurek was right. Their original nature still flickered like a dwindling fire.

Kiirion took the book from me and carried it to a quiet room on the second floor of the temple. Vines blanketed the ceilings and wrapped each pillar. He placed the book on top of a small, creaking table and opened it for me.

"Thank you." I sat on an old, worn chair made from ornate engraved wood with a torn fabric seat.

Kiirion exited through the doorway and stopped on the balcony, overlooking the rest of the temple. There were no doors or windows, so he had good view of below. Voices muttered and people shuffled around.

Below me, Aneirin and my other advisors helped the civilians settle in. The quicker I found what I was looking for, the quicker we could end this war and return to our home at Lake Delendil. We could rebuild the destroyed settlements of the Light Triads.

Although the Goblins granted us safe residency within the temple, if we made no progress with our deal to help them reverse the curse, would Zander and the other Goblins return to their hostility?

I wanted to reunite them with the open world above ground. An aggressive failed alliance with the Goblins was a fate I wished to avoid.

If I found the information in this book like Zander said, we'd be able to devise a plan to collapse the portal. No more Demons could pass through. My child may see light, after all, and a warmth stirred within me.

I flicked through the pages, scanning the scrawled writing, and each page displayed a drawing that translated the text into something visual and easier to understand. A rough sketch of the portal on the next page accompanied a passage.

The words were faded but still legible. Most of them translated into colours—purple, red, green, and each denoted a different type of portal.

My eyes widened when I found the words *Mage* and *blood magic* written on the same line as *red*. My heart thumped.

The Dark Mages were behind the creation of the portal and their portal would have a red haze. We had to find it. I drew out my spell book.

Would it contain anything related to portals?

Scanning the pages, I was desperate to find the answers.

'Portals created by Mages will be produced with red, green, or purple centres, depending on where they lead. Red denotes evil and hell. Green is neutral and leads to other locations within one realm. Purple is the connection between two physical realms.'

This was the evidence I needed. Adrenaline pumped through my body, numbing my fatigued muscles. We needed to go above ground.

I waddled out of the room and grabbed Kiirion by the arm. I've figured it out. Come on."

I dragged him along the balcony and down the stone steps, across the courtyard and into the murky back room of the Goblins' home.

"Zander," I called into the darkness.

"What is it?" he asked.

"Dark Mages have the ability to create portals with different coloured iridescent passageways." I panted. "At the battle of the Badlands, a Dark Mage

266

played his checkmate. He showed all the Dark Triads, and us, what they were capable of doing. The passageway of this portal will be red because the evil entities from the Beyond are crossing over."

"Excellent." Zander's lips curved into a crooked smile.

The Goblins behind him cheered and roared. This was their next step to freedom.

When the cheer quietened, he continued, "What do you suggest we do?"

"We need to find the portal and destroy it." I'd ensure everything was done in our power to rid the land of the Dark Mages's evil.

Kiirion glanced at me with widening pupils and an open mouth. My fingers trembled, and my knees buckled from a mixture of exhaustion and adrenaline. We'd found our way down here and now we had to return to the most dangerous and hostile surface of the realm.

I was pregnant with the prophesied child, and I needed to prepare myself for the interrogation that would soon follow.

If I knew them well, my friends would not allow me to accompany them on this vital journey.

"The Ezen Riders may have found the Orc scouts, and any others who may have been with them. We can assume they'd find the hideaway. We can't risk returning to the surface in case that's true." He gritted his teeth, his face turning as white as fresh parchment. "There's no way up. We cannot go back the way we came. It's too dangerous."

"Have you presumed we are stupid enough to have only *one* passageway back to the surface?" Zander laughed. "Ridiculous."

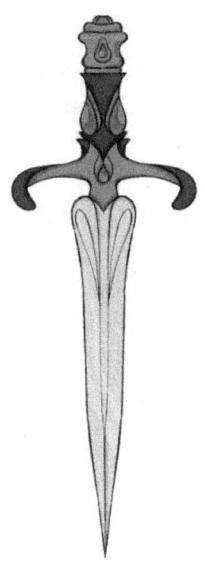

Chapter Fifteen

Inside the obsidian-shaded room, I gathered with the High Elves alongside Aneirin, Laurent, Katrin, and Sofia. Piles of straw and dead vines lined the floor of the den where some Goblins rested. Their faces were cloaked with shadows as there was little light in the lair.

"We have made progress." My voice resonated through the high ceiling temple. "My research has indicated the Dark Mages have opened a red haze portal. It connects this realm to the world of the dead and must be destroyed."

I braced myself for the fire of questions and orders from my advisors. Regardless of my pregnancy, I wouldn't let them stop me from fulfilling my duty.

"You want to return to the surface and search for a portal just to check its colour?" Aneirin's eyebrows rose high on his forehead. "Not on my watch. Not in your current condition."

"Valneris and Theodas have already volunteered, and of course I will stand with my friends." Kiirion lifted a hand. "Perhaps you might join us, Aneirin."

Aneirin, rooted to the spot, was silent. Perhaps the idea of returning to ground level seemed absurd. Or was his power over his civilians keeping him put? If we succeeded in destroying the portal, we'd return to life above the earth, and I'd resume my reign.

"Someone must stay here to look after the civilians," he finally said with a blank expression. His gaze remained fixed on Kiirion, as if staring a hole into his face.

I narrowed my eyes at Aneirin. His mouth twitched. Could he be in search of excuses? If he joined the High Elves on the expedition to the portal, his life would also be at risk, and his attitude made me believe he wasn't prepared for the commitment.

"I will be here, and so will Katrin," Sofia reassured her companion. "We know I am capable. I have proven my skills time and time again. We will all be safe, including Evalyn."

"Do you even know where this portal is?" Aneirin flicked his gaze to me, and he crossed his arms like a small child.

I shook my head at the sight of him. He'd painted a picture of himself as being a hero, a leader, yet

270

refused to act like one or show any enthusiasm towards the idea we might be safe someday.

"That's what I'm about to get to." I glared at him, then took a deep breath and turned to Zander. "The book you gave me was damaged and difficult to comprehend. However, I found relevant information in my spell book. We just need to find the location."

Aneirin emitted a childish laugh that echoed through the den. My pulse quickened with anger.

"Aneirin, that is *not* necessary." Laurent spoke for the first time since entering the temple. "Perhaps the two Mages can perform a location spell."

Zander stroked his chin. "Smart idea. But won't the Great Sea interfere with it? The portal is somewhere back in the Barren Territories."

"With both of our powers combined?" Sofia flicked her long hair over her shoulders. "Of course not. We possess a lot of magic and will be able to see the portal's location with great clarity."

"I don't know the spell." I frowned. "It's far too complex."

"You've been too preoccupied with other matters to focus on your abilities." Sofia's lips curved into a gentle smile. "Do not worry—I'll be helping you."

"You best get to work then." Zander retreated on all fours deeper into the darkness. We took this as a signal to leave and backed away from the Goblins' den.

"If you're certain about this—destroying the portal—then we'll devise a strategy for above ground. We might not get another opportunity to end the Dark Mages, Demons, and Ezen Riders for good," Kiirion said when we were back in the main courtyard of the temple. "Figure out the spell, and we'll be right here when you're ready."

He lingered with the others as Sofia guided me to the room where I'd researched the chronicles earlier. She brought me closer to her and closed her eyes.

"I'm going to tell you the words of the location spell to demonstrate. It won't work without the both of us saying it together, so the quicker you remember the words, the better," Sofia explained. "From north to south, east to west; from where the stars meet the sky and where the dirt kisses the realm; reveal to me, reveal to me… Show me the cross between our world and the world of the dead. Show me the Dark Mages's portal."

I could do this. I needed to for my people, for my child. For Felix.

"That's in our mother tongue." I nodded. "All major spells are written and spoken in the ancient tongue of the Noble Ones."

"Correct." Sofia opened her eyes and gave my hands a squeeze. "Now you know the translation, but for the spell to work, you must recite it in the ancient tongue."

She chanted the spell in the Noble Ones's tongue. Her words blurred together in a fast haze, resembling an incoherent mess of sound. She laughed at my gaping mouth.

"How am I supposed to say that?" My arms slackened in her grasp.

Sofia, however, smiled.

We continued to practice the spell in the correct language. She spoke the version of the spell in our mother tongue until I remembered it word for word. She enunciated every word, demonstrating each shape to create with my mouth and the variety of sounds I needed to make.

My head pounded from the concentration. Rubbing my baby bump, I relaxed into the chair, my eyes blurring from strain.

"We are Mages." She sat with me on the stone bench at the back of the room. "It's in our blood to learn things."

"It sure as hell doesn't come easy." I sighed.

We repeated the spell until the words became a jumble and I could no longer string them into a sentence. With no firm concept of time underground, I took my exhaustion as a hint to stop. A few candles lit the vastness of the temple and its surrounding areas, its dimness lulling me into rest.

———————⌢———————

The civilians had retired to their beds when Sofia woke me. No other sounds resonated through the temple besides her feet shuffling along the concrete floor.

"It's time," she said. "The men are ready."

We gathered in the courtyard of the temple. Aneirin and the High Elves waited with Zander, Katrin, and Laurent. Sofia drew four small candles from within the many folds of her robes and placed them on the floor, each pointed to north, east, south, and west. She lit them and tugged me into the circle.

"If you struggle with some of the pronunciation—" she held my hands, "—then focus on the red haze of the portal's centre as best as you can."

I nodded, trembling with nerves.

I needed to get a grip. They were relying on me. I had to do this.

This was the first step of the plan for freedom and Sofia couldn't do it without me—there were some spells even a High Priestess could not perform on her own.

We recited the spell in unison. I kept a strong image of what the portal would look like to help me through the spell. I envisioned it towering into the darkness above, its hazy red centre beaming light across the ground.

It took us several attempts to get it right. She remained patient, however, and soon, the words rolled from my tongue in the same rhythm as hers.

As if we'd been teleported, Sofia and I stood on a cliffside in an area of the Barren Territories I'd never been. The sights I'd encountered on my brief visit to Zhah were nothing compared to the burned wasteland before us now.

Bursts of fire exploded from craters as I observed the high portal with its unmistakable red shimmer. "What is this place?"

"Southkeep…it never used to look like this," Sofia muttered, her voice shaking with each explosion.

"You've been here before?" I furrowed my brows.

"I lived here for a long time," she answered. "As a prisoner. This place was the home of many Dark Mages. It seems like the power of the portal has made this place even more dangerous."

Her face paled. She'd experienced something traumatic there, and it flashed in her eyes. Yet, I couldn't begin to imagine this place looking better than its current state of decay. I'd grown accustomed to the cataclysmic appearances of the Barren Territories.

"How far is this from the Badlands?" My curiosity was piqued by the prospect of venturing farther into the Barren Territories. I feared what I'd see, and who, or what, I might meet.

"Once we've sailed the Great Sea back to the mainland, we can access the Badlands from the south, so about a day's walk," she explained. "But we'll need to do all those things without running into trouble from either the Dark Triads *or* the Riders."

"You should join the men. You are a High Priestess. You have the ability to heal *and* protect. They are going to need you."

"You are carrying the child of the prophecy," Sofia responded. "I must stay with you."

I didn't answer. My friends made great soldiers but having a healer on their side would double their chances of survival. There had to be a way of convincing her.

The image of Southkeep disappeared, and we reappeared in the temple.

"Well?" Aneirin asked, voice blunt and arms still crossed over his chest.

"Southkeep…" Sofia pressed her lips in a tight line. She recoiled into herself and wrapped her arms around her petite frame. I couldn't imagine the awful images of her imprisonment that must be flashing through her mind.

"Oh," he murmured. "I am sorry you had to return there."

"It's fine." She peered at the many eyes who stared back at her with a frown or arched eyebrows. "You can access the Badlands from the south once you've voyaged the Great Sea. Southkeep is about a day's walk from there." She hurried away, vanishing into a room where some Gnomes rested.

"What was that about?" Kiirion squinted in interest which distorted his striking facial features.

"Southkeep used to be a prison." I provided the small piece of information Sofia shared with me. "The Dark Mages kept her there."

———— ∽⌣∾ ————

Those who'd volunteered to venture across the Great Sea and back to the mainlands gathered outside the temple. Katrin remained with the civilians, ensuring their welfare. Sacks of food were positioned by them, ready to be taken to the boat. Zander and his fellow Goblins emerged from the shadows.

The High Elves, Xurek, Eric, and Aneirin formed a crescent moon shape around the Goblins. My friends, dressed in their armour again, clutched their weapons. Sofia informed them how to get to Southkeep.

"You will pass several settlements, each separated by tall fences," she said, "but when they took me from my home to Southkeep, I was blindfolded for the most part. I can't remember all of it."

She had muttered her directions in a rushed chain of words with her gaze flickering from the floor to the pillars, never making eye contact with our friends. Her face was strained when she talked, and her voice trembled. Her hands mirrored this and shook at her side until she clasped them into fists.

Unbidden, my mind wandered to Felix. What would he think of
this plan, that we held a possibility of being free? Our people safe?

"Since you won't let me come with you, I will produce a teleportation spell for you." I flexed my fingers ready to conjure the spell.

"It won't work. The charm will only work if you go *with* them. It would transport you too." Sofia shook her head.

"I can't stay here while my friends risk their lives. I have to do something." I dropped my hands to my side.

"You must stay here where *you* are safe. Protect your child," she said.

There was nothing I could do. My friends needed to survive the journey to the portal, find a way to close it, *and* return to the temple without being killed by either the Riders or the Mages. It seemed like an impossible plan.

I prayed to the gods, pleading for my voice to be heard, to protect us from the evil that surrounded us to help us restore balance to our realm.

What threats would we face along the way? I couldn't protect them all, and my heart sank.

No Mage would be accompanying my friends on their journey to Southkeep. They needed magic to destroy the portal. Sofia, or I, must join them.

Wrapping my fingers around the spell book, I contemplated learning the spells.

I flicked through the fragile pages. There was a protection spell with a delicate drawing showing several people shielded by an ethereal glistening layer. I sighed in relief at the short paragraph. I knew little of the pronunciation or the Noble Ones's language, but I pushed this away.

My gaze landed on handwritten notes next to the protection spell. *This spell is not to be used in conjunction with any form of weapon enchantment.*

I frowned. This used to be my mother's book, which meant she may have used this spell before, but what could she possibly mean? My uncertainty couldn't hinder me. I mustn't let it.

Soothing my belly with finger and thumb, I continued in my search for a useful charm. Something that might prove useful on our journey to Southkeep.

My gaze fell upon several healing spells, all proving to be tricky to say aloud. The foreign tongue seemed far denser and harder to pronounce, each sound catching in my throat. With more practice, combined with Sofia's help, I may be able to perform them.

With my friends discussing strategy around me, I used this to my advantage. Concealed by their shadows, I scanned for more defense spells. I'd already mastered my first attack chant, having used it against the Demon that attacked Juliette. Yet, I'd been too late to save her and needed the strength and power to prevent anyone else from dying at the hands of the Dark Triads.

I hoped I'd find Felix somewhere in the Barren Territories.

After reading *The Chronicles of the Noble Ones and Arogathean Beasts,* everything seemed to piece together. The Dark Mages had the ability to summon Demons and the Riders from the underworld, and together, they were the strongest clan in the realm. The Orcs were no match for them.

"Are you okay?" Aneirin asked.

I jolted, peeling my gaze from the pages. I stuffed my book inside my pocket and faced him.

"I know I have not said much to you since your arrival, and I know I have a lot of making up to do. Perhaps this journey will solve more things than it will destroy, and we will have the time to mend."

"You don't even want to go." I laughed, rolling my eyes.

"There are many things I fear, Evalyn," Aneirin said gently. His voice dropped a few octaves, creating a private conversation for just us to hear. "There are things above ground I have not seen in a long time."

I'd yet to find a reason to trust him. "You don't make much sense." I cocked an eyebrow.

Aneirin seemed strong and powerful when underground, in charge of his civilians. But when faced with a *true* calling for bravery— returning to the surface to face the apocalypse and the Dark Mages—he cowered.

Laurent, however, discussed his position in the strategy with my advisors. How could Aneirin allow his own advisor to be portrayed as braver than he?

My pulse quickened with rage, and my gaze locked with Aneirin's. He left me alone in the shadows to re-join the men.

"Although we appreciate your offer to come with us, you should stay here, Laurent," Kiirion said. "You will offer protection to the civilians in case the Krears decide to turn against us."

"They've known us a long time, so I hope they will not do such a thing," he said. "However, when their freedom hangs in the balance, I cannot be sure. I'll stay with Katrin and the others."

"Be safe." I closed the gap between Eric and me, then touched his arm.

He brought me into an embrace. "Of course."

"To all of you, be safe."

My friends were ready for their ascension to ground level and unaware of my plans to follow them undercover. If I mentioned it, they would do everything in their power to make sure I didn't step foot out of the temple.

Xurek hugged me. Valneris tapped him on the back with a sense of urgency. It was time to go.

They followed Zander through a narrow corridor to the left of the temple. Each of them disappeared in single file up the slope to ground level.

"Are you worried?" Gnovash appeared next to me, her voice timid and small. She flattened her shaking fingers against her side, and I pretended not to notice.

The memories of her torched village, Westwilde, resurfaced. The urge to protect my people and build them new homes came in thick waves. My heart swelled with fondness. I still had my allies close by, even after all this time and everything that had happened. It gave me hope.

"Yes." I curled my lips into a slight smile. Finbrik came to her and wrapped his arm around her.

"We wanted to thank you," he said, "for giving us a home at Lake Delendil."

"It is my duty, and I am glad a sliver of happiness still prevails. Even in the darkest of times."

Finbrik and Gnovash returned to their room within the temple, and I let a few moments pass before I grabbed my bag, then stuffed the ancient book inside. The Krears didn't need it, but perhaps there was something more in there for me to learn about portals.

I navigated my way down the corridor. My palms grew sweaty, and my chest tightened. I kept my footsteps light and soundless as I followed the men through the long, weaving corridor. Several droplets of water escaped their pipes and glistened on the rocky surface of the walls. Wheezing and holding onto my bump, I kept my hand on the stone walls as I trailed my friends.

My swollen belly hung low. I could understand why they wanted me to remain at the temple. I would hold them back, slow them down. But if I stayed, they may die and fail to destroy the portal.

The flickering torches hanging from the wall cast the men's elongated shadows across the floor, which soon disappeared as they took the final turn towards the stairs. At the end of the corridor, I remained hidden behind the wall as the men ascended wooden steps and exited the hideaway.

I waited a few long and tense moments, then proceeded, holding my breath as my heart pounded. The stairs stretched upwards for ten flights and before long, I could no longer hear their feet thumping against wood. I needed to time this right. I couldn't let them board the boats and leave without me.

Each step was hesitant as I pressed my foot against the wooden stairs. Above me, a door creaked open as the men exited the hideaway. I stood still—they clicked it shut behind them.

How would I get onto the boat without being spotted? I assumed it would be best for me to stay hidden until we reached the water. If I made it to the ship and set sail without getting caught, they'd have no choice but to allow me on their journey.

I climbed the rest of the stairs, panting and dizzy from the workout any pregnant woman would find hard to endure. In my moments of rest, I thanked the Goblins for revealing their secret escape route.

I leaned against the wall, my legs burning and sweat forming along my hairline.

Come on. You can do this.

Above my head was a door built into the roof. I unbolted it and flung the door open, slamming it onto the ground. I peered over the edge to see the men heading towards the water. Waiting, I observed their descent of the slight hill and out of sight.

Would my friends see me as I left the underground sanctuary? From here, I had a clear view of the Great Sea stretching for miles ahead.

Nervous and desperate to remain quiet, I scrambled out of the hideaway, closed the hatch, then followed them towards the boats at the bottom of the hill. My legs burned as I walked, keeping as low to the ground as I could.

I cradled my belly and murmured, "Everything will be all right. I promise."

I passed the spot where the metal entrance once stood, a straw camouflaged plank now in its place.

A small shrub withered at the top of the sloping hill, so I ducked behind it. I surveyed the men as they boarded a boat, then headed to the helm. Eric went below deck with his basket of food.

The darkness swarmed and hung over the realm in a thick mass, as miserable as it'd been the night of the rise of the Ezen Riders. Barren lands stretched for miles on this side of the Great Sea.

What would the mainland territories look like now?

I wondered what the Elementals would do. Where would the Undines and Nereids go? Would their home at the Galae Pools remain safe? The Sylphs in the Highland Trees were protected from the darkness by their dense canopies of branches and leaves, but even trees can die. The Salamanders had their caves, but the apocalypse could still find them.

I waddled down the slope towards the boat and hid underneath the boarding plank.

"Evalyn!" whispered a voice. I jolted, half-jumping out of my skin. Sofia glared at me and slid down the slope to join me under the plank.

"Don't try to talk me out of it." I peeled my gaze from her and stared at the boat. "Come with me."

"I've stored the food next to the pails of water that were left from our journey here," Eric said as he rose from below deck. His footsteps creaked the floorboards of the boat as he climbed the steps to the helm of the ship where Kiirion, Valneris, and Xurek were. At the rear of the boat, I spotted Aneirin, looking across the Great Sea, his brows furrowed.

"I'll sail the ship," Valneris said. "Kiirion, can you raise the sails?"

The men continued their conversation.

"What should we do?" I whispered.

Sofia pondered this for a moment—her gaze fixed on the shoreline. She turned to face me, and a smile curved her lips. "Watch this."

She held her left palm flat in front of her, then used her right index finger, began a swirling motion above her other hand. Leaning close, she blew lightly onto her hands.

My lips parted, and I gasped. A small, spinning tornado formed, and Sofia stretched out her hands, letting the magic float towards the water on her left side. When it hit the sea, a whirlpool swelled and spat water against the boat.

Footsteps thundered across the deck.

"What in heavens is going on?" Xurek's voice boomed.

I peered over the edge to see my friends watching the whirlpool spin in front of the boat.

"Come on." Sofia grabbed my hand, then dragged me towards the plank.

We took the opportunity to tiptoe along the boarding plank, then disappear below deck into a dim lit cabin.

I rested against the wall. She clutched me, acting as support until I found my breath. I decided it would be best to stay out of sight until after setting sail. At least there'd be no way of sending me back then.

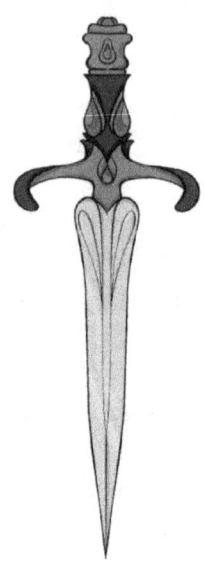

Chapter Sixteen

I stared at the thick, shadow-ridden realm through the small window of the cabin. How much time would pass before someone spotted me below deck? Hidden behind a beam, I held my breath as the stairs creaked and wondered who'd come to find me.

"Evalyn?" I peered round to see his gaze upon my pregnant bump protruding from the side of the pillar. The voice belonged to my father.

I stepped out of the shadows, the light from several candles casting a yellow glow across my skin. What lecture would he give me?

"What are you doing here?" He cocked his head.

I'd painted heroic pictures of his death in battle—a noble death and a sacrifice to save the realm from the clutches of the Dark Triads. But after all this time, there he stood, lungs still breathing, heart still beating. Who could forgive a father's lie? One so preposterous as his?

He had no honour.

"You needed a Mage," I blurted. "So, here we are."

"I would have prevented it if I'd known of her plans to leave," Sofia said, stepping out beside me.

"It's not safe." He frowned.

"Why didn't *you* stay at the temple?" I wrinkled my nose and sneered. "You didn't want to leave, anyway."

"Evalyn," he warned. "I didn't want to leave Newland, but here I am, doing what I should be doing. And you should be doing the same, which is bed rest."

I lifted a brow. "You named it Newland?"

"That's not important." He narrowed his gaze on me. "You are putting your life in danger by coming with us. More so, you are risking the life of your unborn child and the lives of your friends on this very boat."

"You are not in any kind of position to tell me whether I am doing something right or wrong," I snapped, fighting the urge to burst into tears. "Your moral compass was skewed the day you deserted your duty, family, and had everyone believe you were dead."

He jerked back, and his eyes glimmered. I didn't care. My words held the truth. He shouldn't have abandoned his child or his friends, and the pressures of the last few weeks had made it almost impossible to keep my opinions to myself.

He spun around as the rushing sounds of footsteps echoed across the cabin. The High Elves descended the wooden, creaking steps.

Kiirion's eyes widened. His gaze fell upon me and Sofia, then his shoulders relaxed.

I couldn't help but offer him a smile in return. Valneris, on the other hand, kept his feet rooted to the spot. He was older than the other High Elves, with a harsher facial structure. The dim, yellow glow from the candlelight cast deep shadows across the contours of his face and his thin, pressed lips.

"Valneris." My heart sank in my chest, and my gaze fell to the floor in shame. "I'm sorry…I couldn't send you into the Barren Territories without me. Without us." I gestured at Sofia. "I just couldn't."

His face softened, as much as his wizened appearance would allow him. He didn't say anything. Instead, he opened his arms to me. The embrace was the first I'd shared with him, and it spread a warmth through my body.

"No matter what we face, we face it together." I smiled. We returned to the deck, reuniting with Xurek and Eric.

"Evalyn? What're you doing here? I mean, why are you here? Weren't you supposed to stay? Why've you come?" Eric asked.

"Have mercy on our souls…" Xurek muttered. "I can't deny I'm happy to see you, but this is very dangerous."

"I didn't have the chance to stop her," Sofia explained.

"Are you sure about that?" He frowned. "You said you were competent enough to watch over her."

"Enough." I raised my hands to silence them. "I'm not going to leave you alone in the middle of a war. You are my family."

"Hmmm…" Xurek grumbled, then marched towards the steering wheel.

"He'll come around," Sofia whispered.

The others busied themselves on the vessel as we drifted farther away from Newland. Aneirin took my elbow and guided me towards the boat's rail.

He leaned against the handrail and let out a deep breath, gazing across the rippling waves. The Elves affixed torches to the deck for light, but the water ahead couldn't be seen with clarity.

I stared at the water lapping around the boat. What could I say to this man who was a stranger?

"Do you think we will find my mother?" I recoiled into myself.

Aneirin once told me, when I was very young, that my mother was captured by Dark Mages not long after I was born. Just shy of twenty years had passed. Could it even be possible?

"I don't know." He let out a loud exhale. His face softened, and the frown disappeared. His eyes welled with tears.

"But Sofia said she was imprisoned at Southkeep, and she managed to escape. Maybe she knew my mother...there's a chance she could be alive—somewhere—we could find her." If my father was alive after all this time, then there was a possibility my mother was, too.

"Evalyn..." His eyebrows drooped around his glistening eyes, and he shook his head. "She's been gone for twenty years."

"But so had you—there is a chance, however small—she might be alive."

"You may not remember it like it was yesterday, but I do," Aneirin whispered. "You weren't there to see it. When you were young, I refused to share details of her kidnapping because I didn't want to burden you with the same aching pain."

No matter what my opinions were of my father now, he'd spared me the torture. My heart wouldn't hang as heavy as his, and I wasn't haunted by the same vision that tormented him.

I'd no other connection to my father other than my mother and the blood running in our veins. His selfishness made any memory of a bond we'd shared disappear the day I arrived at the hideaway.

Instead of allowing unanswerable questions to cloud my judgement, I locked them away in the far corners of my mind.

"Thank you." I glanced at him, and I smiled. "For sparing me that much."

The boat drifted against the sea, the silence lingering between us. My anger towards Aneirin washed away as we gazed across the black, seamless horizon, where the sky blended with the waves.

———————⌒⌒———————

When the bustle of the deck simmered to a silence and the Elves took their leave to sleep, I conjured a moon dial spell. An ethereal crescent moon hovered above my outstretched palms.

Xurek took his turn to steer the boat and the others left to sleep in their cabins.

I wrapped my cloak around me, hugging myself for warmth against the chill of the night. My heartbeat quickened, and my stomach knotted with anxiety and fear. Would we manage to break the curse on the Goblins to set them free? Or would the Ezen Riders' darkness continue to take everything from the realm until nothing remained?

I created a ball of bright, white light and let it float towards the front of the boat where it hovered, illuminating the rippling water below.

Xurek's eyes drooped with sadness. He'd abandoned his life following the Dark Triads—the same darkness had run through his veins—and offered allegiance to me. I'd make sure I repaid him for his loyalty.

He stared across the water ahead with a deep frown between his thick eyebrows.

"Do you have faith in this mission?" I rested my hands on the rail, the salty air filling my nose.

"We're risking our lives going to Southkeep, and you're risking the prophecy by coming with us." He sighed. "But I'm glad you're here."

A slight murmuring sound surrounded us. He took his hands off the wheel and thudded to the edge of the boat. He leaned over the handrail and held his breath as a slow, soft sound filled the air. I remained, tense and rooted to the wooden floorboards of the deck.

Then songs began. The Undines swam the length of the boat, singing their compelling tunes. Their ballads grew louder. I frowned.

"Why aren't they stopping?" I shot Xurek a look. I crossed the deck and peered over the side of the boat. "Seara…is that you? Are you okay? Listen to me. I order you to stop singing!"

They ignored me and continued. Xurek's eyes glassed over.

"Perhaps they don't know it's you on the boat?" His words lacked conviction. "These blasted songs." He rubbed his eyes and shook his head as if to rid himself of the compulsion.

"How did they get to the Great Sea from the Galae Pools? Another sacrifice?"

The men came from the cabins as chaos descended on the deck.

"Cover your ears!" I hurried to my friends. "I suspect the Undines are no longer our allies!"

As Sofia and I were female, we were immune to the enchanting melodies and could not be affected. I leaned over the boat and strained. The Undines, with their deep-green scales seemed somewhat cursed.

Their bewitching eyes, which were a bright gold, had turned a milky white.

I stared at the Elementals. My spine tingled, and I shuddered.

We were in grave danger. Had the Dark Mages caused the contamination of the Great Sea with their darkness? Is that why the water Elementals were different?

The Undines and Nereids, feral and rabid, clawed at the side of the boat. Some of them managed to drag themselves up with their long, talon-like nails. I winced at the high-pitched scraping as they tore up the side; their bodies writhing and their music screeching unlike their silky songs from the Galae Pools.

Grabbing the sword from Kiirion's scabbard, I spun around, now head on with one of the Undines. She wriggled and slashed her tail, using her arms to pull her body across the deck towards me. With my heart pounding in my ears, I swung the sword through her head, which hit the slick floorboards with a thud and rolled across the floor. The other Undines screeched; their music intensified as they tightened their bodies into coils and attempted to clamber onto the boat.

The men clustered in the centre of the deck with wide eyes and covered ears although it wouldn't fully block out their songs. Xurek's hammer collided full force with the next Undine. More were coming.

Sofia's bright magic bolted through the air, then hit an Undine.

I scrambled up the steps to the helm. With a brief, frantic glance over my shoulder, I saw Seara. Her feral eyes glinted in the dark sky as she gripped Eric's legs. He fell and thudded against the floor. She dragged him towards the edge of the deck.

I screamed and clutched the wheel, trying to jerk the boat around but the attempt was useless. The boat was too large to manoeuvre with such sudden movements. I abandoned the wheel and waded down onto the deck to help fight off the Undines and Nereids.

Seara let out a shriek as I launched a ball of red magic into her. It hurtled her backwards into the boat railing. Sofia shot flares of magic at the surrounding water Elementals until only a few were left.

The remaining Elementals scattered, diving deep. I leaned against the boat and panted, clutching my belly with both hands, cocooning my unborn child.

The men, planted in their places, gasped for breath. Green slime covered the deck. The blood of the Undines and Nereids. The blood of an ally. I grabbed the rail and vomited over the side. Tears rolled down my face.

The week of travelling by boat reached its last stretch. We'd depleted our water supply two days prior. The horses had eaten the last of their hay. Tired grumbles of hunger and thirst spread across the deck. I tapped my fingers against the railing of the boat, staring at the sea ahead. With each passing day, the knot of fear in my stomach tightened. We were growing closer to the portal, the Riders, and the Dark Mages.

I prayed to the gods one last time, pleading that we could stop the Dark Mages, and their army. I wanted peace for my people and a safe world in which we could rebuild.

I huffed, frustrated by the battle of thoughts that created a dull ache in my forehead.

My heart panged. My child might be born into a world plagued by darkness without a father. Would my son ever see the realm?

I stroked my blooming belly, eyes prickled by tears as I issued a silent promise to my sweet child, to give him everything I could, to pave the way for him.

When we docked on the shore of the Barren Territories, an eerie silence enveloped us. The Demons and Riders were nowhere to be seen. No Dark Mages had wandered this far south, either.

The black mass of evil magic hung above us in thick clouds. With fingers clenched into fists, I contemplated lingering on the coast with my friends. Set up camp until I was needed. But thoughts of finding my mother and Felix at Southkeep was motivation enough to keep moving.

Eric and Xurek lowered the plank, joining the boat with the dry land in front of us. Stretched out ahead, were the unfamiliar, uncharted territories of the Dark Triads. Felix and I hadn't ventured farther than Zhah. While Sofia spent many years at

Southkeep, my first sight of it was through the location spell.

The south end of the Barren Territories lay before us, unnerving and gloomy, the dull discolouration of dying lands blending with the darkness above. The image of the portal returned, burning in my mind's eye, a fiery hell pit and a gateway to the dead.

I needed to do this for my people, no matter how much I wanted to hide away.

I repeated this to settle my nerves and gripped the rails of the boat, following my friends along the plank until my feet kissed the charred ground.

"Let's get a move on." Theodas descended the plank with his hand resting on his sheathed sword. "We shall avenge Ascal's death."

Eric and Xurek led the horses off the boat, then towards small tufts of grass that poked out from the cracked ground.

"If anyone sees anything unnatural, be sure to say so." Kiirion walked across the dry terrain. His gaze travelled to mine. "And Evalyn, stay close."

"Kiirion, do you have any useful tools? We need to find another source of water. It gives the horses time to feed as well."

"I *do* have something." He dumped his bag on the ground and rummaged through it until he pulled out two pieces of wire. He bent the wire three quarters at a ninety-degree angle. "Here you go."

I stared at them. "Er…what are they?"

"Dousing rods. Simple yet effective." He beamed. The others stood by and stared at each other with blank, dumbfounded expressions. "You hold them like this…" He held his arms out straight, allowing the wire to point in any which direction it preferred. "When there's a source of water nearby, the wires will cross each other. When they form a straight line, you know you've found it."

"Perhaps we should find some edible cacti." Theodas stifled a laugh.

"No, I'm serious," Kiirion said. "It'll work. I promise."

He guided us across the barren field. Several trees were dotted about the terrain, most were crooked, dried-out or killed from the apocalypse. I scanned my surroundings for any sign of life but only carcasses came into sight. How was he going to find water?

More so, how long would it take for the darkness to take its toll on the races? No one in our group had grown ill, thus far, from the disease brought about by the apocalypse. For the most part, the hideaway acted as a block from the onslaught above. Yet, now, we faced full exposure to the wrath of the apocalypse.

"See! Look!" Kiirion called. "The rods have crossed over. There must be water here somewhere."

He strode through the thick, dying grass towards shrubs and withering bushes. I hung back with my friends and frowned.

Was the apocalypse affecting him? Was he losing his mind?

"I knew it!" he exclaimed.

We strode to the spot where he stood. And as promised, between the rows of shrubs, was a shallow pool of water in a small ditch. It wasn't a lot, but it would fill our flasks for the onward journey.

"We may have found water, but we are exposed." I gestured to open savanna. "If we are unable to find shelter along our journey, we risk being affected by the darkness."

"We will find shelter." He hovered close, gaze flicking to my pregnant belly every now and again. "For your safety."

"There is something more important to consider." Eric lifted a finger. "How are we going to find our way to Southkeep? It's not like there are road signs."

"I no longer have my map." I sighed. "There's only a few of us, so I can perform a teleportation spell."

"No, we can't do that. We'll zap straight into plain sight by the portal. We're better off—and safer—travelling by foot. This will keep us out of harm's way and give us enough time to prepare our attack," Sofia said.

We pressed on, foraging for any edible cacti and berries as we made our way across the land towards a cluster of broken, dead trees.

I squinted, spotting a high wooden fence behind them. It blended well with the darkness but remained visible behind its camouflage of trees. "Over there." I pointed.

The men strained their gazes.

"I don't like this," Valneris panted. "We have no idea where we're going. We're wandering around in the open, in perpetual darkness with the risk of being attacked at any moment, *and* to top it all off, we have to close the portal." He gripped the handle of his sword, knuckles turning white.

He was right. Everything he said made sense. Sofia stood nearby, a frown deep between her brows.

I wondered if she'd thought of a plan. "Are you okay?"

She peered at me. "Southkeep—my prison—it haunts me in my I sleep."

"I'm here." I rested my hand on hers. "We'll get through this together."

We carried on, walking through the openness, guiding the horses by their reins. I imagined it would have been a field once, with life and prosperity. Yet, dead corn snapped under my feet as we passed through the trees.

The unnerving silence continued, stretching far ahead.

We approached the fence, which towered high above us and found the entrance located on the left. A small opening through the side curved around, framed by another fence.

"Evalyn, stay in the middle." Aneirin pulled me between the group of men who drew their swords. "At least until we know what we're dealing with."

We walked down the passageway, and my heart thumped in my chest and ears.

Once on the other side of the fence, we stopped and surveyed the quiet land stretching farther onward. We remained quiet, taking careful steps across the cracked terrain.

Sofia trailed behind, wrapping her arms around her body as she wandered through the land of her prison.

We reached an abandoned settlement of huts.

"This place is known as the Southern Peninsula." Xurek entered one of the huts. "Home to many Orcs and Trolls."

"Where have they gone?" I scanned the deserted buildings.

The shelter in front of us resembled his own in Zhah. His eyelids drooped as he picked up planks of wood that'd fallen loose. He threw them aside with a grunt and plucked more debris from the ground, launching it into other houses.

"Not even the gods know." He ripped a door from its hinges, grumbling to himself as he entered the hut.

I followed him in, leaving the others outside to stand guard. He snooped, touching cabinets. What item could he need from an abandoned home? Xurek hadn't mentioned his family of Orcs, nor any friends he'd once made as a member of the Dark Triads. Why, now, this search?

"Xurek, is this necessary?" I tiptoed closer to him and placed my hand on his shoulder. He winced, then turned his head and met my gaze. "I'm sorry. We can't stay. We need to leave. Whatever this place means to you—what it *meant* to you—will need to wait. We must close the portal."

"Hunh." He flicked through a stash of trinkets and other little things piled on a table against the far wall.

He sucked in a deep breath, then marched out of the hut. As he pushed past the other men, their bewildered gazes caught mine. I shook my head and hurried after Xurek.

"What was that about?" Kiirion leaned into me. He kept his voice low enough so Xurek, who was a few feet ahead of us, would not overhear.

"No idea." I sighed and counted the stones along the path. "Perhaps his emotions are getting the better of him."

Kiirion glanced at me from the corner of his eye, bemused and stifling a laugh. "Xurek, a giant Orc, afraid of his emotions? Not possible."

Eric appeared at my side. The light-heartedness I'd shared a few seconds before with Kiirion vanished. Eric's face was strained, his eyes dry and dull.

"Are you okay?" I gripped his arm and halted in front of him. I scanned his body for injuries or any sign of discomfort. A large, black circle of dying flesh spread across his neck and disappeared beneath his neckline, his armour camouflaging the extent of the plague. "Eric…"

Theodas approached and turned Eric's face to the side to get a better look at the rotting flesh. Theodas squinted, surveying the affected area. "I'm assuming this is what the plague looks like in people," he muttered, keeping his fingers far away from the patch of rot.

"How long does he have?" I demanded.

"A few days." He removed his hand from Eric's neck. "Maybe more."

"I'm right here, you know." He rolled his eyes. "I'm fine. Let's keep walking."

He wasn't fine. Anyone who was rotting away as they were still breathing would not be okay.

Xurek wandered several steps ahead of me, his head down as he stared at the path. My baby shuffled and kicked. I clutched my stomach and gasped.

"Evalyn, are you okay?" Valneris placed his hand on my arm.

By instinct, I took his hand in mine and placed it on the bump. Aneirin watched with a glare.

Stood between my friends, I gazed at my father. He remained rooted to the spot.

———— ⌇⌇ ————

We exited the Southern Peninsula to arrive at a wood and rope bridge hanging over a thin ditch. Had it once been a stream before the apocalypse arrived?

"This used to be a dense forest, can you believe it?" Xurek observed. We weaved our way through the shrivelled trees. "It was home to a lot of wildlife, some very beautiful creatures. And, of course, some dangerous ones…"

As he examined his surroundings, his teeth were clenched tight. Although he'd turned his back against the Dark Triads, I understood his pain. He watched his homeland wither around him. How would I react if I returned to Lake Delendil to the same sights?

The waters the lake may be poisonous now, home to all sorts of dark creatures who'd slithered their way into this realm. A shiver crept down my spine at the notion of the dead crawling back through the natural portal in the lake. Did the Citadel still stand in all its beauty? Or had the Demons managed to breach and destroy it?

Mirroring Xurek's despair, I longed for Felix and his comforting touch. His guidance and wisdom. His love and support. With closed eyes, I pictured him standing with me, cocooned together, and hidden from the world, safe in each other's arms.

My mind wandered to my mother. What would it be like to see her after all these years? I didn't hold a single memory of what she looked like. I needed Aneirin to find her. Had Sofia shared the same prison with her? Would she have known what my mother looked like?

I yawned, dragging my feet across the land. A niggling sensation of nausea in the pit of my stomach swelled and strengthened. I clutched my hands over my mouth and nose to block the stench of death and decay, sucking in small gasps of breath.

"Is it time for us to stop?" Aneirin asked. "You're pale."

He draped his arm around my shoulder to offer support. Instead of resisting his attempts to help, I leaned against him, allowing him to bear my weight.

"Yes." My voice was thin. A wave of pain flushed down my spine.

"Is there anywhere we can stop?" he asked Xurek, who led the way past more abandoned huts surrounding a settlement hall. "Evalyn has done too much. We must rest."

Xurek nodded and peeled a door open for me. We entered a hut, one with its roof still intact. Theodas lit a few stumped candles with the flint we'd brought with us and Xurek drew the curtains. Plumes of dust wafted into the air, causing shimmering light to streak across the room. The dust tingled my nose and I sneezed. The others settled on the floor, pulling scrappy remains of blankets over them for warmth. A warm, orange glow illuminated the cobwebs in all the corners of the hut.

Seated on the floor, with Aneirin and Valneris resting on either side, I tore off my shoes and shoved them aside. Each of my limbs were heavy and a dull ache urged me to sleep.

I stared at Aneirin and Valneris for a moment before removing my cloak and leaning into Valneris. He circled me with his arm, then stroked the hair away from my face with his finger and thumb.

Sofia sat opposite me with her knees drawn to her chin. She wrapped her arms tight around her shins. Her silver hair fell beside her face, no longer tied back with a ribbon. She resembled a child. Afraid of this place. She stared at the floorboards, her gaze never wavering. I took her hand.

"We will get through this." I did my best to soothe her. "I promise you."

Her glassy eyes connected with mine, and her mouth opened but no words left.

"Please be strong for me." I squeezed her hands, the others silent beside us. "I cannot do this alone. I need you. We all do."

"I will help you." She closed her eyes and let out a deep breath. "Let's get some rest."

The others obeyed, lying against the cold floor of the shack underneath the warm glow of the candles.

Valneris folded another scrap of fabric into a pillow and placed it on the floor for me.

"Sleep," he whispered with a glint in his eyes.

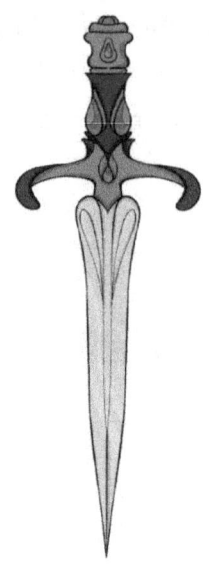

Chapter Seventeen

I stirred a few hours later while everyone else still slept, curled into balls on the wooden floorboards. With a yawn, I stretched and sat up, rubbing my groggy eyes until they focused on an amber light flickering on the other side of the curtain. The burning scent of wood wafted through the cracks in the hut walls. I peeled back the curtain and peeped out the corner of the window—orange flames illuminated the settlement.

Scrambling to my feet, I yanked the thin curtains open. Flames licked up the side of the huts and sparks flew in the air from the roofs. Transparent figures hovered a few feet above the ground, their eyes piercing a bright red against the black of night. Demons.

"Wake up! Wake up!" I ducked out of view of the Demons. The men jolted awake, grabbing their swords with swift movements, their eyes wide.

"What is it?" Xurek gripped his hammer, crossed the hut in two long strides and glanced out the window. "Demons are here."

The other men pulled me into the middle of the group.

Adrenaline shot through me. "They're trying to find us. We need to leave."

The window glazed with ice as a Demon flew overhead. A chill seeped in through the walls and the hairs on my neck stood on end.

Xurek edged the door open and led the way left, out of sight of the Demons. We crept along behind the other huts, one at a time to avoid being spotted.

The birch trees framing the abandoned settlement were ragged and dead, offering no camouflage.

Adrenaline shot through my veins. "Your swords…they won't stop them," I whispered. "We won't be able to take them all on."

The men scanned the area, walking along the path that headed as far left as possible. Xurek kept me close to his side, hiding me behind his bulky frame until we could no longer see the Demons.

The darkness transformed into a thick black mass in the sky.

Hidden by the gathering of dead trees, I peered around the trunks. My body trembled, and I held my breath, begging to the gods we wouldn't be found. We needed more time.

"Where do we go from here?"

Xurek's face creased into a frown as if he were already contemplating our next move. "I'm certain there is a tunnel around here. We'll have to leave the horses behind to reduce our chances of being spotted."

The rest of us waited. I drummed my fingers against my legs.

He placed a thick finger on his chin. "That'll take us out of the line of sight of any threat. You used the location spell to find the portal, but I know how to get to Southkeep itself. This route will lead us there."

"This is risky. We're going to be seen." Eric gritted his teeth.

"It's a risk we have to take as we have no other option," Xurek explained as we snuck along the trail he set. "The tunnel was once used to transfer slaves to Southkeep. We may run into trouble there, but it's our safest option."

"Lead the way." Kiirion shrugged.

We hurried side by side, flanking Xurek through the trees and across several thin ditches that, perhaps, were once streams, home to small fishes and other aquatic life.

Valneris remained silent for most of the journey. He held out his hand to help me across the ditches, staying close by my side. Perhaps he'd been as quiet as I because we both feared the end. We both understood the finality of the singular shot we had at stopping the Dark Mages and closing the portal. We hadn't devised a plan to do so, yet we continued our venture through enemy territory.

I curled my hands into fists and dug my nails in. I wanted another option, another way to save our people and our friends. Casting a glance at Sofia, I yearned for her help, but she'd been quiet for the most part of the journey, but who could blame her, knowing what memories this place held for her?

Ahead, we found a small hut suitable for us to lie down for a few hours of extra sleep. Old, jagged stones poked out from the ground alongside weeds and other wilting plants. A thick layer of spongy, soft moss covered the floor.

"Perhaps we could all sleep in here." I stifled another yawn. "It's a tight fit, but it'll do."

"Good idea," Kiirion said. "We need a firm idea before moving forward to Southkeep."

"I agree," Theodas said.

"We'll discuss plans once we're settled. The night will grow colder, and it's too risky for us to build a fire, so the cozier this cavern is, the better," Kiirion added.

Sofia bit her thumb knuckle, hovering in the doorway. I wanted her to come up with an idea, to understand the importance of our mission.

The High Elves huddled together in the main room of the hut, leaning against each other for warmth and support. Aneirin sat opposite them, where a space for Sofia and I welcomed us.

How different would my life be without them? Would I have gotten this far?

I doubted it.

Eric rested against the far back wall, undisturbed by the rot and mold gathering there. He closed his eyes, body hanging limp from the disease spreading across his skin. He resembled Theodas in more than one way and as selfish as it sounded, I liked to keep Eric around as he reminded me of those first few days I'd spent on my journey with Felix. I'd been so uncertain about my magic and my ability to help those who needed me but with Felix and Juliette, I'd found strength. Eric believed in me too.

Sofia, eyes sullen, tread across the stones and sank to the ground beside me. She whispered a chant in the foreign tongue of the Noble Ones, manifesting a golden orb that spun around in her palm.

She let it hover towards Eric where it fused with his skin. "That should ease your pain and discomfort. I will heal you as soon as we have the time and strength to do so. Hold out until then."

Sofia, with her High Priestess abilities, could cure all kinds of illnesses and plagues. So why did she need to wait?

I stared at her, longing to question her and demand her healing abilities. I couldn't have Eric die. Yet I couldn't find the words to ask her.

How could I demand her to heal my friend when she was suffering—walking straight through the place where she'd been held prisoner for so long?

"Sofia, I know this is difficult for you, but I really need you to heal Eric."

"I can't. Not yet," she said. "Using my healing abilities will weaken me, and I need to be at full strength to destroy the portal."

"Let's hope we do it quickly. I can't let him die."
I glanced at him.

Through the opening of the cavern, I fixed my
gaze on a slight crack in the darkness. A sliver of
light shone through, poring over the dead trees. I
relished the sight of it until it disappeared. I hadn't
seen the sun for a long time, and I didn't understand
how the world hadn't turned into an icy wasteland.
But there was a lot about this realm that didn't make
sense, like how the realm was fused with magic, how
it accepted more evil than good.

Magic ran through the earth, through its trees and
mountains and waters. The legend said Arogath had
a mind of its own and therefore could retaliate if it so
desired. Lake Delendil represented this at its core.
But after all the suffering Arogath endured, surely it
would have done something about it by now if that
were true.

Perhaps the world acted through its Elementals,
but the darkness poisoned the Undines and perhaps
had done the same to many of the others.

I sighed when the light vanished. Would the gods
disappear with it?

"What are your ideas?" Aneirin asked Valneris as
he stifled a yawn.

"I've been thinking…the portal was opened by
the Dark Mages in retaliation to the betrayal of the
Orcs who drained hundreds of them for their magic.
We know that blood magic is connecting them *to* the
darkness and the creatures that have crossed through
the portal," Valneris said, his eyes glistening.

"Evalyn, you don't need to neutralise their magic on your own. Same goes for you, Sofia."

"He's right," she muttered.

My gaze flickered to her, and I relaxed my shoulders, pleased with her contribution to the conversation.

"What do you suggest we do?" Aneirin asked, his face marked with displeasure.

I leaned my elbows on my lap. They wouldn't have brought a flawed plan to my attention. They must have faith in their strategy.

"All we have to do is weaken the enemy," Valneris added.

Then it clicked. A large bulk of the enemy were Demons.

Aneirin tutted, frowning at the Elves before him. "You expect Evalyn to do that on her own?" he questioned. "Are you stupid?"

"We knew you'd say that." Valneris smirked. "I have it all figured out. Evalyn will stay protected at all times. We will defend her and defeat any creatures with a true physical form. Sofia can help. All they have to do is destroy enough Demons to close the portal."

"Then we'd split up," Theodas said. "Sofia will get Evalyn out of Southkeep and to safety, while the rest of us focus our attack on the Dark Mages to stop them from reopening the portal and to end their tyranny once and for all."

"I'm not okay with this." I sat straight. "I was on board with your plan until the mention of us splitting up. That's never a good idea."

"We don't have another option." Kiirion's lips curved in a sad, crooked smile, yet the glint in his eyes remained. "It'll keep you and the baby safe. We have a real shot at ending the darkness and stopping the Dark Mages for good. Then we can start rebuilding this realm we swore to protect."

"Have you thought of a way to get the Dark Mages to reverse the curse on the Goblins?" I asked. They were right. I couldn't offer a better plan.

"We've thought of that too." Theodas tucked a stray piece of golden hair behind his ear. "Once we've slain enough of the Demons, the Dark Mages will be weakened by their blood magic connection. They'll have no choice. Their downfall will undo their curse."

"You think it will work?" Aneirin laughed. He tutted loud in dismay once again, his gaze darting across the room.

"I have an idea." Sofia found her voice. "There will be too many Demons for Evalyn and me to slay alone, let alone the Dark Mages. Right now, no sword can destroy a Demon because they don't have a physical form. I can enchant the swords."

"How would you do that?" Kiirion said.

"It's a spell I've known for quite some time, but of course, never needed it," she said. "Although, I must warn you—it comes with a consequence."

My attention perked. "Sword enchantment? Wait, I read something about that in my spell book."

"What is it?" she said.

I pulled out my book, then flicked to the correct page. "See here? The protection spell will create a dome around my allies, but there's handwriting here. It can't be used in conjunction with weapon enchantments."

"That's your mother's writing," Aneirin said. "I suppose now would be the right time to tell you about her involvement in the last war."

"I know of her involvement—she encouraged the Elementals to help." I glanced at him.

"Well, yes, but there's more to it than that. Your mother enchanted our blades when we needed to fight the Demons during their last appearance. Of course, back then we didn't know the implications that this protection dome would have on the enchantment."

"What happened?"

"Those of us who used the blades could no longer be protected by the dome," he said. "Your mother wanted to use both spells for the ultimate protection, not knowing that they counteracted each other."

"We'll need to be quick about it. We must focus on slaying as many Demons as possible. They're connected to the Dark Mages through blood, so once the Demons are destroyed, the portal will collapse, and the Dark Mages will fall with it."

"Let's hope it works." Valneris bowed his head, then returned his gaze to me. "We'll set out tomorrow, but first, we should all rest. Including you, Evalyn."

He lay flat on his back and turned towards the wall of the cavern. The others followed suit. I, however, lingered on the precipice of consciousness for a while longer, tossing and turning, discomfited by the sheer silence surrounding us. There was no rustling in the branches or across the ground. There was no *life* around us.

We were surrounded by nothing, no signal of our former lives in a beautiful realm. This fuelled my burning desire to fulfil my duty and bring into this world a healthy son who would reunite the realm.

Throughout the night, I awoke, restless. With every waking moment, I gave my word to the gods that I would destroy the portal.

———————～ᵕ～———————

The men stirred from their sleep when a wind whistled through the opening of the cavern. We set off in search of some food on the way towards Southkeep. With no wildlife around to be hunted, we were left hungry. My stomach moaned and grumbled.

My friends rummaged through the remaining shrubs, foraging for any edible berries. What they found wasn't a lot, but it would do for now. Perhaps, when we reached the borders of Southkeep, we'd be able to search a home for some stale bread if we were lucky.

The blackened sky chilled the ground we walked on. The bitter wind prickled the skin of my cheeks. I pulled my cloak tight around me and my protruding bump, and we continued down a winding path through broken, twisted trees until we reached the clearing. The cracked ground opened in front of us, revealing more barren lands and a tall fence ahead.

"Southkeep is just beyond the wall." Xurek pointed into the distance at a low wall made of loose rubble.

Southkeep stretched out before us. Sofia's location spell had revealed this as the place to find the portal.

Fires crackled ahead. My heart thrummed. A low hum rumbled. The portal.

"There will be plenty of Demons." Xurek's gaze scanned the surroundings in search of enemies or any sign of threat.

We neared the fence; the rumbling sounds of movement rose high in the air.

"They're destroying the machines." He gripped his hammer, peering over the wall. We crouched, backs against the stones, awaiting his signal to move. "Can you imagine being locked up in a machine, submerged in liquid that drained everything from you, with only enough left to keep you breathing?"

"Are you going soft now, Xurek?" Kiirion asked.

Although the High Elves had long since welcomed Xurek in amongst them, I wasn't one hundred percent sure they trusted him. Yet, he had given them no reason not to be trusted.

Would Felix react the same way if he were here? I frowned at Kiirion, and he ducked his head.

"Of course not," Xurek snapped. "But everything leads back to the Orcs. They're the reason we're in this mess."

"Let's just stick to the plan *you* put forth." Aneirin waved his hand. "We must remain focused."

Xurek had confirmed the sightings of Dark Mages destroying the machines, but no other enemies. I'd imagined us captured and killed by the Demons, the Riders, or any other foul creation of the Dark Mages by now. Something didn't add up.

Perhaps they lingered within the confinements of Southkeep, building on their strength before dispersing across the realm even further. We hadn't crossed paths with them at all since our departure from the hideaway.

Once everyone else was dead, the Dark Mages, their Demons, and the Ezen Riders would conquer the rest of Arogath. The portal would allow more to crawl through its connection to the Beyond.

Xurek signalled us to rise from our crouched positions behind the stone wall that separated us from Southkeep. Lucky for us, there were many intact buildings offering cover as we moved through the area. Kiirion shielded his eyes with his hand and strained forward, scanning the settlement whilst the others freed their swords from their scabbards, taking each step slow across the cracked mud.

The ground beneath my feet rotted and decayed, and pits of fire burst through the cracks, shooting ash and black smoke to join the darkness in the sky.

Then I saw the portal. The very thing that was killing the realm

day by day. Its dark metal structure curved upwards, a hypnotic sight to behold. My skin tingled in amazement, muddling with the sudden coldness biting at my core.

The red haze confirmed its blood magic connection. It stood upon the opposite slope in the distance with an expanse of land separating us, dipping into a valley, where many Demons gathered.

Xurek's gaze fixed on me. I carried the prophesied child, thus was the main target of elimination. My vision blurred, and their plan wiped from my memory. I remained rooted to the spot.

His gaze softened.

"You'll do well, my queen," he said in a voice no one else could hear. "Have faith."

I sucked in a deep breath before following Xurek behind the dotted buildings, concealed from the enemies' line of sight. The men followed, single file, swords drawn in preparation. I flattened my sweating palms against my cloak.

"Let's get this over and done with," Eric muttered, eyes hollow from the plague. Sofia fused another bolt of her golden, healing magic with his skin.

Dipping my head in acknowledgement, I was unable to offer any words in response.

Xurek halted behind the last building, closest to the portal and still hidden from our enemies. He tossed his hammer from one hand to the other, then repeated several more times.

I placed my hand on his shoulder, and his muscles tensed below my fingertips. His gaze darted to mine, wide and alert.

"What is it?"

"They're here," he murmured.

I peered around the corner of the hut to view the gathering Dark Mages and Ezen Riders.

Jodie Angell

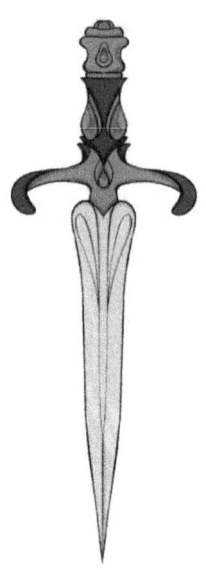

Chapter Eighteen

Demons and Dark Mages patrolled the outskirts of the valley while the Ezen Riders remained close to the portal.

A machine created by the Orcs, stood disengaged at their mercy. The Dark Mages, with one simple burst of colour from their hands, fired their magic at the machine, shattering it into thousands of fragments that rained upon the ground.

Dotted across the valley were huge crates containing the Orcs. How had the Dark Mages managed to capture them?

I narrowed my eyes onto the caged Orcs. For the first time, I longed for them to be freed, to balance the scales and eliminate the threat of the Dark Mages.

"We're outnumbered." I frowned. "Sofia, now would be a good time for that enchantment."

She nodded, then took each sword from the High Elves and Aneirin, lay it in front of her on the ground. She lifted her hands above them, and a green, swirling magic wrapped itself around each blade, causing the metal surfaces to glow.

Once they were ready, she handed them back to each owner. "There you go. We must be quick to prevent anyone not in the dome from being severely injured."

Xurek gripped his weapon, then his gaze fixed upon the imprisoned Orcs. His own kind. "We'll scout the perimeter. Keep an eye out for any weaknesses in their defences."

My shoulder muscles tensed. Thus far, there'd been no sign of Felix. Perhaps he was nearby, and I dreaded to think what sort of condition I'd find him in.

We remained rooted to the cracked terrain underfoot. Someone entered the hut we stood against. Waiting until the door closed, we tiptoed around it and ducked beneath the window to avoid being seen.

We darted behind the next building, making our way around the outskirts of the southern tip of Southkeep, towards the portal. The Demons patrolled the area, weaving their way around the huts and several left through the fence we'd come through.

"Does your magic make any noise?" Eric flicked his focus from Sofia to me, pupils dilated.

"No," she answered.

I pressed myself into the shadows of the buildings and nearby trees. Our surroundings were blurring with the darkness, the red haze of the portal one of few sources of light. I strained my eyes and flinched— fire burst from the cracks in the ground, sending fragments of mud flying into the air.

"Don't forget the Dark Mages have the ability to manipulate you into doing whatever they want. They have the Crimson Kiss." Xurek guided us behind a larger hut with thatched roofing and dusty windows. "We were lucky enough not to have experienced it in the Badlands."

"What happens if they manage to manipulate us?" Aneirin asked. Instead of his usual mockery or presumptions of knowledge, his question seemed genuine. His brows furrowed, and his eyes glimmered. With what, I wondered. Fear?

"Anything," Sofia answered, her icy tone shooting a chill down my spine.

I stared at the dancing shadows of the fire along the floor to the left of the house we hid behind. I held my breath as I heard the whooshing sound of a Demon nearby. A glow emanated from the tainted soul, shining onto the huts as they hovered. I gestured for the men to stay back.

The sounds grew louder as the Demon drew nearer. Then it appeared. An ominous, coal-black being scanned the area with its red, piercing eyes.

Without a second's delay, I imagined a fiery ball of light and manifested it between my hands. Gritting my teeth, I fired the ball of light at the Demon. It disappeared with a shrill scream, and I drew in my next ragged breath. I clenched my fingers into fists to stop them from trembling.

"Let's move," Theodas whispered. "We're right behind you, Evalyn. Stay as far left as you can to avoid them."

I forced myself to move my heavy legs, ignoring the sharp chill that nipped at my neck.

The Dark Mages returned to the settlement hall towering to the right of the portal. If we proceeded with caution, I could weaken the Demons without the Dark Mages realising. The Riders, however, took up post next to the portal.

I continued down the sloping embankment, drawing closer to the valley. On the far left, a crooked building with jagged fencing stood erect. Iron bars barricaded the windows of the building. Could such a structure be a prison? My heart leapt. If Felix and my mother were inside, they'd have to wait until the area was cleared of enemies.

We used the nearby withering bushes and birch trees to sneak across the wastelands. The pits spat their fire and smoke high into the sky around us.

"There they are." Theodas pointed to a group of Demons materialising in front of us. They pierced my eyes with theirs.

I formed a glowing ball of red light within my hands and launched it at the group of Demons. The ball of light swelled larger than any I'd created before, enriched by the need to protect my people.

A loud, screeching sound pierced through the area as they disintegrated into nothing. The others must have heard it. Soon, the Dark Mages would appear, and we'd be in battle once again.

"Keep fighting the Demons. We'll slay as many as we can," Kiirion said, reminding me of our initial plan. "As soon as the portal starts to weaken, you need to get yourself out of here. Go to the prison, search for Felix and your mother. Take Sofia and stay there until we come to find you."

The Dark Mages emerged from the settlement hall. The High Elves, Xurek, and Eric continued to fight the gathering Demons.

I headed to the right of the portal where the Dark Mages gathered. Sofia raised her hands, ready to fire bolts of magic.

Placing my hand into my pocket, I clutched the pouch of gemstones Juliette had once given me for protection. I closed my eyes and visualised a protective dome with a shimmery surface, much like the portal I was close to.

Once the dome materialised, I let it float towards Xurek, Eric, and

Sofia to provide them protection. From the periphery of my vision, I saw the red glow of the portal dim, meaning Theodas and Valneris were right about their theory.

More Demons swarmed around me in a crescent shape,

separating me from my allies

Balls of red light formed in my hands within seconds, and I fired them both at the group of Demons. Their ethereal bodies disintegrated, and their piercing, bright eyes were the last thing to fade from this world.

Focusing on my own mission, I continued to create red balls of light, destroying any Demon that crossed my path. The red glow of my magic, combined with the fierce light of the fire, stood out, bright against the apocalypse in the sky.

I ignored the dull ache in my ankles which began spreading up my calf muscles and stroked my belly to reassure my baby it would be over soon.

'The connection between the Dark Mages and the creatures of the other side were via blood magic.'

A crackling noise filled the cool air. The noise suggested the infrastructure of the portal was breaking down. The Dark Mages retreated to it, then scanned the area. The number of Demons dwindled, threatening the portal's existence.

The Dark Mages' skin was ice white with black and blue scales, deepening in colour over the contours of their face, contrasting with the red and gold appearance of Light Mages like Sofia and me.

A second wave of Demons hovered around me and my friends. I bit my lip until I tasted blood. Although the balls of light formed in my hands, the Demons were fast enough to manifest in front of me. With every crowd I defeated, more appeared.

I rested my gaze on the Ezen Riders in the background, who observed without intervening. The scales on my arms raised.

Once I weakened enough of the Demons, the portal would collapse, demolishing everything else along with it. They needed their blood magic connection to survive this onslaught.

I swear, my gods, this would be the sole time I am grateful for blood magic.

I crafted the balls of light in my hands but before I could fire them at the crowd of enemies, a Demon caught me, gripping my throat. My fingertips tingled; the life was squeezed from me as it stared at me.

My vision blurred, the oxygen in my body diminishing. With burning lungs, I fought to pull in another breath. If I could manifest another ball of light, I'd be able to get it.

Without warning, the Demon disappeared. My surroundings were covered in a layer of bright, white light as the spell wiped out the remaining Demons in Southkeep, turning them into ash. A screech of rage from the caster spread across the land.

I collapsed to the floor, choking and clutching my throat, desperate for breath. I peered up at the person who'd taken out the last of them with one powerful, magnificent spell. Sofia offered her hand to me and pulled me up from the floor. She scanned me, looking for any damage.

I stared at her, at a loss for words.

Chaos swirled around us, no sound reaching my ears for a moment. Even as our surroundings blurred,

I could see her clearly. She held her shoulders back, and there was a brightness in her eyes. A fire.

We faced the Riders upon their black bears. The Riders' vibrant eyes shone through the darkness. A chill shot down my spine.

I'd never come so close to the Riders, and I recoiled. Wrapping my arms around myself, I leaned into Sofia. The Riders remained fixed by the portal. Could they fear death if they weren't even alive?

With a single shared look between Sofia and me, we initiated a stream of light, a combination of her magnificent white light and my red spell. We fired it towards the Riders until our joined magic crackled with their own black magic.

The impact of their spell jolted me back. I dug my feet into the ground and launched my ball of crimson towards them. The sheer brightness of our charm intertwining with their eerie, grey talon-like magic blocked our vision.

My heart thrummed with the determination to see the end of the war. Every nerve ending in my body burned. A sharp pain shot through my temples, and my vision blurred.

I ignored the burning tiredness coursing through my limbs and forced my magic to continue. But my arms collapsed at my sides and within a second, I disappeared into nothing.

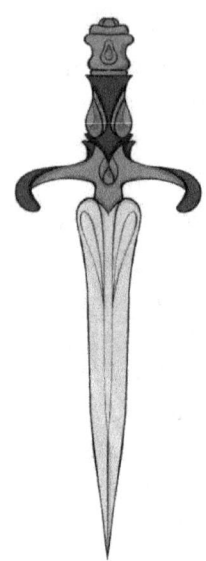

Chapter Nineteen

I'd never given much thought to what it would be like to fall into oblivion, to float around in nothing, to *be* nothing.

Was I dead? Was it over?

I drifted, weightless, in the dark.

I didn't know how long I'd been in this state, but the Ezen Riders lingered in my mind, far away and out of reach. There was no sense of time wherever I was. I hovered through the expanse of nothing. Thoughts weren't whole, nor did they make sense. They were mere resemblances of things I knew.

Jodie Angell

Felix, my mother, the Elves…Lake Delendil…my home.

I was finally free.

"Evalyn?" a muffled voice called from the distance, as if speaking underwater.

A face appeared, indistinct and blurred. I recognised her as Alinar, Felix's old friend. She was unburnt, beautiful, and returned to her elegant Elven self.

So, I *was* on the other side.

"What are you doing here?" She frowned. Then her eyes widened. "This isn't right."

"I'm dead." The words rolled from my mouth with ease, the serenity of this place lulling me into a sense of security. "How do you know my name?"

"I've been watching you," Alinar said with her thin, transparent voice.

"I'm sorry," I reached out to touch her, but my fingers fell through her ethereal form, "that we couldn't save you."

"I've lingered close to Felix's side—he needs you," she said.

"My friends will save him. I promise."

"You must go back. Hurry."

"How?" I gestured to the enveloping darkness. "I'm already dead."

"No," she said. "You're not. This place is Elysium—the Beyond. The place where people go when they're not dead. They just haven't decided whether to stay or to go."

Something panged inside me, perhaps, the strong desire to remain. Yet my need to return to Arogath remained unwavering.

"I'm sorry I can't take you with me." I was consumed by a pain that wasn't mine. Perhaps a guilt—we'd been too late to save her from the fire. "I have to go back."

"Yes, you do." Alinar gazed at me with hollow eyes. Her brown hair cascaded down the length of her torso, floating in eternal Elven beauty. She would be preserved as a Woodland Elf and a servant of the Light Triads forever.

"You need to want it enough. I must go now…" Alinar drifted away, returning to the depths of the Beyond.

"Wait!"

Her figure waned, joining the souls on the other side.

I was alone.

———————⌒⌒———————

Focusing on the burning image of Southkeep and Sofia's fierce face, I returned to my spasming body and collapsed into a heap on the cracked mud. Scrambling to my feet, each step unsteady and shaky, I mustered everything within. Cupping my hands together, I manifested a brilliant, intense red light. It collided with the Ezen Riders and hurtled them backwards. Their wails sliced the air.

With every ounce of energy I could gather, combined with every emotion and memory, I allowed the electric current to course through me. Growing stronger, it became a true part of me. The grey magic of the Riders weakened as their wraith-like forms faded.

"It's working!" Sofia yelled over the crackling of our magic.

I glanced at my hair as it warmed around my neck. It glowed a fiery red. My knees were weak, and my head was pounding, but the spell *was* working.

Their forms flaked away bit by bit, disappearing like dust into the air around them until there was nothing left but the empty space they'd occupied. I staggered into Sofia who caught me in her arms.

"Steady there, Evalyn." She hooked her arms underneath mine.

"I've got you."

"I need...water..."

Sofia pulled the flask from her pouch and lifted it to my lips, pouring its cool contents into my mouth. "That's the first time you've ever done a spell of that magnitude. Well done!" She put the flask away and created a golden, healing orb between her palms. It floated towards me and fused with my skin. "The Ezen Riders have seen this realm once before—a millennium ago—and now they will never see it again. This healing spell should return you to your normal strength until you can rest."

"I should...thank you," I managed. "The Demons are...gone."

The portal's centre was a pale, washed-out hint of red. The Demons let out shrill screams as they fell through the earth, clawing at the ground above as they were dragged back into the other side.

I shot a glance at my allies who were fighting the Dark Mages in the valley. They stayed in their tight formation as they pushed through the crowd. Blood and mud covered their exposed cheeks. The rest of their bodies were protected by armour, and I couldn't spot any other injuries.

I stared at the portal as it collapsed before me. My chest lurched with our triumph.

The portal groaned as it fell to the ground.

Large fragments of the portal structure crashed down the side of the valley, landing a mere few feet away from my allies. Kiirion stumbled amongst the debris, but Valneris hauled him to his feet. He pushed Kiirion to the end of the valley. I started towards my friends with my palms cupped together, ready to conjure another ball of magic.

"We need to go!" Sofia called over the groaning, scraping sounds of steel against rock.

"The worst of the battle is over." She drew me away from the valley.

"What about the Dark Mages?" The sound of swords clinking against swords grew distant. "How long will it take for the bond of blood magic to break?"

"It can't be too long." She hurried towards the prison, leaving our friends behind. "We need to get Felix, and your mother, and get out of here!"

Sofia didn't give me a chance to object. I struggled to look over my shoulder at the chaos below, hoping the gods would allow my allies to survive.

———⌣———

We sprinted towards the prison. Sofia flung open the wooden door, then led the way down the corridor.

"Evalyn, we must be quick," she said. "As soon as the Blood Magic bond breaks, any surviving Dark Mages will be immobilised for a short amount of time. It'll give our friends enough time to catch up with us, but then we need to get back to the boat."

The staircase led us underground to a damp and dark layer of prison cells. Water dripped from the ceiling, creating puddles on the floor. The cells were formed in a maze-like arrangement, made of concrete.

We found Felix in the third cell. His head lolled to one side, and he was covered in dirt and dried blood, the features of his face I'd memorised now difficult to distinguish. His wrists were bloody and chafed from being bound and each finger was covered in a thick layer of blood.

My heart leapt and plummeted in my chest, each breath coming quicker than the last. He was *alive*. He was there, in front of me. In this world of darkness, the gods shed some light by returning him to me.

"He's not conscious," Sofia said. "Help me take him upstairs. Then we'll find your mother."

I reached out to Felix and stroked his arm, shaking. He did not respond. I slumped against the water slick wall, tears falling, and clutched his hand.

I twisted the cap off my flask and pressed it to his dry lips—the water dripping from his mouth.

"You need to be strong for me," I choked out. "I need you." I wiped my tears away and glanced at Sofia. "Together."

We hoisted Felix off the ground. With my heart hammering in my ears, I helped drag him out of the underground floor, and up the stairs.

Xurek, covered in lacerations, blundered in through the prison entrance. Eric, Aneirin, and the Elves trailed in behind him.

"The Dark Mages are immobilised—their blood magic connection is leaving their bodies." He bent, then scooped Felix into his arms. "Find your mother. Hurry."

Aneirin dashed ahead. I hurried after him, down the stairs, then weaved through the underground layer of cells. My chest tightened, and I couldn't breathe. My vision blurred with black spots and the room spun. My mother...I may meet my *mother.* After so long apart. The possibility of it seemed almost farfetched.

Aneirin bent into a cell. I edged closer, clenching my teeth. His back straightened. He was holding what looked like a bony corpse with long, matted hair covering her face. I moved closer still to see a fragile woman.

He carried the woman, and I caught glimpses of her small feet, covered in dirt, hanging over his arm. He walked away before I could see her face.

In a frantic blur, my thoughts swirled until they mingled into one confusing state. I managed to keep moving as my hands sweated with the desperate urge to meet my mother, to *have* a mother I could call my own.

At the staircase, Aneirin lowered himself onto the bottom step, cradling the small woman in his arms.

I stepped closer and brushed the hair away from her face. The thick layer of dirt on her skin and the twenty years of separation made her unrecognisable. "Is this my mother? Mya?"

"Yes," he croaked.

"We need to take her to Sofia—she will heal her." I urged him up the stairs.

When we reach the others at the prison entrance, Felix groaned in Xurek's arms.

"Evalyn," he muttered in a weak, trembling voice. "The baby…"

I glanced at him, and my breath caught in my throat. There were several, large wounds across his emaciated body. I climbed the steps to sit next to him and cupped his cheeks. His eyes were hollow. I swept his hair away from his eyes. He was alive.

"Me and the baby are fine." I traced my finger and thumb across his cheek where his scar would be, hidden beneath the filth. "How are you feeling? We'll get you back to the Citadel as soon as possible."

"I'm…okay," he said, voice paper-thin. He rested his forehead against mine. "We'll be okay."

"Yes." I kissed him, not caring for the muck on his face. "The Ezen Riders have been defeated. The portal is no more."

I turned to my mother, who stirred in and out of consciousness in Aneirin's arms and couldn't find any words to say to her. The gods had given me a miracle and returned her to me. Yet, I had no words to say to this woman.

The Dark Triads held my mother imprisoned and abused her all these years to the point where she didn't know how to formulate a single sentence. She'd been broken into nothing more than a shell.

Sofia rubbed her hands together. "I'll heal your mother and Felix first, then Eric."

She produced a soft, green light within the palms of her hands, spinning it around and caressing it like a small child. Healing magic was the most important, precious magic of all and took time and effort to master. I admired her for it.

She muttered her chant in the tongue of the Noble Ones, and the green light lifted from her hands, floating upwards where it expanded into a light, emerald blanket that fell over Felix and my mother.

"You'll need to keep a hold of Felix and Mya as they will need to rest. Eric, come closer." She gestured to him.

He shifted closer—the plague festering on the upper half of his body.

Sofia healed his wounds with the same spell, then outstretched her arm for him to hold onto. "Will you be strong enough to make it back to the boat?"

"I'll get it done," he said.

"If we have destroyed enough of the Dark Mages, they should be able to reverse the curse on the Krears and return them to their natural state," Sofia said.

"We need to get back to the temple and gather the civilians onto the boats. From there, we can head to Lake Delendil." I glanced at her.

"We should hurry back to the horses," she said, then turned to check on Mya who grumbled and stirred awake. "I need you to keep your eyes open, okay? Just until we get to the horses. Can you do that for me?"

Mya nodded once, then closed her eyes again. Sofia grumbled but performed the spell, cloaking the room in a bright light.

We returned to the horses where we left them. They grazed the sparse shards of grass next the huts. Once Felix was slouched on the saddle, I climbed up behind him. He rested against my chest as I grabbed the reins. The horse beat his hooves into the trodden ground.

Sofia hoisted herself onto her horse and propped my mother up into a seated position in front of her. The Elves mounted theirs. Xurek held Eric steady against them as they rode together.

We galloped away from the abandoned settlement and through the tunnel Xurek led us through.

When we reached the cavern, we dismounted, then helped Felix and my mother inside. An evening wind whistled through the cave, raising the hairs on my neck.

I cradled Felix's head and tipped some water into his mouth, then did the same for my mother while Sofia collected sticks for a fire.

"If we camp here, we can hunt for food." She stacked the twigs, then lit them with a spark of magic. She leaned back against the cave wall and stretched her leg.

"I'll search for something to eat. Berries, cacti—anything at this point," Valneris said, then left the cave. Theodas, Kiirion, and Xurek joined him.

A while later, they returned with a scant number of fat bugs to eat. It wouldn't be as nutritious as meat, but there was nothing we could hunt.

"It's not much, but there isn't much in the way of wildlife or plants around here," Kiirion said. "At least we know why it's called the Barren Territories."

The following morning, embers from the previous night's fire drifted through the cave, fluttering across the dusty floor.

I pressed the canteen to my lips for a drink.

"It's time to go." Sofia stroked my arm. Her eyes were hollow, and bags formed underneath. She, and the others, mounted.

Using the stirrup, I pushed myself up onto the saddle.

Felix rubbed his neck, then stretched his back.

"Can you manage to get onto the horse, or do you need a hand?" Xurek asked.

"I'll manage," he said. "Sofia, your healing magic is impressive."

She smiled.

Felix hoisted himself onto the back of my horse, then placed an arm either side of me. We set off towards the boat, leaving the camp behind. As we rode, I spared no further moment and relayed my journey across the Great Sea to him.

"The Krears sound fascinating," he said.

"They are an interesting people for sure."

When we arrived at the temple, the civilians gathered around. Katrin and Laurent stood close by. The Goblins had already transitioned into their natural, true forms. The Krears. They were a humanoid race with the same bone structure as a Human or an Elf, but their skin was thick and covered in scales, and horns sprouted from the tops of their heads.

The leader of the pack had pale skin, and his horns were the largest of them all. Zander.

The others were tall and slender, with a slight arched spine and as terrifying to witness as they were when in Goblin form. But up close, a kindness formed in their eyes. A glimmer much like the one that glistened in Xurek's eyes beside me—a warm, affectionate glow.

"I can't believe it. The curse is truly broken." Zander's eyes widened. "Thank you."

"You're welcome." I clutched Sofia, who kept her arm wrapped around me. "I must rest now. We have injured people to tend to." He nodded.

I dragged myself towards the room where the Humans were keeping Felix and my mother comfortable. My mother lay flat on a bed of hay with her hair brushed away from her face.

I stayed in the doorway, watching them as they rested.

Felix stirred, his lips tilting into a smile when his gaze fell on me. "You're here. We're together. I'm so sorry I couldn't help destroy the portal."

I crossed the room to his side and stroked the hair away from his face. I kissed his forehead and my heart flipped. "You have nothing to be sorry for. You're here with me, and that's all that matters."

A tear rolled down my cheek, and he wiped it away. I clutched his fingers to my lips and kissed each one. "I will thank the gods every day for bringing you back to me."

Sofia entered the room. "Come with me, Evalyn. They will both be fine—they just need to rest." She took me by the arm and steered me away. "You'll have time to talk to them both later. Now it is time for me to look after you."

I glanced at Felix's hollow, tired eyes. I couldn't leave him when he'd just returned to me.

"Go, Evalyn, I'll be fine," he said.

"I will come back to check on you soon. I promise."

Sofia escorted me to the quiet room on the second floor of the temple where I'd slept before we left for Southkeep.

With the drapes drawn across the windows and doorway, she helped me strip out of my dirty clothes until I stood in nothing but underwear. She lowered me onto the hay bed until I lay flat.

"Let's have a look at how this baby is doing." She pressed her warm hands against my abdomen.

She prodded around the lower area of my belly with her eyes closed and leaned forward. She listened to the heartbeat, although I couldn't hear it myself.

"He's happy." She opened her eyes to offer me a warm smile.

"And he is sorry for hurting your back so much." I laughed, although every inch of my body ached.

"Sofia." I climbed off the bed. "Could we spare some water? I'd like a bath."

"Of course," she said. "I'll get the Humans to run one for you right away."

Sofia left through the doorway and sometime afterwards, several female Humans with a small, steel bath and buckets of warm water entered. They helped me into the bath and poured the water over me. One of the Humans lathered a rag with a homemade soapy yet scentless concoction and rubbed my skin with it.

I stayed in the tub with my eyes closed, allowing the steam to loosen my chest until each breath came easier. I focused inwards on the well-being of my baby.

Kiirion, Theodas, and Valneris were having their wounds tended to by the Humans, mumbling amongst themselves in a whisper I couldn't hear. The healers moved Felix into the other chamber where he could rest with Eric, away from the chatter of the High Elves. Aneirin remained leaning over my mother's fragile form, caressing her hand.

I wondered what he'd say to her when she woke. I couldn't imagine her reaction. It'd be the first time she'd seen him since the day she was kidnapped by the Dark Mages. What would she say to me when her gaze fell upon the daughter she hadn't seen or touched in so long? The prospect of the reunion made me tremble.

My friends *survived*. The war was over. And yet, I couldn't shake the dread I'd been consumed with for the last few months.

The Orcs still needed dealing with, but for now, we *were* safe.

When the Humans finished tending and cleaning the High Elves's wounds, I joined them in the courtyard of the temple.

"There was a moment when I didn't think we'd do it, Evalyn," Kiirion admitted. We sat on the floor of the courtyard with dead weeds sprouting from in-between the cobbles. They were smooth and shiny in some areas and worn with age in others. "There were so many of them."

"At one point, I thought Aneirin was going to make a run for it." Theodas laughed, even though he stared at me with a blank expression.

"You used to be good friends with him." I raised an eyebrow. "You were so overwhelmed with joy when you were reunited with him at the hideaway."

"We were friends twenty years ago." He shrugged. "He has changed, and for the worse.

342

Before the last battle, he was proud, and courageous. We all believed he was dead, but to know he ran away, and lived a whole other life. We still have no idea why he left."

"Neither do I, but I'm sure to find out. I'll speak with him once the dust has settled. I want to ensure my mother is okay first."

A heavy silence hung between us. I stared at the cobbles, trying to believe we were okay, that it was really over.

"How is your mother, Evalyn?" Theodas said.

"I've not spoken to her as she's still resting." I traced lines with my finger along the dirty concrete slabs. I yearned to crawl up into the cot with Felix and sleep in his arms. "I can't imagine what it'll be like to talk to her or what we'll even say."

"You should get some rest," he said. "You need it. For your sake and the sake of your child. We will rouse you if there is further news on your mother's welfare."

I fell in and out of sleep, tossing and turning and unable to find comfort on the hay bed. The images of my mother and Felix lying still flashed in my mind and tortured the minimal sleep I managed to get. Sofia checked on me several times throughout the night and wiped a hot, wet cloth across my forehead and ankles to relieve the swelling.

A while later I stirred as people muttered in the courtyard of the temple. I eased onto my feet, waddled through the doorway, and leaned against the balcony for support. The Krears were stacking their gold into baskets.

Kiirion's gaze caught mine from within the crowd, and he edged his way out to join me.

"What's going on?" My eyes were blurred from sleep, and my body hung heavy and sluggish against the balcony railing.

"The Krears are packing their belongings." He smiled. "We get to go home. It's over."

I nodded in response, glad for the Goblins but unable to speak words of acceptance or agreement. No matter how much I repeated what he said in my mind, I couldn't allow myself to trust his words.

Kiirion was the youngest of the High Elves and although his features were harsh and striking, his smile softened the planes of his face. He became childlike. I didn't want to take his happiness away.

"Where will they go?" I asked him. "The Krears lived underground in the temple for many centuries, but where would become their home now?"

"I'm not sure." His gaze travelled to mine where it lingered. "They'll be doing what everyone else will have to do. Rebuild from nothing. Start again."

"We could send soldiers to each settlement to help with the rebuilding." I thought of our allies who'd lost so much in this war—they gave their time and lives to fight by my side—it was time for me to give back to them. "Everybody's home has been destroyed in this war."

"That's a good way to start." Xurek smiled.

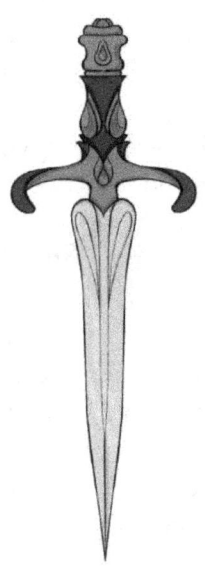

Chapter Twenty

The next day, we left the temple and returned to the surface. The heavy, black clouds hanging over the realm had dispersed, allowing rays of sunlight to burst through and warm my cheeks. It would be a slow return to normality, but life would start to sprout between the cracks in the ground and we could rebuild.

After using the dowsing rods to find more water, we boarded the ships. Sofia tended the injured, manifesting balls of healing magic to soothe their pain. The civilians helped where they could, clearing the decks and lifting the sails in preparation for our departure. The boats sailed along the length of the shoreline for a while. The Elves used old nets to catch fish.

Felix, Eric, and my mother were guided into the cabin where they could rest away from the bustle on deck. Sofia followed them, carrying a pail of water and several cloths. I trailed after her and closed the cabin door behind me. Taking the flint Sofia placed on the wooden cabinet, I lit the candles which blanketed the room with an orange glow.

"How are you feeling?" I helped Felix onto the left cot and propped up the worn pillow.

He took my hands in his and stared up at me with his hazel, almond eyes. "Much better, but my body aches."

I squeezed his hands. "Close your eyes. Rest."

"Listen to your queen." Sofia smiled and tucked my mother under the blanket on the other cot. She lay unconscious, mumbling in her sleep. Sofia looked at me. "She will be fine. My magic will heal her."

I nodded, placed a kiss on Felix's head, then returned to Xurek's side. His bulky hands clasped the ship's wheel.

"I wonder if we will ever return to this part of Arogath." I leaned against the rail. "For as long as we've known, the clans of the Light and Dark Triads have remained on the mainlands."

"You are a queen, Evalyn." Xurek glanced at the lapping waves glistening under the new sunlight. "You can return at any time. The Krears are staying here—they will welcome you."

"I will give this place an official name and put its mark upon the maps. I will suggest a new name for the island. If the Krears are planning on making a home here, I'll want their verdict. They have no ruler—perhaps we can come to some sort of arrangement."

"What are you going to do about your father?" He peered at me from the corner of his eyes.

"I'm not sure…"

The journey stretched, passing slowly yet my heartbeat quickened with each day we grew closer to home. The civilians crowded the deck, huffing and puffing with the eager anticipation of reaching the mainland.

I glanced over the edge of the boat in search of the Undines who'd sought refuge in the poisoned waters of the Great Sea. For all I knew, they'd disappeared. Perhaps the effect of the water had worn off when the blood magic connection was severed.

As Queen of Arogath, I needed to maintain a healthy alliance with the Elementals and would be sure to visit the Galae Pools, the Vesuvius Caves, and the Highland Trees.

———————

When we docked at the shore of the mainland territories several days later, I waddled from the deck to begin the journey north towards Lake Delendil. Eric, Felix, and my mother were strapped to the backs of two Centaurs who'd offered to carry them home for us.

"It'll be best for them to travel this way so they can conserve their energy," Sofia said.

Soon, we reached Westwilde, the burned home of the Gnomes.

"We couldn't be more thankful," Gnovash said as the rest of the Gnomes dispersed around the village, starting to clear the rubble. "You're always welcome in this part of the territory."

I smiled at her. She placed her hand on my swollen abdomen and returned the smile.

"May you have a safe delivery and a healthy son," she said.

"I'll be sure to write to you." I smiled. "I will send men to help you restore Westwilde."

"Please do. I'd like to know how you're doing." Gnovash picked up rubble around her. "I wish the best for Felix and your mother too." She nodded to them.

"They seem better already," I said. "I hope for a quick recovery for both of them."

Their skin appeared brighter, and a rose blush returned to their cheeks. Eric, who also spent his journey upon the back of a Centaur, still slept, recovering from the plague curse. He stirred a few times from his slumber during our voyage across the Great Sea, but nothing enough to prove he was okay.

Sofia placed her hand on my shoulder. "Have hope. He's strong. He will get through it."

"Your Majesty, there's something Laurent and I want to tell you and Aneirin." Katrin glanced at me. "We were discussing living arrangements on our voyage, and we've decided to stay at Bluefair Fort for a while with Eric's permission. We can be useful there and help with the plans to rebuild what's been lost."

"Are you sure this is what you both want?" Aneirin asked.

"We're certain," Laurent said. "Although I must thank you for your friendship, and I hope our paths cross again."

"I'm sure they will." Aneirin embraced them both in turn.

"Farewell, both. You're welcome at the Citadel any time." I smiled.

The next few days were long and consisted of sleeping in uncomfortable barns and travelling northward to Lake Delendil. As we passed Bluefair Fort, we parted with the allies who lived there. Eric however, stayed with us for the rest of the journey.

As we grew closer to Lake Delendil, we rode through Rushdale Forest, the burned home of the woodland Elves, where Alinar's body was found.

Should I tell Felix of my time in Elysium with her? She'd been the reason I came back to this world.

Felix rode beside me, growing stronger every day. He smiled at me as he patted his horse's hide.

Our journey progressed in a blur. The rest stops were frequent, many at my demand.

We approached the trees that revealed the lake before us. The water glimmered under the sun, rippling against the slight breeze. I let out a gasp, and tears prickled my eyes. The stone soldiers were destroyed, stacked, and dotted around the grounds. Piles of debris covered most of the entrance into the

Citadel. Although the bridge and Citadel were made of a multi-coloured glass, unbroken and withstanding the war, it seemed dull and lifeless.

"I see the darkness has taken a toll on our home." Theodas' lips curled upwards in distaste. "Perhaps the new sunlight will revitalise it."

We made our way through the rubble and into the Citadel to see cracks in the glass floor.

With great care, I climbed the stairs to my room. Someone had rifled through my things. All my clothes were scattered across the floor, my drawers pulled out of the dressers, and the bedding shredded.

"Are you all right?" Sofia asked from the doorway of my room. I pivoted to see a brightness in her eyes. "Your mother is waking up, and Felix is doing well, if you'd like to see them. I checked him over to be on the safe side. He's doing perfectly fine."

"Thank you." My pulse quickened as the reunion with my mother grew nearer. Even with the time on our journey back from Southkeep, I'd found it difficult to find the words I would say to the woman who gave me life.

Sofia led the way to a quiet room at the back of the Citadel where my mother, Felix, and Eric recovered. A fire in the corner warmed the space with its comforting orange and red glow.

"Your mother hasn't said a word," she warned. "She's still in shock."

I eyed my mother, unsure whether to edge closer to her side. An impulse fluttered through my body. A need to protect her. "Is there anything I can do to help?"

She was clean now, dressed in a new pair of tan pants and cream shirt that was rucked around the neck. Her face glimmered under the candlelight, like Sofia's iridescent skin. She was here, with me. My mother.

Sofia continued to tend to my mother, brushing her hair across her shoulders. Mya remained still and conscious on the bed and her gaze shifted to mine for a brief moment.

Overcome with nerves and a nauseating knot in my stomach, I flicked my gaze to Felix instead. Perched on his bed, he stretched his arms out and welcomed me into his embrace. I weaved my fingers through his hair, then rested my face against his chest and inhaled his sweet sandalwood scent.

I held him tight. Each of his breaths were hollow as if they were remnants of panic.

I thanked the gods for bringing him home to me.

"I'm glad you're okay, though." He shook his head and kissed the back of my hands instead of probing me further.

"How is Eric?" I glanced at Sofia who smiled at us.

"Although my magic healed him of the plague, his body is still recovering." Her smile disappeared, and the twinkle diminished from her eyes. "But not to worry, Evalyn. I won't be leaving his side."

"I'm going to get some dinner," Felix said, then eyed my mother.

"Of course. I'm going to stay with my mother for a while," I said before he left.

Sofia handed me the brush. I pulled it through my mother's auburn hair. Once it was detangled, I set the brush aside, then lowered myself into a chair opposite her.

"Hello, Mother." I cleared my throat.

She kept her empty gaze fixed on the window.

"I have some news for you." I kept my voice soft and quiet, so as not to frighten her. "You're going to be a grandmother." Her face remained ashen.

I took her hand in mine, then rested it against my bump. My mother's gaze peeled from the window to me. She blinked several times, then jolted when the baby kicked. Her eyes sparkled.

"Do you want something to eat?" I stroked her hand with my thumb. "I can take you down to the banquet hall. Aneirin is downstairs too—he'll be eager to speak with you when you're ready." She gave a small nod.

I placed her hand in the nook of my elbow, then escorted her out of the room and through the ground level of the Citadel to the banquet hall. The servants prepared food, but it was a simple meal of breads and cheeses with a sparse number of grapes. The darkness had done terrible things to this world, killing most crops and plants, and it would take a long time to return the realm to its former state.

"Here we are." I helped her into her seat. I held her hand in my left and placed the fork between her fingers.

Once she managed to curl her fingers around the fork, she reached for a small piece of cheese on the plate. Her malnourished form curved forward as she shovelled food into her mouth. She swallowed a mouthful, then glanced at me.

"I'm sorry," she whispered. "I've missed so much of your life."

Her eyes shined with a regret I couldn't understand. Her capture, her absence, hadn't been one of her own making. I would never understand the suffering she'd endured at the Southkeep prison.

"Shh…" I shifted the tumbles of hair out of her eyes. Her knuckles turned white as she clenched her fingers around the fork. "Another time. Eat."

While I knew I needed to make plans for the restoration work, I wanted to enjoy a moment with my long-lost mother. I sank into the chair next to her. Between mouthfuls of my own food, I scooped more cheese and bread onto her plate for her to eat.

The sunlight poured in through the coloured glass of the Citadel, caressing my cheeks with its light glow. I smiled, beginning to appreciate the things I'd taken for granted. I'd jump out of bed every morning and dash towards the window, expecting the sun to be in the sky, as beautiful as ever, and I wouldn't think twice about it. Children would play in the courtyard while the locals sold game and trinkets at the nearby market. People would work together to pick fruit from the trees and tend to the corn in the fields. But when something so normal, so natural, was taken away from us, I couldn't allow myself to live an ignorant life.

I waited with her until she finished her food, then assisted her outside to the lake. We sat on the dull grass next to the water, overlooking the ripples glimmering under the sun. With shoulders resting against each other, we lay in peace, encompassed by a pleasant silence.

Then my attention pricked at the sound of something delicate. It was a far-off sound, light and soft like a bird.

My eyes widened at the kingfisher fluttering by. Her songs drifted the air as she joined a nest in a tree across the lake. Then the dull patting sounds of marching began. A small army of Elven guards were leaving the Citadel for the damaged settlements of the Fertile Territories. My friends remained home, offering all the protection I would need.

I observed the guards as they crossed the bridge over the lake and disappeared behind the trees. A serenity surrounded us, soothing our souls, and encouraging us to heal. We watched the water for a while until the sun sank behind the trees. We were safe.

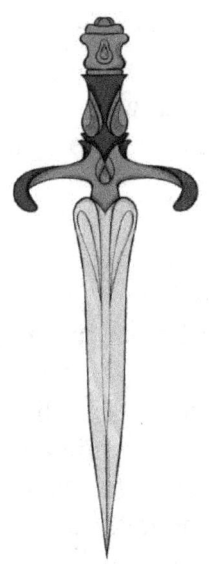

Chapter Twenty-One

"There's a letter for you here," Kiirion said as I sat at the table in the council room a few days later. He passed the scroll to me, which was sealed with the wax crest of Westwilde.

"It's from the Gnomes." I scanned the neat writing on the parchment. My lips curved into a smile. "They send their thanks—the guards have reached them with no cause for concern and they hope to start rebuilding in the coming days."

"We have also received word from Bluefair Fort." Theodas leaned forward and intertwined his fingers in front of him. "The Centaurs have been busy helping the Humans rebuild, as well. Katrin and Laurent have settled in well."

"It seems things may be returning to normal," Valneris added.

A silence hung between us. Could we allow ourselves to believe it?

"Have you heard from the other Elementals?" I frowned.

"Not yet," Kiirion said. His eyelids were half closed with shadows forming around them. He'd taken it upon himself to maintain order in the Citadel and stayed up throughout the night. "I am sure we will soon, my queen."

I sat and appreciated the silence of the council room. There wasn't much to say, which wasn't a bad thing. It made a difference from the issues we'd dealt with over the last few months.

"We've also thought of an official name for the Newland." Valneris' lips curved into a wide, joyous smile.

"*Vrecrai*," Kiirion said. "Juliette's family name."

"That's perfect." I beamed. "It will honour her memory forever. Send word to the Krears—offer them my protection and ask if they accept the new name. We must do something for Ascal and the many other innocent people who've perished."

"We will celebrate their lives," Theodas said. "Their deaths will not be in vain."

I rose. "Have the servants prepare a banquet. We will have an evening of laughter and dance after the service."

———————⌣———————

That night, the Elven servants lit torches around the lake and planted new beds of tulips along the shoreline of the water. Torches were lit and positioned throughout the gardens. Candles nestled amongst flowers in a long, wooden boat at the side of the water.

Felix joined me for the service, the dark shadows disappearing from underneath his eyes. He wrapped his arm around my waist, drawing me against him.

Aneirin sat farther away with his arm around my mother.

The air was silent with the slight breeze of a cool evening fluttering around. Above, the sky beamed with the light of thousands of stars now returned to us.

The three remaining High Elves gathered around the wooden boat bedded with beautiful tulips and roses from Lake Delendil's garden.

"Ascal served this realm for many years," Theodas said as the water lapped near his feet and his eyes swelled with grief. The torches around us lit the area—its warm glow collided with the starlight. "And now his service ends. May he rest in peace in the arms of the gods."

"He has brought honour to this realm and to our queen." Kiirion added his own flowers to the boat, placing them in the centre. "But this is not goodbye forever, my dear friend. Just for now. Until we see you again."

"Goodbye, my brother." Valneris added Ascal's sword to the boat. "It is time, my queen."

I sucked in a deep breath. "It is time to reflect and pay tribute to those who have lost their lives during the war. May each of these candles represent everyone we have lost, and I hope they find eternal peace in Elysium."

My gaze lingered on the candles. One for Ascal, Juliette, and one to represent each clan who suffered at the hands of the Dark Triads. I shunted the boat away, then stepped back.

We waited as the boat drifted farther down the lake until it floated in the middle above the connection to the other side. Although there were no bodies to send across the lake, the funeral would be a mark of honour.

Kiirion handed me a bow and arrow. I kept my chin high as I fired the arrow into the sky. My gaze travelled with it until it collided with the boat. The boat burst into flames, illuminating the sacred waters.

───────◦∽◦───────

We returned to the banquet hall, where the candles shone brightly, and musicians created sweet tunes with their violins. The food was served across the long, wooden tables: platters of sunflower seeds, chestnuts, redcurrants, and blackberries with a small cut of boar and a few slices of cheese.

I danced and feasted into the evening, enveloped by the joyous laughter of friends and family. Aneirin escorted my mother from her chamber to enjoy the event.

"Give her time." Kiirion's gaze fell on my frown.

"I spent some time with her earlier. A light returned to her eyes when she felt the baby move." We were the same person, sharing the same blood and bone with Mage Magic coursing through our veins. "I should be with her."

Aneirin guided my mother towards me. A smile spread across his face. "After all these years, we are reunited."

I embraced my mother, stroked her hair, then let go. "How are you feeling?"

"Stable. The food helps." Her mouth curved into a tired smile. "Evalyn, my sweet daughter. I never thought I'd see you again."

"I'm so grateful you are here." I stroked her arm. "If there's anything you need, call on me at any time."

"Come on now, dear. Let's sit down." Aneirin assisted her into a nearby chair and remained close to her side.

Sofia entered the banquet hall with Eric in tow. His face was pale and pasty, but his eyes glittered.

I crossed the hall to his side. "Oh, thank the gods! Are you okay?"

"I'm a lot better." He pressed his lips into a small smile. "Sofia's spell is literally a lifesaver, but it feels as if I haven't slept in three weeks."

I flicked my gaze to her for her confirmation.

"He'll be fine." She smiled. "Give him some time. He needs to eat."

I nodded and stepped back as she helped him to the table next to Aneirin and my mother.

"Would my queen like a dance?" a voice echoed from nearby.

I spun and smiled at Felix standing before me. My heart burst. To have him here before me, whole and well, made a warmth spread through my body. I made myself a promise: to never let anything keep us apart again.

He wore fine golden robes, embroidered with red and silver threads and small jewels stitched into the collar of his shirt. He radiated warmth.

My smile widened.

He took me in his arms, and as we glided around the room and everything else fell away. We were now cocooned by our own love. No one else mattered in that moment. It was a moment of happiness, something we shared little of during the war. Forced together during the darkest era this realm had struggled through, a bond developed. I closed my eyes and leaned my head against his chest; he led the dance, accompanied by the sweet hum of violins.

The music halted when the wooden doors of the banquet hall burst open, and several guards rushed in.

My cocoon with Felix shattered. I stared at the guards as I awaited their news.

"We must speak with you now, my queen." The leading guard stepped closer to me.

I nodded and turned to the musicians. "Resume your sweet music. Let's not disrupt the celebrations unless it is urgent."

The Elven musicians obeyed and began their songs once again.

The High Elves appeared at my side.

"What's wrong?" I gripped the guard's forearm. My pulse quickened.

"We have received word that a Dark Mage is still roaming the paths near the Badlands, not too far from here," the guard informed us. "A few civilians nearby have reported the sighting whilst remaining undetected."

"Close the gates of the Citadel and have the guards stand post on the bridge and around the grounds of Lake Delendil." I clasped my hands together to hide the trembling. I needed to show I was strong and unbreakable, no matter how much pain and suffering we endured. "I refuse to let any more of my people be hurt by such a poisonous creature."

The guard nodded and whispered to the other guards around him. They hurried out of the hall.

"Go to your chamber, my queen." Xurek appeared at my side with his hammer in hand. He traced the ragged surface of the weapon. "We will keep you safe."

"Inform my parents." I turned to Sofia. "Escort Eric upstairs. He isn't strong enough to fight, and I won't put him at risk again."

"I'm fine, Evalyn," he insisted.

"No, you're not." I narrowed my eyes at him. "Do as your queen commands."

Sofia obeyed and whisked him away. I fled the banquet hall with Felix at my side.

"I won't let anyone hurt you, Evalyn," he said, voice hard and almost feral.

He guided me to my chamber, revealing a warm fire crackling in the corner. The ensemble of orange and red lit his cheeks and cast dark shadows across the plains of his face.

He urged me to the bed and drew the covers. I sank onto the thick mattress and sighed with my eyes closed, hand resting on my swollen belly.

"We've gotten this far," I whispered. "We've managed to conquer the Demons and the Dark Triads. I believe in my friends. They will keep the Dark Mage at bay."

"They'll *kill* the Dark Mage." Felix sat beside me and placed his own hand upon the swell of my belly, and his eyes twinkled when they connected with mine. He brought his lips to my head where he planted a kiss.

I dipped his face with my hands, and our lips met. A desperate need to be whole with him consumed me, but now wasn't the time.

"I'll take care of you." His fingers cupped the nape of my neck. "Both of you."

I closed my eyes and absorbed the moment. I never understood what brought us together so many months ago. The need for survival. A true attraction. Or perhaps the sheer, awful circumstances we'd been forced to endure together. Either way, I wanted him, *needed* him.

I sat back and observed his fire-lit face. He was Human; he did not possess the striking Elven features or the mystical characteristics of any other being that resided in Arogath, but there was still something beautiful about him. He was home. Wherever he was, if we were together, we were home.

Then the ground beneath our feet shook, and my heart leapt into my throat. Felix gripped me, head turning to the sound outside the window.

"What was that?" I clutched his forearms.

"We're about to find out." He took several strides across the room to the window overlooking the lake and mosaic bridge.

"Find the others. Protect the lake." I rose, urging him towards the door. "Please. Most of the stone soldiers were destroyed during the attack, but I will try to produce the protection dome."

Before he left, I caressed his cheek. "I love you."

"I love you too." He brought my fingers to his lips. "Stay here. I'll go and help our friends."

I closed my eyes and envisioned the glistening shield that encompassed them in the valley of Southkeep, trying to make it stronger than before. But the image in my head was hazy, and it seemed very far away. My body shook, and the image disappeared.

"Damn it. Come on!" I scolded, but the dome wouldn't materialise. My friends were not in my line of sight.

The Citadel was full of loud, clattering sounds. Swords. My Elven friends were fighting the Dark Mage. But it seemed, from the heavy footsteps, that there were more than one.

My ears rang. I planted myself against the far wall of the chamber, next to the window. The Citadel went quiet. Too quiet. Clasping my hands, I envisioned a fiery ball of magic, but nothing materialised.

At a slight noise, I stared at my chamber door.

When, the door swung open, I was greeted by a Dark Mage, dressed in a black cloak emblazoned with sapphires. The hood fell over half of her face, showing a small portion of her silver skin and her dark blue lips. She peeled back the hood and bared her face, revealing her piercing, red eyes, and silver hair. Her features were sharp with cheekbones that curved upwards and a slim, pointed nose. Although some features were different in her Dark Mage form, I recognised her face. Makdou.

I stood, rooted to the ground. How would I escape? My magic was dulled, and I had no way of defending myself. What had she done to my friends?

"Evalyn," the Mage muttered in a silky, chilling voice. "At last, we come face to face once again."

"You should leave while you still can." I was unable to keep my voice from shaking. "The guards will be here any moment."

She laughed. "Please. You should've killed me when I was within your grasp." As the words left her mouth, she cupped her hands in front of her and muttered a spell. A spell of Dark Magic. She clutched my necklace in her left hand, the beads glowing the same fiery red as her eyes.

"Why have you taken my necklace? What are you doing?" My heart hammered. Without my magic, all I could do was try to distract her by talking.

"This necklace—it's quite remarkable." Makdou's lips curved into a wicked grin. "It's what I've needed. For the spell to work, I need something important to you, something that holds a piece of your soul."

"That necklace means nothing to me," I lied, hoping she could not hear the trembling in my voice. I fought to remain calm, for the sake of my child, but my entire body shook with fear.

"Don't be stupid," Makdou spat. "I know what it means to you. It binds you to Felix—the love of your life," she mocked. "Together, you have produced a spawn who will destroy my destiny. Although similar things can be said about the rest of your family."

"What do you mean?" I kept my spine pressed against the wall, longing for it to conceal me.

"Me and your father had quite the scandalous affair. He was blinded by love for me, and as he worked closely with the king, who appointed me as chief counsellor. Of course, he knew me as Nieve. My intention was that I would marry into the royal family. One day, I would become queen.

Back in the day, Aneirin was quite heroic and fought in the last great battle with the High Elves. His act of bravery didn't last long as he fled across the sea. I suppose that is my fault—I *did* threaten to kill him if he went looking for your mother. I turned my attention to Atticus, seeing as he was unwed and childless, but the bitter man didn't want me."

"What? No, you're lying. My father would never—"

"Never hurt your mother like that?" She threw her head back and laughed. "We both know that is not true. I informed the Chief Orc of your mother's remarkable Mage abilities. If she stuck around, I'd never succeed in killing you."

My mind raced, but before I could defend myself, the Dark Mage chanted until my ears buzzed, and my vision blurred. The shining surface of a small blade on the mantel of the fireplace caught my eye. It was beautiful, dazzling in the dim light of the fire crackling below the mantelpiece. I found myself sleepwalking over to the knife. In a haze, all reason escaped me.

"The prophecy of your son unifying Arogath will not come to light." Makdou's voice came like sharp knives. "You will no longer threaten my revenge and desire for dominion."

My fingers wrapped around the cool surface of the blade, and I lifted it up from the mantelpiece, drawing it nearer to me. I tried to fight the spell of manipulation. The Crimson Kiss? It must be.

My muscles refused to obey me. I was now controlled by the very spell we'd been fearing since we'd started retaliating against the Orcs.

I buried the knife in my stomach, cried out in pain and collapsed to the floor in a heap. Blood poured from the wound, blanketing the wooden floorboards.

The room vibrated with the eerie sound of Makdou's satisfied laugh, then she was gone as quick as she'd arrived.

As I lay in a puddle of blood, my fogged vision focused on the delicate patterns on the ceiling that swirled and danced alive. The breath I needed became hard to find, and when I tried to scream for help, no sound left my mouth.

With shaky hands, I clasped my belly, stroking the skin as if my touch might prevent my unborn child's death. Perhaps this was my end too.

The prophecy was a lie. A soul-destroying, heart-breaking lie.

My eyes closed, the life dwindling from me.

There was nothing but darkness.

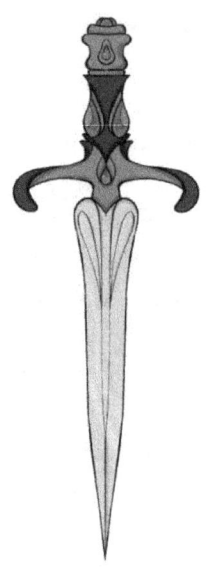

Chapter Twenty-Two

"Evalyn!"

A frantic voice screamed my name, yet it seemed far away. Surrounded by darkness, I floated, waiting for Elysium to welcome me.

A swelling blackness encompassed me, and no light could break through it. What happened to me? My thoughts were fragmented and scattered. I couldn't piece them together. The one thing anchoring me to the world of the living was the excruciating pain pulsating through me. I was dying, falling farther away from the sounds of my friends' urgent pleas.

I'd never contemplated what it would be like to die, to leave the world behind. I was weightless, drifting through nothingness. However, my soul clung to the distant, transparent voices calling out to me.

"Evalyn, you stay with me, you hear me?" a familiar voice demanded. *Kiirion.*

What were they doing to me? Perhaps they were trying to save my life, though I tiptoed on the precipice of death. The tiredness lingered with me over many months of endurance, and I longed for it to be over. Would I join the gods in their banquet? Would I reunite with Ascal and Juliette?

I wondered if they were watching me, too, like Alinar, demanding I stay alive for the sake of the prophecy. But now that'd come to an end.

The distant muttering of a spell brought my attention to the living world. Sofia would be casting her healing spells in attempts to stop the bleeding and stitch my wound together. My thoughts couldn't be formed into anything that made sense, and the haziness was too strong for me to fight. I floated, waiting for my fate to be determined.

My body separated into thousands of hovering pieces. I would pass from the world of living into Elysium where I would reform. The voices around me grew thinner, like a whisper. Then the slipping sensation halted, and tingles returned to my fingertips again. They were resting against the rough surface of a wooden floor. However, I found myself clinging to the edge of life, unwilling to return to the pain my conscience was drowning in.

"It's working," Felix said, voice thick with emotion, as if he held back tears. His fingers wrapped around mine. "Please, hold on."

Sofia continued to chant her incantation, although her words were faint. I imagined my wound spurting blood across the floor. She'd need a powerful spell to stop the bleeding.

I stirred on the cusp of consciousness, eyes fluttering open for a few seconds. Each blink shot agonising jolts through my head as I stared at the strange textured surface of the ceiling.

"Evalyn?" Felix leaned over me, blocking my view. He stroked my hair away from my face, his own expression twisted in pain.

I stared back at him, unable to find the words. Or maybe I didn't want to. I wanted to disappear, and I'd been so close.

"You're okay," Kiirion said as he came into sight. Then he turned to look at a servant Elf. "Take Sofia to the washroom and have her looked after. The spell has weakened her."

"Where is my baby?" I managed to force out. Every part of my body ached.

A heavy silence hung in the air.

My fingers fell to my stomach, no longer ballooning with motherhood, but flat. The memory of the Crimson Kiss replayed in my mind.

As sensation returned to my body, I clutched my healed wounds and wailed. A part of me was stolen.

"What have you done with my son?" Tears fell from my eyes, and my throat burned as I screamed, but I didn't care.

"He has been taken by the servants in preparation for his funeral," Kiirion whispered, his face strained.

"We have failed you," Valneris croaked.

"Get out of here!" Dizzy, I clawed at the floor and tried to steady myself. I attempted to push them away. They'd failed me, in more ways than they could imagine. "Leave me."

I wanted to lock myself away from them all, but I had no strength and every muscle hurt when I struggled up off the floor. The tears continued to fall, and my mind spun. Why had the gods forced this upon me when I'd tried so hard to save their servants from evil?

I bunched my hands into fists, turning my knuckles white with every ounce of pain being suffered for the full sum of its parts.

"Evalyn." Felix lifted his hand to touch and soothe me, but I slapped it away. He'd left me in this room to help fight alongside my friends. But they'd failed.

"Don't touch me," I seethed. His figure was blurry in my disoriented vision. Nothing but my anger remained.

He lowered his head, staring at the ground with shame.

Aneirin burst in through the door, panting and gripping his sword. He threw it to the ground and appeared at my side. He clutched me, without giving me a second to refuse his comfort. I accepted his embrace, unable to gather the strength to push him off.

"My sweet child," he whispered against my shoulder.

I closed my eyes, willing the world to fade away, wishing I'd slipped into the darkness of Elysium, the Beyond, and stayed there forever.

I leaned into my father as the tears consumed me. I'd failed too. I'd failed my child, and hence, failed my realm as a leader. The prophecy was broken. They would have no future leader.

Felix ushered everybody except my father outside, closing the door behind them.

He peeled my blood-soaked gown from my body, dressed me in a robe, then tucked my pouch of gemstones into my pocket. Helping me into the chair by the mirror, he took a brush in his hand and ran it through my tangled mess of hair. My father remained closed, keeping his hollow gaze locked on me.

"I'm sorry I couldn't save him," Felix said, voice hoarse and broken. In the mirror, his reflection displayed his tear-streaked face. "I'm sorry I couldn't protect you."

"He's gone." Tears caused a lump in my throat. "Leave me."

"Evalyn."

"Get out, both of you." My tone was harsh. He recoiled as if stung by the words, then left the room with Aneirin.

I stared at the four-poster bed across from me. I wouldn't find sleep. Even if I did, it would be riddled with nightmares of Makdou.

I remained in the chair for a long time, unaware of how much time had passed, staring at my own reflection in the dusty mirror. How did I deserve to breathe, and my son did not? How was the universe so cruel?

Conjuring a ball of brilliant, red light in my palms, I let the rage bubble within me. I launched the ball into the mirror, shattering it into a thousand tiny fragments. Some fell onto me, but I dusted them off, ignoring the thin streams of blood dripping down my legs.

I grabbed my bag that had been brought in by the servants upon our return. Unburdened by the limitations of pregnancy combined with Sofia's healing spells, I'd returned to full strength. Perhaps my own magic intertwined with hers and advanced my recovery.

This intensified the anger coursing through my veins and set my skin afire. There was something I needed. Something that would help me avenge the murder of my son.

I swatted away the tears falling from my eyes.

Overcome with the desperate need to flee, to cling onto something that would relieve me of my pain, I flicked through the pages of the book I'd taken from the temple.

What was I hoping to find?

Nothing would hinder me on my path for revenge. I would make her pay for the innocent blood she had on her hands.

Adrenaline coursed through my veins as I halted on the pages that referred to portals.

A compelling sensation filled my body, as if my Mage nature knew I would find the very thing I needed. What darkness would it reveal to me?

I plucked a translation dictionary from my shelf and laid it next to the leather-bound book, referring to it each time I came across a new incantation. The bag of crystals dug into my hip. I pulled them from the pocket and tossed them aside.

"You lied to me, Juliette. They protect no one."

I turned the pages over every time a spell translated into something that would be of no use. There were curses of necromancy and blood magic, but I needed something strong enough to kill Makdou. She had the Crimson Kiss. I needed something of equal strength for when I would fight her, one on one.

My gaze landed on something that looked like another portal spell at the end of the chapter. The compelling sensation within me intensified. The portal at Southkeep connected the world of the living to the world of the dead and took a group of Dark Mages to create and open it. I would have to open this one alone.

According to the translation, it would lead to a different dimension somewhere outside of our universe, where our time didn't exist. It was a straight connection to a facility for training of warriors. If a Mage could conjure the portal and cross through it, then they would be welcomed into the facility, acknowledged as a powerful Mage who sought refinement.

Refinement. I wasn't sure if it was what I was seeking. But if I could access a part within me that would strengthen my magical abilities, turn my anger and hatred into something useful, then I would be able to return to Arogath and defeat Makdou. The facility for training could help me defeat Makdou without becoming the very thing I despised—a Dark Mage. What other choices did I have?

I repeated the chant in my head, until I could pronounce each word without difficulty. I needed to be quick.

With my hands spread out before me, I read the spell in full and visualised a portal with a purple centre, one that would lead to another world.

My mind was clear, absent of hindering uncertainties.

The fury pulsed through my body, allowing the portal to form in front of me, glowing a magnificent purple and buzzing with the sound of electricity. I stared at it wide-eyed, the loud buzz filling the Citadel. It wouldn't be long before my friends became aware. I wanted them to see me leave—I'd abandon them as they'd done to me.

Within moments, hurried footsteps made their way towards the room. The door burst open, and the High Elves stood in the doorway.

"What the hell?" Kiirion gaped.

"A portal." Theodas frowned and held his hands up in front of him. "Evalyn, don't."

"It's too late," I shouted over the loud crackling sounds of the magic coursing through the swelling gateway.

"It's not too late, my queen," he pleaded. "Let us help you."

"You cannot help me." The compelling sensation urged me closer to the entrance like a magnet. "You have proven that."

I took my first step towards the portal. The High Elves lunged forward to block me from entering. I launched a fiery bolt of light from my hand, sending the Elves crashing into the glass wall behind them, shattering it as they collided.

"Evalyn!" Felix yelled, appearing at the scene. His eyes still drooped from the exhaustion and torture endured during his time spent at Southkeep, but it made me despise him more. He *was* weak.

They were *all* weak.

Eric, now cured of the plague and evil magic, stepped towards me with his arms open. I hesitated for a moment, contemplating his embrace.

"Let me help you, the way you have helped me," he begged, his voice shaky.

"I did more than *help* you, I *saved* you." I produced more red balls of light in my palms, ready to throw them towards anyone who stepped in my way. "What have you done to repay me? Nothing. You are all responsible for the death of my son."

"Wait!" Valneris lunged forward to grab my arm. I threw the balls of light at him, sending him into the bookshelves on the opposite side of the room.

"Goodbye." I stepped into the portal and darkness consumed me, leaving the traitors in the chamber, far, far away.

I drifted through the dark nothingness that fell between dimensions. Now free of pain, I allowed myself to relish it. Knowing how much I'd wanted to die, how I couldn't bear to live in a world without the very being who had lived within me, I let myself hover through the empty vastness around me.

I floated through the endless void for a long time. Maybe days, months, or maybe even a few seconds. Soon, a small, white light appeared somewhere in front of me. I stretched my hands and focused to bring it nearer. The light grew and swelled, marking the exit of the portal.

Concentrating all my power and ability, I pulled the exit close enough for me to fit through. As soon as my fingertips connected with the surface of the portal, sensation returned. And with that, the burning pain in my chest resurfaced.

Eager to find what I was looking for, I climbed through the portal exit, landing on the cold, concrete flooring of an open temple. A thin layer of sand covering the floor found its way between my fingernails as I scrambled my way across.

Rising, I scanned the temple. I was alone in a room held in place by four pillars and walls made of sandstone. I listened for any noise at all. A voice, or even a movement. No sounds reached my ears, so I edged towards the archway across the room.

I followed the narrow corridor that continued around different bends with multiple other corridors sprouting from it. Staying in the main passageway, I stared at the doorway at the end. My heart pounded and a magnetic sensation within lured me closer.

I opened it, then entered, enticed by the compelling sensation.

The room was lit by an array of candles of all sizes. Its warm glow lit the detailed and delicate battle tapestries that hung on the walls. A man dressed in a black, embroidered cloak sat in a sculpted chair in the centre of the room.

"Ah, Evalyn," the man muttered in a voice so calm, so gentle, it was almost eerie. "I have waited a long time to see you."

I stared at him, unable to recognise his face. Had I travelled all this way for one man?

My voice creaked out in a whisper, "Who are you?"

SEVERANCE
OF
MINDS
SNEAK PEEK

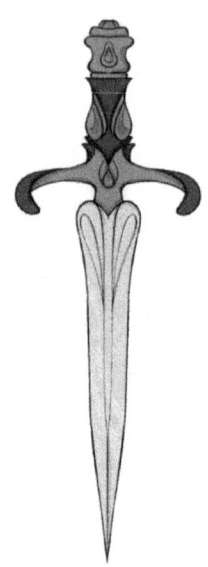

Chapter One

"You've been expecting me?" My voice raised several octaves.

The seated man paused writing and looked up from his work. His face was touched by age—creased forehead and dull, weathered skin, bald head. A goatee sprouted from his chin. Something about him demanded respect—perhaps the way he held his shoulders straight.

Who was this man? More importantly—*where* was I?

"Oh yes, Evalyn." His gold and jewel-encrusted chair was in a room made of simple stone walls without carvings or statues. He held a quill, the tip hovering an inch above a parchment page of a leather-bound book clutched in his other hand. "Your arrival has been written in the sheets of time since the dawn of the Noble Ones."

I eyed him and processed his words. His voice, calm and casual, echoed against the high sandstone walls. Daylight streamed in through the dusty windows and illuminated his olive skin.

My son had been prophesied...and murdered for it. If one foretold fate had failed, could another?

His embroidered robe, not as ornate as the sapphire-encrusted robe Makdou, the deceiving Dark Mage wore, created a wave of nausea in my stomach.

"How do you know of the Noble Ones?" I wandered to the wooden table, then glanced at a small charcoal block positioned amongst some candles.

A lavender flower burned in the centre of the charcoal, swirling its sweet-scented smoke into the air. Above the block, the smoke halted, then flattened as if held in place by something invisible. Within seconds, the smoke disappeared.

I furrowed by brows, trying to understand exactly *where* the smoke had gone. The lavender continued to burn.

"The book promised a facility for training of warriors. Is this the place? Or has the book betrayed me too?" I cleared my throat and narrowed my gaze at him.

"So many questions. Why?" He created a steeple with his fingers. "To answer your first, I am Reuben, the master of this Temple. Why do you frown so?"

"I will stop frowning when I find out all I need to know."

"All in good time, Evalyn. In your world, you were exposed to Elysium, the realm of the dead. For someone who has seen several dimensions, it would be logical to assume you are now in an alternative timeline."

I scooped up a red gem from beside the smouldering lavender and turned it over in my palm. "A place where my time—Arogath's time—doesn't exist?"

The man put his quill and book aside and relaxed in his chair. He spoke of inter-dimensional travel as if I'd arrived with the knowledge of it.

"Tell me, is this the place I've searched for?" My tone was sharp.

Reuben rose to cross the room, his robes gliding along the concrete floor. He lit a new block of charcoal, placed a fresh sprig in the centre, then blew the lavender, sending a cloud of sweet scent swirling above.

He lifted a scroll from its glass cabinet next to an archaic bookcase lined with rolled parchment, and leather-bound books. The scroll's edges were worn and bent as though it'd been handled many times.

"I believe you already know it is." He stroked the scroll's smooth parchment.

"You ought to get to the point." I crossed my arms, my fingertips resting on my scales.

The trees outside the window shook in the breeze and cast long, jagged shadows across the concrete floor.

"At Southkeep, you entered Elysium," he said. "A place you were never meant to go. Prophecies rarely fail to come true. There is a possibility you changed your timeline completely by accident, although I cannot say for certain."

"Does this mean my son died because I entered

Elysium?" I flicked a strand of hair out of my face. Coldness hit me, sweeping over every inch of my body.

"I cannot answer that, nor can I predict events or presume the reasons for their occurrence." He handed me the parchment.

Makdou had stolen my necklace to complete the Crimson Kiss spell. Maybe the runes meant something else altogether.

"What do these runes mean?" I placed my fingers on the symbols. "These here—they are on the necklace Felix gave to me."

"This one on the left is the four elements wind, earth, fire, and water—their individual runic symbols merged to show unity. The middle symbol is the marriage of the individual runes for crown and blood. Ah, this last one—the most important—balance," he said.

I raised my eyebrows. "Are you sure? They sound like—"

"Your life?" He smiled. "The Elements, like your friends. The next one represents your crown and claim to the throne of Arogath and finally, your duty to maintain peace between the triads. I read the scroll every day, so I know what happened to you—what Makdou did. It is unfortunate she is more powerful than you are," he said. "Although, there are some things in this scroll which you will not be aware of."

I turned the scroll round and studied it. Normal parchment. "What could possibly be in here that I wouldn't know? After all, it *is* my life."

"Felix's ancient ancestors came from this realm," he said.

"What?" I gaped at him. "That's not possible. He's

spoken of his family before, and he mentioned no such thing."

He smiled. "This happened many centuries ago, of course. There is a legend amongst our people that tells the story of a Great Mother Tree—a tree with extraordinary healing abilities. Such a treasure needed to be concealed from our enemies. Felix's ancestors played a pivotal role. After all, they were Mages."

"Surely not." A nervous laugh escaped my lips. "He would know if he had Mage blood in his veins."

"Would he?" He cocked his head. "Once they hid Great Mother Tree, his ancestors fled this realm and lived as Humans in your world. Although, I have wondered if this is why Felix sensed you would need his necklace."

I shook my head. "I don't know what to say—this isn't what I expected."

"We can discuss it more later, but we need to focus on what you need to know right now. Refinement is why you are here, and refinement is what you will receive," he said.

"Tell me the name of this place, and I will look at this...*my* timeline." I kept my gaze fixed on the smooth surface of the ivory parchment.

"Indeed. We call it the Temple of Peace."

I untied the string, then unravelled the scroll as far as my arms could stretch, revealing drawings of the events I lived through. The day I left the Eyrie. The fires at Westwilde and Rushdale Forest. My first night of passion with Felix. Heat rose in my cheeks.

"Come." With an air of grace and fluidity, Rueben drifted towards a stone archway, then down the steps on the other side—his robe trailing behind.

After placing the scroll and its string on the glass shelf, I followed him.

"As you mature, meet new people, and encounter new challenges, more is added to the scroll. After the Mages left, the sentient magical energy had no host to channel itself through, so it took to writing the scroll until they returned." He led me out into the open air where several small buildings jutted out into a courtyard.

The smell of molten iron drifted from the blacksmiths to the left and the woody scent of damp straw from the animal shelters hung in the air. Chickens clucked as two servants shooed them into their coops. Dung marked the cobbled floor towards the stables. Trees grew in the centre, and people gathered on the benches underneath the branches. A strange purple fruit hung amongst the green leaves.

I pushed onto my tiptoes, cupped a fruit in my hand, then brought it to my nose. Its sweet, rich aroma tingled my nostrils. Intertwined flowering vines scaled the walls of the temple.

"Why is there a scroll of my timeline?" I skipped to keep up with the man as he came to a stop in front of the brick wall.

He placed his hands on top of the moss-covered surface and gazed at the snow blanketed mountains on the horizon.

"I'm not from this realm, wherever *here* is." I peered over the wall and gasped at the long drop. This new world—somewhere I didn't know—was familiar, situated on a cliffside like the Eyrie in Arogath.

He focused on a single eagle gliding across the sky. "Although the prophecy did not come true, you are meant for something, and this kingdom can sense it. We are here to help you. Please trust us."

The eagle's feathers darkened into shades of purple as it shrank into the skyline.

"This planet is connected to yours in more ways than I can explain," he said.

His words offered no logic. I'd abandoned my home, on the whim of a book, to find I'm connected to another. I hoped this new world would give me a solution. A new life. A new land. A new hope.

Resting against the stones, I surveyed the contoured mountains covered in snow, the glistening river flowing below us, and the clear sky. Cool, fresh air filled my lungs.

"It's incredible, isn't it?" He turned to face me, then clasped his hands. "Welcome to Swynvale."

———————◇———————

The melodic notes of a harp filled my ears as I approached a room down one of the temple's many corridors. Soldiers practiced close-range combat on sackcloth dummies. Older warriors fought in duals with either long bamboo sticks or blades. The sticks thudded against each other as the soldiers parried their opponent's attack.

Curious, I leaned on the doorway and observed the dance-like moves.

Swords etched with curling calligraphy shone under the light from the torches affixed to the stone walls. Fights were followed with cheers and pats on the back after each duel ended. It seemed those who resided in the temple ensured the realm's protection.

I had no such protection in Arogath.

A man fell to the floor with a loud thud, and I jolted. The harpist stopped playing. Blood oozed from a wound on the soldier's arm where a blade nicked the skin above his elbow.

The wounded man's opponent slit the gash open with the tip of his blade. "Aye, it'll be good for you. Best get used to blood being spilled."

I clasped my stomach, wondering if my own belly had been sliced open with a blade. In desperate need of fresh air, I fled to the courtyard, then rested my hands against the wall and glanced to the sky. Each breath was ragged, and my eyes brimmed with tears. I swatted them away.

I needed to learn how to use this anger against Makdou and do what my friends failed to do—put a stop to her for good. They'd let me down.

Had my own belly been sliced open with a blade after Makdou killed my son? I'd returned from Elysium, lying in a pool of my own blood and no baby in sight. Sofia must've cut him out of me and taken him away before I regained consciousness. I fled Arogath, having never laid eyes on him, without saying goodbye. Where was his body now?

"Evalyn," Reuben called from behind me, voice smooth like silk. "Come on, you can't stay out here. Come inside and join the others."

"Give me a minute," I breathed deeply, although my tightening chest constricted each intake of air.

A heaviness ached behind my ribs, right where my heart pounded. Closing my eyes, I focused my attention on the rustle of nearby trees, the call of a bird, and the floral scent of flowers in full bloom.

I flattened my shaking fingers against my thighs

and opened my eyes. "Okay. I'm ready."

He led me to the training room, and the soldiers bowed to him. One soldier was dressed in polished armour, his dark hair pulled into a tight bun on top of his head. He reminded me of Kiirion.

They faced each other, then shook hands. With a bow of their heads, they sparred, each movement quick and sharp as they weaved their way around the other, blocking hits at an incredible speed. The other soldiers watched from the sidelines, dodging out of the way as the fighters came too close.

How quickly would the war between the Triads in Arogath have ended if we'd trained soldiers to this level of skill? When Reuben pushed his opponent to the floor, he bowed, offered him a hand, then plucked him from the ground.

"This is Seth," Reuben said. "One of our finest soldiers."

"He gives me far more credit than I deserve." Seth smiled with an affectionate twinkle in his eyes. His friends gave him a pat on the shoulder before they retired from the training room. "If it wasn't for his shelter, protection, and training, I'd be as ill-skilled as a Human babe straight from the belly."

His words seized my heart, and a tightness formed in my chest that would not loosen. I pressed my lips together, hiding their trembling, for images of my unborn child flashed in my mind. Memories I couldn't suppress, pain that resurfaced in surprising waves.

"You have brought me great honour." Reuben bowed to his companion.

"Go easy on him." Seth laughed. "He's getting old, and frail." He dashed from the training room before he could respond.

"I apologise for Seth's brash behaviour." Reuben faced me to take my hand. He stood like an oak tree, calm and strong, ancient, and wise. His demeanour allowed me peace despite my inner turmoil. "If you are to stay here, then your training will begin."

"My son's murder broke my heart. My friends' betrayal broke my spirit—they couldn't stop Makdou. That's why I came here." A numbness spread through my being as I uttered the words aloud. The truth. I placed my hand over my chest in a feeble attempt to soothe the ever-present ache.

"Do not fear the absence of anger, as it will make you stronger. Swynvale has a habit of doing that." He let go of my hand, then strolled back and forth across the stone floor. "This realm is peaceful and has a mind of its own. It looks after its own and makes them feel the way they should—safe, free."

His last two words fell heavy, carrying a weight of importance and something I desired for myself and my people. The sooner I could learn what I needed to in Swynvale, the sooner I could fulfil my duty to my kingdom.

"It works much like your Elementals," he said. "There is one difference—there are no magical beings to do the work of this realm. The very realm itself will aid you in time of need. It protects the balance of life."

He waved his hand and a ball of light appeared, projecting a view of an ocean forming into a great beast, engulfing and destroying the ships. "The natural magic killed the enemies on those vessels. Although, it will not kill all our enemies as we are not prioritised over the other clans."

The scene changed to an army of Orcs who burned Human civilians in a field outside their homes. Thick clouds of smoke shot into the sky. Crops were set ablaze, and survivors ran through the corn fields, desperate to escape their fate.

"Orcs—they're everywhere."

"Of course." His brows drooped around his eyes. "They have colonised many realms, Evalyn."

"I'm aware of how brutal they can be." The image flickered in my mind's eye.

The Dark Mages and the Ezen Riders stood atop the valley in Southkeep. The Orcs became a mere threat to be dealt with in comparison.

"We all have our enemies." He waved his hand again, and the ball of light evaporated. "And you are here to kill yours—Makdou."

"Then you understand."

He was right. Something was in the ground I stood on, in the air I breathed. I feared nothing.

"Show me what you can do." He strode into the centre of the room, then stopped. With time and age, he'd withered into an ancient husk, yet I sensed only strength.

I concentrated on my cupped hands. A ball of magnificent white light manifested in my palms, swirling and dancing. My white light appeared occasionally when it broke free from the shadows within me. It was more often red, made of fear and sheer determination to survive.

"Good." He frowned, and deep creases appeared around his eyes. He focused on the magic I held, and it turned red.

"How did you do that?" My concentration snapped, and the light disappeared.

"A manipulation spell." He flicked his hand with ease. "The spell reveals the sorrow and the pain you bear alone, every day."

"What are you?" My voice shook. Was he a Mage? Or something else?

"A person made of flesh and blood, like you." Reuben conjured a light of his own, which transformed into a dial with multiple symbols displayed on its ethereal surface. "But I am Human, and you are Mage."

"The magic." I became transfixed by the shimmering blue light surrounding the dial as it turned in slow movements. "How?"

"I am one with the realm," he replied. A few seconds afterwards, his spell dissipated.

"You said this world doesn't have magical beings to do its work, but you are one."

He smiled. Was he right about this world? The magic pulsed through the realm and the green of nearby trees became vibrant. The scales on my upper arms tingled with power that surged through the air. Aware of everything I knew and experienced in my own kingdom, I should be accustomed to the bizarre ways of magic. Something of my father was within me after all. Something Human.

"Join the others." Reuben gestured to the door leading into the courtyard. "Eat, rest. I will show you more tomorrow."

"Aren't you going to eat with us?"

"I must pray." His lips curved into a half-smile, then he ambled towards a narrow archway on the left wall of the training room.

He pulled back the ornate tapestry curtain and revealed a vaulted room illuminated with flickering candles. Sour orange and sweet cinnamon wafted into the training area. Reuben stepped inside, and the heavy curtain fell back into place behind him.

I headed to the grand hall via the walled courtyard. A purple-tinged twilight fell over the Temple. Moths darted towards the flickering candlelight in the windows.

The soldiers from the training room congregated at a table near a door left ajar at the back of the hall. The opening allowed a snippet of the mist-covered mountain to come into sight and the soft breeze to swirl in.

I lingered in the doorway until Seth waved me over. A pleasant smile spread across his mouth. Bowls of meat stew were positioned next to a selection of dates and raisins baked into pies. The sickly-sweet smell of large, purple fruit enticed me, yet I couldn't work up the nerve to taste such an unusual food.

I reclined into the seat opposite Seth and observed the people sitting around the table—Humans with slender noses and freckled faces, some with blemishes and acne marks. I sank further into my chair, made vulnerable by my contrasting appearance.

"You'll get used to Reuben's riddles soon enough." Seth grunted around a mouthful of meat stew. "Don't worry too much about it. You'll understand him someday."

The glare of a woman opposite me caught my attention. In brooding silence, she narrowed her gaze on me. I smiled, but the gesture was not returned.

With the ladle in hand, I poured the stew into my bowl.

"Does your hair always glow?" The woman pointed a dainty finger at the strands of hair draped over my shoulders.

At first, I frowned, drawing a blank. But when I glanced down, my hair shone a warm and radiant red. "No. It's new."

"It's the realm." Seth took a sip of water. He swallowed, wiped his mouth, then continued, "The magic flowing through Swynvale is making you stronger. You were meant to be here."

"You sound a lot like Reuben."

The men at the table laughed.

Surrounded by a room full of strangers, I reflected on my level of endurance, my ability to survive. We'd been unprepared for the Crimson Kiss. We were aware of its purpose yet relied on its absence over the last few centuries to see us through. We failed.

"The Orcs are brutal creatures. Have you not yet found a way to control them?" I asked.

"The feud between Orcs and Humans is as old as the universe," the bald man muttered. His skin was dark, his shoulders broad and toned. "They've colonised many areas of this planet. According to the tomes in our libraries, such colonization has been documented through the centuries."

A silence fell over the table. Would we find a solution to the problem plaguing not just my kingdom, but this one too?

"Lighten up, Dmitri." Seth crammed the last of his meal into his mouth. Even feasting like a pig, he was handsome. A strand of his dark hair fell free from its bun.

I scanned the shadows of the mess hall. Soldiers with blank expressions slumped in their seats.

"They've had a rough time." Dmitri followed my gaze to the table of lifeless warriors. He touched the scar on his face. "Blasted by a powerful spell conjured by an Orc. Some sort of Dark Magic they've used over the past few months."

"I'm familiar with that. Orcs and magic—a dangerous combination."

"Why have you come here?" The woman stared at me. "Why would you leave your own realm?"

"Er." Unable to fathom any other words, I clung to the story they all knew. "You know why I'm here. It's written in the scroll, remember?"

"You don't have to abide by what is predicted to come of you," she said, her voice cold. "You changed your fate, although by accident, and I'm sure it can be done again. Your friends—you left them."

"That's *enough*, Lilith," Reuben ordered as he appeared.

The soldiers around the table jolted, then straightened, now in the presence of their master.

She huffed, shunted her chair backwards, then fled the hall.

Reuben's stern gaze disappeared. Dmitri rose from his seat to bring Reuben a tray of meats and a bowl of stew. Seth glanced at me and smiled.

Lilith's hostility didn't make sense. Even if every part of my being compelled me to question her and demand an explanation for her ignorance, I couldn't. My soul was at peace with this new land. Its magic had fused with mine and locked itself into place.

I needed to let myself heal, regain my strength, then I'd be ready to fight back.

Jodie Angell

DEAR READER

Thank you for buying and taking the time to read *Crimson Kiss*. This novel was born during my second year of university. It was exam period, and I needed to be away from studying. I opened up Microsoft Word, and thought, you know what? Now is the perfect time for me to test drive my favourite genre.

Fantasy gave me the escapism I needed—a world without rules and limitations. I could make my own rules. I love books that transport me into a different world to achieve for my readers while challenging some of the traditional tropes of fantasy.

Now that you've read a teaser of *Severance of* Minds, Book 2 in *The Ancient Spells* Trilogy, I hope you're convinced to follow Evalyn on her journey through grief, acceptance, and recovery.

Jodie

I hope you enjoyed this as much as I did during the writing process. Please leave a review as a way to support me and ensure I can continue to bring readers books to love and enjoy.

Follow me on social media to stay up to date on my writing and #bookish content!
Instagram: @jodieangell_author
TikTok: @jodieangell_author
BookBub: @jodieangell_author

Jodie Angell

ACKNOWLEDGEMENTS

I must start by thanking my mother for giving me words when I could not find them. her vocabulary is extensive, and this is extremely useful for an author. Who needs a Thesaurus?

Next up is my partner, Josh. Thank you for reading early drafts of the book and highlighting typos. He asked me questions, helped me build upon my ideas, and supported me through the publish process and beyond.

And finally, a huge thank you to the whole #bookish community on Instagram. Your support, loyalty, and kindness has kept me motivated and inspired. I'm thrilled to have found you all.